# Daisy Haites

## JESSA HASTINGS

To my Grandma.
Carol, I think you'll hate this more than the
first one. But I love you more than ever.
And close this book right now.
You need not venture any further.

# Daisy

No guns at the dinner table. That's my one rule. Call me old fashioned, I don't know. It's just what I've always said to the boys. I don't care about phones, I don't care if they're texting, I don't care if they're wearing a hat at the table—I just don't want guns while I'm serving them a brisket I slow-cooked for nine and a half fucking hours.

Julian makes us say grace (as though the Lord is listening to him and like He'd actually bless us) and then comes the silence of eating that makes the cook happy.

The volume starts to rise again after a couple of minutes—they're total animals when it comes to food, these Lost Boys[1] of mine. I call them that because that's what they are. You can't really be around my brother for too long without meandering off the garden path, and all of these boys have well and truly strayed. None of these boys are boys, by the way—not in age, not in attitude. Each of them has their own unique set of pros and cons, red flags, warrants and no-fly statuses, and together they comprise the inner sanctum of my brother's outfit.[2]

---

[1] Seven Lost Boys in total, which I'll listen below for your ease of reference:
- Declan Ellis
- Aleki Kekoa
- Miguel Del Olmo
- Jason "Happy" Bardsley
- John "Smokeshow" Macrae
- Booker Cline
- TK Thompsett

[2] Which is much larger than seven men. Hundreds of men work for Julian, but I don't remember their names, and we mostly just refer to the rest of them as the Underlings and the Footmen.

"Oi, Daisyface."[3] My brother nods his chin at me. "How'd you do in your Immunopathology exam?"

"Immunopharmacology," I correct him and he rolls his eyes.

"Did you pass or not?"

"Course she passed," Kekoa tells him proudly. I don't have a dad anymore but when I did, Aleki Kekoa[4] was his best friend.

"First class?" Julian asks.

I frown at him, offended. "Obviously."

My brother tosses me a little wink as he pours himself more wine. "What's next on the curriculum?"

I shrug. "I think we're about to move on to a block on Disease & Therapeutics." Second year med student at Imperial College.

Jules swats his hand. "You don't need to know about that sh—"

"Take it back!" Declan Ellis[5] yells suddenly as he jumps back from the table, staring down darkly at TK, who's seated next to me.

I frown between them. I've no idea what's going on, I wasn't paying attention.

"Nope." Teeks grins.[6]

Declan reaches around from behind him and pulls out his Star Model BM.[7] He likes it, I don't. Too heavy in the hand, too much lag on the recoil.

"Decks." Julian rolls his eyes. "Put the gun away."

He's a bit drunk at the minute, Decks—I can see it on him because when he's drunk or hungover, one of his eyes goes a bit squinty.

I glance at TK and I can already tell he's not going to oblige Declan—whatever it is, he thinks it's too funny to take back. He's got this smarmy, shit-eating grin that riles Decks right up because he's being disrespectful and Declan is, technically, higher on the food chain. He's my brother's right hand.[8]

"Take it fucking back." Declan repositions the gun, now pointed squarely at TK's face.

---

[3]    I used to hate it when he'd call me this. He has all my life. Now I love it.

[4]    6'5" tall. Broad. Samoan born in Hawaii. My dad found him counting cards in Vegas.

[5]    Tall, lean, brown hair, brown eyes, irrational, not a great temper. Good in bed.

[6]    Messy blonde hair, big green eyes, forever a cheeky smile.

[7]    Semi-automatic, 9 mm.

[8]    Arguably my brother's 2IC. At least on paper. In practice his 2IC is Kekoa.

"No." Teeks shrugs, indifferent.

"Take what back?" I frown.

"Nothing." Declan glances at me quickly, but TK and Booker start laughing.

Best friends, huge idiots.

Declan cocks the gun.

"Declan, don't be stupid." I roll my eyes.

"I'm not being stupid, he's being stupid."

I exchange a long-suffering look with Miguel Del Olmo,[9] my bodyguard since I was fourteen.

"I'm not being stupid." TK shrugs. "It's true."

"No it's fucking not."

"What's not true?" Julian frowns.

Declan's eyes pinch as he silently dares the youngest member of their crew to speak out of turn.

A cheeky smile spreads over TK's face. "That Decks has a permanent boner for Dais."

And then...

Gunshot.

I blink a few times, glance down at myself. A very old, very valuable white T-shirt in mint condition not five seconds ago is now sullied with a drop of Californian blood.

TK lets out a small sound of muffled pain—just barely audible—as he'd never give Decks the satisfaction of agony.

"Un-fucking-believable." I slam my balled-up fists down on the table. "What is my one rule?" I bellow at the entire room.

The room goes very still. No one answers.

"WHAT IS MY ONE RULE?"

Some variant of "no guns at the dinner table" is mumbled by everyone present, including my brother and poor TK (who, by the way, isn't dying).

"This is a £4000 shirt."

---

9  Once, when my brother was in Rio, someone shot at him and Miguel—he was no one then, we didn't know him—dove in front of my brother. Got hit, actually. Julian paid for his treatment, brought him back to London.

Smokeshow[10] squints over at me. "Might have overpaid for that one, Dais."

"Oh, did I?" I glare at him. "Did I overpay for this Beatles 'Butcher Cover' Original Promo shirt from 1966?" I cock an eyebrow at him. "On eBay last week, I watched you buy a Hot Cheeto shaped like a gun for £560."

Smokeshow looks over at his best friend, Happy,[11] who is conversely scowling at him. Smoke shrugs like he can't help it. "It looked like my gun."[12]

Julian catches my eye and nods his chin at TK. "Help him."

I roll my eyes, pointing to Declan. "Get my kit."

He nods a bit sheepishly.

Miguel helps Teeks into the kitchen, sitting him down at the breakfast table.

It's a big house. My dad bought out an entire cul-de-sac in Knightsbridge, turned it into a sort of headquarters. The Compound, they call it.

Miguel tosses Declan an unimpressed look as he carries over my medical kit, lips pursed.

"Sorry about your shirt." He flashes me a sorry look, leans in towards me, closer than he probably should. "I'll get it dry cleaned."

I nod at him once, try to give him a bit of a smile that straddles the line of being a forgiving matriarch and not wanting to condone his stupid behaviour.

TK cocks his eyebrow at the proximity Declan (doesn't) place between us and Decks flips him off as he leaves the room.

I give TK a look. "Why would you say that?"

"Because it's true."

Miguel tilts his head, concedes tacitly with his eyes. Not a massive chatterbox, my Miguel. A constant presence and a zingy one liner is what he's known for. He and I have spent years crafting the perfect balance of him being nearby without hovering... he's very aware that I'm never alone. And I'm aware that, by consequence of, he never is

---

[10] An old boy (used to work for my dad). Tall, broad, handsome, a bit like Gaston from *Beauty and the Beast*, but not a prick.

[11] Think 2005 Statham, less handsome.

[12] It didn't.

4

either. There's not always that much to say to him either, he sees it all anyway.

"Either way—" I wipe away the blood around the wound with some isopropyl prep pads. "Do you really think it wise to poke the bear?"

"He's not a bear." TK rolls his eyes. "He's a puppy with an inferiority complex and a small dick."

I toss him a look. "Not that small..."

TK starts laughing. "Go on then, be honest, who's better in the sack: me or him?"

Declan, 100 percent. Completely, undeniably, very good, highly recommend. I was so cross when Julian stopped it. A few years ago right after my ex-boyfriend and I broke up, and it was big and traumatic and I was young.[13] Julian found out I'd been sleeping with Declan, who was not so young[14] and who definitely thought I was twenty,[15] though I was not, and I think Julian told him he had to help him with a job or he'd go to the feds and I don't know what happened on that job but Declan was around forever after that.

Teeks... look. It was a brief thing that coincided with Julian trying to woo him and Booker out of the valley. We don't talk about it, but I think I was the deal-sweetener. My brother does his down and out best to exclude me from as much of his work as humanly possible, but he brought me to California with him on that trip and we spent the vast majority of it wining and dining TK and Booker.

They're the youngest guys who work for Jules by a mile. TK's twenty-six, Booker's twenty-seven. Friends from college. Tech boys who graduated top of their class from Stanford. The Silicon Baddies is what we call them. Jules found them on the dark web when they were tracking down the home addresses of people viewing pornography of "questionable legality" and sending it to the FBI. We liked their style. Jules is a fan of a saviour complex, he has one himself. Me? I like anyone who sees something askew and tries to fix it best they can.

They're fun boys, and TK's got a face on him; sweet and younger than he is actually. Good kisser, great eyes, so-so in bed. I don't have the heart to tell him, though. I can't.

---

[13] Like really young. Like lied-about-my-age young.
[14] Twenty-four.
[15] ˙Seventeen.

5

I stab his arm with some lidocaine.

"I don't know." I shrug coyly. "You might have to jog my memory." It's a shallow offer but he looks pleased all the same, chin in the air and everything.

"Maybe I will." It's a bullshit acceptance.

He won't, we both know that—not anymore, anyway, because—

Someone clears their throat from the doorway behind me.

I glance over my shoulder.

Christian Hemmes leans against the doorframe, arms crossed over his chest, eyes pinched.

"Should I go, then?" he asks, brow cocked, hands shoved in his pockets.

I turn away quickly, my cheeks on fire (I don't know why).[16] I blink a few times, refocusing my eyes on the task in front of me, ignoring Miguel's exaggerated eye roll that seems to me like a betrayal of our forced friendship.

TK holds my gaze, smirks knowingly, but they don't know anything… They don't even know the half of it.

Christian Hemmes walks over to us, stands behind me and subtly squeezes my arse as he inspects the bullet wound for himself.

"What happened here?"

I breathe out, annoyed. "Declan."

"Shot you?" He blinks, a bit surprised.

TK nods.

"Why?"

I glance between the two of them. "Teeks was being antagonistic."

Miguel squints, assessing the validity of my statement.

"Thought they weren't meant to have guns at the dinner table?" Christian folds his arms over his chest.

"Pass me the eight-inch forceps," I tell him. "And they're not."

Christian hands me a pair of Mayo scissors[17] and Miguel rolls his eyes.

I clear my throat, pick up the right tool, and start fishing around TK's arm as Miguel shines a light over me.

"This going to take a while?" Christian asks unceremoniously.

---

[16] Yes, I do.

[17] Christian runs night clubs. I don't know what I was expecting.

"Oh—my apologies." I look back at him. "Are we keeping you from something?"

"Yeah, actually."

He leans down over me, peering into the wound again with me, pressing himself up against me. "I had some plans for you."

My stomach falls down a flight of stairs.

"Oh." I swallow, then squint into the arm of my friend and spot the glimmer of a bullet lodged in his right humerus lesser tubercle. "I actually had some plans for you too but then you went and confused forceps with scissors and my libido evaporated entirely."

Miguel frowns, he doesn't like our arrangement[18]—he hasn't said that in so many words, but Miguel has the poker face of a toddler.

"What are you smirking at?" Christian smacks TK over the head.

Teeks starts laughing but I give him a look. "Bad news." I peel off my latex glove and he groans. "It's pretty lodged in there."

"Fuck." He hangs his head.

"Take him to Merrick's." I nod at Miguel while I wrap TK's arm in gauze, tying it off above the wound. "Tell him I think it might have fractured the bone, or at least splintered it." I flash Teeks an apologetic smile. "Are you regretting signing your life away to my brother yet?"

"Nope." TK squashes a smile. "Time of my life."

I roll my eyes.

"Speaking of the time of one's life…" Christian tugs on my hand and I toss him a look. "Are we wrapping up here?"

"We are." I peer down at the dressed wound one more time. I press the bandage against TK's arm once more for good measure. "Don't poke the bear."

He grins up at me. "No promises."

"Good seeing you, bro—" Christian (semi-) affectionately smacks TK on the damaged arm and he winces. I roll my eyes and Miguel fights off a smile before giving me a nod and leaving me alone with Christian.

Alone with Christian. It's still a bit of a wonder for me, really—being alone with someone. I haven't been allowed to be alone with someone in years.

"You're a dick," I tell him as we're walking up the stairs.

---

[18] FWB's.

7

He rolls his eyes. "He's fine."

But I feel a bit floaty because I think he did it because he's territorial with me. "We don't do jealous, remember?"

"I wasn't jealous." Christian frowns. "What's it to me if you fucked him once a few months ago?"

I glance back at him and find myself balancing not wanting to not be in control with not loving the indifference in his voice about someone else touching me.

"More than once." I keep walking up the stairs.

His eyes pinch and he stops for a minute before he keeps following me up. "Pretty hot, though, Baby Haites."

Baby Haites. What they call me.

"What is?" I stand at the top of the stairs, my hands on my hips.

"You." He stares over at me. "Being a doctor."

I give him a look. "I'm not a doctor."

"You're on your way." He gives me a tall look, almost as though he doesn't like it when I say disparaging things about myself, but if I let myself think that. "Soon you'll be a fully licensed doctor and driver."

I roll my eyes at him, walk away and ahead, try to chase after that stupid heart of mine that's riding off into the sunset with a boy who doesn't like me like that.

We're supposed to be cut and dry, Christian and I.

Just sex. Friends who do it. "Bang one out" as my brother so delicately puts it...

I wish it was like that, that's what I wanted from that first night. I've done it before, I'm capable of that—that's what TK was, that's what Declan was. It's not what Romeo was, but nothing ever will be what Romeo was, so it's not really fair to compare him to anyone else. Anyway, my point is I know how to have casual sex. Christian knows how to have casual sex. He and his best friends are gold medalists in casual sex, but something about that first night for us was so jarringly un-casual—

"Tell me," Christian said as he leaned in towards me late one Saturday at his club a few months ago. "Secret daydream, life goal... some shit like that."

We've known each other for years through our brothers. Jonah Hemmes is one of Julian's best friends, but I guess on that night in particular about four months back I stopped seeming like the kid-sister of his brother's best friend. The Orseund Iris tube tank does that.

8

It was great timing for me because Romeo had just fucked off, and I was sad and I've never really known what to do when he's not around.

I pursed my lips, pretending to think like the answer wasn't already on the tip of my tongue, like it wasn't always, and I found myself blushing at how close his face was to mine. "You'll think it's dumb."

"Try me." He cocked his head. He was more beautiful than I had previously noticed, like I'd never properly looked at him 'til then. Swept over to the side and pushed back to perfection, golden blonde hair. Big hazel eyes. Big bottom lip. Big trouble.

I squinted over at him, feeling a tiny bit exposed. "I'd really like to be normal." He gave me a small, confused smile, nodded a few times.

"I'd like to not have a bodyguard, I'd like to feel alone sometimes, I'd like to walk down the street and not worry that the car that's driving next to me is there to take me, I'd like to qualify for ransom insurance instead of being uninsurable—"

"Fuck." He frowned.

"I'd like to drive—by myself—somewhere. Not be driven, to do it myself."

"I feel like that one's within reach, yeah?"

I pursed my lips and his face faltered, confused, and I gave him a sheepish look. "Do you... not know how to drive?" He tilted his head, looking at me a bit cautiously.

I lifted my chin, trying to look like I didn't care about it. "No."

"Oh." He nodded a couple of times. The corner of his mouth flicked up and now I try to make him make that smile at me every time I see him.

"I'll teach you," he told me.

He would, actually. Kept that promise, but more on that later.

Present day, a couple of hours later,[19] it's 1 am and Christian's phone rings for the second time in under ten minutes. I reach across his naked body—nothing but a heart necklace he never takes off— and grab his buzzing phone from the bedside table.

"Kelsey parenthesis Blonde is calling you," I tell him and his eyes flick. He rolls over quickly, snatches his phone from me, and silences the call.

---

[19] I was right, splintered femur.

He flicks me a semi-apologetic look. Sixty percent apologetic, 40 percent amused.

His angel-boy hair is now all tugged in the ways I've just pulled it and his lips are extra rosy from being pressed against mine. He stretches an olive arm back over and behind his head.

I extend my hand out towards his phone. "Can I read your messages?"

He squints, though he's not really upset. "Why?"[20]

"I'd just like to see what Kelsey parenthesis Blonde and all her slutty friends want from you."

"It's one in the morning." He sniffs, amused. "I think we both know what they want."

"A character reference?" He gives me a dry look. "Their dignity back?" He smiles as he rolls his eyes again. "Just kidding—" I quip. "We all know it's far too late for that." He sniffs a laugh as he hands me his phone. "Passcode?"

"6969."

My eyes pinch. "Ever the picture of class."

6969[21]—I actually do think that's quite funny, but I feel a bit like being mean to him because he's getting booty calls in front of me.

I navigate to his messages. "Twenty-two unread texts. At least fifteen of the senders are female…" My voice trails as I peruse the list. "Kelsey parenthesis Blonde. Melanie Watson. Melissa Nigh. Natalie Lamburg. Natalie Boobs—" I look up at him. "Is that her God-given name?" He stifles a smile. "How big are her boobs for that to be her name in your phone?"

"Double Ds at least."

"Fair enough," I concede as I look back down, reading on. "Aimee Aitkins. Olivia XO—" I look up at him, eyebrows poised.

"I mean it like the club, not the sentiment."

"Much better." I give him a tight-lipped smile that's full of judgement. I hug his phone to my chest. "You get a lot of late-night texts." He tries to squash a smile as he reaches for his wine. "Wow." My eyes widen. "Kelsey parenthesis Blonde has quite the sailor's mouth."

He snorts a laugh. "Yes, she does."

---

[20] I don't know, because I'm a fucking masochist?

[21] Hah.

I take the wine from his hands and take a big sip. "Like that when talking to a girl, do you?"

He cracks a smile while trying to appear contrite. He uses his thumb to wipe some rouge wine that's strayed to the fat part of my bottom lip. Everything he does is sexy. "Can't say we've ever done that much talking."

I don't falter when he says that—I remind myself that I don't care—our two rules are we don't fight and we don't get jealous, so I don't care, I tell myself for the twelfth time this week and avoid the eyes of the Feelings Monster that keeps rearing its head and making me think I feel something for a person whom I couldn't possibly feel for and I don't and, even if I could, I can't anyway.

So I take a breath, steel myself as I stare over at the face I'm growing too fond of. "Henry wants to know if you're coming home tonight," I say to him, eyebrows pointed.

Christian gives me a long look, waiting for me to tell him. "I don't know, Baby Haites. Am I going home tonight?"

I sit up, facing him, pulling the blankets around my mostly naked body. I shrug indifferent, though I'm not. "I don't know, Christian Hemmes. Are you?"

He squints at me playfully. "You tell me, Baby."

My heart skips a beat when he calls me that, but he doesn't mean it how I want him to.

"I mean, I think old Sailor Mouth is hoping you'll pay her a visit..."

He gets the look in his eyes. Equal parts sure and troublesome. "Don't want to pay her a visit."

"Oh?"

He smiles and his eyes fall down my body as he shakes his head. "I'm good here..." His words trail. "Are you good here?"

"For now," I lie and he laughs.

For always, I'm afraid.

## 2

# Julian

I wasn't the most stoked when Daisy started fucking a Hemmes, and I love the Hemmes—Jonah's one of my oldest friends, their mum is a saint as far as I'm concerned—but Christian Hemmes strikes me as a bit of a fuckboy and, as an absolute fuckboy myself, I can say that it's not what you want for your sister.

Learned, though, in my time as her in-lieu parental figure that telling her a flat-out "no" only results in a guarantee of her doing exactly what I don't want her to do. Backfired with Rome big time, and now neither her nor I have ever completely shaken the arsing prick.

"Oi." Christian nods at me as he walks shirtless and sweaty into my kitchen—never what you want to see from the blad who's doing your sister. There's a towel slung over his shoulder—a small mercy, I s'pose—as he wanders to my fridge and pulls out one of my sister's juices like he owns the fucking place.

Look up at him. Nod at the towel. "Tell me you look like that from exercising."

He sniffs a laugh and peers over at me, amused. "Just getting my arse handed to me by your sister."

"Glad to hear it." I snort. "You go easy on her?"

"Nah, bro." He shakes his head, frowning a bit. "At first I was, but—she's fucking hectic."

Yep. Had her trained by the best.

"Krav Maga?" I ask him. Fold my paper.

"And a bit of sambo." He nods. "She kicked me in the head."

He rubs it mindlessly, I try not to look too pleased at the thought. Weird tension here because I do like him, actually. Always have. Pretty good guy. Like him less now that he's fucking Dais, but she's a big girl and she's going to do what she wants to. Has all her life anyway.

12

Lad like him is quicksand to someone like my sister, not a great too many people about who have the balls or the backing to say no to me, but this idiot—unfortunately—has both.

If he wasn't one of my best friends' brothers, I'd have smacked him in the face the day I found out they were hooking up.

Booker told me the morning after it happened—told me like it was his duty to tell me but I know it was just because he'd been on the pull with Dais for months and Christian cut his grass. Made me angrier than it should have that they were sleeping together—not his fault. Not like he knows what happened. But her and another Second—I don't know—I just wanted to keep her safe since I couldn't last time.

After he told me, I tore into her room, ripped Christian out of her bed, threw him against the wall. Pinned him there, forearm against his throat. Ready to kill my best friend's brother for my sister's honour. At least I thought it was for honour at the time. My psychologist has pointed out it was actually more for safety.

"What the fuck are you doing?" I growled.

He glared back at me.

"What the fuck do you think?"

Surprised me, that response. Didn't think he had it in him. Turned to her instead. "What are you doing with him?"

The question was weighted. With him. We can't do all that shit again.

I tried to tell her with my eyes but she just arched her brat-eye-brows. "Having sex."

Christian smirked.

"With him?" I stared at her.

"Yes." She blinked, bored.

"Him?" I repeated louder.

"Him." She nodded.

"Why?" I asked, louder still

Christian pulled a face I could have punched.

"How about because she's nineteen and she wants to?" Christian offered. Daisy loved that. Could see it on her. My jaw clenched. I gave him a dark look as I walked out of her room.

"We're going to have a talk, you and me."

"Can't wait," Christian called after me.

"Not you, you prick." I spat. "Her."

Not much of a talk, really. I told her it was dangerous, she said it wasn't. He has security, she has security, she can fight now, came in with a little Ted Talk about why I was wrong about it and it wasn't the same. They're not in a relationship, there are no feelings, no reason for anyone to kill her any more than usual, etcetera, etcetera. I said I didn't like it, and she told me bugger off. Good for the esteem, my sister. Keeps you humble.

That was a few months back now and these two are still fucking about. Daisy wanders in her gym clothes. Everlast boxing wraps around her knuckles that she unwinds at the sink. She looks between Christian and I.

"What?" She frowns.

I shrug at her. "I'm just glad one of us is hitting him."

He chuckles and I smack him in the stomach playfully. Grab my sister's head, kiss the top of it.

"Alright, I'm off," I say.

"Where?" she calls after me.

Nod my chin at Christian. "Brunch with the boys." Jonah Hemmes and Carmello Bambrilla. Point at my sister. "You've got an afternoon class, yeah?"

She nods.

How many men in my position have their little sister's weekly schedule memorised, do you reckon?

Not enough, probably. Probably why mine's still alive, though.

Kekoa walks into the kitchen and I clock him.

"Take the morning," I tell him. "I'll drive myself."

He shakes his head, face looks a bit serious for my liking.

"What?" I frown.

He shrugs like it's nothing but there's something skimming under the surface. "Just chatter."

Daisy pauses by the sink, her eyes darting between us. She looks both annoyed and frightened. Hate the latter, but she's always annoyed, so…

"Where?" I ask Koa.

"Just had my ear to the ground, Jules—didn't like what I heard."

He's being evasive. Trying to keep my stress levels down. I wait 'til Daisy looks away then gesture between me and my sister, asking wordlessly the question: her or me?

He shrugs again, but I know he knows the answer.

Either way, if someone wanted to get to me they'd go after her. Again. Fuck.

"Right." I nod. "Dais, you take Happy."

"I've got Miguel," she whines, because nothing's ever easy with her.

"And now you have Happy too." I give her a look and she stares at my face for a few seconds, thinks about talking back and putting up a fight about it, but I think I see that night she won't talk about rattle around her mind and then she sighs and says, "Okay."

I point at Christian. "You coming to this lunch?"

He shakes his head. "Nah, I'm gonna work your sister out upstairs."

Says that unflinching, that cocky fuck. Jut my jaw, shake my head at him. "I know where you live, bro…"

He grins. "I'm shaking in my boots."

"Face," I call to her. "Kick him in the head again."

She gives me a thumbs up.

Roll into the Greenhouse forty minutes later. Kekoa hangs back by the door, tries to give me space—which I appreciate. Spot the boys up towards the back and I walk over to them. BJ Ballentine stands up to leave as he sees me.

Reaches out a hand and I shake his with two.

"Jules." He grins. "Good to see you, man."

I nod at the door. "Skipping off already?"

"Just dropped Jo in on my way to something." He nods at his best friend.

"He's off to bang a Miu Miu model," Jonah Hemmes announces.

Carmelo Bambrilla starts laughing, but Ballentine rolls his eyes.

"I'm not." He shakes his head as I sit down next to Jonah. "I'm just giving her some career advice," he tells us and we all start laughing. He walks away, flipping us off as he leaves.

I stare after him for a couple of seconds, wait 'til he's out of ear shot. "He fucking about again?"

Jo shakes his head. Ever the loyalist.

Carmelo looks confused. "Isn't he with that hot one *The Daily Mail* can't get enough of?"

Jonah shrugs. "They're not together."

"Fuck off," I tell my oldest friend.

"They aren't." Jo shakes his head. "She just called it off with her boyfriend-of-the-week a couple of days ago."

"Is it?" Carmelo chimes in, brows up. "Oi, should I go for her?"

Jonah rolls his eyes and Carms is happy to get a rise out of him. Jibes him more. "I'll treat her good…"

15

Jonah folds his arms over his chest. "I'm sure you would, man, but it's still a firm no from me."

Carmelo frowns. "What are you, her chastity belt?"

He could be something like that, actually. Funny mix he's in, that little group of London socialites—the Full Box Set is what the papers call them. All Old Valarians who live in each other's pockets because they all became codependent in their youth. Boarding school attachment issues... Don't know how to process shit apart from each other.

Besides, Magnolia Parks, she's just one of those girls—got everyone in her pocket, and you can live in it pretty happily. I do, anyway. She's got all those boys wrapped around her finger, and Jo's easy to rile up when it comes to her. It's low-hanging fruit but I'm here for it.

"I'm going to take a crack," I tell him, sitting up straighter.

And at that, Jonah cracks up. Good old belly laugh, that smarmy shit.

Pinch my eyes at him, annoyed.

"Sorry, man." Jo laughs, genuinely amused. "But she would never."

I sniff a laugh. Weigh it up in my mind whether I'll tell him something that'd blow his fucking mind. Decide to keep it in my back pocket for another day...

It was a few years back now, statute of limitations and shit. Besides, I reckon it says more about me than it does about her, anyway. That we were on the path for a fucking spectacular night and she started crying over her ex-boyfriend, so we had pancakes in my bed and watched Nick at Nite. Fucking bad for business. Can't have it. I'd rather not have the clout of it than risk anyone hearing that I might actually have a heart.

"Yeah." I nod instead. "You're probably right. Girls like her hate older, powerful men."

"You're twenty-nine, man." Carmelo gives me a look. "Wouldn't start writing your obituary just yet."

Carmelo Bambrilla. Son of Santino. They're the big boys out in Liverpool. A sucker for romance... call it the Italian in him. He's one of my oldest friends. Best one, even. Maybe? Friends is a weird word for us all, but it's the closest thing for what we are. It's a weird life. None of us asked for it... All born into it. Like royalty. Probably fewer perks. More fun, though.

Dated his sister for a second when I was a kid. Gia. Big mistake—huge, actually—but Carmelo's little brother and Daisy were childhood sweethearts—a lot of history there. Too much, actually. More than I'd want there to be and definitely more than there should be.

Toss the waitress a smile as she hands me another drink. Very pretty. I'll take her home later.

Carmelo smacks me on the back. "Anything notable on the horizon?"

I shake my head. "Meeting next week. Don't know what about. Potential job."

"Art or arms?" Carms scratches his chin.

"Art, I reckon." I tell him with a shrug.

"Oi." Jo nods his head back towards Kekoa.

"What's your shadow doing here? Everything all good?"

I swipe my hand through the air. "Everything's grand."

Daisy
10:39 PM

> Babbyyyy

> Where are you?

On my way

> Hurry up.

> What do you want to drink

The usual

> Greyhound?

Yes please x

> Are you impressed I remembered that?

Not really.

A few days ago I memorised The Pathologic Basis of Disease.

Yeah, but you're a genius

Yes.

And you are not.

Hah

I'm here. Where are you?

In my office

Without me?

Waiting for you.

Coming.

You're about to be.

!

# 3

# Daisy

I like doing laundry. That's weird—I know. I know I could send it out but I don't, I just like doing it. It feels like something normal people do. Teachers do laundry. Social workers do laundry. Secretaries do laundry. Mechanics do laundry.

A few years ago I asked Julian to have them build for me my dream laundry room. I've got two of the Samsung 6.0 cu ft. Smart Washer with Flexwash[22] as well as the Samsung 7.5 cu ft. Smart Electric Dryer with FlexDry, both in the Fingerprint Resistant Black Stainless Steel. An ironing board and a farmhouse-style folding table in the centre, which someone puts white tulips on every day, but I don't know who.

It's my safe place in here.

The washing machines are actually devastatingly quiet now.

When I was a kid, if there was something happening at the house that no one wanted me to see or hear, Julian would bring me into the laundry room. He'd put on our old washing machine, even if it was empty. Sometimes he'd put coins in there so it made a louder sound.

At the time I thought it was cool and sort of a weird thing my brother and I did together, but now I think there was probably someone dying somewhere in this house and this was their way of keeping it from me. It's quite hard to un-hear someone dying once you've heard them. I hear my parents dying most days still for no real reason other than simply because that's the sort of shitty thing your brain tries to fill a silence with. Mostly it's the sound my dad made when he fell on the sand. Most of it was swallowed by the sand but there was a dull thud that plays on a loop in my brain.

---

[22] The machine has two separate washing machines inside each one so I can have four loads going at once. It steam-washes. It's app-controllable.

Anyway, I have a reclining leather chair and a stack of cooking magazines by the big bay window that looks out from the utility room and onto some of the grounds out back that Happy tends to,[23] though that's not a part of his mercenary job description.

A cup of tea, the barely there hum of my washing machine[24] and I can lose hours in here.

I think it's the instant gratification of prewash sprays.

Or maybe it's the everything getting clean in here.

I do the whites tonight.

Picking things out of the basket and treating them.

My favourite kind of stain remover at the minute is Vanish Gold for Whites. Also, I like their soap bar, because it's so tactile. And bleach. I love bleach. Everything about it. How it smells. How it brightens. How it removes all traces of sin.

Do you know what original sin is?

It's this theological concept that we were all born innately sinful and my brother loves it.[25] Says it's one of his two "get out of jail free cards".[26]

That we were all already born sinful so he's just living up to his nature.

But I don't like it. I don't like the idea that we're born bad because if we're all born sinners, I don't know if we can ever really wash ourselves clean.

Do you believe children carry the sins of their father? Have you heard of that? Generational sins, ancestral sins—do you believe in those? My brother does. Because our dad did what he did—that's Julian's second pass. He's already wearing Dad's sins—what's a few more?

He says it's just the family business but I call it the family sin. He doesn't like it when I say that, but I think he thinks I'm right, he just doesn't know what to do about it. Neither of us do. We are who we are, and what we are is all we've ever known.

We have rules I made up when I was little that we don't break,

---

[23] White and periwinkle hydrangeas, a ridiculously beautiful crabapple tree, a magnolia tee (vomit), rosemary, crocus and some white English roses.

[24] Annoying.

[25] Of course he does.

[26] Of course he does.

things Julian promised he'd never do that makes everything we do seem a little less bad.

People we won't work with, no matter what. Sapanta Asad, Mata Tosell, Roisin MacMathan—people who fuck with people how they fuck with people, it's a no-fly zone for us. Julian would never. I need him to never.

And it's then I pull out a white T-shirt of my brother's from the laundry basket.

I shouldn't let him buy white, I always tell myself every time I do the laundry—stop letting him buy white things. There's really no point, it's just money down the drain—it's a waste of time and white is unsalvageable for the best of us. Boys will be boys is what I used to tell myself... Boys will be boys and gang lords will be gang lords.

It's a nice T-shirt. I bought it for him.

It's from Mastermind Japan. Plain white.

And I pretend my heart doesn't sink as I inspect it all stained.

It doesn't take a med student to know this, just anyone with a working pair of eyes could tell you: there's too much red on the shirt for the person it came from to still be alive.

Julian
4:02 PM

The girl at breakfast was different to the girl at lunch.

That's astute, Daisyface... very good.

They teach you that in med school?

No

Do you know what they do teach us about in med school though, Julian?

Communicable diseases.

I'm clean as a whistle.

21

That seems both categorically untrue and factually inaccurate.

So I guess this is a no to me bringing a hot bartender home for dinner tonight?

3 for 3?

Are you joking?

….yes.

Ew

Firm no, then?

EW!!!!

# 4

# Christian

I'm lying down on the couch at home when the door knocks. We weren't expecting company—not that I knew of, anyway. Henry heaves up from his arm chair and wanders over, swinging it open.

Magnolia Parks walks on in, followed by Paili Blythe; I barely notice her, though, because, fuck, Magnolia is beautiful.

Our eyes catch even though they shouldn't. She drops them as she walks towards me before she drapes herself around Henry.

She thinks she's not tactile, but she's always touching one of us. Her sister says it's because we're all codependent. I'm pretty sure it's just because Magnolia doesn't know how to be alone.

"Where are the boys?" Magnolia says with a glance around the room, all innocent and shit. What she actually means is "Where's BJ?" and the question pisses me off, so I sit up, crack my back and yawn before I answer.

"Jo's out with Banksy and BJ's on the pull with Feaven Lusk."

Magnolia's face freezes, all pained and tight like someone's smacked her, and I get a shot of satisfaction from it—that's fucked up of me, I know—I can't help it, but...

"The model?" she clarifies with a blink. I nod. "But she's an American." She pouts, like that fucking means anything. I shrug and Henry's giving me a look I'm ignoring because I know what happens after BJ hurts her. "Right, well, then..." She clears her throat.

And it works like a fucking charm. She switches into what me and Hen call FYBJ (Fuck You BJ) Mode and she's out for blood. Her eyes drift over to mine just like I knew they would because she's like this.

She crosses her arms over that beautiful chest of hers and sits down bang next to me. Leans in way closer than she needs to. Puts her head right on my arm.

She purses her lips, steeling herself for a few seconds.

I nearly feel bad for a second because it's all over her face how hurt she is—imagining what the person she loves is doing with someone else, it fucks you up. But you know what? Join the fucking club, Parks.

I've felt like this for three years and I want some company, so I shrug a bit and say, "She's pretty hot."

Paili throws a book at my head from the other side of the room—doesn't hurt much because it's a softcover but I don't appreciate it—and Henry breathes out loudly through his nose. Bit of a bad sign from him—he only lets me take this shit so far.

Parks's eyes look glassy. Fuck. If I make her cry, then Henry'll fight me—not that he'd win. Not a fair fight, though, because he's never had to learn to fight like I have. He's decent in a brush, though, even for a boy who grew up in Belgravia…

I stretch my arms up, put them behind Magnolia—not around her—behind her. An important clarification.

Henry squints over at me. He knows me too well. I know this shit with us puts him in a weird position. Me and Beej. Me and Parks. I love her, just. And it's not all fucked up all the time.

Magnolia and Henry were best friends in nursery, they have a real sibling vibe. Hard for him sometimes, I think, working out whom to be more loyal to. His brother or his best friend? Usually it's her. He'll cover BJ's tracks sometimes, but I suspect that's more to do with what would happen if Magnolia found them.

But us four—me, Henry, Magnolia and Paili—we're the originals. The three of us became friends in year one. Paili moved to our school in year two. And it was just the four of us 'til we got to Varley. Jo and Beej were around, but they were bigger, grade above. Didn't give a shit. I mean—BJ gave a shit about Magnolia because he's been fucking obsessed with her since he was six.

Parks used to love me. Loved me first, actually.

Henry was my best friend and she was Henry's, and she followed me around like a puppy. I'd kiss her at lunchtimes and parties and when I was bored like you are when you're a shit-kicking kid away at boarding school. And then all it took was just one fucking summer to fuck it all up.

Lil and Ham took us all to Saint Barts for three weeks.

That was the summer Parks fell for BJ. Also happened to be the summer I fell in love with Magnolia. Yeah, yeah, bad timing, I know. It's my fault. I left it too long, whatever.

24

I always liked that she liked me before she liked him, it made her feel a little less his in my mind's rationale for feeling how I feel about her, which is—for the record—in love but pretty fucked off about it.

"What are we watching?" Henry nods his head at the TV.

I glance from him to Magnolia. "Scary—"

"No!" she whines. "I hate scary movies!"

She looks over at Paili for help, who shrugs, God bless her. "I like them."

"Well, I don't." Magnolia crosses her arms, huffing. "And I'll be scared and then I'll have to go home alone."

Henry stares over at her, blinking. "Your dad's 6'2". He has weekly training sessions with Leon Edwards."

"He's in Atlanta!" she cries, her head falling back on the couch behind her. It lands on my arm. She leaves it there for a few seconds. Swallows. Sits back up. "And Bridget says she knows taekwondo but I've never seen the fruit of that, and allegedly—" She pulls a serious face and I'm laughing because she's insane. "Bubushka defected from the Soviets, so she might be useful but also, she's pretty old and also, maybe that's who's coming for us anyway."

"Yeah." I give her a look. "My ear on the ground says that the Soviets are just waiting to pounce on the elderly of the WII…" She glares over at me. "Stay here." I shrug. Her face freezes up at the suggestion. Henry cranes his neck, staring at me with wide eyes. "With Henry, I mean—" I say quickly.

I can feel my cheeks turning pink.

She swallows again and looks over at Henry. "Can I, Henny Pen?"

He sighs out of his nose, annoyed. "Yes."

Like he'd ever say no to her. Like any of us can. I don't know what it's about, why we can't—why making Magnolia Parks sad for a second feels like you're betraying your country. Happens to all of us, though, even Jo, and Jo doesn't give a shit about making anyone sad.

"Yay." She claps her hands together. "Sleepover!"

"Good luck, Henry." Paili nods solemnly. Magnolia frowns over at her. "Sorry, babe—you're just… so horrible to share a bed with."

Magnolia looks from Henry to me, casting a line out. Henry gives her an apologetic smile. "Yeah, you are."

Magnolia peers back to me, blinking a lot. Her eyes look hurt already.

"You are," I tell her.

She turns around to face the TV, arms folding over her chest, having a little strop. "You never seemed to complain before," she says under her breath, eyes on the television.

I lean down to her ear, stare straight ahead and whisper. "I wouldn't complain now."

We watch Texas Chainsaw Massacre, Parks is jumpy as shit the whole time. It's cute. She grabs my hand a bunch, then she lets go every time she realises she does it.

Midway through she drops an M&M down the front of her top.

She stares down at it, frowning.

I stare at it for a few seconds too, quickly clocking Henry and Paili—neither are paying attention to us—so I grab it.

Pick it up with my index and my thumb, toss it into my mouth, smirking.

She stares at me, eyes bright and wide.

I think about her body against me the whole night, don't pay attention to the movie.

It's such a benign version of physical contact, I know—her head on my shoulder and her cuddled up against me, one of her oldest friends in the world. I'm probably reading into everything, but maybe I'm not.

Daisy texts me midway through, and I look at my phone—seeing Magnolia see that she's texting me. She looks away reflexively, trying to give me privacy or some shit, but I don't hide it. I like her seeing other people want me in the ways she won't have me.

It's also fake because Magnolia Parks is the fucking nosiest girl in the world. She's angled her head, but she's trying to read my messages out of the corner of her eye, I can see it. She's straining so much she's going to get a bloody migraine.

what are you doing

Leave it for a minute. I don't know why. A bit of a prick, I guess.

chilling

come over?

maybe?

Not maybe. I'm not going anywhere… Not with Magnolia next to me like this.

> what are you doing, Baby Haites

Dickhead, I know, but it is what it is, and we are what we are.

Me and Daisy? We're friends. Actually, we're good friends these days. Friends who fuck. My mum would have a fucking conniption at that, but here we are. I'm shagging the sister of Britain's most notorious crime lord and I'm blowing her off, but we're friends, just so it's okay. Daisy doesn't care, we've been hooking up a few months now—not exclusively, obviously. The Haites don't do exclusive.

Fuck, I don't do exclusive. Except that one time and it went to shit. She's sitting right next to me three years later like a deadweight wrapped around my heart's fucking ankle.

nothing.

playing GTA with the boys

> which boys

Booker and TK.

I frown and get a pang of jealousy. Weird.

She's slept with TK. Has she slept with the other one too? I can't remember—they're the youngest ones of the Lost Boys. The Americans. Good looking enough. I think she does it to annoy her brother. I think that's why she slept with me.

My chest goes tight for a second. Weird.

> who's winning?

who do you think?

She's just my friend, but she's very, very hot.

> hah. I can't tonight

27

ok

tomorrow?

maybe

I pocket my phone and see that Magnolia's looking up at me, a look on her face that I love, but then again I love all her faces. "Well, well." Her lips purse. I sniff. "Is that a thing, then?" she asks, eyebrows up.

And because I'm shit, I let it hang there for a second and hope it makes her feel how I feel whenever she's with someone else. Then I scrunch my face up. "Nah."

"Oi, Parks," Henry interrupts, staring over at us. "Bedtime."

"Fuck off, man." I laugh. "I think she can figure out her own bedtime."

Henry gives me a look that makes me feel like shit, makes me feel like I'm being the prick here.

He ignores me and catches Parks's eye. He cocks his head towards the stairs, then starts walking up them.

"Night, Pails," he calls back. "Text when you get home, yeah?"

She stands, kisses me and Parks each on the cheeks, and lets herself out.

I glance down at Magnolia and she stares up at me. I do my best not to kiss her. Find myself preparing for it anyway, lick my bottom lip, swallow down the heavy feeling of how much I want her. I'm a pro at not-kissing her now, though. Been not-kissing her for going on three years.

Her eyes drop to my lap. A rogue M&M sits around the fly of my jeans.

Her eyes flicker from mine to the M&M and back up to me. She drums her fingers on her mouth, eyes big and less innocent than you'd think they are—she's staring at it and my whole body feels electric.

Then she plucks it up, tosses it in her mouth, bites down on it with a crunch and a grin.

My mouth falls open as I stare after her walking up the stairs, looking back over her shoulder at me with a small laugh.

I have a shit sleep that night. Something about her being here and not with me fucks with me a little. I'm used to her not being with me at this point, obviously.

Her staying here isn't dead unheard of—better her in Henry's bed than BJ's—but how many beds will she go through before she circles back to mine?

She'll crawl into it in the morning anyway, that I know.

She finds it less threatening to lay on my bed in the daylight, like she doesn't trust herself with me in the dark.

The next morning I wake up how I thought I would—with Magnolia Parks flopping down next to me, staring up at the ceiling.

I roll in to face her, but she's all eyes on the roof. Picks up the stuffed lion she gave me when I was six that still sits on my bed even though it shouldn't anymore and tosses it up in the air, catching it mindlessly.

"Is Feaven good in bed?" Magnolia asks the ceiling.

I look over at her. She's such a bitch. A bitch for asking me and a bitch for feeling like she can. I know what she wants me to say, I know how I could respond without hurting her, but I'm kind of keen to sting her for it because fuck her for asking.

"She's pretty good in bed, yeah." I nod.

Her face falters as she looks over at me. "Better than me?"

I sit up and raise an eyebrow. "We never slept together, remember?"

She purses her lips, staring over at me.

This bit's always shitted because if we're being technical—and I want to be—because if we are, maybe we've had sex. But she doesn't count the Maserati as her first time with Beej, so she doesn't count whatever's happened with us as sex either. And I don't know how much Beej knows, but she'd spin it to him different anyway, waving it around like a banner she's proud of—that we never properly did it—like she's one up on him. Like she thinks she's betrayed him less than he betrayed her because she and I never did what he does with everyone else all the time. But there's a wide open plain of sexual possibilities between kissing and literal, actual penetrative sex, and Magnolia Parks and I explored the entire fucking savanna.

And she'll say it as loud as she can anytime it suits her—that we never had sex—but what she strategically leaves out is that we tried to. All the time, and every time we did, she'd cried.

So when she's on that fucking high horse of hers spouting that "we never had sex", the giant black abyss that trails behind her sentence is: "but it wasn't for lack of trying."

And I'm an idiot, I know, because if that isn't a fucking red flag, I don't know what is.

Because I'd never force her, most of the time she'd initiate it—and she wasn't crying because she wasn't ready. She wasn't crying because she was drunk. I know now—I get them, how fucking tied they are to each other and their monumental levels of dysfunction—that she was crying because she was trying to have sex with someone who wasn't BJ. I should have known that, should have seen it, but she'd already got me by then. I was all in, all in love and shit. She could have fucked me or fucked me over, it wouldn't have mattered either way. I wasn't going anywhere.

I still haven't gone anywhere.

I don't think Beej knows that part—don't even know if he should know. I don't want to be the one to tell him either because it's our chink; if we'd kill each other over anything, it'll be her. He can't see straight about her, but neither can I. We both love her and neither of us can do shit about it.

She's angry at me for saying that, though—reminding her that we didn't have sex. She can remind everyone else, but all fucking hell breaks loose if I remind her. We've had this argument before, if you want to call it that. It's more of a nonversation and I reckon it shits her because it either invalidates us to her or because it makes her feel deficient. Neither is true.

The fact that she's the only girl I've ever been with whom I haven't had sex with says more about her than if we'd actually done it.

And there's not a fucking thing that's deficient about her.

There's a knock on my door and it swings open without waiting for an answer—Henry nods at Magnolia. "Just buzzed BJ up."

She sits up, eyes all wide and hopeful and pathetic. She tucks her hair behind her ears like a dog whose master's coming to the door.

She skips out and she's so happy I want to fucking vomit. Henry stares over at me, then points. "Tighten the fuck up, mate."

I roll my eyes with a sigh, then follow them out.

BJ walks through our front door. Parks's cheeks go pink.

He gives her this half smile that gets her every time—fucking sad that I know that—but you know what? I am fucking sad. In love with my best friend's girl.

I'm a piece of shit.

"Hi." She gives him a shy smile, skipping over to him to hug him.

He wraps his arms around her, puts his chin on her head before he peers down at her.

He tugs on the oversized T-shirt she's wearing that's obviously a man's. Doesn't let her out of the hug. "Whose is this?" His eyes flick from me quickly back to Parks. More insecure than he'd want me to know he is.

"Henry's." She frowns up at him like it's a fucking ridiculous question. He nods once.

"You stayed here last night then?" he asks her but doesn't let her go. She nods, looking up at him.

"Why?" he asks and looks straight at me.

It's a casual question with sharp edges.

"Because we watched Texas Chainsaw Massacre last night, Bushka's on the USSR's hit list, apparently, and Magnolia can't defend herself for shit," Henry says with a shrug. He doesn't look at me as he says it, but I know he's covering for me, even though nothing he's saying is untrue. "Worst sleep of my life." Henry stretches his arms over his head, hamming it up.

"Hey." She pouts.

Beej tilts his head at her, eyes all soft, looking at her like she's just his.

"You are a bit hard to sleep with…" BJ concedes and she shifts in his embrace. Yes, they're still holding on to each other. Yes, they're that fucked up.

"She's hot, she's cold, she's scared, she's hungry." Henry sighs and then gives her a pointed look. "No wonder you're single."

Hen's the only one she'll take that shit from without getting stroppy. It's just how they are.

BJ shakes his head. "You've got to have a granola bar in your bed-side table for her or else she's a pain in the arse."

Henry ruffles her hair as he walks past them. "She's a pain in the arse either way."

BJ sniffs. "Come on, get dressed." He hooks his arm around her neck, pulling her upstairs with him. "I'll take you to breakfast."

"Okay, I'll just take myself to breakfast then?" I say.

BJ looks back at me. "Yep."

# 5

# Julian

I stare over at my *View of the Sea at Scheveningen*. The Van Gough Museum says they recovered this one. They are lying. We planted the fake. The real one hangs strategically in my office on a wall where that bloody nosy copper won't see it when he pokes his fucking head in to perv on my sister.

My office is pretty sick, though... Pieces of art I've "accumulated" over the years.

I've got an Edvard Munch, a Kandinsky, two from Franz Marc, an Egon Schiele and the Van Gogh. The circumstances surrounding the acquisitions of the aforementioned pieces might be of precarious legality, but who's gonna stop me?

Dais hates expressionism, so my office is the only place I can keep them.

Impressionism, Fauvism and expressionism—me.

Renaissance, rococo and romanticism—all her.

I'm sitting at my desk, Dais is playing darts. Kind of with Declan, kind of not—if they're playing, she's creaming him. If they're not playing, she's still creaming him.

It's no secret around here that he's into her—besotted with her, always has been. They dated once, briefly. Not long after her and Rome—bit of a rebound, if you ask me—but they're all rebounds for her, I think. Decks was at university too, not studying medicine. Law, I think.

Slept with her. Took her on a date. Had no idea she was seventeen to his twenty-four 'til I showed up.

Hardly his fault, though. How many seventeen-year-olds are at university? The whole thing was pretty fun. Made a few threats, threw my weight around. Kind of liked him by the end of it, brought him into the fold not long after that. A happy by-product of that was, and remains, that Daisy becomes acutely uninterested in men if they work for me. She dropped him pretty quick, but he never really got past her.

A bit painful to watch him around her, and I reckon she does her conscionable best not to feed into it, but then Daisy's been the centre of everyone's focus since the day she was born.

'A flower among thorns," my dad would say. And then Mum would say that daisies are a common flower, and every time I think of that I feel a weird sense of relief that I don't have to navigate that shit anymore. Not that you ever want your parents dead—I don't—but Mum with Daisy was a fucking lot. Probably why Daisy doesn't know how to interact with other women—though I suppose that's partially my fault. Not a lot of matriarchal influences out on the London crime scene, just Delina Bambrilla (who is undoubtedly all of our saving grace). Rebecca Barnes too, Jo's mum—a good woman—but at the time we could've used her she was heavily distracted by the death of her own daughter. Wasn't a great year around these parts, really. Remy Hemmes and then our parents not too far apart.

All of that feeds into my sister's pathology—why she is who she is, why she can't seem to make a friend who's a girl, why she gravitates to men how she does. Didn't mean to do it, but I guess I just raised her that way.

Daisy hits the bullseye again, like she does almost every throw, and tosses Decks a smug look over her shoulder, but it's unnecessary because every man and his dog knows Declan thinks she strung up the stars.

My office door swings open and in saunters my sister's best friend from school. He falls back into the armchair by my desk.

"Is that celebrity stylist Jack Giles?" I grin over at him as my sister bounds over and plants herself in his lap.

A good man, that Jack Giles—been dealt a bit of a shit hand, but he's made the most of it. Made a name for himself despite everything. And he's a fucking looker. Turns heads everywhere he goes, breaks hearts left and right, but I reckon his heart's pretty fucked up at the minute all on it's own.

"Ey." I nod my chin at him. "How's it going with you and Hot John?"

Giles looks over and grimaces.

"He still fucking you around?" Decks asks from the other side of the room, folding his arms.

"Always." Daisy rolls her eyes, pushing some hair behind Jack's ears. "But Jacky did go on a date with a certain gay celebrity the other night—"

"It wasn't a date." Jack rolls his eyes.

"He asked you out after you styled him!"

He tosses her a look. "To say thank you!"

"Who was it?" I lean in, interested.

"We shan't be saying," Daisy announces, brat nose in the air. "But rest assured it was regrettably not Anderson Cooper, but we'll get there eventually."

There's a knock at the front door.

Dad bought out an entire cul-de-sac in the middle of Knightsbridge in the 80s. The Compound. Looks like a bit of a palace. You wouldn't know what goes on in here other than the stuff of legends. You can't tell from the outside that it's so much more than just a fucking big house. Indoor pool, basketball court, gym, rooftop bar, rooms for my boys, couple of panic rooms and a biosecurity safe where we keep a bunch of shit I'm not going to tell you about. It just looks like every other bougie house around here. The heightened security might get a couple of extra looks, but for all anyone knows around here we could just be royalty.

"You get it," I tell my sister, nodding towards the knock. Whoever it is has already been vetted by security. Besides, I know who it is.

Dais rolls her eyes at me, trots over to the door.

I get up after a second, walk to the doorframe, watching as though I don't know, like I'd ever let her open a door if I didn't.

It's him.

It's 9 pm on a Wednesday night.

It's always him.

And he's a sucker for her.

"Tiller, we have to stop meeting like this!" She beams up at him, batting her eyes.

Killian Tiller, a detective with the NCA who's been jonesing for my sister since the second his American arse laid eyes on her. As if I didn't have enough on my fucking plate, now I've gotta keep an eye on a fed who's trying to get into my sister's pants.

Trouble is, I reckon she'd let him. She's always been a sucker for boys who look like the blonde one from Fast & Furious, and that's this lad to a tee.

"What?" He gives her a look. "Me turning up at your house because your family's under criminal investigation? I agree."

"Perfect." She smiles at him coyly. "So Friday? Dinner at eight?"

She's too fucking good at this. Makes me feel a bit nauseous.

He snorts a laugh. "What are you, sixteen now?"

"Don't tease, you know I'm twenty." She scowls at him.

"Do you want a prize? Or are you all set with the one that comes with your Happy Meal?"

She frowns at him. "I don't know why you're speaking about Happy Meals in a disparaging way. They're perfectly portioned and completely delicious." Cocks an eyebrow at him. "You know they're my favourite…"

"Do I?" he asks, smirking down at her.

She nods at the folder snug under his arm. "You can stop pretending that file isn't just a million photos you took of me, you big old perv."

He bites back a laugh. "Ah, you got me."

"I look quite fresh in that navy lingerie, don't I?" she says, nose in the air.

Fuck. I want to die. Persevere with my spying anyway.

Tiller tilts his head, looking down on her more affectionately than a man investigating her family should. "I wouldn't know."

"Okay," she tells him, using air quotes and finally he cracks a proper laugh, face lighting up.

Fuck me, I haven't even asked her to work this guy, she's just doing it herself.

He shakes his head, drawing himself back to something approaching serious. "Where was your brother two nights ago?"

She gives him a tight smile and a shrug.

I shift a little, make sure he can't see me.

"Know anything about some missing art?"

"No." She shakes her head emphatically. "But that sounds very serious…"

"A Fernand Léger painting worth £150,000 went missing that night."

She inspects her nails. "I don't like him, do you?"

"Your brother?"

"Léger." She glares. "Not a big fan of pop art nor abstract."

"Who was your brother with two nights ago?"

"Where were you two nights ago, Tils?" She bites down on her bottom lip and he rolls his eyes. "Every time you point a finger, there's three pointing back at you!" she tells him merrily. He rolls his eyes again, exasperated.

"You'll strain those if you keep doing that." She nods at him.

"Well." He gives her a look. "It's hard to control around you."

"You can't control yourself around me?" She flutters her eyelashes at him and I shake my head, trying not to laugh. "So adorable." She sighs.

The copper gives my sister an amused look and she nudges his arm playfully. "So where did we land with Friday?"

Tiller squints at her. "I don't date criminals."

She leans her head against the doorframe and sighs. "I love it when you talk dirty to me."

He sniffs a smile then shakes his head then walks down my front stairs.

"I don't either, by the way..." she calls after him.

He looks back. "What?"

"I don't date criminals."

"Just fuck them, do you?" His eyes are sharp and his tone is daring.

Her lips round out in surprise—she's enjoying the attention too much, like she's starved for it.

"My, my!" She squashes a smile. "That is a comprehensive little folder you've got there. If you know that, then you really do know how good I look in navy lingerie."

He stops and squints for a second, then shrugs. "I liked you better in the white."

Her jaw drops and she lets out a single laugh, but I want his fucking head on a platter for that one.

I walk back over to my desk, sit on it like I wasn't eavesdropping on them, and she meanders back into my office.

"Who was that?" I ask, pretending I don't know.

"Tiller."

I roll my eyes. "What'd he want this time? Besides a date with you."

"Unfortunately," she sighs, "as is ever the story of my life, I fear it's not me he wants a date with."

"Is Inspector Tiller gay?" Declan asks from the other side of the room, his eyes wide with earnestness. "Giles, have a crack, mate!"

"A court date, genius." She rolls her eyes.

"Wait—are you talking about the Sexy Policeman?" Jack asks, sitting up.

"We are." Dais nods.

"I mean…" I frown a bit. "I wouldn't call him sexy." I shrug.

Daisy gives me a look like I'm an idiot. "Then I would call you blind."

"He is stupid hot." Jack nods, not looking up from his phone. "Should have been a model. What's he being a policeman for? Making me disrespect the badge for a peek."

Feel myself frown a bit, try to cover it because I don't want another lecture from my sister about how I have to be the most attractive person in the room or else I apparently shit a brick. Not true. Besides, I've never been in a room where I wasn't the best looking.

"Anyway." Daisy plants herself in front of me, arms folded over her chest. "Did you steal some art this week, Julian?" She squints at me.

Yep.

I did. Well, not me personally.

Some of the footmen.

She'd rather not know about the comings and goings of our family business, and I'd rather keep her out of it as much as possible. Safer that way.

"I don't steal, Face." I give her a look. "I acquire."

"That sounds like 'educated thief' for 'steal'." She gives me a curt smile.

I match it. "Right, and what's 'nosy sister' for 'fuck off'?"

"*Casse-toi.*"

I smile. "Nup—" Shake my head at her. "That's what it is in 'pretentious sister'…"

Magnolia<br>
10:26 AM

> Morning champ

Hi

> How are we feeling

We've felt better

We can imagine

What happened

You know what happened

Remind me

He slept with Taura

brought her to your mum's launch.

Pricky

You got shitfaced.

And then...

And then nothing.

Henry was on pupil watch and I got the always-fun task of sloshing you home

Was I very sloshy

Yes

Sorry

It's all good.

What are you doing? Me and Hen are gonna go to Annabels for lunch

Beej and I are on New Bond St. We'll call you in a bit xx

Cutie update please

I don't know a cutie, sorry.

Angelic-faced gang lord, impeccable arse.

Not a gang lord...

Because that's what counts.

Arse is impeccable though

Worthy of poetry, I'd say.

Impeccable Arse is fine. Blew me off.

Is that a sex thing?

Don't answer that.

Hilarious.

Why'd he blow you off?

Because he's an impeccable arse.

Way to really bring that home. 10/10

I think we're going to get drinks tomorrow night.

Sexy

Fingers crossed.

# 6

# Daisy

It was my birthday a couple of months ago. I didn't tell him about it, but the day after Christian just turned up on my front steps, unannounced and uninvited, wearing a grey T-shirt, shredded jeans and Vans. In his arms were the biggest bouquet of daisies and chamomiles I've ever seen.

He grinned at me proudly.

"What are you doing?" I eyed him suspiciously.

"It's your birthday." He shrugged. "Figured you wouldn't have plans—"

I frowned at him. "Wow."

He pointed his thumb towards my brother's office. "Where's he letting you go two days in a row anyway?"

"He could—" I glared. "Be letting me go places."

I frowned and he paused, his eyes flickered up and down my body. I was in the Pure-Wrap knitted jumpsuit from Calvin Klein's underwear range and I know he knows I wear that to bed.

He smirked, that cocky prick. "Do... you... have... plans?"[27]

"Well, no, but—"

"Now you do." He walked into our foyer and spun on his heel, mouth twitching into a smile.

I rolled my eyes, closed the door, and folded my arms over my chest. I tempered my face and tried to not look a little bit pleased.

I was worried my cheeks were going pink so I snatched the flowers from his hands and wandered to the kitchen to find a vase.

"So, what are you thinking then?" I looked over at him, filling the Baroque and Roll vase from Versace with water from the sink. My mother decorated our home before she died and Jules never really

---

[27] That dick.

changed it. She was really into the froufrou vibe,[28] a lot of marble and gold. You could close your eyes, raise your hand, and spin around, and nine times out of ten you'd be pointing to something Versace.[29]

"I've got a plan," he told me coyly.

"Well, what is it?"

"Surprise."

"I hate surprises." I frowned.

"Do you?" he asked, a little miffed.

And I don't know why, but him looking a little deflated made me feel a tiny bit happy. "Not really," I conceded, and he perked right back up.

"Good."

"Just tell me?"

He smiled and nodded his head towards my room. "Go pack an overnight bag."

"For where?" I pouted.

"Can't tell you."

"How will I pack then?"

"Oh right," he groaned. "Okay, I'll go pack for you then."

"Well, wait," I yelled after him as he headed to my room. "Don't just pack underwear."

"Great idea!" he called over his shoulder. "Definitely only packing you underwear."

I followed up after him, deciding that wherever we were going, I should probably change.

I tugged on the black Le Skinny de Jeanne jeans from Frame and rummaged through my drawer for an overpriced plain white tee.

Christian glanced over at me, a fist full of underwear in his hands just to spite me, then shoved it unceremoniously into the duffle bag he'd found with a grin.

He tossed me a pair of shoes. Low top suede Star Kicks from Converse. "Let's go." He nodded to the door.

"Where's Miguel?" I asked, following him down the stairs.

He shook his head as he trotted back down the stairs, then turned back at me, eye to eye because the steps let us be. "No Miguel."

I gave him a look. "He has to come, Julian makes him."

---

[28] Aesthetically, not musically.

[29] Is this a brag? I don't know.

Head shake. "Not today."

I looked at him skeptically. "Julian's letting me go somewhere without Miguel?" I blinked. "Somewhere with an overnight bag?"

"Yes."

"But—"

"He trusts me," he told me.

I gave him a look. "Since when?"

Christian shook his head decidedly, brows creased in a way I've come to learn means he's not playing. "I won't let anything happen to you, Dais."

We got into his car[30] and just drove.

I don't know where. North.[31] We'd been driving for about fifty minutes, out of the city and he was singing away pretty tunelessly to Leon Bridges and I couldn't believe he knew all the words because I'd pegged him purely as a doof-doof music lover[32]—then he pulled over to the side of the road.

He turned off the ignition and looked over at me and—imagine with me for a second, will you? Christian's face. It always looks a little bit tense. Always a little squinty, always his jaw looks a little clenched—but when he looked at me there in that car, for a split second it was like someone had thrown some silk over his face. A wisp of gentle.

"This is the hand brake." He pointed to it. "This is the gear stick. This—" He kicked his feet. "Is the brake." He glanced at me with stern eyes. "Important." I rolled my eyes, trying not to smile too much, trying not to mount him on the spot, trying not to melt into loving him accidentally. "And the accelerator. The steering wheel, obviously." He gripped it and I was jealous. "Some people say ten and two, but fuck it, hold it how you want to." He shrugged. "Indicators and lights. Windscreen wipers." He talked about the mirrors and the

---

[30] Mercedes jeep, G-class, black.

[31] Whitby, up in Yorkshire, so it would turn out.

[32] I don't know why. It was incredibly two-dimensional of me to think that, I know. I think when you're trying not to feel a certain way about people, sometimes it's easier to keep them flat on a page, but Christian singing all the words to "Beyond" made me feel nervous because I wasn't sure who he was singing about, and, no matter how much I wanted it to be, I was 99.99 percent sure it wasn't me.

seat position. About the engine lights and what they all meant. Blind spots. He nodded at his door. "Come around this side."

I obeyed, oddly quiet and a little too wide-eyed for my own liking.

He opened his door, grabbed my wrist and yanked me down onto his lap.

"I'm going to do the pedals, okay?"

"Okay," I barely said as I barely nodded.

"You just do the wheel. Focus on the road. Get a feel for it."

I nodded. Heart thudding, but that was likely because I'd never operated a vehicle before and not because I could smell John Varvatos on him and I loved it.

He reached around my body and the engine revved to life.

"Okay," he said quietly. "Indicate back onto the road." I nodded. "Check nothing's coming, then roll out."

I did—ultra carefully, but smoother than I'd imagined, so I was actually pretty pleased with myself.

"Good," he said. "Put your lights on." He gestured to the darkening sky.

I nodded and did.

I loved it. Driving. Instantly I loved it. I felt in control for the first time in my life.

It felt like breathing.

My eyes danced across the road in front of me, checking for dangers that couldn't possibly exist in a world where Christian Hemmes was teaching me to drive a car alone in the middle-of-nowhere-England, and no wonder Miguel always drives, no wonder he's never offered to teach me—that greedy bastard, saving all the magic up for himself.

"This is the quietest you've ever been," Christian told me, jerking me out of my brain's diatribe. "Should have taught you to drive ages ago…"

I sniffed an indignant laugh, and he reached around my body again, nudging the wheel a little.

"You're hugging the right a bit."

I nodded, not really knowing what that meant; all I knew was he had a big ass car and I was afraid I'd hit someone so I kept veering away from the other lane.

He nudged the wheel again. "Little more to the left."

I nodded but ignored him.

He waited for about ten seconds, letting me hug my right, then he eventually slipped both arms around me, sliding his hands on to the steering wheel and over the top of mine.

"Loosen these up." He tapped my hands.

I did.

And then he kept them there. His on mine. Keeping me left.[33]

He rested his chin on my shoulder and I liked the way his breathing sounded.

I hadn't thought about his breathing before that day, but there and then, our hands on the wheel, his chin on my shoulder, I realised I liked it, that I'd grown accustomed to it, the steadiness of it. My cheeks started to flush and I worried that my hands might be sweaty—why would they have been sweaty? Was I sweaty? No.[34]

"Left," he reminded me gently.

I nodded quickly to silence him.

I remember worrying we were so close to each other in that moment that he could hear my thoughts. Transference by osmosis?

"You're a very serious driver," he told me and I could tell he was smirking.

"Is this really the best way to teach someone to drive?" I asked him, eyes on the road.

"Definitely not," he conceded quickly, a smile in his voice. "I just thought it might increase my chances of sex afterwards."

I left that hanging for a bit. "It has."

He started laughing and a piece of his laugh snagged on my heart and I didn't want him to stop.

We stayed like that for a while, at least a quarter of an hour, his hands on mine. Me on his lap, his chin on my shoulder.

We didn't speak. He wasn't singing along to the music anymore even though it was playing still.[35] It was a little bit exquisite if for no other reason than because it was the most by myself I'd felt since the morning my parents died, and the aloneness was riveting.

"Alright." He eventually nodded towards a stretch of upcoming road. "Let's pull in here for a second."

"Why?" I pouted but complied all the same.

---

[33] Or, maybe a little bit, just keeping me.

[34] A little bit, maybe.

[35] Bobby Long, "Being a Mockingbird".

"Why do you think?" He gave a single laugh, killing the engine.

In a move that was so smooth he had to have done it with a multitude of others, he reclined the seat with one hand, and flipped me so I was facing him with the other.

I collapsed on to him, pushed myself up enough to peer down. "How many times have you done that?" I asked skeptically.

"First time." His eyes twinkled, all pleased.

"I don't believe you." I rolled my eyes.

He gave me the serious look. "I wouldn't lie to you, Dais." Then he cracked a smile. "Was it that smooth?"

I let out a frustrated sigh. "Yes."

"Oh." He grinned like the cat who got the cream. He ran his hands along his jaw. "Do you think I've found my calling in life? Driving instructor?"

"Have you taught anyone else?"

"You're my first."

"How many years has it been since you've been able to say that?"

"Oi!" He chuckled.

"You were quite a good teacher," I admitted, resting my chin on his chest, which wasn't something I normally did.

"You're pretty easy to teach," he conceded.

"Really?"

"Yeah, I mean, you were rubbish when we first started sleeping together and now you're—"

I smacked him in the arm and he cracked a laugh that I caught because his laugh is a bit like that. He shook his head a tiny bit. "You're good at everything you do." He gave me a slither of a smile. "It's annoying, a bit."

"Hey." I pursed my lips together. "Thank you. For this."

He gave me a half smile then slipped his hand behind my head—which I remember thinking at the time, hey, you don't normally do that. His eyes flickered from my eyes to my mouth, unable to decide where to land. Eyes, eventually. "I said I would."

Jack
8:34 AM

Tell me everything you know about Gus Waterhouse.

45

Friends with Jules. Very handsome. Likes boys. Not seeing anyone.

That I know of.

Interesting...

Want an intro?

No, you're not very subtle

I beg your pardon?

Love ya. Great friend. Top notch chef. Very studious. But the last time I asked you to make a subtle introduction you clicked your fingers in the face of Luke Evans, drew a heart in the air and pointed at me with a wink....

Sue me

I wish I could.

# 7

# Julian

I stare at my best friend sitting on my couch—all bleeding, that fucking prick—I do my best not to look annoyed about it but it's a £46,000 Art Nouveau Settee by Georges de Feure from the early 18th century. It's black, at least—I tell myself. Still pains me a bit, though…

Carmelo peers down at his bleeding arm. "Well, go on then." He nods his chin towards the door. "Get her."

St Daisy's Hospital for the Deranged and the Desperate, that's what she calls it when they come here, and a lot of them do.

She's more central than Merrick half the time anyway, who's all the way out in Clapham.

"Daisy!" I call for her.

Brief pause.

"What?" she bellows back from somewhere in the house.

"Get in here," I tell her. "And bring your suture kit."

Another huff from that girl I've raised since she was fucking nine years old. A few seconds later, my sister drags her feet into my office with the enthusiasm of a prison ward.

"What now?" She glares over at me.

I nod my chin at Carmelo, who flashes her the gaping wound slashed down his forearm.

She pinches her eyes at it. "And what happened here?"

He purses his lips, thinking. "Floor is lava," he tells her.

"Bullshit," she tells him, unflinching.

I try not to smile.

"Fell through a glass table?" he offers as an alternative.

She inspects the gash. "Now that I believe."

"Doesn't matter anyway." Carmelo sits up straight and catches my eye as he gives me a shit-eating grin. "Not important. What is important is this: Daisyface, when did you get full-blown sexy?"

I roll my eyes. Fucking Italians. Daisy's about to rip him a new one herself when there's a voice from my doorway that I always have mixed feelings about.

"What are you talking about?" Romeo Bambrilla says as he looks her up and down. "She's always been full-blown sexy."

Somewhere between hateful and grateful is how I feel about Romeo Bambrilla.

And my sister—she stares over at him, eyes wide with the sort of hopefulness that you never want to see someone you love sporting because you know it'll never be met.

"Rome," she says, blinking a lot.

"Dais." He cocks a small grin and their eyes lock how they always have.

Feel bad for a second for all the shit they've been through, all the ways I've kept them apart, but then that night rattles around my head and the feeling disappears on the spot. I did the right thing. Keep her alive, that's the gig. Happiness is irrelevant, you can't cater to happy, ask any parent. It's ephemeral. Keep her safe, that's the important part.

"When did you get back?" Daisy swallows.

Me and Carms trade looks, and Rome stares over at her for a few seconds before answering. "Couple of days ago..."

Daisy's head pulls back and she's snapped out of it. Not a massive change in her demeanor, but I notice it and so did he. Neck tall, bottom lip sucked in, eyes pinched. "And you didn't call?" Tight smile.

He wanders into my office, scratching his chin. "Last time I saw you, you weren't too happy to see me..."

"You were fucking Tavie Jukes."

"So?" I jump in, a bit because I don't want my sister turning into some idiot, possessive girl. "Face, you broke up like two years ago."

"Yeah." She stares over at me for a few seconds. "And whose fault is that?"

My jaw juts a bit and I drop her eyes because I can't. Don't want to look at either of them because I don't want to see it—that splintery hurt that's always there between them, the one that I might have wedged in there.

Daisy grabs some gauze and holds it against Carmelo's arm.

"They were in my bed," she clarifies and I look over at Rome, eyebrows up, tongue pressed into my top lip. The fucking nerve.

"*Idiota…*" Carmelo breathes out, shaking his head.

Romeo lets out this little puff of a laugh that makes me want to kill him.

"Can we have a chat?" He nods his head towards the door.

Daisy glares over at him, makes him wait a few seconds. "Fine."

"Hello?" Carmelo waves his good arm about. "I'm bleeding out here."

My sister rolls her eyes. "Oh, does the gang lord have a little scratch on his arm and need a Band-Aid?"

"No." Carmelo frowns. "I need a stitch."

"Actually," Daisy considers, "you need about twenty. Keep the pressure on that." She points to him. "I'll be back in a sec."

They walk out of my office and I toss Carms a long-suffering look, neither of us particularly ready for round 9000 of these star-crossed idiots. Not like we have a choice. Not like they do either, actually.

# 8

# Daisy

He just left. There's more to it than that, I suppose.[36] The short version is that I found him in my bed with my nemesis,[37] I threw a lamp at his head, we yelled at each other for a bit, and then in the morning he was gone. A few days later he was in New York surrounded by a bevy of women.[38]

The long version is he is my family. I grew up with him. I fell in love with him when I was, I don't know, all of eight years old. He's my oldest friend. He's my best friend.[39] We've been through more shit than I wish we had, but I don't want to talk about it. We ended properly probably three years ago, but define "properly". There's too much water under the bridge for properly, there is no properly. He and I will only break up properly when one of us is dead. No one likes it when I say that, though, least of all him…

Now, Romeo Bambrilla leads the way from my brother's office and into my kitchen. He knows this house like the back of his hand; every corner and crook memorised from a million games of hide-and-seek when we were tiny, and later utilised for more adult reasons when we weren't really adults—but what did they expect with how they raised us? Never denied anything, raised by my brother,[40] gang lords for parents...

He's muscular, lean, 6'1", brown skin, brown hair, brown eyes. That's under-selling him, but I have to, to keep how much I miss him at bay.

---

36  There always is with us.
37  Tavie Jukes. Younger sister of Danny, and the Jukes being the movers and shakers out in Birmingham.
38  Again.
39  Don't tell Jack.
40  I was raised by my brother, not him. Romeo had real parents.

He leans back against my kitchen bench, and he's as beautiful as his name makes you think he'd be. Mixed. His mother is Eritrean, his dad Sicilian. Romeo stares down at me with his pinched eyes that are more bronze than brown. Eyes the colour of a new 1p coin, just as shiny too.

"Happy to see me?"

"I'm always happy to see you," I tell him with a nod, and I think that sentence is true.[41]

I take a step closer and he tugs me towards him a tiny bit more. His gaze flicks from my eyes to my mouth, and I press my thumb into his neck. There's a scar there from where the blade was and he holds my hand against him for a second before he takes it and kisses it without thinking. Kissing without thinking, that's sort of our thing these days. He gives me a half smile but his eyes are full soft.

"Not always." He's trying to goad me because that's what we do, it's always been what we've done, even when we were together we fought. Fight and make up, push each other away just to pull back as close as we can get—this is our bread and butter, really. But I still feel off about what happened the last time I saw him. I'm not ready to pull him close again—I also don't want to feel far away from him again just yet either, so I side-step his invitation to fight and clear my throat instead as I take a concerted step away from him. "How was America?"

He clears his throat too, straightens up. "Good."

I give him a suspicious look. "How good?"

He cocks a small smile. "Better than you'd like it to be."

"Wonderful." I give him a glib look and Rome tilts his head, trying to catch my eyes again.

"Still came back, though..."

"Yes, I can see that." I fold my arms over my chest and give him a curt smile. "And to what do we owe the pleasure?"

He squashes a smile as he reaches for my hand. "I missed you."

I roll my eyes at him as I push past him to get to the sink. There's nothing in the sink I need, I just wanted to push him. "Bullshit."

"I did," he insists with a shrug.

"Okay." I nod once. "You missed me and...?"

Romeo starts laughing and I love it when I make him laugh. There

---

[41] Or at least mostly true. I'm always something to see him.

was once a time in our lives when I treated that like it was my full-time job.

He runs his tongue over his teeth, smiling and amused. "I missed you and... the girl I was seeing in New York was fucking mental. I had to get out of there."

I snap my fingers. "There it is."

He pokes me in the ribs. "Did miss you, though..."

I roll my eyes at him. "You didn't call, you didn't text."

"Fuck off." He rolls his eyes. "I tried calling you every day for the first few weeks."[42]

"Well," I start unpacking the dishwasher, "you know how I feel about phone calls..."[43]

"I bought you a ticket to come out to see me but—"[44]

I turn my head over my shoulder and give him a look. "Yeah, because Julian does ever so love a spontaneous trans-Atlantic journey."

He sniffs a laugh.

"You were trying to make it look like you were trying to make it better, but actually all of your attempts to make it better were just different ways for you to avoid me." I give him a look.

"Well," he concedes, "you were very angry."

And he's right, I was. More than maybe I should have been—or maybe my response was right on the money for seeing what I saw, but that's hard to confirm when I don't think you can quantify what we are. I can tell you in about forty-five different languages what we are not, but I'll pull up blank if you ask me that question the other way around.

Rome shoves his hands in his pockets, his eyes flicking over my face. "Dating anyone?"

"No," I say.[45]

"Really?"

"Really." I shrug.

He juts his chin a bit. "People talk... about you, to me..." He shrugs. "I don't know why. Why would I want to hear about you naffing some guy?"

---

[42] This is true, but I was really angry.

[43] Not good.

[44] I don't fly commercial.

[45] Technically true.

"Some guy?" I give him a look, feeling offended.[46] "He's your friend."

He gives me a look. "That's so, so much worse—Face, how do you not realise that's worse?"

I start laughing at his distress because it's cute and I still miss him. He looks annoyed that I'm pleased, does his best not to smile but fails. "What are you doing tonight?"

I roll my eyes at him. "Not you."[47]

"Come on—" He reaches for my hand again.

I let him take it.

"It doesn't work between us," I tell him, our hands still in each other's.

He lifts my chin with his thumb and holds my eyes up with his. "Your head is fucking cut, bro—" I smack him in the arm because I hate it when he calls me that. "Of course it works between us, Daisy. That's why we're always in this fucking mess."

He interlocks our fingers. I keep letting him.

"We don't work," I tell him again, not moving.

He moves in closer. "We work okay."

"We didn't last time."

He lifts his eyebrows with a sort of hopefulness that probably made me love him in the first place. "We might this time."

"We won't." I give him a sad smile and he matches it with a tall-browed look.

"We could…"

I pull back a little. "We can't."

He takes an unconscious step back from me, his face faltering like I've hurt him, like I've told him something he didn't already know. He stares at me for a few seconds, looking over my face. "Is this about Hemmes?"

"No." I cross my arms over my chest defensively. "Why? What have you heard?"

"Oh," he shrugs airily, "just my deepest fears rushing to the surface of reality."

---

[46] Which I know I shouldn't, because we are not one. Someone being dismissive of Christian is not someone being dismissive of me, but there's that motherfucking Feelings Monster again!

[47] I mean, probably not him.

I lift up my brows. "Such as…?"

"I don't know." He shrugs, annoyed. "You're sleeping together?"

I shrug again. "We are."

He nods once and he looks away.

"What?" I look for his eyes. "You were celibate in New York?"

"Obviously not—" He starts and I interrupt him.

"Right! So why would I—"

"I didn't say you couldn't—"

I scoff. "You think I need your permission?"

"No." His head rolls back, annoyed.

"That I'd just wait for you?"

"No."

"Then what?" I ask, giving him a pointed look.

Romeo frowns and grabs me by the wrist. "Let me take you to breakfast tomorrow."

"No." I snatch my hands away from him for no real concrete reason other than that I know he'll reach for me again.

He leans in like he's going to kiss me, and I duck away from him—holding a wooden spoon out threateningly.

"Why?" He smirks.

"Because." I frown. "I have uni."[48]

"Lunch?" Romeo offers as an alternative. "Dais, say yes—come on, I'm going to show up either way…"

But I don't actually have a Christian, I don't think. Not the way I wish I did.

I purse my lips, pretending to think about it.

"I'm not free 'til Friday."

He looks outraged. "That's almost a week away!"

I ignore him. "I have forty-five minutes between classes. Be there at 1:15." I poke him in the chest with the spoon. "Be on time." I poke him again.

He nods obediently with a little grin. "I'll be early."

I roll my eyes at him. "You're never early."

Then Julian clears his throat from the doorway and I glare over at him.

"Right then." He gives us an annoyed look. "If that embarrassing lovers' spat is over, would you mind coming back to sew up his stupid brother's ruddy arm?"

---

[48] And Christian. I have a Christian.

54

Jack
7:25 AM

He's back.

Who.

Rome?

Yes.

Shit

Yes.

Shit.

How do you feel?

Fine I guess.

I don't know.

You were a bit of a mess when he left

A sloppy, dumb mess

Yes Jack, thank you, I recall.

Why's he back

He said he missed me

Line.

I know.

55

A line but also the truth, probably.

Did he say sorry?

No

Fuck him

I mean, I probably will but don't you think that might send a mixed message?

Oh, look who's funny now that her boyfriend's back in town.

How does Impeccable Arse feel about the ex-boyf being back?

Impeccable Arse doesn't know. Nor do I suspect Impeccable Arse would care.

The Impossible Twat underestimates the power of her own Impeccable Arse…

# 9

# Christian

"Plans tonight?" Henry looks over at me from the couch. "Or you with your missus again?"

"Not my missus," I say, tone unflinching as I shoot his Call of Duty character.

"Right," he says, knowing full well she's not. "So—plans?"

"I've got to go into work tonight for a bit. Show my face."

He lights up a bit. "Boys' night?"

"Er—" I pause. I don't want to give him the satisfaction, but he knows and starts chuckling. "Sorry—I already invited her." I tell him apologetically.

"Course you did."

I look over at him for a few seconds. "Do you not like her?"

"No, Chris, I love her." Henry smirks over at me. "Do you love her?"

"Fuck off." I pelt the remote at him.

"Is she meeting us there?" he asks. I shrug. "Is she coming here after?"

He shoots my player.

I shrug again. Probably. Hopefully.

"Could you not have weird, loud sex?"

"We don't have weird, loud sex." I frown. "Is she loud?" I ask, a little stoked.

He gives me a disparaging look. "Fuck, you're needy."

Fiddle with my heart necklace absentmindedly.

Parks gave it to me.

Gave one to all of us, actually. Back in school. Tiffany's dog tag heart necklaces with our last names on it. "Best friend necklaces," she called them.

Hated it at first, kind of love it now.

"How's it going, anyway?" Henry asks, looking at the TV. "With you and Baby Haites?"

"Not going," I tell him, bored.

I see him roll his eyes.

"I like her," he tells me, even though I didn't ask.

"You want to date her then?" I joke, but watch him close for the answer.

"I'll leave that to you." He scoffs.

"We're not dating." I sigh, bored.

"If you say so."

"I say so." I say so like I've said so nineteen hundred fucking times. Doesn't stick with Hen, though.

Henry looks over at me. "Hey, quick question—"

He pauses the game and tosses the controller down on the couch.

"What?" I glare.

"How many other girls in your rotation come to our house to hang out and not have sex—"

"We always have sex," I interrupt.

"Yeah," he concedes. "But you don't bring others here, full stop. And you definitely don't bring other girls here to hang out for nine hours before you have sex with them."

My eyes pinch. "What's your point?"

My best friend gives me an annoying smile. "No point." Shrug. "Just an observation."

Later that night at work, I feel more keen to see Daisy than I want to say. I haven't seen her in a few days. Missed her for a second, that's all—which is weird, sure—but I guess we spend a bit of time together these days.

She walks on in about an hour later than I tell her to be there, Miguel trailing behind her because she can't go anywhere without him, apparently. They love a bit of theatrics, the Haites, whether it's valid or not (it's not). Julian runs a tight ship.

I lock eyes with her from across the room and she is, I cannot stress this enough, stupid hot.

Cropped brown hair, brown eyes, a bit tan, smiles with her eyes like a girl who's never heard the word "no" once in her lifetime.

She gives me a small smile and I walk over, grab her by the waist, press my mouth against her ear. "Tell me you're coming home with me tonight."

She gives an indifferent shrug. "We'll see."

I cock an eyebrow. "You got other plans?"

"Could do…" She smiles coyly.

"Baby Haites!" Henry Ballentine cheers. He tosses an arm around her, pulls her in for a hug.

Her face lights up and she buries her nose in his neck.

"What a surprise…" Henry eyes me, giving me a look over Daisy's head that I hope she doesn't see and if she does, I hope she doesn't get it.

He's a fucking pain, thinking I'm into her. Probably wishful thinking on his behalf because his life would be easier if his best friend didn't like his brother's girl. Sorry, mate, here we are.

Daisy pulls back from him a bit to look up, but doesn't let go. "How'd your exam go?"

I'll pause here to say: girls fucking love Henry. All through school into uni. He doesn't sleep around at the same pace as the rest of us, but it's not from lack of opportunity. Any given night out, I reckon Henry leaves with about seven girls' numbers that he doesn't ask for.

Bit annoying, actually—Parks is like this with him too—different with them, I suppose, because of all the years they've been around each other and shit. But Daisy only knows him through me and she's always throwing herself into his arms, always happy to see him.

Henry cringes down at her. "Maybe upper second? At very best."

"That's not so bad!" Daisy shrugs. Only these two idiots would think an upper second was bad—the man with the work ethic of a Marine and her, the tiny genius who graduated Upper Sixth at sixteen and then went straight into studying medicine at Imperial.

Henry nods at Daisy and finishes his drink in a gulp. "You?"

"She only gets firsts," I tell him, sounding more proud of her than I should because now I won't hear the end of it.

I avoid my best friend's eyes so I don't have to see the look I know he's giving me and decide instead to pay attention to some other girls because every time he tells me he thinks I'm into Daisy it fucks with my head. Because I'm not. It's not like that. I don't love Daisy and I need to make sure Henry knows that. I tap her on the arm and say I've got to do a round in the room (for work) but immediately beeline for a table of models.

I think Dais looks hurt for a minute, but her bounce-back time is second to none, and she leans over the bar to order a drink, grinning at the bartender.

They're all gorgeous, these models, as models often are, I guess. They're all over me, laughing at everything I say, touching my arm, hungry for attention—one of them is so forward that she actually starts restyling my hair. I hate it when girls do that, it's so fucking obvious. I don't care how some girl from Miami thinks my hair should look, and I'd stop her myself if I wasn't completely distracted by Daisy and my fucking bartender having the chat of their God damn lives.

I didn't leave her there to talk to Matthew the Hot Australian Bartender. I left her with Henry, whom I know she'd never shag, but now he's gone and disappeared and it's Daisy and the bartender, whom I heard someone refer to last week as "Fuckable Matt".

Daisy's perched up next to the bar now, cross-legged and laughing. She's swooping her hair behind her shoulders, and I swipe my hand through the air to silence the bloody chatterbox next to me who's been banging on about a movie she saw and she laughed when she shouldn't have, and it's the most fucking benign story I've ever barely heard, because I'm not listening to her. I need her to shut the fuck up so I can lip-read what Daisy's saying to the bartender.

"You right there?" Henry grins as he plops down next to me.

"What?" I blink. "No, yeah—I'm fine. Why?"

"Dunno," Henry smirks. "You just look a bit agitated..."

I glance at him then back at Daisy. "I'm not, I'm good. I'm fine, I am. Is she alright, though, do you reckon?"

"Who?" he asks, smirking.

"Daisy, you git—who else?"

"Who else, ey?" He snorts and I toss him a look. "Do I think Daisy's alright over there with the sexy Australian lifeguard-bartender? Yeah, man—I think she's fi—"

I'm already on my feet before he finishes the sentence.

Don't like it. Not at all—

And I'm not jealous, but it's just fucking inappropriate.

Everyone knows me and Daisy are together. Well, not together, but you know—whatever. We're—you know. And he works for me.

It's fucking disrespectful.

I'll cop it from Henry later for this, but I don't care. I walk over to her, still perched on the bar, and I spin her around to face me.

I stare past her, eyeing down the bartender whose eyes fall to the ground and he moves away quickly. Watch him go away from her, away from us, wait until he's gone before I look up at her, override the urge in my brain to kiss her. Kissing in public isn't the vibe. Instead, I've got a hand on each leg, rubbing them a bit mindlessly, before I slip them around her waist and boost her down off the bar.

"Wanna bounce?" I push some hair behind her ear.

She swallows, nodding wordlessly.

I like it when she goes like this. She goes quiet when she wants me.

I slip an arm around her waist and lead her over to the door where Miguel's waiting.

I can never tell whether he likes me or not, her bodyguard.

His eyes look me up and down as I pull her over towards him. He looks a bit annoyed at me, if I'm honest—don't know why—so I smack him in the arm, playfully because I want to be on his good side. My sex life is gonna go to shit otherwise.

"How tight's the leash tonight, my man?"

Miguel cocks an eyebrow and looks between me and Dais. "Who's asking, you or the bartender?"

Daisy bites back a smile but I'm pissed—try not to show it, though. I give him a look out of the corner of my eye. "Who do you think?"

"I think he spent more time with her than you did," he tells me, and my head pulls back, surprised.

Daisy gives him a stern look and Miguel flicks his eyes, annoyed. Feels a bit like they've had this conversation before.

He nods his chin at me. "You drive here?"

"Yep."

"Where are you headed?"

"Mine."

He nods once. "I'll wait outside."

I shake my head at him. "She's going to stay the night," I tell him, even though she and I haven't talked about it yet. She will. And I want her to.

Her bodyguard friend gives me a tight smile.

"Then I'll wait outside all night."

# 10

# Daisy

After dinner one night,[49] I head back to Christian's with him and Hen—Miguel too, God bless him, it's about his third night this week sleeping in the car out front. I try to send him home—he won't go. Christian invites him in every time, but all Miguel sort of does is gives us a grimace and says, "Yeah, no thanks."

Anyway, we walk into their house, into the boys' living room, and I switch on the light, but nothing happens.

I peer over at him apprehensively. Force of habit, I guess. I wish it wasn't, I wish I didn't immediately think someone might be trying to kill me, but here we are.[50]

"Oh." Christian swats his hand dismissively. "Light's blown."

"We need to get the maintenance in," Henry adds.

I relax. "Or you could—you know—change it yourselves?" I frown.

"They're eleven-foot ceilings." Christian points up. "And we can't find the ladder."

"Boost me." I shrug. "I'll do it."

Henry and Christian trade dubious looks, which I find personally offensive.

"Do you have a globe?" I ask, ignoring them, more determined than a moment ago.

Christian frowns. "Er—"

"It's a bulb made of glass." I make the shape in my hand. "Which when heated becomes so hot that it emits a light..."

Christian squints playfully. "Genius..."

Henry goes to find one as I take off my knee-high boots. And

---

[49] Enoteca Turi. Get the Tonnarelli al Chitarra and the sea bass. Thank me later.

[50] Is it nice not to always wonder if someone is trying to kill you? I'm asking for a friend.

then with an ease that makes my stomach curl with hunger that isn't related to food at all, Christian lifts me.

I fiddle around with the light socket, trying to jimmy it in, before peering down at them. "Why didn't one of you just lift the other and do this yourselves?"

"Thought about it," Henry says from below. "Just wanted to give Christian the opportunity to look up your skirt."[51]

I glance down, smirking at them for a second before refocusing on the task at hand. "Feels like a lot of planning. Could have just asked."

"Would you have said yes?" Christian asks brightly, looking up at me.

I maneuver the bulb in and the room lights up.

I shrug my shoulders. "Yeah, probably. If you bought me dinner before."

Christian lowers me back down slowly and carefully, but slower than he needs to and I can't even begin to imagine how strong he must be to do such a measured descent—it's all intentional—where his hands are placed, how they move down me, grip me.

He lowers me to a point where I'm about a head above his, looking down on him and he's holding me against him when Henry lets out an uncomfortable whistle. "Still here, guys."

"Then leave," Christian tells him without looking at him.[52]

"Been your best friend for twenty fucking years and that's how you're gonna talk to me?" Henry gives him a look. "How pussy-whipped are you?"

"Right now? Very." Christian nods once, still not looking over at him[53] and I feel like my head's in the clouds because they're talking about me and I love him[54] when he goes like this, so serious and so solemn, precision-focused on the task at hand, which happens to be me.

Henry gives both of us an unimpressed look. "Don't have sex on the couch."

Christian looks at him now, frowning. "You always have sex on the couch."

Henry shrugs. "And you never do, so why start now?"

---

[51] I'm wearing cute knickers, don't worry.

[52] OMG.

[53] Oh. My. God.

[54] I mean it. I love it when he goes like this.

63

Christian stares over at him then peers back at me, nodding. "We're going to have sex on the couch."

"Well, then I hope you make a baby," Henry calls as he walks away.

After, I'm laying on top of him. We're under a blanket, TV's on— *The X Files*—I don't know why that's what we're watching lately, but it is. It's maybe the ridiculousness of it? It's the one where they think they've found the frozen alien, and I'm actually pretty invested in the series at this point, Christian is too, but he's not watching it, he's watching me. Staring, just looking at my face. Inspecting it, almost like he's seeing it for the first time.

"What?" I ask, feeling self-conscious.

He shrugs. "You have nice eyes."

"They're brown."

He gets a little closer, shakes his head. "Bit of gold in there." He squints at me. "You have a freckle on the corner of your lip," he tells me.

I sniff a laugh. "We've been hooking up for—what?—like, four months now and you've just noticed that?"

"Five." He gives me a little look and I mirror it back, then he covers my eyes with his hand. "Alright, go on—where are my freckles, then?"

I find myself loving that he doesn't hesitate to touch me—that somehow we've crossed that imaginary threshold where touching each other becomes second nature, thoughtless, almost—so I reach out my hand and touch his face, blindly getting a feel for it, grabbing it more than necessary just because.

I feel my way to below his mouth and to the right, then point. "There." A little further down, a little more right. "And there." I feel my way back up to his left eye, pat my finger gently around the area, discerning where I am by the socket and then move it left. "And there." Then I trace my finger down a little and move it right. "And there."

I shove away his hand from my eyes and look up at him, and he's staring down at me—brows low, face serious and all ripe with the kind of confusion one might have when you realise someone likes you more than you like them and I feel shamefully see-through, like I just gave all of me all away. And he's all surprised that I know his face, but what he doesn't know is that how he looks in the morning time is burned into my memory and one day, when all this is over and we're not hooking up anymore and he's with someone else and I've figured out how to move on and past him and we're not together anymore[55] because I don't think he has room in his heart to see me like that when all he can see is her, even if sometimes now it feels like maybe[56] he could—even then, I will see his face when I close my eyes.

---

[55] Not that we ever were.

[56] Maybe.

## 11

# Julian

I'm a businessman, first and foremost. A bunch of other adjectives might be used to describe me as well, but fuck them, because I work hard.

Legally, I'm an arms dealer. We also control almost every channel on and off the British Isles for produce and contraband, but what I really love is art.

Love it. I love art. Always have. Love looking at it, love taking it.

And we've got a reputation now—anything you want, we can get it for you. Doesn't matter where it is, doesn't matter whose eyes are on it or whose thumb it's under—if anyone's going to be able to get it, it's me and my boys.

It's fun—like a game, figuring out how to rob a high-end facility. High stakes, high pay, good times, usually. Sometimes it's museums, sometimes it's private residences—different sides of the same coin, and I've not tanked a job yet.

Anyway, I'm on my way to a meeting with a new client—that's what Dad always used to call them. "Clients."

Don't know what kind of client this is… whether he wants his hands on weapons or stolen goods, or if he just wants to bring some shit into England and I'm the only way through.

Tried to send Declan out first, but he only wanted to speak to me. Ballsy.

Kekoa didn't like that—insisted I bring the entire fucking cavalry. Him, Declan, Happy and Smokes follow me in to the speakeasy Jonah has under one of his more legitimate venues upstairs.

This one's so off the map it doesn't even have a name, but we all just call it Downstairs.

Easy to spot, all the geezers who want to work with me but haven't before—

Always with this need to prove themselves, and this motherfucker is sitting in the corner drip-drip-dripping Fendi head to toe, but he's too old for it. Looks like a fucking idiot.

As I approach him, he looks me up and down, like he's scoping me out—doesn't love my garms. A fisherman's beanie, tattered jeans and a T-shirt. He thinks I'm unprofessional—which is fine because I think he's a fuckwit and I haven't even spoken to him yet.

I take a seat down opposite him.

"Julian?" He gives me a polite smile.

I lift my brows. "And you are?"

"Ezra Brown." He offers me his hand to shake, I peer down at it, shake my head. I lean back in my chair.

"And why have you requested an audience with me, Ezra Brown?"

"Because I'd like to work together."

"Would you, now?"

He looks past me and nods to the Cavalry. "Do you always travel with a wolf pack?"

I shake my head, a bit bored. "They're here for show. Rest assured, if need be, I could kill you all by myself."

He gives me a tight, somewhat apologetic smile. "That won't be necessary..."

"We'll see." I interrupt.

He swallows.

"What can I do for you?" I ask him as the waitress puts down a top-shelf glass of scotch in front of me.

I don't know what it is, but she knows what I like—in multiple ways. Her name's Lacey. Pretty. Great mouth. Dauntless hands.

"There's a piece of art I'm interested in... procuring." He chooses his words wisely.

I nod once. "And which piece of art might this be?"

"Gustav Klimt's *Adam and Eve*," he tells me with a straight face.

I snort a laugh, and I can hear the boys a few tables away chuckling to themselves.

"Yeah, good." I nod. "And after, do you want me to just grab the *Mona Lisa* as well, or...?"

Ezra Brown gives me a tight, unamused smile. He folds his hands on the table. "That piece is very important to me."

"I'm sure it is at $100 million..." I give him a look.

"Money's no object."

"Is it not?" I sit back, nod my chin at him. "What's your name again?"

His jaw goes tight. "Ezra Brown."

"If money's no object, why've I never heard of you, Ezra Brown?"

"I've just come into it."

"Convenient."

"I want that piece," he tells me.

"You can't afford me," I tell him with a shrug.

He doesn't look too happy with that statement. "Try me."

"My fee is 50 percent of the total value."

"That's fine." He nods and I look over at Declan, wondering if he's buying this.

"Plus cost," I say, just because I don't like him.

He shrugs. "Fine."

I lick my bottom lip and frown over at him, pointing to Smokes. "Give him your number. Telephone, passport, license and NIN—"

Brown's eyes flicker from me to Smokeshow. "Why?"

"Standard procedure to vet someone before we get into bed with them."

"Right." He nods.

"Love a good Thursday lunch and this was a shit one." I stand and walk away from the table, pointing back at him. "I hope for your sake you haven't just wasted my time."

## 12

# Christian

I take Dais to a cafe by her university some mornings when she stays over. I don't usually let the girls I'm shagging stay the night, but like fuck am I telling Julian Haites's sister to leave.

After I have sex with someone, usually I'm pretty keen for them to just fuck off, feel a bit off after it sometimes—don't know why—because it's not Parks, probably.

Fucked up thing about that is it's never been Parks and even still, I'm having sex with other girls and after I hate myself a bit because I'm with a girl that isn't the girl I never even had to begin with.

Daisy's different.

Don't tell her because she's already pretty up herself, but she's probably one of my favourite people now.

Funny, clever, so good looking, and she knows she's hot shit. That makes her hotter somehow.

Anyway, I don't care when she stays and she's stayed over a few nights this week, actually. Bit weird, but I sort of didn't want her to go. Don't know why, I just have fun with her, I guess. Maybe I even just like it when she's around.

I like getting breakfast with her. Like how her hair looks in the mornings, how puffy her lips go. I like how she never orders the same thing, ever, even when I can tell she wants to get what she had the day before, she won't. There are strange things she does, learned, I think from the weird world we come from.

I asked her about it once, the never ordering the same thing twice, even if she loves it.

"Harder to poison me." She shrugged like it was nothing. Kept on eating her raspberry tartlet even though she doesn't like raspberries that much.

Sort of thought she was joking at first, but turns out she wasn't—like I said before, they're pretty dramatic.

I don't know why, maybe it's that Julian's scared of something happening to her, like what happened with their parents.

Daisy's barely ever not with Miguel. Sometimes Julian lets me and her kick it just us, but it's a rarity. It could be getting less rare—he trusts me a bit these days.

Not today evidently, because Miguel's sitting a few booths away from us, giving us whatever space he can and sucking in the extra reading time. He ploughs through a book a day. Find me a more well-read bodyguard, I dare you.

He's actually a bit of a saint. Still in the clothes from the night before.

So is Daisy, come to think of it. Less of a saint, though—especially after last night's performance.

I like her across from me, back in the clothes I took off of her last night. Makes me feel tall.

I'm trying to convince her to come to one of my rugby games on a Saturday morning—never had to convince a girl to come to one of them before, they're usually just happy I asked them to—but she's complaining about the weather and the cold and the time.

"You're up at 8 am on Saturday anyway for Krav Maga," I tell her.

"Yeah." She sighs. "But then I'm so tired after and I like to have the option of just going back to bed if I want to, and I've actually g—"

She stops mid-sentence, looks up, and smiles brightly at a man I've never seen before.

"Tiller." She bats her eyes.

He's good looking, this guy. Big, tall, light hair, looks like a surfer. One of Julian's guys, I wonder?

He smirks down at her. "Dais." He looks over at me, waiting for an introduction.

"Christian, this is Killian Tiller. My stalker."

I frown between them, not getting it but she laughs it off.

"Tiller's an agent with the NCA who's perennially interested in my brother."

I frown more. Fuck that. He's perennially interested in her, I can spot it a mile off.

He nods his chin at me, glancing between us but doesn't say anything.

"Don't be cagey, Christian," she tells me brightly. "Tiller knows all about us because Tiller's obsessed with me."

She beams up at him and I don't like the air between them. It's too playful.

Tiller snorts. "Daisy wishes."

I jut my jaw.

"Daisy does not." She folds her hands in front of her. She's enjoying the attention. She's good at flirting. Too good, even. Makes me feel like shit because she's making him feel like a fucking million bucks, and she made me feel like that a couple of minutes ago so I'm fucked off for a second and then I chill out because we're not together and I'm in love with someone else anyway, so fuck it.

"Daisy wishes to eat her breakfast in peace."

"Christian wishes Daisy would stop speaking in the third," I interject.

Daisy shoots me a glare.

Tiller sniffs a laugh, licks his top lip, nods his head at Dais. "Where was your brother last night?"

Daisy shrugs dismissively.

Her life is pretty different from mine, even though it's similar. I don't have coppers apparently knocking down my door every other day. Then again, I don't look like Daisy.

I don't believe for a fucking second that this twat's here just to give Dais a pop quiz on her brother's whereabouts, this clown's doing a fly-by because she's got honeypots for eyes and he wants in on them.

My face pinches a bit as I watch him watching her.

"Where were you last night?" he asks her.

"With me." I eye him down.

"Ah." He nods, looks a bit annoyed about it. "Convenient."

I stretch my arms over my head. "You've obviously not spent any time with her because she's about as convenient as a prostate exam—"

She rolls her eyes. "Get a lot of those, do you?"

I give her a play-glare.

Daisy frowns at me.

"What were you doing last night?" he asks Daisy a bit loudly to get her focus back and I think he's a prick for it.

She goes to answer him but I cut her off.

"What do you think, mate?"

Tiller gestures towards her, scowling at me a bit. "You going to let her talk for herself, or...?"

Daisy presses a little finger into her mouth, tosses the poor bastard a few slow blinks. "We didn't do a lot of talking last night, if that's what you're asking, Tils."

He sniffs a laugh, shaking his head. She nods her chin at him with an eyebrow cocked.

"You come all the way down here to ask me about my sex life?"

He matches her face. "So what if I did?"

I smack my hand down on the table—loud—to get his attention. I give him a curt smile. "I reckon you're done here, man." I hold his stare, wait for him to back down. Daisy glances between us, almost like she's unsettled.

He holds her eyes, ignores me.

"I'll see you soon."

She nods and he walks away.

"Hey," she calls after him and he looks back.

"Can I borrow your night vision goggles? There's a sexy policeman I want to spy on."

He flips her off without looking back and she's stoked.

She looks over at me, smiling, waiting for my approval. I toss her a smile that's weak at best.

I can't say I loved that, which is weird. We don't do jealous. And I'm not anyway—why would I be?

It was just weird.

I wonder whether they've kissed.

I wonder if they've done more than that.

"Are you on birth control?" I ask her, frowning a little.

She peers up at me from the menu. "Sleeping with each other for—what, four months?—and you only think to ask that now?"

"Five," I correct her, a bit annoyed. Then I shrug, wanting to come off more casual than I feel—don't know why I don't feel casual, to be honest. "I mean, I always have stuff with me."

"Stuff?" She blinks, surprised.

"Keep a minimum of five morning-after pills on my person at any given time." She gives me a despondent look and I grin over at her. "Kidding."

She shakes her head at me, trying not to smile. Trying and not failing.

Some girls at the booth behind ours are staring over at us, whispering. It's either about me or her, hard to tell which, though—me, probably. Box Set shit. Besides, no one's stupid enough to whisper about Daisy. Still, she glares over at them in a way that'd make your hair stand on end and they shut the fuck up.

"I am." Daisy nods, reaching over and taking my coffee from my hands. She takes a sip. She's already drunk hers and patience isn't her strong suit.

I sit back and look at her like she's ridiculous. "Why are we using condoms then?"

Her face falters a little and she sniffs a laugh. "Uh—" She purses her lips. "Have you heard of sexually transmitted diseases—"

"Yeah." I shrug. "But I don't have any—" I give her a look. "Do you?"

"Doubtful." She rolls her eyes.

I blink over at her. "What's that now?"

"I mean…" Her face pulls. "You have a lot of sex."

Woah.

My head pulls back, blink a ton—why did that feel like a slap? She's not wrong, I guess. But kind of, she is. Yeah, in general I probably have a lion's share of sexual encounters, but not lately. Like I have fucking time to shag multiple girls when I'm shagging this idiot.

But Daisy, she stares over at me all confused, frowning over at me as she shakes her head.

"I'm sorry, were you under the impression that you came off… virginal?"

I run my hand over my jaw, brows furrowed. "You think I'm a slut?"

She cracks a laugh. "I mean—it's almost a goal for boys like you, is it not?" She looks confused again. "Are you offended?"

What the fuck?

I can't believe that's how she sees me.

I frown. "Is that really what you think of me?"

She smiles a little apprehensively. "Sort of?"

I press my lips together and nod, coolly. "Good to know."

"Seriously?" She laughs once. "Am I wrong?"

I don't answer, I just give her a scoff.

You know what fucks me off? She looks delighted.

She's pissed me off and she's sitting over there happy as fucking Larry that she's shitted on my morning, and all that does is make me angry.

Making me feel like I'm a slut when she's off fucking around with a bobby that looks like a 90s teen heart-throb—fuck her.

73

"Alright." I give her a look. "So if I'm slutty, what are you?"

She gives an unimpressed look. "What are you asking?"

"You know what I'm asking."

"Clarify it for me." She nods at me with her chin.

We glare at each other across the table and I don't even know what we're talking about anymore. What are we arguing about?

"Can we get the bill?" I touch the arm of a waitress who passes us.

"Are we fighting?" Daisy whispers as she leans across the table.

"We don't fight," I grunt, looking away.

She kicks me gently under the table, looking over at me with big eyes and fuck her with those big eyes that make me swallow heavy. I don't know why.

"It feels like we're fighting," she tells me.

I shake my head, disinterested. "We aren't."

A silence hovers between us.

We have silences a lot.

I like them usually.

Usually with her being quiet feels like I'm alone, and I never feel like I'm alone when I'm with someone else.

"So is there a magic number that you hit and you become slutty, or is it just a vibe I give off?" I glare over at her.

She looks up at me, surprised at the sharpness in my tone. People don't talk to her sharply. How could they? They'd die usually.

"Okay." She squares up and I get the distinct feeling I'm in hot water. "Let's play a game. Give me your phone."

"No." I scowl, placing my hand over it to keep it from her.

"Why?" she asks, eyebrows tall.

I sigh, annoyed, and slide my phone over to her.

She unlocks it. "6969—" She looks up at me. Gives me a look. "Exhibit A."

I roll my eyes. "It's the only number combination I remember."

She glances up at me. "Of course it is." She gives me a dry smile and I bite back a laugh because I don't want to give her the satisfaction.

She makes her way to my contacts, squeezes her eyes tight shut and then dramatically scrolls up then taps randomly on the screen—flashing it to me.

"Have you had sex with this person?" she asks brightly.

I flick my eyes down to the screen—Casey Hayes—then back up at her.

Fuck.

"Yes."

She does it again. The big scroll. Flashes me the phone again.

"How about this person?"

Jamie Davis.

I squint, annoyed. "Yes."

Scrolls again. "And this one?"

Leah Warshawsky.

I'm glaring at her now, jaw tight as my eyes. "Yes."

"This one?"

Pierce Norton.

Hah. I give her a triumphant look.

"That's a boy."

She runs her tongue over her teeth and moves her finger down a centimetre. Raises her eyebrows.

Her finger lands on Pippa Moore.

Fuck.

"…Yes," I tell her through gritted teeth.

I'm so annoyed at her.

I also want to take her into the back of my car.

She places the phone face-down on the table and slides it back over to me.

I pick it up, shoving it into my pocket.

I sniff a defensive laugh—why am I defensive?

"What's your point?" I ask, eyeing her.

"No point." She shrugs dismissively. "I'm nothing but a beneficiary of your sexual appetite."

She flashes me a bratty smile and I fucking hate her.

Also feel like kissing her.

"How so?" I nod over at her, trying not to give her a smile.

"You're quite good," she tells me, taking another sip of my coffee.

"Quite?" I blink.

"Very." She nods earnestly.

I eye her. "Better."

She points to herself. "Best."

# 13

# Daisy

I walk out of my Immunopharmacology class[57] and round the corner with very low expectations, but there he is, leaning up against the wall across from me, arms folded over his chest, wearing loose fitted jeans, a backwards cap, an old Vans sweater, Old Skools, and sporting a smug little smile.

It's not so good for me, I think, that I can't look at that mouth of his without thinking about a summer when I was fifteen and we were on his family's yacht[58] in Scala Dei Turchi on the Sicilian coast, his brown skin, and how red his mouth gets when he goes in the sun and how much more I wanted to kiss him because of it, and I did—a lot that trip. We did a lot that trip.[59]

"You're here." I try not to sound too pleased and he nods, impressed with himself. "On time." I blink. I can scarcely believe it.

He looks at his watch. "Actually, I was early."

I go and stand toe and toe with him and pinch my eyes.

"Surprised?" he asks and then looks past me to Miguel. Rome leans forward and shakes his hand. Surprisingly, Miguel's always been a fan of Romeo Bambrilla. I guess Rome has earned his stripes in the eyes of my bodyguard, and I guess he kind of deserves them.

"I am surprised, actually." I shift my books in my hands before Rome takes them from me mindlessly. We start walking the same way we used to in school.[60]

"I'm a changed man, Face..."

---

57  Which is really more of a Immunotoxicology class at the minute.
58  Benetti, Oasis £40M.
59  A lot, but not everything.
60  For a brief and thrilling time during my adolescence, I went to actual school with my actual boyfriend.

76

"Shame—" I glance over at him. "I liked the old you."

"Oh." He gives me a look. "Is that why you threw a vase at my head?"

"It was a lamp," I clarify.

"It was marble."

"Belle Époque period, 19th century."[61]

He grimaces. "Jules pissed then?"

"Oh, yeah..." I cringe. "Part of a set. I offered to throw the other one at you if it made it better."

"It didn't?"

I give him a look. "We both thought about it."

He leans down and flashes me the side of his forehead where there's a little scar. "Four stitches."

"Don't be a baby." I roll my eyes, but actually I'm fighting the urge to tug his head down so I can kiss it. I've kissed all his scars. Most of them are my fault, but I guess isn't that the way with first loves?

I give him a look with eyes rounder than I want them to be, but it's him, so I guess I don't care. "Why'd you do it in my bed?"

He sighs. "I don't know."

I give him an exasperated look. "It's my bed, Rome."

He shrugs. "You were fucking around with Booker."

"So?"

"So you were fucking around with Booker."

I roll my eyes at him. "We just got drunk one night and kissed."[62]

"In front of me."

I purse my lips. "I thought you'd left..."

"Daisy—" he sounds annoyed. "I don't leave you alone at parties."

I give him a look. "The party was at my house."

He shakes his head. "I still don't just leave you at parties, Dais."

"Well, you did that night," I cut in.

"Because you were hooking up with Booker!"

"Because I saw you touching some other girl's face!"

"She had something in her eye"—

"Bullshit"—

---

[61] Which, if you're stupid, is about 1871–1914 and is an era heavily defined by pre-war optimism coupled with economic prosperity and technological and scientific progressions in much of the developed world.

[62] ...ish.

"She did!" he tells me, stubborn.

"What was it then?" I cross my arms over my chest.

"Glitter," he tells me, defiant.

I make a sound at the back of my throat[63] and Romeo rolls his eyes all exasperated, but you don't need to worry—this is just how we are. Kind of always have been, too much tension to know what to do with.

"I'm helping this poor girl who can't fucking see—"

"Alright, alright. Calm down," I talk over him. "It was glitter in her eye, not acid—"

"And you're getting slippery in a corner with the fucking American bad boy!"

"It's the Silicon Baddies."

"I don't fucking care, Face!"

"It was just a kiss!" I yell, loud enough for Miguel to glance over disapprovingly.

"You just kissed?" Romeo eyes me skeptically.

"Yes."

"Just kissed?" he repeats condescendingly, like I might have forgotten what constitutes a kiss.

"Yes," I over-annunciate.

"You didn't have sex?"

I look at him, unimpressed. "No."

This settles in and manifests upon him like a frown. A strange relief and an uncomfortable revelation.

"Fuck." Romeo pulls a face. "I might have overreacted then..."

I blink at him. "You think?"

He sighs and turns to me, grabbing my wrist. "I was jealous. What was I supposed to do?"

"Literally anything but that." I scowl up at him. "I had to throw the bed away."

His face falters a little. "That was our matrimonial bed."

I cross my arms over my chest. "Yes, it was."

He's frowning now, like I've wronged him. "And you just threw it away?"

I scoff. "As did you, figuratively, when you slept with Tavie fucking Jukes in it."

He purses his lips and nods once. "Sorry."

---

[63] Girls who wear glitter on their face deserve to get it in their eyes.

I give him a pointed look. "We don't work."

His eyes still don't meet mine, but he nods. "No, yeah—you're right." He gives me a quick smile. "We don't." Romeo sighs, shoving his hands in his pocket like he doesn't know what to do with them now that he doesn't think he can touch me. He's an idiot, though, he can always touch me. "How's Jacky-Boy?"

"Having a bit of a rough go at the minute, actually."

"Same old prick?"

"John?" I clarify and Rome nods. "Yeah—still a grade-A arsehole."

About twenty minutes later, we're at the diner and Romeo reaches over to my plate and shovels a bunch of fries into his mouth.

"You and Hemmes—what's that about? Is it a booty call?"

"I don't know." My face falters a little—the question hurts me, but even still, I know the answer.

"I guess?"

He nods, thinking to himself. "Will it stop now that I'm back?"

I roll my eyes. "Why would it stop now that you're back?"

He takes more of my fries and grins at me. "Because I'm back."

"We just clarified that we don't work—"

Rome swipes his hands through the air. "Different."

"Different how?"

"Because it's different. We can't date, but..." He pulls back, giving me a look. "Did you really just think I took sex off the table for us?"

"Yes—well, I mean, I took it off."

He gives me a look like I'm an idiot. "You'd never take it off."

"Well, it's off now." I eye him in faux-offence.

He rolls his eyes. "It's never off with us."

He's right. It never is. There are lots of different metaphors for things that I could compare him to, but the best one I can give you is inosculation.

Once upon a time, we were two trees, and then our branches touched and our bark was abraded away, our cambium mixed[64]—and then we bent around one another and our limbs fused and neither hell, high water, nor Haites has managed to successfully hack us away from one another. Julian's hacked away bits of what we were, forbidden us from being what we wanted to be, but we still have this.

---

[64] This is not a weird sex thing. Though it is an appropriate sexual metaphor.

"If I didn't go to New York, would you not have hooked up with Christian?"

"Which time?"

He lets out a dry laugh. He has a penchant for flittering off, Romeo. His first New York spell was the last nail in our coffin, I think. This one might have just ushered in the Age of Hemmes.

"This time." He gives me a look.

The answer is probably yes, but I don't want to tell him that so I dodge it.

I let out a whistle. "You're really hung up on Christian, aren't you?"

"Yeah." He nods emphatically. "I am."

"Why?" I bat my eyes like he needs a reason.

"Because it's him and you—and you're you. And I'm…" He trails and I lift my eyebrows up, waiting for more. His eyes pinch at me. "You're enjoying this."

"I am." I smirk then give him a little shrug. "You had sex in my bed."

He smooshes his mouth together and nods once. "I had sex in your bed."

Julian
2:10 PM

Face.

You cooking tonight?

I can

Yep

What do you want?

Wouldn't say no to some salmon…

Salmon roulades?

Yum

80

How many for

The usual

That means nothing to me

Me, Koa, Migs, Declan, Baddies.

Jack's going to come.

x

# 14

# Julian

Daisy and me go to the Bambrilla's for dinner at least once a week usually. Have since before our parents died. Santino Bambrilla was one of my dad's closest friends, so they took us in after what happened.

Delina has always been important to Daisy, Carms said his mum saw something in the way our mum was with Dais—tried to cushion it with lunches and dinners and girl dates that Gia Bambrilla, her own daughter, wasn't necessarily stoked on but they were good. They're good parents. And these Monday night dinners for Daisy probably were the only glimpse into the outworking for a semi-normal family.

Half the time Daisy will get there early and cook it herself. She says it's because Delina is a rubbish cook (she is), but we all know it's because she just loves Delina and wants the time with her.

My sister looks nervous as we drive over to their place in Little Venice, rubbing her thumb with her index finger—her nervous twitch since she was tiny—Rome does this to her, that fucking arse. He didn't used to. It's hard to describe what they were before—something between the friend you've had all your life that you sat in muddy puddles with when you were small to that strange infatuation you have with the first person you fall in love with. I had a girlfriend in Lower Sixth. Loved her. Big mistake.

Daisy combs her fingers through her hair, tapping under her eyes and fussing with her face. I toss her a look.

"You look fine, Face."

She turns to me, scowling. "I don't care."

I sniff a laugh. "Okay."

When we walk in, Delina flitters over, takes my sister's face in her hands, kisses both her cheeks. "I've missed you," she tells her—sounds mostly British these days, a hint of her Eritrean accent still there but not really. "You missed our lunch last week."

"I know." My sister sighs. "I had a Microbiology paper on Pathogenic Resistance due that got away from me."

"Did you pass?"

"Always, Mum," Rome says, staring over at Dais from the bottom of the stairs.

Their eyes catch and I breathe louder than I mean to. Delina gives me a look, and Dais floats on over to him.

"Hi." He stares down at her, biting back a smile.

She doesn't say anything back and just beams up at him, somehow without moving her face at all.

I roll my eyes and Delina takes my arm, pulling me out of the room. She gives me an unimpressed look.

"You're unhappy." She nods her chin in their direction and I give her a look.

"I'm not unhappy—it's just the same old shit with them."

"It could be time we let them be?" She shrugs demurely, batting her eyes up at me. She's excellent at getting men to change their mind. Difficult woman to say no to for a multitude of reasons, least of all is the fact that she looks quite a bit like Halle Berry. Different hair, but a dead-ringer otherwise. Delina taught Daisy everything she knows. Bloody Santino thinks he's the shot caller, that poor fucker, but twenty seconds with Delina and you know she's the neck turning the head whichever way she wants it.

Not this head, though—I shake it. "Nope."

"They find their ways regardless," she tells me.

I pull a face. "We don't wanna know anything about those ways, Del—"

She sniffs a laugh and her face goes thoughtful how a mother's does. She watches them from where we're standing. "They're happier together."

I nod once. "Always have been. That's not what tended to be the problem..."

She gives me a long look and I watch her remember why we keep them apart and she nods once, moving past me back towards them.

She hugs them both at the same time. "This makes me happy."

"Mum—" Romeo shoves her away, a bit embarrassed the way kids can be of their parents when they still have them around.

Delina slips her hand into Daisy's. "Come." She tugs her towards the kitchen. "I cannot cook a chicken if my life depended on it."

# 15

# Daisy

I don't know why, but one morning after staying at his house, Christian and I head to Holland Park Cafe. It's not that close to the boys' place and it's a tiny bit benign. Part of me likes the banality of it—it's so regular, so normal-person. Nothing showy or gang-lordy about it.

And Christian's being sweet, actually—he's not not usually sweet. Actually, that's a lie—he's not a sweet guy—you wouldn't say he was either. But sometimes he's thoughtful and notices things like haircuts or that I'm wearing a different colour on my lips. He doesn't know what's different about me, but he can always seem to tell that something is. He's always well mannered, though—holds doors open, pays for everything, blah blah blah.

But today he's sweet. He put his hand on my lower back and guided me through the doorway of the cafe and there were these seven glorious seconds where I was enamored and completely enraptured by the feeling of his hand on my body in such a genuine, couple-y way that I started to wonder whether maybe he was starting to like me back in the way I so desperately want him to. And it was exactly then that I saw her.

Her.

Magnolia Parks.

At a table with her sister.[65]

She's completely wretched, everything about her.[66]

The way she brings her coffee up to her mouth, the way she tucks her hair behind her ears—fuck, even how she blinks.

Her movements are willowy and somehow innately likable and captivating. God, imagine having that as a sister. The sister's beautiful

---

[65] Bridget is her name, and I know that because, despite persistent rumours, I'm not a bitch.
[66] Magnolia, not Bridget.

too, I'm not saying she's not, but there's just something about Magnolia Parks, I guess. Something you think only really belongs in the movies, but it's real in her. Like she's the real-life version of Helen of Troy or something. Her eyes dance around the cafe, bouncing from corner to corner, probably flashing those stupid eyes of hers at every person possible, and then they land on us. Fuck me, what a nightmare.

Her eyes go wide and her mouth falls open in surprise and maybe even delight, and I hate her more than I did before because she looks actually happy to see me and I don't want her to be happy to see me because I'm angry as fuck to see her.

She jumps to her feet[67]—how annoying. God, she's the worst. So fucking graceful. Like she's a bloody elven princess that's high on cocaine and dressed in Miu Miu.

"Christian!" she yells, waving a long, brown arm.

Christian gives her a nod with his chin. He doesn't look surprised to see her, not at all, and that's when I know with a great certainty[68] that us bumping into her wasn't a coincidence as much as it was the intention.

He puts his hand on my lower back again to guide me over to her. I understand and this understanding washes away how I felt just a few seconds before, all hopeful and doe-y and stupid, and my hate-fire for Magnolia burns ever the brighter because now his hands on me feel tainted now that I know they're not on me for me at all.

"Parks." He leans down and gives her a kiss on the cheek. "Bridge." He ruffles her sister's hair.

He's too familiar with them. My heart starts sinking in my chest.[69]

"Daisy." Magnolia stands, giving me a big grin, tossing her arms around me. I don't hug her back. For one, I don't hug people. But also, I definitely don't hug people like her.

"Hi." I give her my dullest-edged smile.

"Sit, sit." She blinks and her eyelashes flap like butterfly wings and she becomes more loathsome by the fucking second. It's as though she hasn't noticed how much I don't want to be there, that or she doesn't care.

---

[67] Somehow with the poise of someone who's been trained at the Royal Ballet.

[68] And a quiet horror.

[69] I'm being hyperbolic, not literal. If I were being literal, I'd probably be dying.

"...Oh—" I stare at the spare seat, not wanting to take it. "We don't want to interrupt."

"Oh, no, not at all." Her hand breezes through the air. "Bridget's a terrible conversationalist. Please, I beg of you, you'd be saving me from a tragically miserable breakfast."

The sister rolls her eyes and Christian sniffs a laugh, licks his bottom lip, and sits down.

I sigh out of my nose, plop down next to him.[70]

Magnolia gestures to Bridget Parks. "Do you know my sister?"

"We've met a few times, yeah." I nod. "Hey."

"Hey." Bridget smiles. "You're studying Med at Imperial, right?"

"Yeah." I nod. "You're Psych?"

At least this Parks is smart.

She nods, about as invested in this conversation as I am, but fractionally more friendly and then... nothing.

Nothing at all.

This weird, massive silence hangs over us like a shadow. Christian's staring at Magnolia in a way that makes me feel voyeuristic to be witnessing, but she's just staring back at him like it's nothing, like it's a regular Wednesday, batting those stupid eyes-like-jewels away at him and as though her very presence in the world isn't sinking mine like an eight ball.

Magnolia Parks flashes me one of her stupid, award-winning smiles. "How's school?"

I shrug because I'm not here for it. "Fine."

"Are you enjoying it?" she asks brightly.

I shrug again. "Sure."

"What's your favourite class?"

"Mortuary procedures," I say, deadpan.[71]

She looks nervous. I try my best not to laugh. She glances at Christian uneasily, and it annoys me that she looks at him to steady herself. "Cool."

The sister's watching on, intrigued. Christian thinks it's funny, but I can't tell which part; the part where I'm making Magnolia Parks squirm or the part where everything she does, even prattle on

---

[70] Magnolia Parks has never plopped a day in her life, I can tell you that.

[71] Haven't taken it that class.

86

incessantly like she has the worst case of verbal diarrhoea the world has seen since Trump left Capitol Hill.

"Is that… what… you want to do…?" Magnolia folds her hands in front of herself demurely.

"No." I look at her like the idiot I'm convinced she is—the idiot she must be to not want Christian the way he obviously wants her. Although, I do get the Ballentine thing, I guess.[72,73]

Magnolia bites down on the bottom lip that sits on her face like a summer strawberry. "How's your brother?"

Of course she'd fucking ask about my brother, that sneaky slut—she'd love him. Toffs like her love a bit of rough. This annoys me extra because Jules has always had a bit of a thing for her,[74] so I give her a bit of a dirty look because I give all the girls who are interested in my brother dirty looks. "Fine."

"And your parents?" she asks, I think just because she's flailing now. On autopilot.

Christian's body tenses up next to me. He's uncomfortable for me.[75]

"Dead," I tell her tonelessly.

Her eyes go wide, and she swallows—even gulps, maybe.

"Cool…" she squeaks.[76]

The sister makes a weird sound that I think is some convergence of excitement and horror at watching her sister conversationally flop around like fish on dry land.

Christian's pressing his hand into his mouth and trying to keep it together, and I like the feeling of making him laugh.

"Okay, okay." She lifts her hands like I'm trying to arrest her. "Slow down. No need to waterboard us with information…"

Christian chuckles but I don't.

I just stare over at her, face straight, completely unamused even if

---

[72] Won't tell Christian that.

[73] (Or will I?)

[74] More than she'd realise, actually. He told me they nearly hooked up once, but I catch him on her Instagram all the time, which is a bit weird now in context of Christian, I'll give you that.

[75] Don't read into it because I can't either. It doesn't mean anything, it's just the side-effect of us both having deceased family members. It's awkward when someone mentions them.

[76] If I didn't hate her, that response might have sent me over the edge. "Dead." "Cool…" That's actually pretty fucking funny. But fuck her, she's the worst.

I do find her a tiny bit amusing,[77] but I think it's in the way where a cat finds a mouse a fun thing to play with.

She lets out a small, bewildered laugh. "…So glad you guys sat down."

"I didn't want to—" I jump to my feet, crossing my hands over my chest. "Christian made us."

Magnolia stares over at him, frowning. "Made you…?"

She sounds confused at how anyone wouldn't just die to be in her stupid presence.

"Bye," I call back to her as I start to walk away.

Christian jogs after me a second later, grabs me by the wrist. I like the feeling of him running after me, it tricks me again into feeling like we're a couple and we've been having a bit of a tiff and now I'm stroppy so he's come to chase after me. I'll have to make him work hard for a minute, but not too long, because I'm constantly fighting the compulsion to run my hands through his hair. Or at least that's how I think it might feel if I didn't know all that's just a trick of my head and that none of that is real…

"Baby Haites." He laughs, shaking his head. "My little wallflower."

My.[78] I swallow heavy, try my best not to read into it because he doesn't mean anything by it and I know for sure why he brought me there.

I stare up at him, annoyed I can't call him on his shit.

He doesn't know I know.

No one's ever said anything to me about it, it's not like it's a known thing either—actually, I don't know if anyone really knows at all—but I pieced it together over time by myself from normal conversations, the absence of conversations, and just plain old eavesdropping.

Here's what I've worked out: Something happened between Magnolia and Christian,[79] and whatever it was, however it went down, it made everything for that group of boys strange and shitty. I also know that it's something that they all ignore now, pretend like it never happened, except it fucking did happen, and now it's just a thing that

---

[77] Reluctantly.

[78] Calm down.

[79] I wish I knew what. I want to know exactly what, where he touched her, how he touched her, how many times he touched her, and if she touched him. And where? And when? And how long before me?

happened that they don't acknowledge but move around like a corpse in a room.[80]

It lays there, decaying, stinking up the whole place, and all they've done is throw a blanket over it and pretend that there's no whole-arse elephant rotting away in the middle of their friendship group.

For a little while, that was all I knew, but I needed to know more because I'm nosy and I realised I had a crush on Christian Hemmes,[81] and that was my mistake,[82] but it was what it was and it is what it is, and I needed to know what I was working with.[83]

We were at a party that Jonah threw maybe two or three months ago—one of those infamous Park Lane ones. [84]

I'd been wondering about Magnolia in regards to Christian for a while by then, just bits and pieces I'd picked up on here and there, but when Christian and I first started hanging out,[85] Magnolia was fake-dating some Australian guy to cover her obvious[86] feelings for BJ Ballentine, and anyway, she came to the Park Lane party without the boyfriend.

When I got to the party, Christian spotted me almost straight away from where he was standing. He walked over to me and kissed me more than he needed to—it was this big, earth-bending kiss where it felt like I was falling with him, the sort of kiss where your breath goes and you see stars—but the thing was, he was standing there with BJ, who had his arm draped mindlessly around Magnolia, and to kiss me, Christian glided in front of them (he could have gone behind, brushing past them to get to me was a choice) and he walked over to me and slipped his hands around my body, and kissed the fuck out of me.

It was one hell of a kiss with one hell of a motivation. I could feel it in the kiss that it had absolutely nothing to do with me.

---

[80] I know a few things about corpses in rooms.

[81] Understatement.

[82] Understatement.

[83] Very little, so it would turn out.

[84] Did you know magazines write about those? Not just the ones you'd expect like *Tatler*, but *GQ* listed them as one of the Top 5 Parties to be invited to in London.

[85] Read: sleeping together.

[86] As fuck.

"Hey, Baby," he said a little louder than he needed to, and actually—to give him credit—I did see Magnolia make a bit of a surprised face.

She thought he meant "baby" like I'm sure BJ calls her baby when no one else is around them, but that's not how Christian means it. I know it and he knows it, but she doesn't know it—and Magnolia Parks not knowing why Christian Hemmes calls me baby might be the entire reason he calls me it. And that actually, in all honesty, kills me a little.

Christian touched my face, looked out of the corner of his eye to see if she was looking. But she wasn't because she doesn't see anything but BJ.

It's fascinating, actually, being in a room with them.

It doesn't matter who they're around or what they're doing. It's almost trance-like, the way they move towards one another.

Like moths to flames.

Romantic, nearly.

She didn't see Christian hoping she would notice his hands on another girl, she didn't see him cupping my arse or his nose in my neck because she was all eyes for Ballentine. She reached over and found a reason to touch his chest, do up a button or something—put something in his pocket, maybe, I don't know—just a non-existent reason to touch him and this jealousy rattled through me because I wanted to be able to touch Christian like that, but I couldn't and I can't, because it's not me he wants. And then BJ nodded his head towards the stairs down to his bedroom and she followed him down. They stayed there the whole night. So, just to recap for you, not only is she detestable because the boy I like[87] likes[88] her and because she's beautiful, but also because she was cheating on her fake-Australian boyfriend with Christian's best friend.

And I could see it on him, that it wrecked him a bit.

He drank a lot. Got a bit distant and weird. He kissed me in a way that made me feel sad and not excited, because by then I knew.

I'd like to state here that I didn't attend the party that night planning on extracting information from a very drunk Henry Ballentine, but the way Christian kissed me made me feel like I needed to know, because at that point in time, I could feel myself on the knife's edge of liking him.

---

[87]  Fine. Love.

[88]  Loves.

Actually, I think—if my memory serves me correctly—I ended up sleeping with a Formula One racer to prove to myself that, actually, I didn't like Christian, which actually failed spectacularly because, as I would realise a few days later, I had already fallen in love with Christian Hemmes.

Before that, I thought I didn't really care either way whether I liked him or he liked me—it was just fun, that was what I kept telling myself. He was my friend with a huge benefit[89] and that's all he was, but then that night he kissed me in front of them and it was a kiss that meant one thing to me and another thing to him, and then I needed to know.

I spotted Henry Ballentine in a corner with a girl from Varley.

'Hello.' I gave her a tight smile.

"Hi." She smiled warmly. "I'm Tibby."

"Like the cat?" I blinked.

"That's a tabby." She looked annoyed.

"Sorry," I said with a shrug, though I wasn't.

"How do you know Jonah?" Tibby asked.

"Her and Christian—" Henry yelled, though there was no need.[90] "They're, you know…" He attempted a wink.

"Why are you yelling!" I yelled back, mimicking him.

Tibby made a drinking motion and pulled an uncomfortable face.

"I'm sober as a judge," he told me proudly.

"Is the judge an alcoholic?" I asked and Tibby laughed.

Henry glared at me as Tibby looked past us and muttered something about "Is that Perry?" and excused herself.

I poked him in the ribs. "Are you drunk?"

He squinted at me. "Yes."

"Oh, good." I smiled.

"Why? I don't dip my pen in the company ink."

I shook my head. "Not an applicable expression."

He thought to himself for a moment. "I don't borrow coins from Christian's piggy bank." He grinned.

I pointed to my chest. "Am I a coin?"

Henry nodded and then his face looked mortified. "Please don't have your brother kill me."

---

[89] Pun intended.

[90] He's a chaotic drunk.

91

"Wow." I blinked and then laughed.

"Please no!"

"No—I mean, really—wow."

"Really, though?"

"Okay." I laughed. "I won't."

Henry sighed and downed the rest of his drink.

"So." I leaned in towards him.

"So—" He mirrored me.

"What's the deal with Christian and Magnolia?"

"Aye!" He smiled, coy. "How do you know about that? No one knows about that."

I folded my arms over my chest. "Because I don't have the deduction skills of a blind toddler."

"Well deduced!" He pointed at me with a drunk, spindly finger. He leaned back against the wall. "Whadda you wanna know?"

"When did it happen?"

"Three-ish years ago."

"How?"

"Here's the thing—" Dramatic pause. I smiled, loving his theatrics. "Parks used to have a thing for Christian back in the day. I'd say roughly from the age nine 'til she was fourteen, she loved him. We all knew it. She was infatuated with him."

I frowned. "How'd she end up with BJ?"

"Christian didn't want a bar of her when we were kids. And then... I don't know what happened, but something did and Parks and my brother fell in love in the stupid way that they are. Until, you know— There's just been a vibe with Christian and her."

"Okay." I pursed my lips. "But when did they actually start... whatevering?"

He sniffed a laugh. "Whatevering." He squinted, remembering. "Beej and Parks had been broken up for a couple of months. Beej was so gutted, so we never saw her—then I think Christian and Parks bumped into each other, caught up one day. Then they kept hanging out on the down-low. Hooked up a few weeks later, kept hooking up, and then they got caught—and Beej and Jo... Bad—" He shook his head at his own private memory. "Really bad."

"What kind of bad?" I frowned, hating the thought of bad things happening to him.

"A&E the next morning bad." He gave me a look.

I was horrified. "Why didn't he fight back?"

"Christian doesn't fight anymore." Henry shrugged as if it were simple.

"Why?" I frowned again.

Henry gave me a strange and serious look. "He's too good at it."

The sentence hung there and I wondered if it meant what I thought it meant, but I didn't ask because I didn't want to get distracted from what I was trying to learn.

"So that's it? Then they broke up?"

Henry shook his head. "Then they dated in secret."

"Oh." I sighed. "For how long?"

He shrugged. "Couple of months." He took a sip of a drink that I don't know how he acquired.

"Why'd it end?"

Henry squinted, thinking, and stared over to the other side of the room.

BJ and Magnolia in the kitchen for a post-coital snack, I presume. Her perched up on the bench, him directly in front of her, her swinging her legs, his hands on either side of her body, her index finger pressed into his nose.

Henry nodded over to his brother.

"Because they look at each other like that." He smiled far too tenderly for a boy as cool as himself. "Always have—" He shrugged. "They've never not loved each other."

"Even when she was with Christian?" I blinked.

Henry gave me a look. "She has never not loved my brother." He shrugged again. "Christian just worked that out too late."

And then I saw Christian watching BJ and Magnolia from the other side of the room, and, honestly, my heart surged for him.

I know the feeling now myself. Now I live with it.

He looked so sad. So hopeless. So stuck.

And so here's the fucked up thing: seeing him love her made me like him more than I liked him before.

Not because I'm a masochist, but because my Friend with Benefit became a Human with Heart. I could see through his heart and I knew that loving his best friend's girlfriend would kill him, I could see it in the way he watched them—this fresh pain all over him, him trying his best to hide it.

If I had the foresight, I would have known what all this meant—him trying his best to hide it would mean he'd have to rip my heart from its chest, rub my love all over himself to cover the scent and throw them off. If I had the foresight, I would have known it would kill me.

But, with or without foresight, I would let him again and again and again.

"One to ten it for me: how in love with Parks is he still? I'm guessing like an eight." I poked Henry in the ribs. He shook his head loyally. "He still loves her," I said to Henry as I watched Christian watch them.

Henry looked guilty, like he'd accidentally told his best friend's secret.

"I didn't say—"

I shook my head, cutting him off. Then I gave him a smile that was sadder than I meant it to be. "That wasn't a question."

Daisy
11:44 PM

Where are you?

Out

Oh!

Out!

Excellent.

Where, Daisy.

Romeo's.

Calm down.

Without Miguel?

Yep.

94

Are you fucking joking? Come home now.

No.

I'll come get you myself.

Romeo
11:46 PM

Relax Jules.

We're on our way back.

"We're"

It's the compound word for "we are"

I have not missed you.

:(

# 16

# Christian

Memories are funny, don't you think? Creep up on you, break through the ground of your mind like a weed, even when they don't have permission to be there.

Me and Jo, couple months after Rems had died. Mum and Dad had gone to shit, couldn't talk to each other, didn't know how to. I was standing outside Dad's office, I was probably twelve by then. Dad and Mum were tearing each other apart, blaming each other, crying, throwing shit—and I was just standing there, watching through a crack in the door—pretty scared. I'd never seen them like that before. Beginning of the end for them, I guess, even though they're still technically married today. Anyway, Jo came up behind me, put his hand on my shoulder.

"It'll be okay," he told me.

I looked up at him, not sure, and he handed me a backpack. "Lily's on her way," he said.

"We're going to stay there for a bit now."

Our parents didn't ask Lil to take us for a while, it was Jonah who asked her if we could. He's a fixer, Jo, always has been.

I think about that moment every time I walk past that office. Dad's still in there, barely ever leaves it now. I don't really go home much. It's a part of the St George's Hill estate, and it's nice—big and like a castle. A lot of land that's sick for practicing chipping and driving four-wheelers but the whole house feels depressing. They should have sold it forever ago, but I think Dad keeps it because he wants to feel closer to Remy. Like leaving the house behind is leaving her behind.

BJ's face when he saw me and Parks kissing at Box. That memory crops up a lot. Whenever me and Parks have a minute to ourselves, it doesn't take very long for that one to rear its head.

It was weird, I was almost relieved to be caught, to be found out.

I'd never lied to the boys before that, though I guess I lie to them all the time now. I could be sick over how he looked, though. It would have killed him to see her with anyone else, but me? One of us? Fuck.

And then I've got this one of Daisy and I don't fully understand why it's there. About a week before we started hooking up, I saw her out. We were at one of Jo's clubs. She was with the Lost Boys, I was with the Box Set, and I didn't even talk to her—but I remember looking across the room and seeing her—she was talking to Booker, and he said something and the way her head fell back as she laughed, the way her mouth pulled wide when she smiled, it didn't curve up, I just remember seeing her and thinking she was like, stupid beautiful, and I wondered if I should go talk to her, but then BJ pissed off Parks and she snapped into FYBJ mode and my hands got pretty full pretty quickly. How Daisy's looked that night lives in my brain, rent-free, 365 days a year. Ordering coffee: Daisy's face. Filling up my car: Daisy's face. Buying milk: Daisy's face.

Just a good face, I guess.

I blink a couple of times, shake her out of my mind, focus on now. We're at Seven Park Place—Magnolia's favourite—and it's dinner with the whole set. They've got us where they always put us. I'm in the corner next to Hen. Beej is across from me, his arm slung around Parks's chair.

I'm invisible tonight. Haven't had a fucking look in.

She's chattering on to Henry about why she thinks alligator skin is "the fabric equivalent of controlled diamond supply" when a song plays overhead and she goes still and then our eyes catch from across the table.

I never meant for it to happen, me and Parks.

When Beej and Parks broke up it was a complete nightmare.

They were together one day—couldn't have hacked them apart with a machete—and then they weren't.

The signs were there if we looked. There was a party and Magnolia wasn't there, but honestly, because of them and how they were, it never even crossed my mind—it was so out of character for BJ back then. He loved her, he was mad about her, she was his every waking thought, he'd kill someone for giving her a look sideways.

My feelings for her at the time were on the back burner, still warm but not bubbling. I'd come to terms with it fairly quickly once they'd started dating. I had missed my shot, I knew, and we were never going to happen. I could tell because they looked at each other then the same way they still look at each other now.

I didn't call her after it happened. Them breaking up was a weird fracture down the middle of our group. It was like she didn't know how to be around any of us anymore, she didn't even really talk to Henry for a few weeks, that's how far she pulled away from all of us.

It'd been a couple of months or something, everything still felt weird—her and the P's fell off the face of the planet—and then I saw her through the window of Papillion, eating breakfast by herself. That was weird. She doesn't know how to be by herself, never has. The empty chair across from her felt like an invitation. Fate, maybe, but definitely not Fortune in retrospect.

I walked in, sat across from her, and we didn't talk about the break-up, I didn't even ask her how she was—I just ate her toast, told her about this shitty date I'd been on the night before with a girl from James Allen's, and she started laughing. Then she told me about her mum and some marchioness getting trapped in a stable at three in the morning, and then we saw a movie and I dropped her home.

And it wasn't conscious, I didn't mean to start liking her again, it's just that the pot moved from the back burner up to the main and then everything started to bubble again.

I was pretty sure it was all in my head at first, the things I thought I was feeling spark between us. It was a bunch of dumb shit—little looks, hands grazing, shoulders touching when we were next to each other, eyes holding longer than they should—things that aren't things and could actually just mean shit.

But then there was that one day where we got caught in the rain and I pulled her into a phone box and she was completely soaked and she looked so fucking beautiful. I pushed the hair from her face and I felt like I could kiss her—and even before I did it, I knew I shouldn't have done it—but she was staring up at me, looking at me like she was waiting for me to do it, bit down on her lip even, and you know what? When I think back to that moment, I can feel a cloud rolling in over the horizon. There's that low rumble of thunder that's less something you hear and more something you feel under the ground, and I was scared because it felt heavy and massive, and then I kissed her anyway.

It escalated pretty quickly from there—we nearly had sex in the back of my car that day. That probably should have been the red flag, because that was so unlike her—she'd never been with anyone else besides Beej and then one kiss in a phone booth and she's undressing me in the back of my car?

I can see for the most part what we were: she was on fire, being burnt alive. I was the silver blanket she wrapped herself in.

And that would have been fine if that was all it was. I even reckon that I could get past it. But then there was one day I told her I loved her and she told me she loved me too, and I believed her. She did. Does? I can't tell.

The song is "The Tennessee Waltz", and when Magnolia hears it in Seven Park Place her eyes go rounder than they always already are and she swallows.

She glances over at me and I can't cover the smile I've got on my face before BJ catches the whole thing and his eyes go to slits.

He nods his chin at me, eyes darting between Parks and I. "What the fuck are you two smiling at?"

Then the whole fucking table shifts uncomfortably.

"Nothing." Magnolia shrugs it off the same time that I swat my hand through the air dismissively. "Nothing, man."

"Nothing?" Beej repeats.

Henry shifts uncomfortably next to me.

"Yeah." Parks gives him a breezy smile and he stares at her for a couple of seconds before he moves his arm from around her chair.

BJ glares over at me. "That wasn't a fucking nothing smile, mate."

"Beej—" Magnolia touches his arm and I feel sick.

"What the fuck was that smile about?" he asks her as he stares her down, and to be honest, I don't love how he's talking to her. Neither does Hen, whose jaw is now set and his eyes are watching close.

Beej gets like this when he's drunk. Turns nasty, remembers that once upon a time Parks wanted me too and he can't deal with it. Worse, there's this nervousness in Magnolia's eyes tonight that I don't want to toy with. She looks so sad. Fucking hate it when she's sad. I just want to make it better for her.

"When we were together, we went up to Gwynedd. It was raining like crazy. We got bogged in the mud. Only thing around for miles was a chippy, so we went inside. They were playing this song—that's all." I shrug like it's nothing.

Magnolia swallows heavy because she knows it wasn't nothing.

We slept in my car, fogged up the windows, held her against me all night. Probably one of the best nights of my life, dancing in the chip shop with her to this song.

This doesn't placate him, though, if anything he looks angrier now.

"BJ—" Magnolia grabs his arm. "It was so long ago."

"Yeah, right. And you're over everything I did ages ago too, hey?"

She looks at him, surprised. "That's not the same thing."

Beej pushes back from the table, looking from me to Parks. "You can both get fucked." And then he delivers her his final blow. "I'm going to."

Then he saunters to the bar.

"Are you okay?" Paili whispers to her, but she's not listening—she's staring over at BJ, who's picking up a girl at the bar already and I wonder how this night's going to go. Is she about to switch into FYBJ mode or is she going to dissolve into a puddle that Henry's going to have to slop home and look after all night?

Parks looks over at me, her hands pressed into her cheeks, a little dip in her eyebrow that happens when she's stressed.

"What are you doing later?" she asks me with a weak smile and I don't know why that feels like a smack right across my face, but it does.

Feel myself scowl at her. "Fuck you," I over-annunciate to her. She pulls her head back, surprised. "Like, genuinely, fuck you."

I grab my drink, toss it back in one gulp, and walk the fuck away from her.

Pull out my phone.

Text Daisy.

> hey

hey

> Whats doing?

Watching a movie

> Where?

Home

> Want me to come?

> No, I've got a friend here.

I blink down at my phone screen in surprise.
A friend? What the fuck.

> Cool.

Shove my phone back into my pocket and pull out my keys.

"Oi." Henry jogs after me. "You good?"

I nod, jaw jutted out.

"Off to see Daisy?"

I give him a look. "She's with someone."

"Like a hookup?"

"I don't know—" I scowl. Kind of hate the thought of it, though, and what the fuck's he asking me that for?

He gives me a little smile. "You annoyed about that?"

"No." But yes. I frown. "I don't care."

Henry rolls his eyes.

I nod my head back towards inside. "Where's the puddle?"

"They left the back way." He shrugs.

"Together?" I can't help but sound surprised and thumb back towards them. "I leave for five minutes and those two become a functional couple?"

Henry considers this. "I wouldn't exactly say functional…"

I sigh, clench my jaw. Why the fuck isn't Daisy free?

"That sigh for Magnolia or for Daisy?"

I scowl at him. "Neither."

"Bullshit."

"What friend?" I ask.

"So, Daisy…" Henry says under his breath and I ignore him.

"Like, what friend is she with that she'd rather be with than me?"

"I thought you weren't together?" He points at me, pretending to be confused. I give him a look. "Are you?" he pushes.

I point to myself. "You know I'm the 2IC of the second-biggest crime family in England."

"Ooh." Henry wriggles his shoulders sarcastically.

I roll my eyes at him as I start walking towards my car.

101

"Just hook up with another girl." Henry shrugs.

Not really the kind of advice I'm used to getting from him, so I peer over suspiciously.

His eyebrows are up, an annoying look on his face—he's goading me. Trying to prove a point.

"No." I shrug indifferently.

"Why?"

"Don't want to." I shrug defiantly as I climb into my car.

Turn the ignition on as quick as I can so there's a sound filling the space in my head, but the question comes anyway: why don't I want to?

Jack
1:12 PM

Impeccable Arse update please.

no update

Seems implausible.

He's still into her.

Magnolia?

Yeah.

How do you know?

I just know.

You might just be reading into things.

I'm not.

# 17

# Julian

We've got our fingers in a lot of pies. Most of the ones you'd expect—bit of racketeering, extortion, party drugs. Mostly it's just opening channels for other people to do the work, work in and throughout my jurisdiction. The arms dealing was my dad's thing, so I keep it up but my personal sweet spot is the arts. I like planning the heists. The harder to steal, the more fun the time.

I've got a reputation—dangerous guy, stay away, a lot of drama—I'll kill someone if I have to, probably rather not, though. I will say if someone's got to die, I'll be the one to pull the trigger, though. I don't like people doing my dirty work. It's all dirty work. Weak to get people to do it for you. If you don't have the stomach for it yourself, you don't deserve a seat at the table.

I've got a little boat over at St Katherine Docks. A little black Rivamare.

Most of the time it just sits in the dock. I like it for sunning and it's a pretty smooth alternative to a hotel to take girls back to when Daisy's being a shit at the house. Loves to be a shit, my sister. Thinks it's her personal mission in life to tank as many dates that I bring home as possible. The other week she told a girl she found in my bed that she reminded her of our mum. Really flattened the mood.

The boat's good for thinking too. Quiet, even when it's not literally. The sun and the water do that for me, and I like the combination. Like how it hits the water, makes my brain feel good, looser.

Art does that to my brain too. At its best, it takes me out of whatever I'm doing at the moment, pulls me to another time—at worst, it makes me tilt my head and look at everything a bit differently.

I like Klimt. *Judith and the Head of Holofernes* is my favourite. Had my eye on that one for a while now.

"You gonna take the job?" Declan says as he glances over at me.

I look from him to Koa, who's shirtless in the sun at the bow of the boat. He props himself up on his elbows and peers over.

"I don't like him," he tells me.

I shrug. "I don't like him either."

"It's not worth £60 mil, Jules." Kekoa shakes his head.

"No, it isn't." I lean back, stretching my arms up over my head, looking at him out of the corner of my eye. "It is worth a £100 million, though."

Declan looks confused, but Kekoa stands and walks over, squinting down at me. "You're going to take the Holofernes?"

I nod. "I'll jack a Klimt on another man's dime."

Kekoa nods, thinking it through.

"Up for it?" I glance between the boys.

Decks shrugs. "Always."

Kekoa shrugs again. "Yeah, sure, why not?" Then he sits down next to me and looks out the corner of his eyes. "Oy, how are you feeling about Rome being back?"

It's a strategic question because Kekoa is the closest thing I have to a father and it's a hat he wears with caution and pride.

"How are you feeling?" I ask him because it's probably the more important question. He gives me a steep look.

"So is he *back* back?" Declan asks.

I nod. "Yeah, that's what Carms said."

Kekoa sighs.

"Trouble, you think?" Declan frowns.

"With those two?" Koa lifts his brow. "Always."

Someone smacks my boat twice with the palm of their hand and we all sit up straight, Koa with his hand on his gun.

"Who's in trouble?" Killian Tiller asks, his partner behind him. The dumb one. Hoover or something. Some kind of vacuum.

"Oh fuck off, Tiller—" I sigh. "Daisy's not here."

He folds his arms over his chest. "I'm not here for Daisy."

Declan jumps to his feet. "Bullshit you aren't."

Tiller gives him a surprised little look and I tap Decks on the chest to quieten him.

"What do you want?" I ask as I stand to my feet.

"A girl from Watford went missing last night."

"And you're asking me about it?" I pull back, offended. "Fuck off," I spit.

Tiller looks surprised and I glare over at him.

"We don't do that shit," Kekoa tells him when I don't say anything else.

"Really?" Tiller says, cocking an eyebrow.

"Really." I stare him down.

We don't.

Never have, never will.

There's good money in trafficking, the slave trade's booming—but I don't have the stomach for it. Drugs and arms? Sure. Art? All day long. People, fuck no.

We have a hard line and there are three things that never happen under my watch: No human trafficking. No sexual assault. Nothing to do with kids, not even kidnapping. These are the rules Daisy gave me when she was ten. What sort of ten-year-old knows about human trafficking?

I follow the rules. My men follow them. If they don't, they're not just out, they're dead. Tiller's accusation isn't taken lightly for a reason.

He watches me for a second, gauging me. Nods once. "Okay." He starts to walk away.

"How old is she?" I call after him.

"Twenty," his partner tells me.

Jut my jaw. Too close to home. Fucking hate that shit.

"If you hear anything…" Tiller eyes me.

I nod. "Yeah. I'll let you know."

And I will.

+44 7724 771 959
4:32 PM

Hey

> Hi

> Are you well?

Yeah. Fine. You?

> Good.

I'm just checking in.

Cute.

You're not 20 are you?

I'm not, no.

How come?

No reason.

Okay... haha.

Rather mysterious...

Are you okay?

Yeah.

No, I'm good.

Okay.

You know you can call me, if you need to.

If something shit happens. You can call me.

So I've heard...

18

# Christian

Been a few days since me and Daisy spoke. Bit weird, I guess. Felt weird the other night, but I didn't feel like reading into it so I didn't— but I did wonder about who she was with that she wouldn't blow off for me. Doesn't have a lot of friends on account of the fact that she's not an overly friendly girl. Jack? Probably just Jack.

Didn't message her the next day, though, just to let her know I wasn't thinking about it, thought she'd message me first. She didn't.

Decided not to read into that either, because why would I? It's not like we're anything.

Instead, I'm at one of my favourite clubs—Nysa. It's like a Midsummer's Night's Dream in here—Magnolia's idea, actually.

Speaking of, that's all turning into a bit of a shit-show. She's taking someone new—classic. Loves a good deflection. I give Tom England a month.

Nysa is pretty vibey tonight, good crew; I'm surveying the land when an old, familiar face walks in.

I crack him on the arm, smiling big.

"Rome!" I grin at him.

"Hemmes." He hugs me.

"So good to see you, man. When'd you get back in?"

"Not too long ago." He shrugs.

"I didn't know you were coming by, man—" I take a sip of my Sazerac. "I would have organised you a table. Who are you here with?"

He gestures to someone behind him and then her head pops around his shoulder.

"Daisy." I blink.

"Hey!" She smiles brightly.

Woah. Fuck. Why fuck? Shit. I take that back, no fuck.

107

"Hey." I give her a smile but it feels forced. I glance from Daisy to Romeo and my brow goes lower than it should.

Then I say nothing—why am I saying nothing?

They used to date, didn't they? I knew that. Haven't thought about it in a while, though. I don't really think about her having dated anyone, if I'm honest—don't read into that, though, because I don't think about anyone dating anyone except for Magnolia, so I mean, that tells you everything you need to know.

Daisy shifts a little. "How are you?"

"Yeah—" I nod. "Good. Yeah. Busy. I've been busy, but I'm good."

Her face falters. "Good."

"I'm good too," Romeo announces, shoulders a bit square.

I look over at him, trying not to seem too annoyed.

Daisy looks between us uncomfortably—it feels fucking awkward. "Also good."

"Bro!" Julian grabs my arm, thank God. "Sick jacket!"

"Thanks, man." I look back at Daisy. "Do you want a drink?" Make sure I look at Romeo too because it'd be weird if I didn't.

"Yeah," Romeo nods. "I'll have an Old Fashioned, and she'll have—"

I cut him off. "I know what she likes."

Daisy goes still.

"Yeah." Rome's jaw juts out and he nods once, unimpressed. "So I've heard…"

Julian lets out a low whistle and then hooks his arm around his sister's neck, laughing as he pulls her away.

Rome and I stare at each other for a few seconds, then I nod my head towards the bar.

Weird air between us. Been friends for years, though admittedly it was probably a situational friendship. Like, how many other people could I possibly know get the family shit that comes with being who we are?

I guess Daisy has a type.

Not that me and her are… whatever. You know.

I order a round of drinks and turn back to him.

"How was New York?"

"You know." He shrugs. "Always fun."

"Lots of trouble to be had there…"

He scoffs. "Kind of the point of it—"

I scratch my neck, trying to suss him out, figure out what he came back here for. "That why you're back?"

His eyes pinch a bit. "No."

"I mean—" I shrug. "It's cool you're back, man."

"Yeah?" His tone is weird.

I nod mostly with my chin. "Yeah."

I'm bigger than him. And taller. I'm 6'3" and he'd only be… who gives a fuck? I'm taller. Older than him too.

I let out a carefree laugh and shake my head. Super casual. "I forgot you and her had a thing…"

Romeo watches me for a second.

"Bullshit," he says and I can't believe it. The fucking stones on this fucking guy.

I press my tongue into my bottom lip, blink a few times. "Sorry?"

"As if, lad—" Rome shakes his head. "We were together for, like, six years. You didn't forget—how could you forget?"

I look at him like he's an idiot. "Actually, until a couple of months ago, I honestly thought of you both still as kids."

"Yeah?" He glares over at me, resentment skimming just below the surface. "What happened a few months ago?"

I give him a quick smile. "I found out Daisy was twenty and started fucking her."

His jaw goes tight.

I could beat him in a fight, easy, any day of the week, with my eyes closed.

I don't like fighting, if I'm honest. Good at it. Too good. I killed someone once. A fight in a back street behind one of Jo's clubs. Stupid. He didn't deserve to die and I didn't mean to kill him. Doesn't change much about it, though. He's still dead and I still killed him, so I don't fight now. Not unless I have to.

I wonder if Romeo's going to try to start something. Carmelo wouldn't let it get too far. Jo would kill me, but I'd take a crack in the face for Daisy. Not that this is about Daisy. Even though it's a bit about Daisy, I s'pose.

And then someone grabs me by the arm and swings me around to face them. Someone. Like I don't know who. Cute little hands. I recognise her touch.

Daisy Haites's cross little face is glaring up at me, her hands on her hips.

I frown at her, offer her her Greyhound.

She ignores it. "Did you fire Matt?"

Fuck.

I purse my lips. "Yeah."

She raises eyebrows. "Why?"

I let out one uncomfortable laugh, flick my eyes back over to Romeo, who's frowning and watching us.

Daisy folds her arms over her chest. "Was it because of me?"

My face falters. "No," I tell her, feeling a bit dirty at the question.

"Then why?" she persists.

I glance from her back to Romeo again. "Could we talk about this later?"

"No." She shakes her head, obstinate. "We can talk about it now."

I don't love being told off in my own club, so I nod my head towards the hallway. "My office then, yeah?"

Romeo scoffs and rolls his eyes.

Daisy touches his wrist—don't like that—catches his eye. "I'll be back in a second." He nods, looks annoyed.

I lean over the bar, clicking to get the bartender's attention. I point to Romeo. "Whatever he wants, it's on me—"

The bartender nods, then I put my hand on Daisy's waist, guiding her down the hall.

Take her wrist once we round the corner, pull her into my office and close the door.

I don't let go of her wrist. I know I probably should. I can't say I really want to, though—a bit weird.

She leans back against the door, glaring up at me.

Her eyes glance down to where I'm still touching her, our eyes catch again and I kiss her heavy enough that she bangs backwards.

It's a real heavy kiss—angsty and she's pissed off at me, I can tell, but she's taking it out on my mouth. She sort of just melts into me. My hand slips up her dress and she's pulling me in towards her. I do like kissing her, I have to admit. More than I like kissing other people, which could be a strange thing to be aware of, but she's also just better at it than anyone else I've kissed in recent memory.

I spend a lot of my time thinking about kissing her. What parts of her body I could touch, how she goes when I do. How it feels when her mouth brushes over my shoulder... I reach over and lock my door

110

and the sound of the lock snaps her out of the moment. She shoves me backwards a bit, glaring at me again.

"Why did you fire him?" She tugs her dress back down, straightening herself out.

I'm breathing heavy, reach over, push some hair behind her ear. "Why are you upset that I did?"

"Why did you?" She stomps her little foot and I glance down at it, amused.

I scratch my neck, uncomfortable, then shrug. "It just wasn't working out."

"Because…?"

I shrug again. "He was putting other people's drinks on my tab."

"My drinks!" She gestures to herself.

I frown. "Yeah, so—"

"So we're sleeping together!" she interrupts. "A month ago you fired that Belgian man who tried to make me pay for drinks!"

I give her a look because it's not the same thing. "Yeah, but that's because you're my—" I stop short. Fuck.

Her eyebrows shoot up, instantly drunk with power. "I'm your what?"

I shift on my feet, folding my arms over my chest. I think I feel my face falter. She's my what? I don't know. I don't know what the fuck is going on with me.

I shake my head. "I just didn't like Matt."

"Why?" She shrugs, all annoying and shit. Kind of want to kiss her, but—"What was the reason?"

"No reason."

"Of course there's a reason. You're not so unreasonable that there wouldn't be an actual reason as to why you'd fire a perfectly good barten—"

"Not that good—" I shake my head.

"Completely good—one of your best, actually. The only one of your staff here that can make a perfectly balanced Long Island—"

"Such a shit drink." I roll my eyes. "No one orders it."

"You had one two nights ago!" She stomps her foot.

Fuck. Why is she so observant?

"What was the reason!"

"There was no reason—"

"Tell me the reason!"

111

"Because I didn't like how he was looking at y—" I press my mouth shut. Fuck. Where the fuck did that come from? My mouth squashes into a smile that I wish wasn't there and her fucking eyes light up like a God damn Christmas tree. That smarmy shit.

"How he looked at what?" she asks all haughty.

I squint over at her, jutting my jaw out in amused discomfort.

She stretches her eyebrows to the ceiling, waiting.

"You're really going to make me say it?" I sniff, trying not to smile.

She nods proudly and I fight the urge to kiss her even though I want to.

"Really?" I blink, trying to look unimpressed.

"Mmhm." She gives me a tight-lipped smile, still waiting.

I scoff, shake my head at the brat in front of me. "I didn't like how he was looking at you," I say it quickly and with a shrug.

"Ohhh," she sings and I roll my eyes. God, she's exhausting.

"Stop!" I laugh, shaking his head.

"No." She shrugs, grinning up at me. "It's just interesting is all, because I didn't think we did jealous."

"I wasn't j—" I start and then I stop again, because I'm just digging myself into a hole. Instead, I let out a dry, annoyed laugh. "Fuck! Could you be any more smug?"

"Probably, if I tried." She smiles up at me playfully. She looks so happy. I like it when she looks happy.

She wanders over and perches on the desk. "I mean, you do realise that you fired your best bartender because you didn't like how he was looking at me whilst you were busy feeling up the leg of some gross, super average Geordie Shore girl?"

I lick my bottom lip and cock a smile—let it hang for a second. "Didn't think we did jealous?"

She frowns quickly.

"I wasn't jealous," she tells me.

I give her a look. "Sounded jealous."

She rolls her eyes. "'I know what she likes,'" she says, impersonating me.

I jut my jaw out a bit, pinch my eyes, nod my head towards the door.

"Is he the friend you were with the other night?"

A frown blows over her face. "Yes."

"Okay." I nod. I sound unimpressed.

"What?"

I shrug. "Not really your friend, though, is he?"

She looks offended, like something I said actually hurt her. I don't like the feeling. "Of course he's my friend."

"What kind of friend?" I ask her and I don't know why.

I don't really want to know the answer anyway, and she's once again offended by the question.

"My best friend," she says quietly, and I don't know why, but that being her response makes me want to fucking throw up and I think I hate Romeo Bambrilla, which is weird, because a half an hour ago I didn't have one bad thing to say about him and here I am now shrugging all dismissively in the face of his alleged best friend, talking shit about him.

"He's a fuck boy," I tell her. I don't know why.

She scowls up at me. "And what are you? A lumberjack?"

I roll my eyes and stand closer to her than I need to, look down at her on my desk.

"You don't really like him," I tell her.

She sniffs this laugh that makes me feel dumb. "Do I not?"

"No." I shrug. "How could you? He's a fucking tosser. He's not doing anything with his life—"

"Oh, that's right," she cuts me off, snapping her fingers once. "I forgot about your Nobel Peace Prize…"

"At least I have a job." I give her a look. "He pisses off for months at a time, blows through money like a coke whore."

Her eyes go dark. "Shut up."

I don't. "With a new model every month. Going nowhere—"

"Don't talk about him like that." She shakes her head.

I duck down so we're eye to eye, and I don't know why I'm fighting with her, I don't want to stop, though. "What's that now?"

"I said don't talk about him like that," she says in a low voice.

I scoff, because apparently I'm petulant now. "I'll talk about him however I fucking please."

She pushes past me, shaking her head. "Not around me, you won't."

"And why is that?" I walk after her, grabbing her wrist and spinning her around to face me.

She looks a bit stumped by the question. She frowns, collects her thoughts but doesn't share them. "Because he's important to me."

I look her up and down. I don't like it. "What's the deal with you two?"

"No deal." She shrugs like it's simple, but I can tell already that it's not.

"Bullshit," I tell her. "I knew you too when you were... whatever."

I hope she doesn't regale that to him.

Her face goes funny, falls to this faraway, hopeless place. "I don't know. He's just... that guy."

Hate that. I nod. "What guy?" My voice sounds impatient.

She shrugs like she can't help it. "That... one... guy."

I stare over at her and for the briefest second it feels like someone kicks a piano down the stairs and it lands on me.

"Well," I give her a look, "your one guy's a fucking joke—"

And then she looks me dead in the eye. "That Fucking Joke saved my life."

I pull back. "What?" I reach for her wrist again but she snatches it away. "From what?"

She doesn't say anything, just glares over at me and I hate myself. My mind is reeling—what the fuck does she need saving from? I feel sick thinking about something happening to her, and I don't know what she means—I don't want to know what she means, either. If he saved her, then they have one of those fucking mythic connections and I don't want them to, so all I can do is to make light of it. "Saved your life like you were about to eat a bad bit of steak, or...?"

She gives me a dark look, crossing her arms over her chest, then she turns on her heel. "Fuck you."

# 19

# Daisy

It took all my willpower after my weird fight[91] with Christian not to kiss Rome. He made me so angry, and he was such a prick, and he was so mean about Romeo—all out of the blue, for no reason whatsoever. And I know he's in love with Magnolia, so I don't know why he went like that, but it was weird and I was upset afterwards and I wanted to do something to upset him back, but I don't know what that would be, because I have the ongoing suspicion that he'll never give a shit about me, not how I do about him.

Anyway, hands got sweaty and my face went hot, and before I even got a look in with Rome, Julian took one look at me and made Miguel take me home.

Christian doesn't text me, he doesn't call. He doesn't ask to come over. We haven't had sex in a couple of weeks now,[92] and I guess that's fine, but a wave of nausea hits me when I think of that because if he's not having sex with me he is without a doubt doing it with someone else, and I want to throw myself through a window when I think of someone else's mouth dragging over his body.

Romeo shows up the next morning, though.

Curly hair all a mess, tired eyes, hands in the pockets of his baggy jeans. He slips his arms around my waist without saying a single word and puts his chin on my head and I don't know why.

I can feel a sadness on him, like he's worried about something.

The hug lasts longer than it should, and I'm glad no one can see us because it really pulls at the seams of my whole "we don't work" argument, because right now, in this particular moment, that seems like a lie. But as we all know, that's only one part of the equation.

---

[91] "We don't fight."

[92] Sixteen days, but who's counting?

The great tragedy of Romeo and I[93] is that once upon a time, we did work. And I'm educated enough to know that there are a million reasons that could explain away the connection we have: similar upbringing, shared trauma, circumstance, proximity—all of those things can be true, and none of them matter anyway because Romeo is frozen in my brain as a seventeen-year-old boy with the sun setting behind him on Formentera. His shoulders are pink, his hair's all a mess, there's sand on the bridge of his nose, and I'm standing on his feet the way little kids dance with their dads.

That's who he is to me. He's also the boy in the bathroom who, knife against his throat, who mouthed to me that he was sorry and he cried while someone else tried to kill me.[94]

I don't know whether we work now, if we can, whether we should even try—but I do know that there are few safer feelings in existence than his head on top of mine.

He's the sexiest security blanket alive. To me, at least.

Romeo stays for the day.[95]

My brother conceals his displeasure that Rome's back around again—but only barely—because they also have a complicated relationship.[96]

Julian likes him, ultimately.[97] That's the bottom line.

We just can't be together, it doesn't work, that's what my brother says.

Anyway, we're all in the theatre room watching a Marvel movie when the doorbell rings. Julian checks his watch. "That's probably for you, Face."

"You just don't want to get up." I roll my eyes and walk out of the room.

He yawns. "Yep," he calls after me.

I swing our front door open.

"Tiller."[98] I bat my eyes up at him as I smile big—the stern expres-

---

[93] Or at least one of them…

[94] There is so much you don't know.

[95] Actually, he stays for lots of days. He just keeps showing up in the mornings, even if I'm not going to be there. He just drives me to school with Miguel.

[96] As I imagine one does with the man who took his sister's virginity.

[97] He's saved me too many times for him not to like him.

[98] Yay!

116

sion on his face falters, mouth twitching as he does his best to be a good law-enforcer.

"These doorway dates are becoming a bit of a weekly occurrence!"

"Yeah, they're a real highlight for me too, Dais." He peers past me. "Is your brother home?"

"Nope."[99]

"Do you know where he was last night?"

"Nope."[100] I smile tightly.

"Do you know who he was with?"

"I think you know where I'm going with this, but I'll say it for you because it's our thing: nope."[101]

He presses his lips together and shakes his head. I lean mine against the doorframe, gazing up at him.[102]

"How's that girlfriend of yours?"[103]

Tiller eyes me for a second. "How do you know I have a girlfriend?"

"Inter-work relationships are so complicated." I grimace at him and then he shakes his head at me.

"That's not how this works."

"What do you mean?" I blink, feigning confusion. "The entire basis of our relationship is you asking me questions about me and my family that are none of your business… Are you telling me this isn't a two-way street?"

"It's actually a real one-way street, Dais. I'm an investigator with the NCA, remember?"

"Ooh." I smile playfully. "I'm shaking in my boots."

He looks down at my Ugg slides.

"New?" He looks up at me.

"Yeah." I grin, happy he's noticed. "Like them?"

He chuckles and drags his eyes back up my legs and eventually back to my eyes. "Sure."

"Everything okay here?" Rome says from behind me.

I glance back at him and I feel my face flush. I'm not sure why.

---

[99] Yep.

[100] Yep.

[101] Yep.

[102] He is sickeningly handsome.

[103] Brown, wavy hair, brown eyes, a few freckles, sort of pencil-looking. I'm much prettier.

"Yeah," I say quickly.

Tiller straightens himself up out of his trademark doorframe lean.

"Bambrilla." He nods his head at Romeo.

Romeo frowns at him. "Yeah, and who the fuck are you?"

Tiller sniffs an amused and indifferent laugh.

"This is Killian Tiller," I tell Romeo. "He's investigating Julian."

"Well, fuck off then," Rome scowls.

Tiller and I catch eyes. I don't smile at him even though I want to.

He walks backwards down our front steps. "Tell your brother to call me, okay?"

"I won't."

Romeo folds his arms over his chest, waiting for Tiller to leave.

"Tell him I came by," Tiller says instead.

I give him a tiny smile. "I won't do that either."

He rolls his eyes and then trots backwards down the steps

"I don't have a girlfriend,"[104] Tiller says once he's at the bottom of the stairs. "Not anymore."

Rome tenses up, but I clasp my chest in faux-excitement[105] and Tills rolls his eyes again, but this time they're bright and playful. He waves his hand through the air in a nondescript way and then walks away.

And, look, I'd be lying if I said I hadn't wondered what it would be like to date someone like Tiller... someone just entirely normal. Completely regular, not wanted by any state or federal agency, just your run-of-the-mill sexy citizen. I think he thinks I'm exciting. I wonder if I am to him what he is to me—a complete escape from our realities and our everyday lives; him to me, a normal person, and me to him, a criminal.[106] Just a strange kind of daydream, something that could never actually work, but might be really fun to try. Not that we ever would or could, but sometimes I think about what it'd be like to jump in his car one day and just tell him to drive. Sometimes I think he'd do it, that he'd kiss me and peel out and not look back. Other times I think he'd drive me straight to the penitentiary.

Forget I mentioned anything. I don't have feelings for Tiller, I just have feelings for being normal.

---

[104] OMFG.

[105] A tiny bit of which is genuine.

[106] At least in his eyes and to his standards.

118

Rome looks over at me, eyebrows up in the air.

"So, how does Jules feel about you having a thing with a copper?"

I roll my eyes and brush past him. "I don't have a thing with him."

"Sorry—" He gestures back to the door. "That was a fucking thing."[107]

I give him a look. "It's just flirting."

"With a policeman?" He looks incredulous.

"It's benign." I give him a look.

He sniffs a laugh and heads back to the media room. "You underestimate how good you are at flirting."

---

[107] Was it?

# 20

# Christian

I feel off-kilter. I don't completely get what happened between me and Dais—I made her sad, I know that. She hasn't called me, she hasn't asked me to come over. And I don't usually care, but I'm pretty in my head about it. It's almost like I miss her, but I couldn't. Why would I? I think it's because we're friends. Weird friends, I'll give you that— but friends, still. She's the person I tell all my shit to, you know? And she left my office the other night, like, pretty angry, and I don't care that she's angry, she's been angry at me before—she will be again because she's got a bad temper and I think it's pretty funny to piss her off and I like the way she works through her frustrations—what I do care about is the way her mouth went when I made her sad. Her dumb mouth has turned into a fucking pothole in my fucking head and I can't think about anything else for more than a fucking minute without thinking about how her bottom lip went all heavy, and now that she's not speaking to me I can't kiss it better.

Anyway, I'm at the Park Lane house, Henry, Jo and Jules are all playing GTA and Hen's complaining about them having unfair advantages considering our familial backgrounds. Beej is downstairs with a girl and I'm doing fuck all.

I make a cheese toastie, sit down on the couch and then I don't eat it—I stare over at Julian for a few seconds, try to nut up and just ask him.

I clear my throat. "Can I ask you a question?"

"Yeah?" he says, not looking away from the TV.

"Um—" I scratch the back of my neck. "What's the deal with your sister and Rome Bambrilla?"

Julian rolls his eyes and pauses the game. "Oh, well, that depends— do you have forty-eight hours for me to apprise you with the most overdrawn love story of all fucking time?"

I roll my eyes and he watches me, looking a bit interested.

"You know the other night, you could have just pulled your pants down and measured your dicks on the spot." He gives me a look. "Probably would have saved us a lot of time in the long run."

My brother smirks, amused.

"I don't care—" I start.

"Bullshit." Henry coughs. I ignore him but Julian sniggers.

Jonah unpauses the game. "If you don't care, Chris, why are you asking?"

"Because she said something weird, that's all." I take a bite of my sandwich.

Julian pauses the game again. "What'd she say?"

"Nothing." I shrug. "Just that he saved her." I watch Julian's face for the answer.

"Oh," he says and he looks sad for a second. He nods, then looks back to the TV. "Yeah. That's true, he has. A few times."

I frown. "From what?"

Julian unpauses the game and shrugs. "Shit."

That's all he offers me. "Shit."

I stare over at him.

"Shit?" I repeat. "What kind of shit?"

Julian groans and pauses the game again. "Aren't these questions you should be asking my sister?"

Henry perks up, looking over with eyebrows reaching to the fucking ceiling.

"Yeah, Christian," Henry nods, "aren't these questions you should be asking his sister?"

I ignore Hen and zone in on Jules. "Was it bad?"

Julian gives me a long look and I think for a tiny second I feel the heaviness he carries for her. "Yeah, man—" He sniffs a laugh like I'm stupid. "It was bad."

"Bad like how?"

"Fuck," Julian sighs, exasperated. "Bad like someone tried to grab her at school once, bad like someone tried to shoot her at that shitty theme park up in Cheadle."

I stare at him. "What?"

"Yeah, on the log ride." He shrugs. "He killed them both times."

I think I can feel the blood draining from my face and then, because I want all the reasons in the world to sever her from him, I say, "That was only twice."

Julian stares over at me. "There was one other time," he says and then he doesn't offer more than that.

Henry stares over at us in disbelief. "Is she okay?"

"Yeah," Julian shrugs. "She usually does better when Rome's around, I guess."

That makes me feel like shit and I think it shows on my face because Julian stares at me for a few seconds. "She's done okay around you too."

I take the bait. "How do you mean?"

"I don't know." He unpauses the game. "Daisy, when you come up behind her or whatever, she'll fuck you up. Throws a punch, wakes up swinging." He shrugs. "Does it less nowadays."

I nod, try not to smile. I do a bit anyway. And then I wonder—

"Romeo been hanging around your place much lately?"

Julian glances over out of the corner of his eye and laughs. "Yeah."

Fuck.

My eyes pinch and Jules chuckles. "Are you into my sister, Hemmes?"

"No." I shake my head and toss him a crooked grin. "I'm just using her for sex."

He gives me a long look. "You sure about that?"

# 21

# Julian

I was a fullback at Varley, fucking good too. Got scouted. That's what I wanted to do. I knew it wasn't on the cards in reality, this life we have was the only life I'd ever have, but I wanted to be the best, so that I knew for myself that if I wanted to be something else, I could have been.

I was eighteen, Dais was eight.

Saturday afternoon, pretty close to me finishing up at school, we were driving home from a rugby game.

Varley's up Kent way, so it's about an hour's drive on a Saturday, and it was just a cracker of a day.

I played well, the sun was out, and Daisy used to get pretty fidgety in car trips longer than twenty minutes and there was only so many times you could listen to the *High School Musical* soundtrack before you just wanted to end it all, so Dad decided to stop by the beach on the way home.

We had security with us, always did, but back then they gave us a lot of breathing room. They were with the cars, waiting for us, watching for us. Dying for us, so it'd turn out.

There were four men with us that day. The only one that was alive by the end of it was Kekoa.

My dad was running around, chasing Dais, and Mum was trying to take photos of her and I when a man approached us.

"Excuse me," he said with a smile. He smiled, don't you think that's fucked up?

My dad eyed him and offered him a cautious smile because that's the sort of man he was. You'll hear people talk shit on my dad, and while he was a lot of things and wore a lot of hats, Hadrian Haites, first and foremost, was a good man.

"Hi," Dad said, instinctively stepping towards him. "Can I help you?"

The man looked back at the carpark. "Is that your black Range Rover?"

Dad nodded, and then it happened real quick—the man pulled two guns out from behind him. Pointed one at Daisy, one at my Mum.

Then, without even thinking, Dad dove in front of Daisy right as the guy pulled the trigger.

Mum was shot, fell to the ground, started bleeding out.

But my dad, he didn't fall, he stood, shielding Daisy as the man shot him again and again and again.

Dad looked at me with ragged eyes.

"Take her and run," he said as he lunged for the shooter.

I scooped up my sister and ran as fast as I could up the other end of the beach. The man shot after us, missing as my dad wrestled him.

Hid Dais behind some boulders, grabbed her by the shoulders.

She was white. The most scared I've ever seen her except for that one other night.

"Are you hurt, Dais?"

She shook her head and I grabbed her face, inspecting it. I still do that to her. I can read her like a fucking book.

I looked up, looked over at where our parents were lying motionless.

She peered around to where our parents were.

"He's gonna come for us, Dais." I nodded at her, and I hated myself a bit because even though she nodded as brave as she could, her bottom lip was shaking.

I shook my head at her. "I won't let anything happen to you."

I'll never let anything happen to her. Not a day in her life.

I thought for a minute about what to do. I didn't have a gun. He was pretty big. I could maybe take him, but the gun element—he could have shot Daisy while I was wrestling him—I knew that.

The best plan I could come up with on the spot was stones.

I found two big ones that I could grip well in my hands and then we waited.

It felt like fucking forever.

Our parents were dying on a beach somewhere, my baby sister was in my arms, waiting for the same fate.

I'd peek out from behind the boulders every couple of seconds.

Tried not to look scared, I didn't want to scare Daisy any more than she already was.

I was pretty sure we were going to die anyway, but I didn't want her to see me scared in my dying moments.

And then I finally saw him coming towards us—I don't know what he was doing all that time, he took a while. There was no one else around.

I took my sister's face in my hands again and looked at her as seriously as I ever will. "If anything happens to me, Daisy, you run. Don't look back. Don't stop. Don't check on Mum and Dad. Run. 'Til you find a family, a mum, a dad and two kids—do you understand?"

She nodded.

And then a shadow fell on the sand around us.

I kicked a stone in the opposite direction and the man peered around for us.

"Close your eyes," I whispered to her, and I hoped to God she did, because I can't really stomach the idea of my sister seeing what I did after that.

Lunged for him from behind, smashed the rocks into his temples over and over until there was blood and he fell. Then I kept hitting him until his skull caved in a bit and there was gray matter and I knew he was properly dead.

I found his gun, pocketed it, and—covered in the blood of the man who killed our parents, the first man I ever killed myself—I ran over to Dais. I remember her little tear-stained face looking at me, I think she was looking for something familiar, maybe? And I was crying, I didn't even know I was crying until she took my face in her little kid hands and brushed them away, and even though we didn't know for sure at the time that our parents were dead, I knew it. I could feel it, this change in the air like that Daisy was mine now. My responsibility.

"Come on." I scooped her up and carried her away. Carried her cautiously and quietly down the beach towards our very still parents. It wasn't 'til we were a few feet away from them that we realised they were both still alive.

"Daddy!" She jumped out of my arms and dove on our dad.

He was covered in blood, all pooling from his stomach and down onto the sand and I hated it, how it soaked in and made clumps. Can't look at sand the same now. All I see is the red.

"Mum?" I rushed to her. She was well on her way to dying, a kill shot. We'd later find out it nicked her heart.

A miracle she was still alive when we got there. "Mum, you're going to be fine—" I lied.

"I love you, son," she said, held my hand to her face. Looked over at Daisy for a second, and then nothing.

She said fucking nothing.

I let go of her hand.

"Julian—" she called for me.

I shook my head at her.

I regret it now.

She was dying. I should have been more gracious. Shouldn't have made her die alone like that, but it's done now.

"Julian," Dad croaked. I reached out, ignoring Mum's cries, took his hand.

"It's all yours now," he told me.

I swallowed, nervous, but nodded anyway.

"She—" Dad coughed and some blood dripped from his mouth. "is yours now."

I nodded quickly, tears again.

"Daisy," Dad whispered, his voice failing him. She started crying. "My flower. You are—" He took this shallow breath. "Your brother's—" Breath. "…Keeper."

His eyes did this thing where they couldn't focus, and his speech started slurring. His breathing started to sound wet and laboured and then—silence.

Daisy says she counted eight gunshots that day.

I've not ever had the heart to tell her that once Mum was down, the shooter used both guns on Dad, so it was fifteen bullets in him in the end.

Fifteen—fucking excessive.

Someone was making a point.

I'll never let anyone make a point with my family again.

Daisy
11:51 AM

Oi

Hey

I'm home.

126

were you not before?

went to Prague.

oh, cool.

Good trip?

Yep.

Boys trip

Nice

Want to see you...

Yeah?

Yep.

Come over tonight.

x

# 22

# Christian

We had this fucking weird dinner the other night, the Box Set and Tom England.

Weird. Beej didn't handle it well. Practically chucked a wobbler on the way there and was a child the entire dinner. It was embarrassing, really.

We wound up in Prague after it, spent the weekend there. I don't know why. It's where I go to process shit. Actually, it's where I go to avoid processing shit.

I tried to make it a boys' trip, but it wasn't really because Beej wouldn't come.

Tom's away, see, so he and Parks are back to business as usual. Bit annoying because I've always got this shitty secret hope that on one of our trips Beej will push the boat out too far and he'll fuck it up for good and she'll be proper done with him, but it doesn't seem to matter what he does or how many times he does it, she always still wants him anyway.

I know that's shit of me, by the way—wanting him to lose her so I can have her, but I love her too, and fuck it, she loved me first.

One massive pro of Beej not coming was everything was way more chill. No one babysitting anyone, Jo not counting his drinks, me and Henry not on pupil-watch. We just went as hard as we wanted, not worrying about anyone overdosing because Beej is the only one reckless enough to do it.

We go out for good meals. Kiss some pretty girls. I hook up a couple of times. It was all a bit weird, though, and I don't have that much fun, which was strange because I normally love this shit.

I'm annoyed about Tom, sure, but it's not Parks my mind keeps wandering to—it's Daisy.

She hasn't texted me—not at all. Didn't even ask how my trip was.

How didn't she know I was in Prague? Does she not watch my stories? It's weird, she's been on my mind a lot, which Henry would read into, but I guess I just miss my friend. I was pretty happy when she told me to come over. Filled my day with a bunch of shit so I didn't head over too soon and come off eager. I do feel a bit eager, though.

I watch her for a few seconds from the doorway, she's lying on her bed, studying, legs kicking in the air. Biting down on a pen, her nose in a book.

It rattles around my mind for a second, what Julian asked the other day. "You into my sister, Hemmes?"

And I wonder... I can't be, I know I can't be, because I still love someone else and it doesn't feel the same.

I knock on the door and walk in anyway.

"Oi."

She glances up and her face goes bright when she sees me. That's a good feeling.

"Hi." She sits up.

I sit down on her bed.

"Been a while." I eye her then chuckle.

"Yeah." She sighs, faces me. "Avoiding me?"

I frown at her. "You're avoiding me."

"Am not," she pouts.

I love her mouth—fuck. I mean it—no, I don't.

She sighs, folds her arms over her chest.

It wasn't like this before. It was easy before, but now this feels hard.

I'm thinking about all the other girls who messaged me today, all the invitations to go to houses and dinners and not one offer sounds better to me than trying to pick a fight with Daisy Haites right now.

"How was your weekend?" she asks, closing her book.

"Killer." I nod coolly. Don't know why I'm being cool, it might be to combat that impulse I have to tilt her chin up and kiss her.

"Yeah?" She gets out of bed, does an indifferent little stretch.

"Yeah. Went pretty hard in the Old Square." Don't know why I said that. It's true, we did, but I didn't really enjoy myself.

"Oh—" Her mouth pulls tight. "Cool?"

I can tell that made her feel insecure, and it's weird because part of me instantly feels shit making her feel shit, but another part of me feels a bit glad, like it's some sort of relief to push her away a bit because I don't even know why she was on my mind so much anyway. I'd honestly probably be relieved if she'd fuck off out of it.

"Yeah." I nod, watching her closely. "Slept with the hottest girl…"

…And thought of you the whole time. That, of course, is part of that story I don't offer to her. I couldn't say that to her, could I? Because what the fuck does it even mean? I have no idea. I'm not proud of it. And it's not a fucking compliment, is it? It's weird either way. Either way I'm fucked up.

And I regret it instantly, telling her that.

Her mouth's fallen open, it looks a bit like I hit her, she blinks a bunch of times and breathes out. Gives me a cold smile.

"Atta boy," she says.

I feel shit after that. Don't like hurting her but it's too late now.

I reach for her face to push some hair behind her ears because I know she likes it when I do—I like it when I do it too, come to think of it—but she smacks my hand away with a scoff.

"Seriously?"

"What?" I scowl at her.

"You slept with the hottest girl?"

"I did—"

"But why would you tell me that?" she asks.

I make this sound like I think she's an idiot even though I don't. "Why wouldn't I?" Even though I know the answer. "We're friends."

She rolls her eyes. "Yeah, sure, but—"

"And we don't do jealous—" I remind her. "Are you jealous?"

"Do you want me to be?" she asks, her hands on her hips.

"No," I lie. But yes.

Shit. Why do I want her to be jealous?

"Okay, then why are you telling me?"

"Because we're friends!" I yell.

"Okay, friend," she says it like it's a swear word. "I'm really glad you had sex with a super hot girl this weekend."

"Thanks." I give her an uncomfortable smile.

"I'm really glad you went so hard in the Old Square."

I nod along, smiling tightly, sort of nervous that I've poked a bear.

"Maybe I'll go hard this weekend," she tells me with a look.

"Great." I shrug. Not great.

"I haven't been to Italy in a while…" She cocks an eyebrow. "Maybe I'll skip over there…"

"Good," I tell her, but it's not good.

"Have a killer weekend with the boys," she says with a tight smile that's all hurt, no happy.

Fuck.

I purse my lips and look at her for a second. "Which boys?"

She looks at me like I'm stupid and points to the door. "Get the fuck out of my room."

Jack
11:33 PM

Should we go to Italy this weekend, y or n.

Yes.

But no.

Jaaaaaackkkkk

I'm sorry! I can't.

whyyy

( REDACTED ) wants to fly me to Paris.

!!!!!!!!!!!!!!!!!!

To go shopping.

!!!!!!!!!!!!!!!!!

....for his boyfriend.

Oh.

Yes.

Well, that's quite the turn of events.

Yep.

Does (REDACTED)'s boyfriend know about what happened in the bathroom?

I presume not.

Well, fuck him—come to Italy then.

I already said an enthusiastic yes to Paris before he clarified it was for his boyfriend.

If I back out now he'll know I'm keen on him.

Sorry—

But do you not think he might have known you were keen on him when you slept together after that dinner? And in the bathroom at the shoot?

Unhelpful.

I think ditch him and come to Italy.

I gotta save face, Dais.

Would you like me to send one of the boys to (emoji) him.

Daisy.

I'm joking.

(I'm not joking)

(Do you actually want me to?)

She's joking @scotlandyard

Hi Tiller @scotlandyard

LOLLLL

@Tiller daisy loves you

@Tiller I do not

@Tiller she would like to shag you though

@Tiller semi-true.

# 23

# Daisy

I spin it to Jules that the boys haven't had a break in a while[108]—I knew there was no chance of me getting away by myself, no convincing him that Jack and I would be fine over there by ourselves, and Jack's busy anyway.[109] In order to have my big weekend, to have that killer time I'd dangled over Christian's head, I knew was going to have to make it a whole Lost Boys' experience.

Booker and TK were immediately on board and helped lobby my plea to the Elder Statesmen,[110] as we call them.

Once Koa thinks something should happen, it's pretty much guaranteed to happen.

"Please, please?" I ask Julian with puppy dog eyes. "We haven't relaxed in a second, I've been working so hard at school, Happy's completely lost his tan—he looks awful!"

"I do," concedes Happy.

"And I'm barely smoking," Smokeshow declares and Julian rolls his eyes.

"Italy's so beautiful this time of the year, and—"

He shakes his head. "I have a meeting tomorrow, Face."

"Skip it," I tell him.

Julian rolls his eyes.

Kekoa shrugs. "Push it back. He's a cocky bastard, he can wait."

I give my brother pleading eyes.

Julian leans in towards me. "How much of this impromptu holiday has to do with that little boys' trip that Hemmes took last week?" He

---

[108] Which they haven't. Not in at least four months.
[109] Drama with that cute-boy celebrity he's "not" seeing.
[110] Kekoa, Happy and Smokeshow. All the ones who worked for my dad.

asks quiet enough for no one else to hear him. His brows are low as he assesses my face without my permission.

No point lying to him. He already knows.[111]

"It has a tiny bit to do with it," I tell him quietly, which is an understatement but that's okay. He knows it and I know it, and I just need to prove to Christian I don't give a shit about him the same way he doesn't about me.

He nods. "Fuck it, we're going to Italy."

A few hours later, we pull up to the London Elstree Aerodrome to our waiting jet.

I get out of the car and my eyes fall on a pair of black Vans. Baggy jeans, open red flannel shirt, white T-shirt under it and a backwards hat. Hot boy shit, you know the look.

"Hello." Romeo Bambrilla grins over at me.

I fold my arms over my chest like I'm not the tiniest bit relieved to see him. "What are you doing here?"

"I'm your authentic Italian guide."

I walk up to him, standing closer than I need to, and I try not to breathe him in because he smells like home. "I don't need a guide. I can speak Italian." I give him a look. "My ex-boyfriend taught me."

"Pretty sure he taught you French." He smirks.

I roll my eyes at my childish ex-boyfriend who is cuter than I want him to be.

"Say it, though," he says, following me onto the plane. "You're a bit happy I'm here."

I sit down in the back corner of the plane, he sits opposite me.

He leans forward, I lean back, not saying anything with my mouth, but I suspect my face is giving me away some anyway.

"I'm not, actually." I give him a pointed look. "I came here to make sexually reckless decisions with a gorgeous man."[112]

He leans forward, offering me his hand. "Romeo Bambrilla, at your service."

I give him a look, smack his hand away. He laughs and it makes me happy and I try not to picture him in my bed, laughing as we watched *Drunk History* under the covers.

"No one kisses me when you're around," I pout.

---

[111] He always already knows.

[112] Julian grimaces in the background.

"Just like God intended." He beams.

"Rome—"

"I'll kiss you!" he tells me cheerily.

"You will do no such thing," I growl.

"Okay," he says, air-quoting and I laugh.

I stare over at him. Mop hair, cheek bones you could cut yourself on, mouth so pink it almost looks dumb against his brown skin—almost, but within the large expanse of that almost resides the miserable fact that in actuality, it's just downright sexy. And I do miss him.

And there is an ease between us that there isn't with anyone else. Not even with Christian, with whom I so badly want there to be an ease—I'm dying for there to be an ease, but there's not, it's just a slog and me alone in it while he's off having sex with the hottest girl in Prague.

Then, Rome... I mean, never mind that Julian forbade us from being together, we've found ways around that before—complicated, sweaty, sealed-section-of-the-magazine ways around it—but I know I was sadder about Tavie than I should have been. I know Romeo and I weren't together then. But we sort of were.

Sort of always been 'til then.

Romeo stretches his arms back over his head, watching me. "Do you actually not want me to kiss you?"

"Rome—" I sigh because it's all I can muster.

There are much, much worse ways to spend your time than kissing Romeo Bambrilla, I can tell you that much for free.

"Come on, Face—" He kicks me playfully. "Think of how much it'll upset your brother." I glance over at Jules, who's on his phone trying his best to ignore us.

"That is true..."

"Oi." He looks up. "Don't even think about it, you two."

"Oh, Jules—" Rome gives him a steep look. "I think about it all the time."

Julian rolls his eyes and Rome keeps going. "When I'm with other girls, when I'm in the shower, when I can't fall asleep at night, it's an honest-to-God miracle it hasn't just fallen off."

I roll my eyes because he's just being antagonistic and he's always like this with my brother, but Julian jumps over the aisle of the jet to tackle him to the ground.

It's 97 percent playful, but there's that 3 percent that shines through with a proper smack in the face.

Julian shoves Rome into the floor again for good measure before settling back in his own seat.

"Why did you invite him?" I gesture to my ex-boyfriend who uses the tackle as an opportunity to shuffle the seating arrangements so we're next to each other. Rome tosses an arm around me.

"Didn't," Julian says, nose back in his phone.

I glance over at Carmelo, who gives me an apologetic smile.

"I already regret it." Carms nods. "If that counts for anything—"

"It doesn't," Julian and I say in unison.

Our place is right on Lake Como, our grandfather bought it in the 70s, then Dad renovated it not too long before he died, so I think now we'll probably never change it. It's completely beautiful. The high, ornate, painted ceilings are heavily influenced by the Renaissance— it's probably why I love that period, actually. Because it reminds me of here. It's palatial.

Ten bedrooms, but it turns out that's still one bedroom short.

Julian counts us all on his fingers, frowning.

"Fuck," he growls.

He counts again and then swears under his breath.

"What?" Declan frowns.

"We're a room short."

Declan counts again, like he'll get a different result, and I roll my eyes at him.

Rome steps forward, tossing an arm around me. "Me and Dais will take one for the team."

"Yeah, right." Julian rolls his eyes.

Romeo waves his hands through the air dismissively. "It'll save me from having to sneak in there later anyway."

I give him an unimpressed look and he smirks down at me.

But I can see it on my brother's brow, the conundrum resting. Because he doesn't want me to share a bedroom with Romeo, but it's not like he's going to share a room with me either.

As for everyone else here, he could just bark at them and they'd have to share a room, but he doesn't do that because he's not like that.

He's very demanding of them, but I think he does try to never be unfair to them. Of everyone present that he'd actually consider inconveniencing by making them share a room, I know I'm top of the list.

Julian's eyes pinch, looking between us.

"Fine," Julian concedes and Rome's already grinning. "But you're sleeping in the room next to mine—"

I roll my eyes at my dumb brother.

"Jules, listen, friend to friend." Romeo walks up to him and grabs his arm playfully, and Julian glances down at it as though he's annoyed by his touch. "I just want to say, historically speaking, being in close proximity to our respective guardians hasn't really been a massively successful sexual deterrent."

Julian's jaw goes tight at the same time as I elbow Romeo in the stomach.

"Shut up," I tell him

"If anything," Romeo shrugs and he has a face on him now, "how quiet we have to be really spices things up."

"Oh my God." I shake my head.

Carmelo looks at Romeo like he's mad—and he is—only person I've ever met who taunts my brother and has lived to tell the tale.

"He will kill you." Carmelo thumbs in Jules's direction. "And I'll help him if it'll shut you up." He gives his little brother a warning look.

I let out a big sigh to tacitly say that I'm done with the conversation, pick up my bag, and carry it up the stairs.

A few seconds later, Rome jogs up behind me and takes the bag out of my hands.

He knows which room is mine.

When we were together and we'd come here, my room used to be our room.

He puts my bag down on the bed.

He stares over at me. "Do you still sleep on the same side of the bed?"

I nod. "You?"

"Nah." He shrugs.

I give him an incredulous look. "What?"

"Yeah." He shrugs like it's hopeless. "I sleep on the left side now too, so I guess we'll both have to sleep there—"

"Romeo." I stare at him unimpressed and then he chuckles, rolling his eyes.

"Fine, I'll sleep on the righthand side—" He sighs, plugging his phone in to that side of the bed. Then he peeks up at me. "I'd sleep on a bed of nails if it meant I got to sleep next to you, Daisyface."

# 24

# Julian

I don't date.

I have dated. It's always complicated and ultimately not worth it.

I have a reputation, I know I do. I'll go to a bar and make good on it tonight—heart breaker, lady killer, call me what you want—all of it and none of it is true.

And I could do big-man talk, say it's all about the sex, that I'm a free agent, no one's holding me down, whatever. It's a tiny bit that, and those things do have their merits, but it's not enough of a reason. I actually like commitment.

I can be committed, naturally I'm inclined that way because commitment and loyalty are two sides of the same coin, and I am loyal as fuck.

If raising Daisy taught me anything, it's that I can be committed to something—I hadn't even finished school when our parents died. Nearly done, but not quite yet. Applied for special circumstances and did majority of the rest of the work from the floor of my sister's bedroom.

She didn't talk after it for months—not to anyone but me. She wouldn't leave my side, became a sticking plaster to me. She slept in my bed, she'd eat on my lap, she'd wait outside the bathroom for me while I showered. She was so fucked up from what she'd seen, she had nightmares every night—that is if she slept, which she did her best not to. She became a little insomniac, that eight-year-old shadow of mine.

We did a lot of therapy—together and then eventually apart. Worked towards her being comfortable around not just me, but eventually Romeo and Kekoa, and then not just me and them, but then also Happy, and then Smokeshow, and it took a while, but she got there in the end. It was a lengthy process, hardest thing I've ever done. Probably the most worthwhile, though.

So I know I can commit, I just don't.

The honest-to-God truth? It's just one less pressure point.

The second my parents died, the weight of Britain's crime empire fell on my shoulders. Make no mistake here: to our people, in our world, Daisy and I are royalty.

But unlike those ones who wear the crowns, our dynasty can be toppled and the way that happens in a world like ours is murder.

And I'll die one day and, God willing, it'll be in my bed at the hands of age, time, and no one else. I don't care if I die, honestly, though I'd prefer not to do it soon. I have a lot of fun being alive, but I'm not one of those men who's stressed about leaving my mark on the world—the world went on fine before I was part of it, it'll keep being fine after I'm gone. None of that shit worries me, what worries me is keeping my sister alive.

She is the pressure point and there's nothing I can do about it.

Can't get rid of her, can't love her less—she's just this wide, exposed, gaping nerve I have for the whole fucking world to press on. So I do what I can: security details, bodyguards, self-defence classes, surround her with people I trust, forbid her from being with people I deem dangerous. About that—it's not that Romeo himself is dangerous, it's just that after the third time where they were together and someone tried something, it became apparent that they were a bit of a two-for-one deal as far as assassins go.

So after that one night—the particularly bad night that none of us talk about—we broke them up, me and Carms—mostly me. They've been what they are ever since.

About two thirds of the way to being a couple, but not quite.

It's a moot point now, I know. And he loves her. He'd die for her, which I care about. That counts for something.

But so would Christian, I reckon, though I don't think Christian knows that yet. Then again, neither does my sister.

Christian
9:37 PM

How's your big Italian weekend going?

good.

Good.

Big?

Massive.

Great

How's your weekend?

Fine.

Cool...

Are you ok?

Yeah fine.

Why?

Nothing.

Ok.

Ok...

what?

are we fighting?

We don't fight.

# 25

# Christian

Me and Henry walk into Harry's Bar, the Knightsbride one, and I look across the restaurant only to see a smiling Taura Sax waving us down to the table the Box Set usually sits at.

"Hello, what's this?" I throw Henry a look. "How's your best friend Magnolia Parks feel about you spending time with her self-confessed nemesis?"

"Don't know." Henry shrugs, pinching his eyes. "How's my brother feel about you being in love with his child bride?"

I grumble at him, don't feel like it's the same.

She's been around more and more these days, Taura. I see her both with Henry and with Jo.

Magnolia would care if she knew that either of them were spending time with her, but she'd care extra about Henry. Wouldn't say anything, but I know she'd be sad about it.

"Oi." I sit down next to her. Kiss her cheek.

Henry sits on Taura's other side and gives her a hug. I notice she lingers in his embrace—interesting.

"How are you?" she asks Henry exclusively.

"Yeah." Henry nods. "I'm good. Uni's been full on, but I'm fine. I like the stretch." He does too, that weirdo. He has since school. The smartest one of us all in an annoying, natural aptitude kind of way.

"And you?" Taura nods at me. "Recovered from your little Fuck It weekend?"

I roll my eyes. "Nothing little about it—" I nod my chin at her. "How'd you know about that anyway?"

"Jonah." She shrugs.

And I wonder if I see it on Henry's face, a flicker of jealousy.

I've asked him about Taura a few times lately, mostly because she just keeps cropping up. He says they're just friends—and to his credit, he is the only one of us who hasn't slept with her—and don't start with me, I know it's weird.

Boarding school and London's social set, it's a finite pool.

I reckon Jo's a bit keen on her actually, and I think it's a bit reciprocated—but now that I'm sitting here with these too, I'm not entirely sure Taura's not also vibing with Henry.

"It was fine." I shrug, annoyed that she brought it up because now that Taura's brought up Prague, I'm thinking about Daisy in Italy, which is all I think of at the minute, which—fine, I admit, is kind of strange and definitely annoying, but it also doesn't mean anything other than we're probably spending too much time together. "It's Prague, you know? Always good..." I look around the restaurant and then back at them, frowning. "Why'd we come to an Italian restaurant then, hey?"

"What?" Henry looks at me confused.

"Italian food—I fucking hate Italian food. "

Henry's frown deepens. "You love Italian fo—"

"It's just that Italy is so shit, don't you think? There's all those old buildings. Everyone makes such a big deal about them, but it's like, build a fucking new building, you know what I mean?"

"Um." Taura glances from me to Henry, back to me. "No, not really."

"And why are they so proud of that stupid leaning one? Basking in the failures of a man, that's so fucked up."

Henry frowns. "Okay..."

"It's just overrated as a nation. It's dumb. So basic—three colours on its flag—"

"How many colours do you think our flag has, then?" Henry interjects.

I ignore him.

"And pasta? Fuck me! Get a new thing to talk about."

"Right." Taura nods, chin in hand, a bit riveted. "And how do we feel about pizza?"

"Fuck pizza," I growl.

"Okay." Taura grimaces.

"What's going on?" Henry leans towards me.

"Nothing's going on, I just don't know why everyone loves Italy all of the sudden. Like, it's stupid, it's small—historically, it's never done anything that impressive. Name me three impressive Italians—"

"Da Vinci, Galileo, Robert de Niro, Michaelangelo—"

"Isabella Rosellini, Guccio Gucci, Valentino Garavani, Giambattista Valli, Salvatore Ferragamo—" Taura butts in.

"I said three," I growl. "You're forgetting, though, they're not all good…" I give the two idiots across from me a steep look.

"Okay?" Taura nods, waiting.

I shrug. "Mussolini."

"Sure." Taura nods again.

"Al Capone—"

"Sorry," Taura interrupts, "was he not an American?"

"An American-*Italian*," I clarify.

"Right." She nods. "Also, are you not in the same line of work as him?"

I scoff. Yes. But I don't say that out loud. "Wasn't that nice a guy, though, was he? Which is my point."

Henry folds his arms over his chest and nods once. "Yep, okay—what's going on?"

"Nothing—I just don't know why we came to an Italian place tonight."

"Because you love Italian food," Henry tells me, annunciating it all. "You love Italy! You once physically fought a man who threw a piece of garbage into the Trevi Fountain."

"He was being disrespectful," I scowl. "Two hundred and fifty years old and he's just going to throw in a Coke can? Not on my watch, man." I feel my point getting away from me. "Still hate Italy, but…"

"A week and a half ago you flashed me a villa on Lake Como and said, 'Give me a few years and I'll retire here.'"

"Did not," I scowl. Definitely did. "Fuck Lake Como."

Henry lets out an exasperated breath. "What's wrong with Lake Como?"

I shrug for the billionth time.

Taura looks at me with pinched eyes. "Is your girlfriend at Lake Como without you?" she asks, that astute bitch.

"Not my girlfriend," I tell her, jaw set.

She rolls her eyes at me. "But you do like her."

"Don't." I shrug.

"He does," Henry tells her.

"I don't." I shake my head. "Do we sleep together sometimes? Yes. Is she in Italy this minute? Yes. Do I separately hate Italy? Also yes."

144

Henry gives me a look. "Seems a bit intertwined, man."

"I'll intertwine your fucking face." I give him a look and he yawns.

I make a note to only spend time with people who know who I am in context of what my family does from now on. The sheer disrespect I'm getting off of my sodding best friend is unparalleled.

"So is she in Italy having her own Fuck It weekend?" Taura asks, and I glare over at the nosy girl whom I don't know why I'm having dinner with. She pulls an uncomfortable face. "Take that as a yes."

"Take it as whatever the fuck you want, because I don't give a shit. I don't like her like that, I—"

"Prove it." Taura gives me a tight smile.

"What?"

"Prove it," she over-annunciates.

Henry's beaming away, enjoying this all too much.

I roll my eyes at her. "How?"

"Kiss someone." Henry shrugs.

I give him a look, rolling my eyes. "I'm not just going to grab a girl and kiss her. Read the global room, you idiots—I don't feel like being cancelled today."

"Kiss me," Taura says with a shrug.

I pinch my eyes at her.

"What?" She gives me an indifferent look. "Nothing we haven't done before…"

"Yeah, but—"

"Unless you don't want to," she cuts in.

Henry leans in, smiling in a way that has me wishing I could hit him. "But why wouldn't he want to? He's single, you're single…"

"Completely unattached." Taura nods. "Unless—are you emotionally attached to someone?"

"No."

"Right." She nods. "Okay, let's do this."

I roll my eyes and feel eager to get this over with, to get them off my back.

They're right, though, because I am single, and I don't like her, so it's fine—I should just kiss Taura. She's hot.

I should want to kiss her. I mean I do, so I will. Kiss her. Now.

I swallow once, move in slowly towards her—feel a bit sick as I do, though, if I'm honest. Which is weird, because we have kissed before. More than kissed before, actually, and it was great. Fine. And I kiss girls all the time—haven't in a while, I guess. Except for Prague, which was the best, except that it wasn't, but it just wasn't because I was stuck in my head about Daisy, and that was Henry's fault, because he said that the girls I was tuning that night all looked like Daisy, but like that's fucking my fault—Daisy just happens to look like women from the Czech Republic. That's on her. And I wouldn't have thought about her if Henry hadn't said that, but then she's all I thought about and it ruined it, but it's not that it meant anything, you know? Like this, now, means nothing to me—it's just a kiss, I just have to kiss Taura.

She's a good kiss. Great mouth, good eyes, bit greener than Daisy's, which are more like honey than anything, if you asked me their colour—which you didn't, I know. Good mouth too—I mean, it's fine. Daisy's is better. Bottom-heavy. More fun to kiss. Still, I lean in more because I'm happy to get Henry off my fucking back, and it's like—my mouth is hovering just a couple centimetres off hers, barely that even, I can feel her breath on me. I swallow. My stomach lurches as I lean in and our mouths brush and I think about how Daisy looked at me the last time I saw her, looked at me like I was stupid—and I am—I like it when she thinks I look stupid. I feel like she'd think I'm stupid now, wonder how she'd feel about me kissing Taura Sax to prove that I don't have feelings for her—which I don't—except that... do I?

I pull back from Taura and stare at her, frowning.

She cocks an eyebrow, waiting for me to arrive there.

"Oh, fuck," I say, mostly under my breath. "Shit."

Taura claps her hands quietly and whispers, "Yay!"

"Shit." I stare over at Henry. "I like her."

"Yeah." Henry nods.

"No." I shake my head, push my hands through my hair. "Fuck. Shit! How did this happen?"

"I don't know." Shrugs Henry. "Because she's great?"

"Who's great?" Jonah says from behind me.

Forgot he was coming. Bad timing, as per usual.

"No one," I tell him.

"Daisy," Taura tells him and I throw her a dark look.

"Oh." Jo's face falters a little. I can see him processing some information he's got rattling around in that head of his, whether to tell me or not. He weighs it up. Jo can be an arsehole, he can be antagonistic, he can be a typical, shit-head older brother, but he cares. In his own weird way. He leans in towards me as if to give me a hug hello.

"She's there with Rome," he whispers.

I pull back. "What?"

He scratches the back of his neck—eyes flicking from me to Hen and Taura—I'm louder than he thinks I should be. Keeps all his cards close to his chest, but especially his heart cards.

"The Bambrillas went last-minute on the trip. Carms posted a photo of them on a boat—" He cringes. "They kind of look together."

I scoff and shrug all at once. "Well, they're not. "

"Fuck, that's shit timing." Henry grimaces.

"Yeah, but it's not true." I tell them, the back of my neck getting hot.

"How do you know?" Taura asks unhelpfully.

"Because it's fucking not," I growl.

I hope.

## 26

# Daisy

The Bambrillas own a few bars along the Italian Lakes, from Como all the way up to Cazzanore, and all of them have a reputation for being "underworld-adjacent". Not because there's anything unbecoming about them, nor is it because what they charge you for an aperitif is—dare I say—as close to criminal as you can get, but because they're the sort of exclusive, off-the-beaten-path places that you only seem to find if you're brought there, and you're only brought there by people who know that these places exist, and you only know they exist if you're one of us.

We walk into one of their bars, one not too far from our house, that's tucked away in an old manor that looks right at home in the foothills of Blevio.[113]

Rome and I have been exactly how I thought we'd be on this trip, which is: like no time has passed at all. I've been staunch about us not kissing and even more staunch about the pillow barrier between us at night time.[114]

He has wandering hands and I have very low willpower when it comes to turning him down, especially because the honest-to-God truth is that I don't want to—I never want to say no. Romeo Bambrilla's hands on my body feel to me like a towel coming straight out of the dryer after a hot shower on a cold day.

It's not necessary, I can survive without it, but it is one of the nicest things.

We walk and he hovers closer to me than the friends I keep telling

---

[113] If you don't know what it looks like, Google immediately. There are these crazy green hills that fall into the lake and are knotted with scattered buildings and homes. It's perfect.

[114] Because I can only trust myself so much.

him we are, close to me how he has since we were kids—since before we were too little to know he needed to. He's always just hovered around me. Just little kids who latched on to each other, who crawled under the tables during their father's meetings, who hid in the cupboards so they didn't have to say goodbye to each other, who found dead bodies in those cupboards and started to understand the nature of the family business. Every horrifying thing I think I've found out about the world, I found out with Romeo. It was his hand that covered my mouth when we found that body. It was my hand he squeezed when we were in his dad's office when no one knew we were there and we heard his dad kill a man who had failed him. Romeo was the only person I spoke to besides Julian after what happened to my parents.

In the end, who he was to me back then made who he became so much worse.

I look back over my shoulder at Rome and lean back a little, and he lets me rest there because we don't have very good boundaries.[115]

"Greyhound?" Rome whispers closer to my ear than he needs to.

I nod and he leads me over to the bar.

Our brothers and the Lost Boys fan out, take over the place, spill into corners and out onto the balcony.

Rome's hands are on my waist, sometimes in my hair.[116]

We're holding hands a bit,[117] and it's hardly my fault because maybe I love Christian or maybe I don't, but I know for certain he doesn't love me back. But Romeo does. And yes, there's been an insurmountable amount of shit that has happened between us, I know that, but he'd die for me, kill for me, keep me warm on cold nights.

I rest my chin on his chest as I look up at him, and he pulls my hair as he kisses my forehead.

And then someone yells from the other side of the room, "Romeo Bambrilla!" And he goes a bit still.

It's not even that the voice is all that familiar, it's his reaction that tips me off more than anything. Something is about to go horribly awry.

His face sort of morphs into a grimace.

-------------------

[115] Can you really blame us, though?

[116] Because, boundaries.

[117] A lot.

149

"Well, well," purrs the voice of Tavie Jukes.[118] "Look at what we have here."

She doesn't sound like a typical West-Midlander even though her family runs the Birmingham outfit. She went to school in London like the rest of us.

She's older than me, the same age and year as Rome. She always made sure I knew she was older than me too. She wears those two years Romeo broke up with me to be with her like a badge of pride, even though he only said he did it because Julian made him.

I don't know whether that's true or not—I've never wanted to ask—I don't want to know that my brother did that if he did.

I was a kid anyway. "Broke up" is such a stupid way of putting it, but I suppose it didn't feel stupid then.

He lost his virginity to her, not to me. I kind of hate that part.

"Tavs." Romeo nods, clears his throat. "Hey."

"Rome—" She presses her cheek into his and then looks over at me, giving me a tight smile. "And little Daisy Haites. What a surprise."

I give her a bored smile. "Is it?"

Tavie gestures vaguely to the Lost Boys littering the room. "I see you've got the whole cavalry here. How sad that you can't travel by yourselves…" She gives me a curt smile that lands mostly on Rome. "It must be so hard for you to get any alone time." And for a moment I wonder what he's told her about me. About us. I feel insecure and a tiny bit panicked, but my acute stress response[119] is all fight, so I strap on my pink Everlast gloves and take a swing.

"I know." I sigh, pretending to be rueful about it. "It must be such a relief not being important enough to need security."

Her smile drops and Romeo sniffs a laugh next to me.

I position myself in front of him, guarding him.

I'm not a good sharer. But quite honestly, with him, I don't feel like I should have to be.

"Rome." Tavie steps towards him. "Remind me, when was the last time we saw each other?"

I roll my eyes at her. "In my bed, I know."

"No." She shakes her head, snapping her fingers like she's trying

---

[118] Tavie Jukes being the girl he had sex with in my bed.
[119] AKA fight or flight response.

to remember. "That's not it," she says that while staring at Romeo, waiting.

I look up at him, frowning a bit and waiting for more. When he doesn't offer it and all he gives me is a grimace, I look back at her.

One more snap of her fingers and she points at him like she caught the thought she was chasing. "In New York, a few days before you came back to London."

I look over at Romeo, eyes a bit rounder than they should be in front of the likes of Tavie Jukes, bitch-harlot extraordinaire.

"Really?" I look up at him.

"Dais—" he starts.

"I didn't ask you to come back." I shake my head at him. "I didn't ask you to tell me you missed me—I didn't even ask you to come to Italy. You came back, you walked back into my life, I was fine." He reaches for my hand and I throw it off me. "Don't touch me."

"Dais, it didn't mean anything—"

"That is true." Tavie nods, flicking me a look. "Although, he did say to me midway through that 'Daisy would never do something like th—'"

And then I just walk away. I can hear Rome calling my name as I do, but I keep walking, go right over to my brother whom I know Rome won't approach because Julian would take a chance to hit him any day of the week.

He's sitting at a table with Declan, Carmelo and Booker, and I practically hurl myself into Booker's lap.[120]

Julian's face falters for a second, confused. He looks around the bar and his eyes fall on Tavie and in a second he's caught up without needing a single word. He rolls his eyes at me all annoyed and then yanks me off of Booker's lap into the empty chair next to him.

Julian's brows are low as he looks past me. "You alright?"

"Fine." I shrug.

"She say something to you?"

Our eyes catch and my eyes say "yes" even though my mouth doesn't and then he knows. I wonder whether we'd be like this if we'd been afforded the opportunity to just be a regular sibling duo,

---

[120] He's pleased to have me there, by the way. Gives me a pleasant smile, drapes his arm over to me. We've done this dance before—probably will again now that Romeo's back.

the kind who fight about who sits in the front seat or him holding a snack I want just beyond my reach instead of nearly dying in his arms and him raising me by himself at eighteen.

His brow's low. "Do you wanna leave?"

I shake my head. "I said I'm fine."

"Fine." Julian shrugs and points to Booker. "But you're not kissing him."

"Already have," I tell him, my nose in the air.

"Not tonight you aren't."

"Fuck you," I scowl. "You can't tell me whom I can and can't kiss!"

My brother nods his head towards Booker.[121] "I can tell him, though."

I let out a cross little growl and push back from the table, wandering to the other side of the bar—far away from where Rome is standing still with Tavie, watching me with sorry eyes.

I don't know why he's still standing there with her like an idiot. I don't know why I care either, because I like Christian[122]—but maybe a little bit of me always likes Rome too.

Not anymore.

I lean over the bar, order a drink right as a brave soul approaches me.

Tall guy, big. Olive skin, some freckles from the sun that you can tell wouldn't be there without it—looks like he might play some sport.

"Can I sit here?" he asks.

"Yeah, sure." I stare up at him, already a bit bored. "Yes."

He sits on the stool next to me and I take a big sip of my drink.

"Are you fighting with your boyfriend?" he asks.

I stare straight ahead. "He's not my boyfriend."

"Then who's that guy talking to that girl who's not as pretty as you?"

I look at the man, then over to Rome, whose brow is low and set how it is when he's on guard.

"That is my ex-boyfriend with his ex-girlfriend." I take a big drink.

The guy chuckles. "Sounds complicated."

"You have no idea." I take another sip.

---

[121] Who sort of reluctantly concedes to this sad reality with a tight smile.

[122] Who doesn't like me, but that's besides the point.

"So tell me," he says and I let out a dry laugh before I stare up at him.

"I don't tell strange men my secrets."

"Well—" He touches my hand. "What if we found a way to get more acquainted?"

I pull my head back in surprise, looking up at him. "No, thank you."

He sniffs a laugh, nods once, and removes his hand.

"Can I buy you another drink anyway?" he asks. "You look like you need it." I purse my lips, thinking, then I shrug. "Okay."

He orders me another Greyhound and himself a rum, neat.

"Cheers." He slides me my glass—and I swear to you, it's the quickest sleight of hand and a tiny plop you'd probably miss if people hadn't been trying to kill you all your life.

I hold the drink in my hand, staring at him.

He gives me a quick smile, wondering whether he's been caught.

I stare at the glass. "Was that Rohypnol?"

He sniffs a laugh, shaking his head. "GHB."

"Fuck." I sigh, rubbing my eyes tiredly. "Why would you do that?" I look up at him, shaking my head. I sigh again. "Why?"

He shrugs carelessly, sniffs like he thinks it's funny, and I'm glad he did this to me. Imagine if he did it to someone else. Better me than them.

And then it happens quickly, quicker than he could have anticipated, I think—

I kick his stool out from under him and slam his head into the bar on his way down.

This man will die tonight, there's no two ways about it.

Julian has a hard line with sex offenders. He'll kill them on the spot without thinking twice, thinks they rot the world.

Julian thunders over. "What the fuck's going on?"

"He put something in my drink," I tell him.

Julian looks down at the man on the floor with a bleeding nose[123] glaring up at me.

"The bitch is crazy—I didn't, I just—"

Julian drags him up by the collar of his shirt and Romeo's at my side. "What happened?" he asks me and I ignore him.

---

[123] Definitely broken, in my semi-professional opinion.

153

Julian slams the man's head down on to the bar,[124] then drags his head the entire length of it.

"What happened?" Romeo asks, grabbing my wrist and ducking for my eyes. I jerk away from him.

Julian cracks the guy across the face then spring-kicks him in the stomach. He goes flying backwards into a table of people.

And then it all sort of goes chaotic from there.

He had friends there, I think. The man. Because then someone else grabs my brother, tries to hit him.

Happy pulls him off and then someone else tackles Happy.

Carmelo snaps his fingers twice to get my brother's attention, signaling to take it outside.

Julian catches the eyes of Miguel and Kekoa, then nods his head towards me. They know the drill: get me out of here, home safe at all costs.

"Why didn't you call me?" Romeo asks, grabbing my wrist on my way out.

"You had your hands full." I glare at him.

"No, I fucking didn't—you walked away from me. I was just standing there." Rome's face strains. "Did he touch you?"

"No." I frown. "I'm fine."

Romeo gestures to my brother, who's smacking the guy in the face, and gives me a quizzical look.

I shake my head. "He just tried to drug me." Romeo's jaw goes tight and he nods once. "Rome—" I call after him, but he's ignoring me now, marching right on over to my would-be assailant and picks him up off the ground where my brother is beating him and hurls him down some stairs.

"Romeo!" I call again, but Kekoa shakes his head at me, hooking his arm around my neck and pulling me towards the car.

"You know how this goes, babe." He gives me a sorry smile. "You don't want to hear this."

He puts me in the car and closes the door as quick as he can so I don't hear it, but I do. The sounds of bones breaking on my behalf, of a body being beaten. I hate this part.

There are so many variables to it, so many ways in which these things can go wrong, and they're doing it for my honour, but my

---

[124] Onto a glass on top of the bar actually, if we're being specific.

greatest honour is if everyone I love would just remain safe and alive, but it's never a sure thing around here.

"You okay?" Kekoa asks, looking back at me through the rear-view mirror.

"Did you drink any?" Miguel asks, shining his phone light in my eyes.

"I'm fine."

"Are you sure?" Miguel frowns.

"I watched him put it in." I fold my arms over my chest. "I didn't have any, I'm not an idiot. I'm fine."

"Fine and grumpy." Miguel gives me a look and then climbs into the front seat to get away from me. I roll my eyes at him and then they talk about me like I'm not there.[125]

It's a long couple of hours between us leaving the bar and the boys trickling home, and I pace a hole in my floor the whole time.

I see headlights flood the driveway and I look out the window.

My brother gets out of the car and I breathe a sigh of relief. I wait for Rome to follow after him, but he doesn't.

I purse my mouth, frowning.

I'm sitting on Julian's bed, waiting for him as he walks in.

A graze on his face, bloody knuckles, the neck of his white Lanvin T-shirt stretched and ripped.[126]

He stares over at me for a couple of seconds, sighs, then sits down next to me.

I wriggle in closer to him and he tosses an arm around me.

"Are you okay?" I lean my head against him.

He shakes his head at me, like my priorities are all wrong. "Are you?"

"I'm fine."

"Did he touch you, Dais?"[127]

I shake my head. He sighs.

"Where's Rome?" I look up at him.

---

[125] "She gets like this when Romeo's in town." "You know how she goes around Tavie." "Needs a nap." Impossibly rude shit like that that only the people closest to me would be brave enough to say.

[126] If I've told you once, Daisy, I've told you a thousand times: do not buy him white!

[127] He knows about the one time. I think the one time haunts him.

155

Julian purses his mouth, thinking, then peeks down at me. "He dropped Tavie home."

"Oh." That's all I say.

"Don't think it meant anything—" He sort of cringes.

I nod. "Right."

I stand up, walk towards the door.

"Don't be a bitch to him when he gets in, yeah?" Jules tells me and I give him a look. "He just put a man in the ground for your honour, Face."

"I didn't ask him to." I shoot back.

My brother shrugs. "And he did it anyway."

Then my brother waves his hand towards the door, gesturing for me to leave. I give him a disparaging look and roll my eyes, slamming the door behind me.

"Love you—" he calls through it as an afterthought, and I don't say it back because I'm feeling petulant and angry at Romeo.

I go back to my room and sit on the bed—no more pacing because I know they all survived, but it's almost a full forty-five minutes[128] before my bedroom door opens and Romeo walks in.

His lip's cut, shirt dirty, smeared with some blood.

"Where have you been?" I ask.

He gives me a look. "I know he told you."

I nod once, looking at the ground. "Did you…" I can barely look at him as I ask it. "…You know?"

He frowns. "What? Now—? With Tavie?" I nod again. "No, Dais—fuck. What's the matter with you?"

I jump to my feet and poke him in the chest. "With me? What's the matter with you?" I poke him again. "You're the one who came back to London declaring you missed me—"

"I did—"

"While still shacking up with your ex-girlfriend?" Poke.

"It was a one-time thing," he yells loudly.

"How many 'one time things' have you and Tavie had in the name of missing me?" Poke.

"Well, Dais—" His jaw goes tight. "You can be sure as fuck that I don't miss you anymore."

I frown up at him, my feelings a bit hurt.

_____

[128] There is so much you can do in forty-five minutes.

"Daisy." He sighs, exasperated. "We weren't together."

"I know we weren't!" I snap, poking him again. "We're friends."

He gives me a ragged look.[129] "Clearly."

I glare up at him and then, suddenly, he grabs my face with both his hands and kisses me quickly.

There is something about kissing Romeo that doesn't happen with anyone else, and though I'm not Alice and I've not fallen through that looking glass, I am falling, and it is through something like time and space. He has hands that feel like an infinity, and the way he presses his body into mine feels the same as it has since we first started doing this back when we were too young to be doing this. Except bigger, his hands are bigger. And he's taller now too. Our bodies fit different than they used to because I stopped growing when I was sixteen and he hasn't stopped yet, but the way his hands feel on me, they always feel the same. Heavy, like a heat pack.

He lifts me off the floor and walks backwards to the bed, falling on to it, bringing me down with him, and he breaks the fall just how he's done for me for every fall I've ever taken.

He stares up at me, holding my face in his hand, smiles, and then puts his hands behind his head, waiting for me to unbutton his shirt.[130]

I do, taking my time, button by button, ignoring the blood on it that's all been spilt for me, and then the shirt spills open.

He's always brown because of his mum, but today he's extra because we spent the day on the lake and he gets dark so quickly.

"What are you looking at?" His face falters, a bit amused.[131]

"You," I tell him bravely.

He sniffs. "What about me?"

"Nothing—" I shake my head. "You're just... my favourite sweater."

He tugs me by my hair down towards him so we're nose to nose, forehead to forehead.

"I'll never stop missing you, Dais." And then he kisses me.

---

[129] It's mean when his eyes go like this, because they're too beautiful to ignore.

[130] Very presumptuous, but I suppose we are with each other.

[131] And definitely a bit pink.

hey

Hi

Been a minute.

I know. Are you well?

In Italy with the boys.

I didn't ask where you are, I asked if you're well.

Hah.

Fine, yeah. A tiny scuffle.

Are you okay?

Yep. Always.

Why do you always message me after your 'tiny scuffles'?

Don't know. Just do.

Cute.

No.

How tiny was it?

Miniscule.

Did you get hurt?

Nope.

Anyway

What's going on with you?

Same old...

Heard you're seeing someone new.

Hah. Haven't you heard? I'm always seeing someone new...

When are you going to see me then?

Goodnight Julian.

x

## 27

# Daisy

Two and a half times later, Romeo looks over at me, chest heaving, his hand still in my hair.

"We're fucking rubbish friends, ey?" He chuckles.

I sniff a laugh that is mostly sincere. "Yeah."[132]

His face goes a bit serious as he pinches my chin to face him. "You are my best friend, though, do you know that, Face?"

I nod.[133] "I know."

"Go on," He scowls at me. "Say it back, then—"

I stare over at him for a few seconds just to be annoying and then I bury my face in his chest so the admission comes out all muffled. "… You're my best friend too."

He tugs my hair back so I look up at him.

"Better than Jack?" He asks, eyebrows up.

"No—" I growl and then I concede. "But yes. I guess. Just because of—"

"I know." He interrupts.

I'm glad I don't have to say it. I hate saying it.[134] I nod, try not to cry as I look at him. "No one else gets it."

He nods back at me. "I know."

"Thank you," I tell him, slipping my arm around his waist.

"For what?"

"For what you did for me before."

He flashes me a sad smile. "Anytime."

---

[132] "The stupidest fucking friends I've ever seen," Miguel would later tell me when I go downstairs to get a snack. And I'll say, "Sort of technically we are fucking friends." And he'll give me an unimpressed look.

[133] Solemnly. And it is a solemn thing because I think it would be easier to leave each other behind if we didn't love each other in this multi-layered way.

[134] Nearly as much as I hate remembering it.

# 28

# Julian

I sit down opposite Ezra Brown for our second meeting.

We're in one of Carmelo's dad's establishments in Islington. Best Italian food in the city up front, best Il Cardinale you'll never get to try because you won't get in.

Today Mr Brown is wearing a garms from Phillip Plein that's too busy for this geezer and a pair of Yeezys—hate them, don't care if they're fashionable, they look like fucking geriatric shoes—and he's such a pretentious wanker and not just because he's dressed how he's dressed. Dress like Big Bird all you want, big boy, I don't give a fuck, but he's still a wanker and I know it.

Looked into him. Had to.

Everyone has shit, I get that, but listen, the older I get the more sure I am of this: the most dangerous kinds of people in the world are the ones who don't have a solid grip on who they actually are. People look at me like I'm bad news because all my shit's all out on the table—yeah, I'm impulsive and I'm reckless and I'll sleep with you and I won't call you back—I'll cut you as easily with my words as I would a knife, but you wouldn't feel afraid sitting next to me at a restaurant because you know what you're getting. I'm an open book.

No point in being ashamed at what I've done, I've done it. Do I have some regrets? Sure, yeah—but who doesn't? Fact is, I'm myself 100 percent of the time, take it or leave it—so I take issue with anyone who's pretending to be anything other than what they are.

Take Ezra Brown for example: a straight Google will tell you he's a married father of two, a businessman respected in the community, donor to his children's non-denominational private school, and sits on the board of two different Fortune 500 companies.

Get the Silicon Baddies on the case and it's a different ball game.

Failing business but ran into some money after the death of an extremely wealthy grandparent, shitty marriage but a committed father and a burgeoning interesting in the black arts market, thanks in large part to...

"Lyra Iordanou." I give him a tight smile and rest my hands on top of the table.

His face pulls and he clears his throat. "Sorry?"

"Your mistress," I remind him with a smile. "Lyra Iordanou. Great shag." I give him a look.

His face falters. I've upset him. Bonus.

Lyra Iordanou is the daughter of a Greek shipping tycoon who most recently was linked to Stavros Onasis. Daisy was hooking up with an Onasis for a minute, I think, but Lyra has a penchant for a certain demographic of male I fall right into: rich and powerful.

How her bar's fallen so low as to now be the mistress of this disempowered fuck I'll never know, but God bless and Godspeed to him, because Lyra Iordanou is a fucking handful.

"I was wondering," I nod my chin at him, "how you came across my name. We don't run in the same circles—or so I thought—but Lyra, I mean, you don't really fit the type, old man." Glance over at Decks for tacit confirmation. "Money, I guess."

Brown's jaw goes tight.

"Hey, bro, listen." I shrug defensively. "Love is love, you do you. I don't care if your girlfriend is with you because your grandfather died and left you that wholesome, homegrown, hand-picked teabag company that won all those ethical awards, and now your tea pickers are practically slave labourers—that shit has to sit on your conscience."

He breathes out his nose. "What's your point?"

"My point is, you're not an art collector."

"So?" he says through gritted teeth. Doesn't like being insulted. Who does, though?

"So this is an expensive gift for your mistress." I give him a look.

Brown sniffs a laugh and sits back in his chair. "That's not really your problem, though, is it?"

"No." I shake my head merrily. "Just wanted you to know that it will be yours if you can't make good on this deal." I give him a look. "Last chance."

Ezra Brown casually takes a drink of his Amaretto Sour. "Are you overwhelmed by this job, Julian?"

Declan's chair makes a noise as his eyes pinch, watching Brown from a table over. I snort, amused. "I think I'll be okay."

"You're just talking a really big game over there." Brown smiles. "And you've delivered no results."

Declan and Kekoa stand, and I wave them to ease.

"I'm so sorry, man—I guess I missed that £70 million down payment for my services..."

Brown gives me a tight smile. "I'll pay you when you do something."

"You'll pay me when I fucking tell you." I lean forward, looking him in the eye. "I know you're new around here, and I know you know my name—it's why you came to me. I'm as good as they say I am. I'm not the man for the job, I'm the only man for the job. Only person who has the team and the skillset to break into the fucking Belvedere—all of that is true of me, but so is this: cross me and I will kill you. Disrespect me, and I'll kill you twice."

He swallows, shook, and I toss back my drink, push back from the table and walk away.

"Oi." I pause at the doorway and look back at him. "My fee for you just jumped another £5 million."

## 29

# Daisy

I spend the rest of the weekend being rubbish friends with Romeo because that's what we do.[135] I've never thought before that it's maybe not something we should be doing, and I'm not even saying that I think that now—I don't know what I think now,[136] if I'm being completely honest.

I'm single, not dating anyone, and yes, I might have feelings for someone else,[137] but I've loved Romeo all my life.

And there is this thing about Romeo that makes him a bit like quicksand for me. Easy to fall into, hard to get out of. Maybe loving anyone is like that—I don't know. It's hard to untangle how I feel about him from what happened because they've fused together, the memories and the emotion behind them, and there's nothing I can do about it—it doesn't matter if he disappears for months at a time,[138] it doesn't matter if he sleeps with Tavie in my bed[139] to get back at me because he thought I was doing something[140] I wasn't, it doesn't even matter that once upon a time I loved him and he loved me and my brother broke us and then Rome left and broke me. All of that's true and none of it matters because Romeo still saved my life three times[141] in horrible, terrible ways, and when I wake up at nighttime and I feel that man's hands around my throat,[142] I don't yell for my brother, I yell for Romeo.

---

[135] Each other.

[136] That was a strange double-negative.

[137] Understatement.

[138] Even if it does matter.

[139] Even if it does matter a lot.

[140] Booker.

[141] Once would have been enough, but three?

[142] I'm not ready to talk about it yet.

I wish I didn't.[143] I wish I didn't feel bound to him like I do, like we're tethered together, tied by bad things that happened to us. I wish I called for Christian,[144] but I don't—I call for Romeo, and when we're apart there's this horrible stretch that I feel inside myself, like I'm pulling at my seams and then when we're together again, the pulling stops and there's no uncomfortable stretching and I know, okay? I know what this is. I'm med student and I'm not an idiot. I have attachment issues and abandonment issues and Romeo has a saviour complex[145] and I don't know—maybe he's driven by a subconscious, constant desire to right wrongs, make different decisions, not leave me behind, not fuck all of the Upper East Side to get over me because I said I wouldn't run away with him when I was sixteen years old.[146]

There is a part of me that worries we're on a track, loving each other in this stupid way, hating each other in the moments between and we're just... what we are. This disfigured, maladjusted version of a committed couple, but the commitment isn't necessarily by choice, it's just an unbreakable habit that makes you feel better and worse in one fell swoop.

And if you were to ask me if it's a habit I want to break, I don't actually know what my answer would be. I don't know if I want to stop. And even if I did, I don't have any idea how I would start something else.[147]

---

[143] I really, really wish I didn't.

[144] Then again, Christian's never saved me from anything.

[145] Not dissimilar to my brother.

[146] And don't think I don't wonder about that. I wonder almost every day what it would have been like, if we would have made it out, and then worked out how to be normal. The truth is, I don't think Romeo wants normal how I want normal. There's too much about our lives that he loves. He loves the power, he loves the money, he loves the drama—and maybe he didn't used to. Maybe he does now because I didn't go with him before and this lifestyle can be addictive. I've seen it destroy so many people. Or maybe it is just him. Maybe it's always been just him but when we were smaller we didn't know it yet. Whatever the truth was then, the truth is now that Romeo doesn't want normal.

[147] Miguel says there's a lady back in the town where he's from who deals with girls like me and she can break anything or anyone off of their lives and he has thrice offered to bring me to her. I don't know if she is a witch doctor or a healer or a therapist or just like a fucking bad arse but I'm scared so I say no every time.

165

Back in Knightsbridge,[148] there's a knock on my bedroom door and then Christian pokes his head in. His eyes fall on me over at my desk and he does this quarter smile that makes my heart gallop faster than if should from just a look from a boy who doesn't care about me.

"Hi." I get up and sort of just stand there stupidly.

He walks over and his eyes fall down me. "Hey—" He leans in almost tentatively to kiss my cheek—super weird. We don't kiss on cheeks. We kiss in darkened hallways and under bar lights and in the back of cars. Our kisses are always dotted with desperate, wandering hands, but not this one. This one is quick and sweet, no wandering hands, just the lingering smell of John Varvatos and the feeling of my heart in my throat.

He takes a step back. "You're tan."

"It was sunny."[149]

A smile flickers over his face. "Did you have a good time?"

I nod. Missed you a lot, I don't say.

I tried my best not to think about him and the Dutch girls, tried my best not to imagine all the things he was doing in London without me, him here with Magnolia Parks and Taura Sax and Vanna Ripley and all the other girls I know he fills his time with.

"Did you get up to much this weekend, then?" he asks, folding his arms over his chest.

"Nope." I shrug.

"How was it?" he asks pleasantly.[150]

"Fine." I shrug, and I know I sound evasive, and maybe I am. "Good. Pretty chill. Hung out by the pool, went on the boat, went to bars, played Sticky Fingers."

His face falters. "What's that?"

"Oh—" I swipe my hand. "A game me and Romeo invented when we were kids. Kind of like the Floor is Lava, but you're trying to jack something that's surrounded by a bunch of shit you can't knock over or disturb... It's just a dumb game."[151]

---

[148] A few days later.

[149] Obviously. I don't know why I say that. Stupid, really.

[150] And I wonder if he's being weird because he's asked a variant of the same question like four times now.

[151] It's actually not, it's my favourite game in the world. Romeo and I beat everyone every time.

He nods coolly. "Anything happen while you were away?"

My face pinches a little, curiously. "What do you mean by 'anything'?"

"Anything—" He shrugs. "Like, anything eventful? Or important?"

"Oh," I nod, kind of getting the question now. "You heard about the guy who drugged me—"

His face shifts. "Wait, what?" He shakes his head.

"Oh—" I pause, shrug it off. "Nothing."

"No, what?" He shakes his head more and then he grabs my wrist and ducks so we're eye level. "Someone drugged you?"

"No, he tried—" I shake my head. "I'm fine."

"What happened?"

"Nothing—"

His jaw goes tight. "Where's the guy?"

And I give him this look, all weighted with a reality only a few people but us know.

"Oh." He nods, shifts on his feet a little. "Well, good." He gives me a tiny smile that's all strained with a worry I'm sure I'm imagining,[152] then he pushes his hand through my hair in that way he does without knowing he's doing it. "Are you okay?"

I nod. "I'm okay. I saw him do it—it didn't, you know—"

He nods a bit, placated. Then keeps nodding. "So, nothing else happened while you were there?"

I frown a bit confused. "I mean—it was sort of a big deal, I guess?"

"You just said you were fine—"

"I am!" I shake my head at him, feeling confused. "I'm not hurt—it's just, what sort of other event were you anticipating?"

"No, like, I mean…" He rolls his eyes. "Did anything happen with you and—" He blows air into his cheeks. "…Anyone?" I frown at him. "Or anyone and… you?" he asks and I frown more. "…Or anyone and anyone!"

My face scrunches, confused. "What?"

"Nothing—" He shakes his head and his whole face pinches. "So nothing, then?" He swallows and I stare over at him,[153] wondering

---

[152] Because why would it be there?

[153] Does he know about Rome?

if he's actually asking me what I feel like he's asking me. "If there's something you want to ask me, Christian, just ask me."

He juts his chin out stubbornly. "There isn't."

"Okay."

He nods coolly. "Okay." He takes a few steps backwards and then he licks his bottom lip and squints at me. "Did you fuck Rome?"

The question catches me off guard even though I'd wondered if that's what he was trying to ask me.

There's an angularity to it, a sharpness that I feel around the edges of it. My mouth falls open a bit and I stare over at him, trying to work out within the few microseconds of strange silence between us a few different things:

1. Why is he asking?[154]
2. Why does he care?[155]
3. Why do I feel bad?[156]

And I don't know any of the answers.

I press my tongue into my top lip. "Yes."

And I wonder if for the briefest second his face falls a little. It's so fast, a blink-and-you-miss-it kind of thing, and it's probably in my head because I want Christian's face to fall when he thinks about other people touching my body too, but then his jaw sets and he nods. "Okay."

I look all over his face for a clue as to why he's even asking me in the first place but there's nothing, the stone wall's up and I can't ever see over it.[157]

"Why?"

He shrugs. "Just asking."

"But why?" I ask.

"Because it's good to know."

"What is?" I straighten up.

His mouth shrugs. "That you're doing that."

"What are you talking about?" I give him a look. "You went to Amsterdam last week."

He tosses his hands in the air like, "so what?" "Yeah…?"

---

[154] And how did he know?

[155] And does he actually care or is he just being pig-headed and territorial?

[156] Because I do. Like I've betrayed him, but I haven't=

[157] He won't let me.

"Shagged a million girls." I remind him and he shakes his head.

"Two, but anyway—"[158]

"Is there a problem?" I ask loudly.

"No."

My brow lowers. "Did I do something wrong?"

"No." He's sounding more tetchy by the second.

"Are you jealous?"

His jaw sets. "I don't fucking get jealous," he over-annunciates.

I nod once. "Okay."

Christian gives me an airy shrug that isn't airy at all. "I'm glad for you."

My head pulls back and I blink a bit. "You're glad for me?"

He gives me a tight smile. "Yep."

"Okay." I give him a weak shrug, feeling a bit dizzy, like I've been hit over the head.

I hate fighting with him—even though we don't fight—I hate it when we do.[159]

Christian sort of nods to himself for a few seconds. "You're sleeping with him," he tells me, I don't really know why.

I give him a look. "I'm not sleeping with him. I slept with him."

"Semantics." He shakes his head.

"No." I shake mine back.

"Well, I'm sleeping with other people," he tells me, eyebrows up.

I press my tongue into the roof of my mouth, swallow, make sure my eyes don't well up at the terrible thought of it. "I know, I assumed you were—"

"Why would you assume that?" He gives me a dirty look so I give him one back.

"Because you're you."

He sniffs a laugh. "This again?" He gives me a look. "You're here calling me a slut when you were the one naffing your ex on some lake?"

"Hold on—" I pull back, eyebrow cocked up. "Are you calling me a slut?"

"Fuck—" His mouth goes tight and he shakes his head. "No—I take it back—"

---

[158] He definitely made it sound like more before…

[159] And we seem to more and more these days.

I point to the door. "Get out."

"No." He scowls at me. "Can you stop telling me to 'get out' every time you get shitty at me?"

We stare at each other—his arms folded over his chest, my hands on my hips—I feel like there's an entire subtext beneath us that neither of us have been briefed on.

"Is there a reason it's bad that I had sex with Romeo?" I ask him, and then it sits there, thick like a horrible cloud, but the cloud isn't the horrible part, it's the silver that hems its edge, hanging there all hopeful and glistening, and I wonder for the smallest second if maybe the answer is yes.

Then he purses his mouth and shakes his head. "Nup."

I stare up at him, ignore how winded I am by how indifferent he is towards me, remind myself that I'll always have Romeo and maybe that's better anyway—safer, fenced in, predictable. I don't like feeling like this about someone, this unbridled, free-falling, slippery, fragile thing that it is to love him because he—Christian, who is standing right in front of me—is never going to want me how I want him. Even if sometimes if feels like he might for a second, it's just a trick. It's the oxytocin talking and nothing I think I see on his face is real, because I'm looking at him through the eyes of someone who loves him and those eyes can't be trusted.

And neither can he.

I nod once and sit back down at my desk, looking at the journal I'm reading: impact of mono-culture vs. co-culture of keratinocytes and monocytes on cytokine responses induced by important skin sensitizers.[160]

"Daisy—" he starts but I just point to the door.

He sighs, stands there for a few more seconds, and then he leaves.

I wait 'til I hear my front door slam shut and then I burst into tears.

---

[160] Venkatanaidu Karri, Carola Lidén, Nanna Fyhrquist, Johan Högberg & Hanna L. Karlsson (2021). "Impact of mono-culture vs. Co-culture of keratinocytes and monocytes on cytokine responses induced by important skin sensitizers", *Journal of Immunotoxicology*, 18:1, 74–84, DOI: 10.1080/1547691X.2021.1905754

# 30

# Christian

I wake up the next morning and press my hands into my face.

I felt sick immediately—immediately—the minute I left her house. I felt this weird dread in me, not just that I'm a fuck-up but, like, I've fucked up. So, so bad, and I don't know how to fix it. So I came home, sank a bottle of red—I don't know what kind, it was Henry's. He cares more about wine than me, about the undertones and the stems and all that fucking shit. Anyway, then I passed out in my bed, slept 'til morning, and I'm lying here now and that fucking dread is still here.

I press the heels of my hands further into my eye sockets, groan, and then roll out of bed.

I trot down the stairs, barely dressed, nothing but dark grey Les Tien trackpants, and I'm vaguely irritated to find Henry sitting down there with Magnolia, who's all chipper and bright as the fucking morning star.

"Hi." She smiles, eyes all sparkly as shit.

Henry gauges me. "Rough night?"

I don't say anything, just sit down on the armchair and stare over at them.

She's sitting cross-legged facing him, reading him flash cards for university. In his lap is a packet of those Skinny Dipped chocolate almonds Magnolia ships in by the crate-load from America, aiming and tossing them into her open mouth from the other side of the couch.

She catches it—surprisingly—and grins over at Henry proudly. She reads another card, "What are the limitations of economic growth?"

He starts listing the answer off his fingers.

"The exclusion of non-market transactions. The failure to account for or represent the degree of income inequality in society—" She nods and he keeps going. "The failure to indicate whether a nation's

171

rate of growth is sustainable or not." She nods again. "The failure to account for the costs imposed on human health and the environment of negative externalities arising from the production or consumption of a nation's output."

"Very good." She smiles over at Henry proudly and he tosses another one. It hits her in the face and she bursts out laughing.

She's only like this with Henry, not even Beej. Must drive him mad, I reckon, that she's like this with his brother but not with him. Sad, but I think she thinks it was her fault, something wrong with her or some way she fucked up that cracked opened the door for BJ to cheat on her—and I think she thinks that she has to be perfect around Beej, completely put together all the time, totally in control, and maybe if she can do that then maybe they'll work out eventually, but they won't because she's not the fuck-up in their scenario. I don't think she knows that about herself.

She looks over at me, more beautiful than anyone should be in the morning, and she gives me a light smile. "What's wrong with you?"

"Nothing." I scowl at her a bit.

Don't feel like her being nice to me today.

Henry tosses me a look, annoyed. It never goes over well with him if I'm short with her. "Are you hungover? Do you want me to order you in something?"

I shake my head.

"I'll make you a tea?" she offers.

Shake my head.

"Come on." She gives me a look. "I'll put in two sugars—"

I roll my eyes at her, but give her a permissive wave. Two sugars in her tea is the nicest thing she can offer a person. It's also all she knows how to make.

"Go on then," I tell her.

She gives me a happy smile because she likes being needed and flits off to the kitchen. Henry swings his legs around and faces me. "Right, so—what happened?"

"Nothing."

He sighs. "We're going to do this dance then?"

"What dance?" I frown.

Henry rolls his eyes, bored already. "'What's wrong?' 'Nothing.' 'No, tell me.' 'I'm fine I said.' 'Why are you so shitty then?' 'I'm not shitty.' 'Yes you are...'"

I glare over at him. "I'm not shitty."

He waves his hand impatiently. "Out with it, go on—"

I give him a long look and then breathe out, frustrated. "Daisy's back..."

"Right?" He nods.

"She slept with him."

"With whom?" he asks, not tracking—the idiot! What the fuck else is he tracking? Fuck economic growth, this is the important shit.

"Romeo," I say through gritted teeth.

"Oh." He pulls a face. "Shit."

I breathe out heavily. "And like, why?"

He looks confused again. "Why what?"

I let out an exasperated groan. "I just don't know why she's fucking Romeo Bambrilla—"

"Who is?" Magnolia asks, handing me the tea.

"No one," I say quickly.

Hate the idea of Parks knowing Daisy would rather be with someone else over me. History repeating itself and shit.

"Daisy," Henry says anyway and I shoot him a look.

"Oh." Magnolia's face falters to a frown. "I thought you two were..."

Shake my head dismissively. "Not exclusively."

"Oh. Right." She nods and looks confused. "Well, then what's the problem?"

I scoff and roll my eyes. "I just don't get why she's sleeping with him."

Then Magnolia pulls a face I fucking hate. "I mean—you have eyes, don't you?" She glances between me and Henry. "He's completely, totally gorgeous—"

"What are you even doing here?" I snap.

She pulls back instantly, a bit hurt, and I wait to get that old rush I usually do when I hurt her but I don't get it.

Magnolia stares over at me, waiting for me to take it back.

"We said we'd all get lunch today," she says a bit weakly, and I'm happy she looks hurt because fuck her—he's completely gorgeous? Honestly, fuck her—so just I shake my head at her and put down that tea she made me. Too sweet. "I don't want to get lunch with you."

Henry stares over at me and I can tell he's pissed. It's weird when you piss off Henry because there's always something weighted about it. He's pretty stoic, pretty level-headed, pretty reasonable—though maybe less so when it comes to Magnolia. BJ likes to think he's her protector, but he's wrong, he fucks her around too much to have a real shot at being her protector. It's Henry, and he's angry at me for this one.

He says nothing, but I know I'll hear about it later. Hen glares over at me, gives me this long look, then pulls Parks up from the couch.

"Come on." He nods towards the door, giving Parks a gentle smile. "I'll take you to lunch."

# 31

# Daisy

In another life,[161] I'm an art historian.

A professor of art history or maybe a conservator of artworks, but this is where I'd be. Surrounded by beautiful things, things that inspire you and move the world forward and speak to what it means to be human, and there would be nothing bad, no one would be dying, and if they were it'd be two-dimensional. There would be no blood, just red paint, and love would be straightforward because there are so many different kinds of love in the world and art captures a moment in each of them. And it's just a moment, not a whole picture—I know that—but there's something lovely about that, isn't there...? About a snapshot moment for all the world to look upon frozen the way the person who painted it saw it and felt it, like that forever for us to try to see it and feel it the same way, hanging in the annals of time and it is what it will be and it will keep being that for everyone until someone like my brother steals it.

We're in Paris this weekend. Julian's baiting Interpol.

He didn't tell me that he's baiting Interpol, but I know that he is.

A big job like the Belvedere—he just needs to lead them astray. If Interpol thinks we're planning a job in Paris, then they're not looking at Austria.

He doesn't much like me involved in jobs, but sometimes I have to be. I have a better eye than any of them, except maybe Julian's.

We specialise in different eras. He's likes impressionism and expressionism, and I like romanticism and the Renaissance, and this

---

[161] My normal life, where I live in a small town in Sweden or Nova Scotia after I graduate. And I have two dogs, and a husband and friends and we pay bills and I drive myself to the supermarket and I don't have security and I don't wake up from nightmares of things that happened to me when I was young.

has fared well for us professionally, although we do argue a bit about what pieces go up around the house.[162] Julian prioritised my art education more than anything else. I had private tutorials with all the best curators from all over the world, and now it's hard for me to tell whether he did that because he's passionate about it or because he saw an opportunity.

I don't know whether you can tell this about me, but I didn't have much of a childhood. I spent most of my time studying. Studying books or Romeo, those were my two things, and I don't know if I believe in eidetic memories, but if I did, I'd have one. People think I'm smart—I am, I definitely am—but also I can recall things in thick and marvelous detail. My dad and I, our thing was cooking. We'd stay up all night watching cooking shows, and he'd let me do all the easiest parts of making a dish and then tell everyone I made it and I would feel so proud. And I guess like that, when I was little, I used to think art was our thing, the thing Julian and I did together. We've visited galleries and museums all over the world, listening and learning, both up front and behind the scenes. I've handled relics and documents I had no business being near and I've watched my brother fall for pieces of art like I've never seen him fall for any woman. I think it's his true love.

I think the way he loves it is why I love it how I love it.[163]

And so I'm happy to be here, happy to be in Paris, happy to be distracted from whatever the fuck is going on with Christian, but also, not really—because the City of Love isn't all that good at making you not think about the person you love. So I've thrown a blanket over my feelings for him and now it sits there in the corner of me... This big, misshapen lump of a man I refuse to love but obviously do, and he overshadows everything now[164] and I hate it, this pathetic version of myself that loving him has turned me into... How I scroll past his photos on Instagram without checking because I don't want to

---

[162] You will notice that there is no impressionism or expressionism anywhere where I have to see it, except his office because my jurisdiction only goes so far.

[163] And I really do love it.

[164] I think of him every time I'm in a car, every time my hair falls over my face. Every time I taste coffee, I try to work out whether he'd like that particular cup or not. I hear a Ziggy Alberts song and wonder if he loves it. He's never not on my mind.

know that he's in Greece with Magnolia and all their stupid, beautiful friends.[165]

My heart's mind is a little disaster, that much I know, because in the car on the way back from the airport, Romeo's on one side and Christian isn't on the other and that's what I'm thinking about. And when Romeo kisses me at night in the bed that Christian isn't in, I'm thinking about that—and, you don't need to tell me, I know that it's fucked up.

Miguel says it a defense mechanism because Romeo hurt me too many times before and I said, "Yeah, but Christian's hurting me now" and Miguel said, "I know, you're an idiot," in Spanish.

I hate the feeling like I'm doing the wrong thing, though. And I feel like I am all over.

Which is weird, I get that. To you, my whole life is doing the wrong thing, a series of wrongdoings—both in and out of my control—but indisputably tied to, around, and done for and by me. I try my best to be better whenever I can. Try to tilt the scales back in our favour. I always give money to the homeless. I never litter. I tried to stop drinking dairy for a while but I can't drink the milk of an almond, I'm sorry—I just can't.[166] I have a little notebook in my drawer by my bed where I try to keep track of how many people my brother's killed so I can at least save that many and maybe that will balance everything out a little in the universe and we won't go to hell for everything we've done.

Not today anyway, today we go to the Louvre.

And I know what you're thinking: who the fuck is letting that lot into the Lourve?

Soleil Cousineau. Newly appointed president-director of the Musée du Louvre and, conveniently, the ex-lover of my brother dearest.

And I will admit, of all the girls Julian has bounced around with, Soleil was my favourite by far because, well, firstly—French girls are so chic. Plus, she wasn't all that concerned with impressing me, which made me want her approval. She's a solid ten years older than my brother and all-around just felt like an intelligent choice.

That, and she once brought a real Sandro Botticelli[167] over for me

---

[165] Why is he in Greece with Magnolia and their stupid, beautiful friends?
[166] It's too watery.
[167] *Portrait of a Young Woman.* 1480–1485. Tempera on wood. 82 cm × 54 cm.

to have a look at while it was out for repair. She won me forever with that.

"*Mon ange fille!*" She holds her arms out for me and I skip into them merrily. She kisses both my cheeks and nods her head covertly towards Romeo behind me. "*Que fait le garçon ici? Je pensais que tu avais fini?*"[168]

I make an uncertain gesture. "*Comme ci comme ça.*"

She laughs and kisses him hello.

Romeo is here for no real reason that I can excuse away. We've just been spending a lot of time together, that's all.

I was coming to Paris and he said, "I'll come to Paris" and I said, "Okay" at the same time Julian said, "No!"

But we ignored him.

Soleil greets all the boys, saving Julian for last, whom she kisses in a way that she probably shouldn't in the steps of her workplace[169] and then she leads us inside.

There is a plan afoot here and that plan is Johannes Vermeer's *The Lacemaker*.[170] The plan is also Soleil. The kiss she gave him, I don't know whether she's in on the plan or whether Julian's just that good—but she's the plan.

I never know whether women know what they are to Julian, which, by the way, is nothing.[171] They're vehicles to the destination of his desire.

What he desires in this instance is to trick Interpol into thinking he's planning on stealing the Vermeer.

A part of this plan, I'm gathering, is letting Interpol think he's involved again with the director of the Louvre and that she's going to help him.

I don't know if she would.

Soleil is one of those people whose base nature presents itself as a mystery but I find that to be the case for many people who dip their toes into the pools of fine art.

The water is beautiful—these out-of-this-world blues that invite you to slip into them, but the caverns are deeper than you think and I

---

[168] "What is this boy doing here? I thought you were done?"

[169] But also, to be fair, it's very French.

[170] 1669–1671. Oil on canvas. 24.5 cm x 21 cm.

[171] Soleil mightn't be completely nothing, but the vast majority are.

don't know many people who do what we do who haven't used someone else's limp and lifeless body to keep their head above the water fine art makes them tread.

"He's unbelievable." Rome nods his head at my brother who's got Soleil pressed up against the wall.[172] I give him a look and he tosses his arm around me. "Come on." He pulls me away. "We don't need to be here for this—"

And he takes me for a walk. We're holding hands.

I don't know when that happened, but that's how touching is with him, how being with him is, I guess.

Like when you don't realise it's raining. And it doesn't feel sudden, not like the sky was blue and you turn around and then it's pouring—but like, it's been overcast the whole time, and then it's one drip, and then another, and then another, and then another and then you're saturated and you can't really tell which drip saturated you, but it happened slowly and snuck right past you.

That's what it's like to have Romeo's hands on me.

We wander down the Denon wing because it's my favourite. Forget the *Mona Lisa*. She's small and unexquisite and she's stolen the show for too long.[173]

Now, *Virgin and Child with St Anne*, who nary gets the appropriate attention or time, that is a painting I'm interested in. Because it's weird.

How the baby Jesus is grappling with the lamb, like they both know what's ahead, but the two adults are at peace about it? About him dying? What kind of bullshit is that?[174]

My mouth pulls right and my ex-boyfriend is watching me closely.

"You came here," he tells me, giving me a look. "I didn't make you come and stand in front of it."

"I know—"

"It riles you up."[175]

"Well, the Christ story always riles me up."

---

[172] Hand up her skirt, in her hair—Julian's incorrigible when it comes to many things, women and art to name a few—but the combination of the two? Dear God.

[173] I said what I said.

[174] Many bullshits.

[175] He knows me too well.

"Here we go…" He rolls his eyes.

"They set him up," I say for the thousandth time. "The system's wroughted. Tilted for blood, someone was always going to have to die. It's not fair. God's mean."

He slips his arms around my waist and tugs me in towards him. "He's saved you and me a bunch of times."

I give him a long look. "You've saved me a bunch of times."

Romeo sighs and swallows, his eyes flicker from my eyes to my mouth and then he kisses me softer than he should but I kiss him back the same out of habit.[176]

"Oi," my brother says, leaning up against a statue he's definitely not meant to lean against. "Watch those hands."

"Why?" Rome grins, slipping them lower as he nods his head towards Soleil. "You didn't."

"I'll box your ears 'til you bleed, you little shit—" Julian says as he darts over to him and puts him in a headlock, punching him (mostly) playfully in the stomach.

Soleil and I trade looks as Romeo springboards away from my brother, laughing.

"Come on," Jules gives me a small smile as he nods his head down the hall. "Let's go see your friend."

Hersilia.[177]

I've always loved her. I don't know why. Just felt a kinship towards her, since long before I knew what "kinship" meant.

How pure she is, like there's not just a light on her but a light in her, and she feels in the depths of her a commission to bring peace.

She stands between the two great loves of her life, Husband and Father, with her babies between the warring men at her ankles—a hopeful reminder that they have more in common than they think they do.

And it works.

Love wins.

I like it when there's conflict, and women are brave enough to throw themselves in the centre of it to end it.

I like it when love wins.

---

[176] Or maybe because I'm the worst—I don't know.

[177] *The Intervention of the Sabine Women* by Jaques-Louis David. 1799. Oil on canvas. 522 cm x 385 cm.

"You and this fucking painting." Romeo rolls his eyes.

All I mumble is a distracted "Mm," ignoring him and letting her speak to me instead.

There's a calm focus about her, about the two men, too—everyone else is in anguish or distress but not them, and she's why. She's what ties them down, holds them together. What kind of woman does that in Ancient Rome?

I know it's pretend, just part of the myth of how Rome was built, but I still love her and I still think she's the most important woman in the Louvre. I hope I can be like her one day.

"Want me to grab it for you?" my brother asks in a low whisper.

I give him an amused look as I glance back up at the oil on canvas that's easily twenty square metres. Nicking it would be quite the steal.

"Well," I grin up at him, "if it won't be too much trouble…"

"Alright—" He nods his head towards Soleil. "You distract the Parisian and I'll just—" He mimes lifting it off the wall and then gives me a little wink. I roll my eyes, amused.

"For your next big birthday," he tells me and I wonder if he will. Hell of a job. Sounds sort of fun, though.

We're done by the time the sun's setting and we take a fire exit out the side of the Denon building where some of the boys are waiting for us with the cars. As we walk out, there stands my favourite American against a souped-up black 508 Peugeot Sport.

Grey T-shrit, baggy blue jeans and Converse.[178]

Romeo rolls his eyes, annoyed, and I give him a look to quieten him.

"You're up, Face." My brother gives me a little shove towards my favourite police officer.

"Tiller." I give him a playful smile as I walk over.

"Dais."

"Don't your eyes look all extra blue lit up by the Seine and everything?"

He glances back over his shoulder. "It's a bit dirty today."

"Just how I like it." I give him a little look and he rolls his eyes, laughing.[179] "That was me flirting with you," I tell him.

"I know." He gives me a look of fake-exasperation.

---

[178] Handsome.
[179] But his cheeks go pink.

"Taking our little dates international, I see—"

"Not dates, Dais." He folds his arms over his chest. "I'm gathering evidence for an ongoing investigation—"

"Okay." I use finger quotes and he laughs again.

Tiller nods that glorious head of his towards my brother. "How long's he been involved with Cousineau?"

I shrug my shoulders playfully.

"How much of their relationship has to do with her becoming the new director of the Louvre?" I shrug again.

"Does she know who he is?"

"Everyone knows who he is," I remind him and he rolls his eyes. They're a crazy sort of blue. Girls lose their mind over my brother's eyes—midnighty, this strange sort of dark blue you don't get in eyes very often—but Tiller's are something else. Like a royal blue with the water refracting through them.[180]

"What are you staring at?" he asks and I feel embarrassed because I didn't realise I was.

"Nothing." I blink away any awe I have and press my hands into my cheeks without thinking—they're all hot.

His face changes for a minute and I feel sweaty on the back of my neck because I know my brother and Romeo and all the boys are watching and so I make myself go taller and smack Tiller's arm playfully, regaining control of the situation.

"Oh my God," I say, back in charge again. "I can't believe we haven't talked about this yet—" His eyes pinch at me. "Tell me everything about your break-up."

He gets a look. "Nope."

"Your call, her call?" I probe. "Just kidding—" I shove him. "Who's breaking up with you with that face?"[181]

He tries not to smile and rolls his eyes. "You're incorrigible."

I point to myself, inquisitively. "Incredible?"

He breathes out loudly from his nose as he opens the door to his car.

"You're the one following me around exotic European destinations."

"Hardly exotic—"

---

[180] The sort of eyes you might drown in, actually.

[181] It was her call, by the way. That's what my snooping has uncovered.

"Just romantic." I give him a small wink and he lets out a single laugh.

I start to walk back towards the boys.

"I thought you didn't date criminals?" he calls after me and I look back at him. He nods towards Romeo.

I flash him a grin. "Who said anything about dating?"

He scoffs, shaking his head as he closes his car door.

Our eyes catch through the glass and there's a smile on his mouth that shouldn't be there—not when my brother can see it, not in general, so he drops it and peels away.

I turn around and Julian has an eyebrow cocked and his arms folded over his chest.

Romeo's already gone[182]—I don't know where—one of the other cars, I guess?

"What?" I ask my brother defiantly.

He presses his tongue into the cheek of his mouth, shaking his head a bit.

"You're a fucking mess."

<br>

Jack

2:48 PM

How is Paris so far?

Lots of sex with the ex?

We've been out of London for like 48 hours.

I know, and knowing you two, that's plenty of time.

Well, you're wrong.

Just once on the plane.

Bit of a mish with Jules there, no?

---

[182] Weird.

Absolutely.

Did he know.

I bloody hope not.

How's (REDACTED)

Well, his boyfriend is very well dressed.

Also. Why wasn't I invited on this trip.

Because you aren't a criminal.

Speaking of...

How is Impeccable Arse.

I don't want to speak about him.

Dais...

g2g. Byeee

# 32

# Christian

We decided to take a last-minute trip to Greece because it turns out Parks's old man has been doing the dirty with her nanny for the last however many years and Magnolia's taking it about as well as you'd expect...

Let it slip to the outlets, tipped off *The Sun*. Hell hath no fury like a Magnolia scorned, I'll fucking tell you that much for free.

The flight over there's long and I think about Daisy the whole time, how I wish I was good at this feelings shit—that I knew how to say sorry, say what I really think. I can't say it out loud. I can't risk it.

I've loved a girl who doesn't love me back for going on three years now—being aware of my feelings hasn't gotten me anywhere, and I was fine before—before I knew I was into Daisy—fuck, I've probably been into her for months unawares, and for months and months I've been fine, and then fucking Henry caught a whiff of it and ruined it by bringing it forth into my consciousness, that shitty prick.

So Daisy's just what I think about now, that's who I've become. I just think about Daisy Haites all the time, and I'm angry about it all the time.

I mean it. I stew on it the whole way there.

Doesn't help that Parks and Beej are holed up at the back of her boyfriend's plane and she's touching him in that way she does where she doesn't even know; it's fully unconscious. Her hand falls into his lap and his eyes never move from her and it makes me angry because I'm fucking sitting right here, and I don't know why that makes me angry, but I'm angry.

Angry at her, angry at him, angry at Daisy, pretty angry at myself, actually.

The hotel is nice, though, I'll give Parks that.

They're never not nice, she'd rather feed her hand to a fucking sea lion than stay somewhere with four stars.

But this place is pretty sick. Hotel Kinsterna. Kind of looks like an old village all tucked into the foothills of a mountain, but it's fancy as hell inside.

I stay in my room for most of the afternoon. Can't be bothered to watch Magnolia flit between BJ and Tom, and besides it's pretty shit reception by the pool and I keep checking my phone to see if Daisy's texted me.

Which she hasn't, by the way.

"Just give her her own fucking text-tone." Henry gives me an annoyed look when I dive on my phone as it vibrates.

"No—" I scowl at him. "I'm not pathetic."

Henry gives me a long look. "If you say so. Come on." He nods towards the door. "We're going to be late for dinner."

The dinner's what you'd expect: The Magnolia Show, part 9000.

Everyone is talking about the affair, how they can't believe it, how's her mum doing, how's Bushka doing, a bit about Jonah's Lower Sixth infatuation with Marsaili (loves an authority figure, my brother. More on that another day.), a lot about the shittiness of her dad…

And then eventually Paili folds her arms over her chest and leans in towards Magnolia. "Do you remember, about a year ago when we were at an event—something for your mum—and we nicked off to the bathroom, and Marsaili walked out of the disabled room all flushed?"

Magnolia pulls back, disgusted. "Oh my God—"

"And you said, 'She looks like she just had an orgasm'—and your mum was flitting around asking where your dad was… I bet they were shagging in the loo." Paili nods to herself and BJ makes this weird choking laugh.

Henry gives him a look. "Like you're one to talk, man—you've had so many orgasms in disabled toilets."

"Oi. Not just disabled toilets," he clarifies. "All toilets, I don't discriminate."

Magnolia didn't like that one, though, her face goes pouty. Looks sad.

Perry holds up his wine glass. "Never have I ever had an orgasm in public."

All the lads and I take a gulp.

I nod my head at Beej, giving him a look. "You better drink that whole glass, mate."

But he ignores me because his eyes are on Magnolia, trying to gain her approval again for a stupid joke he made and it shits me.

"And you," I say, even though I shouldn't. I eye Parks down from the other side of the table. "You should have had a sip."

She pulls her head back, eyebrows up. "I beg your pardon?"

And I know it immediately. I have woken a lot of bears—she's instantly pissed but so is Beej, so is Henry and so is Tom, but I don't really give a shit.

I'm angry. I feel like fucking her off, feel like fighting with someone so I can get my mind off of Daisy and her hands on Rome.

"Come off it—" I tell her. "We all know you had an orgasm in public."

BJ glares over at me.

"We all know?" she repeats, staring over at me, fuming.

"Yep." I nod.

Henry's Vulcan-nerve-pinching me under the table and Paili urgently whispers for me to shut up—but Parks, her nose is up in the air, and it fuels me. "Well, I didn't."

I shrug, indifferent. "Except you did."

More than once. I'm not going to say the times with me because I don't feel like dying in Greece tonight, but then again I might already, what with the way Beej is glaring over at me.

"I'd never—" Magnolia's cheeks are flushing, she's panicking. She doesn't know where I'm going with this. "That's so improper."

"Yeah." I give her a look. "You were real focused on societal proprieties at the time."

And I am a bit drunk, I'll admit that.

Drunk and shitty at them all, and when I'm drunk I love to get under her skin because it's the only thing of hers I get under these days.

"The speakeasy in Paris. You and him—" I nod my head toward Beej—don't look at him, though, because I reckon if I do he'll hit me. Kind of want it to happen... maybe I'd fight back this time. I'd win. I'd always win if I fight back. "Back corner. His hand. Under a table."

BJ presses his tongue into his bottom lip and Parks tenses up next to him.

"Christian," Paili—Magnolia's lapdog tonight and always—tries her best to squash it. "How would you even know?"

And that little line Paili spews is something that shits me to my fucking core. I'm furious that Parks made whatever the fuck we were sound like such a fucking load of nothing to everyone we know, so I stare Magnolia in her stupid eyes and say, "Because I know what she looks like when she's having an orgasm."

And I do know. I know it well. Better than any of them realise.

Henry stares over at me. "What the fuck, man?"

Beej is shaking his head, breathes out, tired and I feel bad for a second. "Hate that—"

Tom's staring down at his hands in his lap. "Can't say I'm a fan either—"

Beej is thinking about hitting me, I know he is. Weighing it up in his mind. I think the part that he's really grappling with is the implication that I've given his precious Parks an orgasm.

I've never known what she's told him about us—not very much, evidently.

Sometimes I feel bad for it, for how she and I fooled around, how shit a friend that makes me for hooking up with the girl my best friend loves, but I love her too so fuck it. It is what it is and she's the problem, not us.

Magnolia's just frozen at the table.

Can't tell if she's about to cry or not. I wonder if BJ's going to jump in to defend her—if there are tears he will, because her eyes go stupid beautiful when she cries and he's a sucker for it. Me too, I guess. It's sort of why I like making her cry, just so I can watch her, give her a cuddle, say sorry, make it stop.

Beej pushes back from the table. "I'm going to grab a drink—"

Tom gives me a dark look before standing himself. "Yeah, I'll come with you."

Magnolia stares over at me with those wounded eyes, biting her lips.

"Prick," she calls across the table.

"Bitch," I spit back barely before Henry heaves me up out of my chair.

"Alright, that's enough—" He shoves me towards the exit, shaking his head.

Parks watches me as I turn back and glare at her over my shoulder and Henry shoves me again.

"Enough!" He grabs me by the shoulder and turns me to face him. "You don't fucking speak to her like that—"

"I'll speak to her however the fuck I want," I growl back.

"No you won't, Chris—" He shakes his head. "She's my best friend, and—"

"She's my best friend too," I interrupt and Henry pulls back.

"Oh! You could have fooled me—" He points back behind him. "You don't talk to your best friends like that—and I get that shit has happened between you two, and I know you're not past it, but you can't just—"

And then he's cut off by BJ rounding a corner and shoving me.

"What the fuck was that?"

I sigh, genuinely tired of all this now, and look over at him. "Don't be an idiot, man—you know we hooked up—"

Beej cocks his head to the side. "Say that again to me."

And I shake my head at him, not in the mood today to pull my punches to keep this tosser's ego in check.

"You're going to talk about you giving Magnolia orgasms at a fucking dinner table in front of me—" Lets that hang there for a second. "And her new boyfriend."

I give him a dismissive shrug. "Didn't say anything about me giving her an orgasm."

BJ shoves me. "Bullshit you didn't—"

I shove him back.

"Oi!" Henry pulls BJ back from me a little. "Easy."

"Did I fucking lie?" I ask him, jaw tight.

"Christian—I don't know how the fuck I can spell this out for you in a way where you're actually going to hear it and get it through your fucking head—" BJ gives me a cloudy look. "She is not yours. She's never been yours. Never will be. Whatever you briefly had with her—" He waves his hand towards the mirage of my past. "It was about me. It wasn't about you, it wasn't because she wanted you, it was because she missed me and she wanted me and we couldn't be together, yeah?"

You know those videos on TikTok of that hydraulic press squashing everything you could ever possibly imagine being squashed?

I am every single thing in every video they've ever made. Every ball, every water bottle, every lollie, every cake, every candle—I'm all of them.

Flattened.

Nothing I can say back.

Everything he's just said out loud to my face is everything I've thought quietly inside my head since she and I ended.

Every fear, every paranoia—and he just called it out like the fucking Powerball Jackpot.

Henry smacks his brother in the chest twice—telling him without telling him that it's enough—and pulls him away, looking back at me as he does.

Henry's eyes look sorry for me—fucking hate it when people are sorry for me—then I turn to go back to my room.

Fuck.

Magnolia
12:03 AM

Why did you say that?

Because it's true.

Which part?

All of it.

You did and I do.

Are you trying to hurt me?

Nope.

Are you trying to hurt him.

Which him, Parks?

Wow.

Are you and Daisy having a row?

Fuck you

Oh thats so funny—

I was under the impression you already had.

# 55

# Daisy

We have a house in the 16th arrondissement in the Seine-Village d'Auteuil-Paris. A white chateau with a dark slate mansard roof and dormer windows popping out.[183] Julian isn't big on hotels (for obvious reasons), he thinks there's too much room for error (and historically, this has proven accurate).

Romeo's sitting on the bed we've been sharing in the room that we're also sharing—not because we need to this time, there are enough rooms here—just because we're like this, even when we shouldn't be, and I get the distinct feeling that maybe we shouldn't be with the way he's looking at me.

"What the fuck was that about?" He nods his chin towards the door and I assume he's talking about Tiller.

"What?" I ask anyway.

He stands. "Are you sleeping with him?"

"No." I frown, offended.

"He's a dibble."[184]

"I know—"

"And you're there chirpsing him like a fucking idiot!"

I pull back a little. "What's the matter?"

"He's a fucking coppa," Romeo says again.

"Are you jealous?" I frown up at him. "Why are you jealous, we're not exclusive—"

He looks a bit surprised. Offended, maybe? "Are we not?"[185]

"No." I tuck my hair behind my eyes, feeling a bit nervous about where this is going.

---

[183] And don't even get me started on the gardens!

[184] Which is derogatory slang for a policeman.

[185] Shit.

He cocks an eyebrow. "I can sleep with other people?"

I shake my head at him. "You've always been able to sleep with other people—"

"Oh, yeah?" he snorts. "Is that why you threw a vase at my head when I was in bed with Tavie—"

"My bed!" I yell over him.

"So you would have been good with it if I slept with her in my bed then, yeah?"

"You have slept with her in your bed—" I tell him loudly. "A million times."

He stands. "And you were okay with it?"

My face pulls, more strained than I want him to see.[186]

Rome waves his hand at me. "Exactly..."

I sigh and shake my head at him. "I don't want to do this right now, Rome—"

"What, Dais?" He tilts his head. "Talk or fuck? You're not that good at either these days—"

My mouth falls open and I stare over at him, hoping to God it doesn't show on my face how much of a fucking slap that actually was—that all the insecurities I have about him and me and sex and Tavie being his first time and me being the less sexy second and that she's better at it than I am and that's why she's still around all these years later—that none of that is dancing over the surface of my face, but I think it all must be because he looks sorry instantly.

"Shit, Dais—" He shakes his head. "That's not what I meant. I didn't mean it like that—"

I wave my hand towards the door. "Just go away."

He shakes his head at me and holds me by the wrists. "I didn't mean it like that—"

"Okay."

"I didn't, Dais—" He sighs again, shoving his hands through his hair. "I meant, like, you don't talk to me how you used to and it's only me who comes on to you now."

"That's not true. " I shake my head.[187]

"You used to lie in bed with me and you wouldn't shut up, you

---

[186] Because, no. A thousand times no. No, never, I hate it. I hate the thought, it fucks with my head but he can't know that because he'll read into it.

[187] But maybe it is.

never stopped talking. You told me everything, all this shit I never wanted to know, you'd tell me because it was you and me and—" he waves his hands between, "us. And it's different now."

I give him a weak shrug. "It is different now."

"Why?" he asks, breathing heavily.

"I don't know." Even though I do.

"Hemmes," he tells me.

"No—" I say quickly, but he interrupts me.

"Bullshit."

"You've never in your life not wanted us to be exclusive, you've always wanted to be together and now you're done."

"No." I shake my head as I reach for him.[188]

"Just admit it." He shakes his head at me. "You've never really forgiven me for leaving." That much is true. I haven't. Not the first time he left, not the last time he left and none of the times in between. He shouldn't have done it.

I shouldn't have to wake up in the morning every day and wonder if he's still in town, wonder if this is the morning he'll be gone again.

I cross my arms over my chest defensively. "And you've never forgiven me for not running away with you," I tell him.[189]

"Of course I haven't, Face!" he yells. "It would've been different—we would've been different! We could have worked. And instead we're whatever the fuck we are, and you're in love with another fucking man—"

"I-I don't—" I stutter stupidly and he lets out this sad, incredulous laugh and shakes his head.

"You don't think I know what it looks like when you're in love with someone?" His eyes look a kind of heavy I haven't seen in them for years. "For fuck's sake, Daisy, it's what I see in my mind's eye every night before I go to sleep."

And my little heart sinks like a stone.

"Romeo—" I reach for him and he kisses me in this sort of sad and wild and desperate way—both hands on my face, moves me to a wall and presses me against it, holds my face like it's his.[190] His chest

---

[188] And maybe hearing it out loud scares me.

[189] But that's not a revelation. I've known that all along.

[190] Like it used to be.

heaves against mine as he kisses me from my mouth down my neck—
but then, I'm not sure he should be kissing me anymore at all…

He pulls back a little. "He's a phase, Dais."

I shake my head at him.[191]

"He is—you and me—we're it, you know? We're always going to
be it, we'll always come back to each other.[192] So yeah, I might fuck
around with other girls, and yeah, I slept with Tavie in New York.
And you know, I'll probably do it again when you do something
shitty—but it's you and me, Dais. No one has what we have. No one's
been through what we've been through. So go—" He waves his hand
dismissively. "Fuck about with the Hemmes boy. I know what we are."

I stare over at him, my chest feeling tight, my breath all gone. I feel
dizzy and sick. I can't completely put my finger on why, but I suspect
all of the reasons are fear based.[193]

"What are we then?" I ask defiantly, putting some distance between
us which he crosses with one step anyway. He kisses my cheek.

"Each other's."

---

[191] I don't know which part of that scares me more. Romeo being wrong or Romeo
being right.

[192] And up to this point of our lives, this much has been true.

[193] Fear of the track we're on. Fear of losing him for good. Fear of never having
Christian at all.

# 34

# Christian

Went for a run after my run in with Beej.

When I got back to my room, I still hadn't heard from Daisy—Magnolia texted me, though, all angry and shit. I tried to sleep for an hour but couldn't, so I just went for a run.

Ran 'til my feet bled actually, but it was a good distraction.

Everything BJ said is everything I've always thought anyway. I've worried it was true, even though I don't think it is—there was more to me and Parks than he thinks, than what she lets him know.

Whatever version of our story she's offered him is watered down and weak. I don't know if she'd done that because she's a fucking sneak or because what we had meant shit to her. Maybe both.

She said she loved me. I feel like that's worth saying, something I can hang my hat on, I guess. Something I can hold over her. I don't think he knows.

She would never tell him that. I don't want to tell him that either because I go back and forth in my head about how culpable I am in all this and how shit a friend I must be to have let it happen.

Depends on the day, depends on the moment. I like to think that a lot of it comes down to her and that thing she has that's like gravity, where men are just like moths to her flames, and she's this force to be reckoned with, a storm we're trying to chase. That's not her fault—not really—but I won't say that to her. I won't say it to him either, because I wanted to love her. It was easy to do, I was happy to let myself.

And I hate that about me—that this is what it's turned to, that loving her for me a lot of the time feels like hating her, but it's where I am and it's what I've got.

It's why Daisy's such a nice distraction from it all, she's like this reprieve from all this shit my chest feels choked up with all the time. And I know it's not the same with Daisy, I know that I love Parks

195

and not her, it's not the same, it doesn't feel the same—I know what being in love feels like and it's not this. It's too easy with Daisy to be love. It is good, though. And it's weird, I float between being in my head about Daisy, thinking about everything I say to her, everything I want to say, all the things I want to talk to her about, and then when I'm with her I don't really think of anything.

Daisy's that feeling you get when you're floating on your back in a pool and there's so much fucking noise around you until you put your ears under and it all goes quiet. That's how she feels to me.

I've probably fucked it up with her anyway because I couldn't just tell it to her face that, actually, there was a reason why it was bad that she's sleeping with Romeo. I should have told her I don't want to share her with anyone.

I hate sharing in general, but I especially hate sharing her. I'm done sharing her. I don't know why I couldn't find the words to tell her that—I wish she was here, but she's not, and she's not texting me and I know I should text her, be the first one to make the first step to us talking again, but I can't.

I've spent too many years giving a shit and trying to be close to a girl who doesn't want me. I can't put myself out there how she wants me to, because I don't reckon I could handle how it would feel a few months from now if she turns around and decides she likes Romeo more than me after all.

A few good months, that's all I'm good for, I reckon.

That's all I was for Parks.

The next morning I go for another run and wind up at the pool. I spot Gus first—headphones in, lying on his back—and then her. Hot pink triangle bikini with these green bottoms, eyes closed, all stretched out and too hot for any good to come of it for any of us.

I walk over to her, stare at her a few seconds longer than I should because I'm only human and she isn't, and then she opens one squinty eye and glares up at me.

I kick her gently and nod at the sun-bed next to her. "Can I sit here?"

She props herself up on her elbows. "Oh, of course—" Waves her hand dismissively. "However, you must be careful, as I have been known to orgasm spontaneously in public—oh wait, no—you know what that looks like. You'll be fine."

I let out an annoyed breath. "Don't be a bitch."

I sit down next to her and sigh to the sky.

She gives me a sharp look. "I beg your pardon?"

I sigh again. "I'm sorry."

She folds her arms over her chest. "I should think so."

I groan as I lean back on the bed and I can feel her stupid, big eyes boring into me.

"Why would you do that?" she asks quietly, like I've hurt her.

I grind my jaw, shoving my hands through my hair. "I don't know."

But I do. Because I hate her as much as I love her and I don't know how to let her go, so I keep us all tangled up.

"It's fun—" I shrug, like a bit of a dickhead. "To fuck with you."

"Oh." She nods, eyes all wide. "Excellent."

I breathe out my nose. "You know what I mean."

She glares over at me. "No, Christian, I actually don't. I don't like fucking with people."

"Really?" I scoff. She's actually fucking unbelievable. "You don't like fucking with people? You've dated, like, five guys in the last two and a half years—present company excluded—and you weren't fucking around with them?" She opens her mouth to say something but I cut her off. "You were fucking around with me."

She looks sad. "No, I wasn't."

"Then what were you doing?" I ask, swinging my legs around to face her, daring her to prove me wrong. I'd fucking love her to prove me wrong—

Her eyes pinch. "You know what I was doing."

"Nope." I shake my head. "I know what I was doing—" I give her a look and I'm worried that my face is too raw, too obvious that I still love her now how I did then. "But you, Parks, I don't have a fucking clue."

She looks tired, takes a staggered breath. "Are you done?"

"Nope." I should be done, I can feel myself crossing a line that I shouldn't, the one where I get angry at her and yell because it's the embers of the fire we had that I used to be able to stoke in different ways and now yelling at her is all I've got left. I give her a defiant look "What about Tom?"

Parks rolls her eyes. "What about Tom?"

"Are you with him or aren't you?"

She scoffs, glaring over at me, chin low. "How is that any of your business?"

That felt like the slap she meant it to, a tacit reminder that she's done with me in the way that I'm not done with her. I hate her for it.

I pull my head back, indignant. "How's that any of my business?" I give her a look. "Really?"

Her eyes go to slits. "Yes, really."

"You're a piece of work, Parks. You know that?" I stand up, jaw tight, and I cross the line I've been dancing with. I love crossing lines with her. "It's funny—I think the only person you think you're not really fucking over is Beej, but you are. You're fucking him over, he's fucking you over. He's also just fucking—"

"You should walk away, man," Gus says, standing up—honestly, I forgot he was there…

I look over at him, smirking a little, amused.

"Should I?"

"Yeah." Gus nods again coolly. "You're a real big man about her when your brother's not here to keep you in line."

I sniff a laugh, looking away, because I can't fight him. It's not a fair fight—which is some bullshit, by the way. I'm the best fighter in every room and I won't do it because I did once and it wasn't worth it. It's the worst feeling—someone dying at your hands. The way the body goes limp, all the blood that comes from a head—heads bleed so much.

"Go on." Gus nods his chin back towards my room. "Fuck off and cool down."

I give Magnolia a long look, shaking my head at her again as I turn to leave.

"Have a great date with Beej today—" I call back. "Or is it Tom? Or is it Beej? Or is it Tom—? Or is it—"

"Either way, it's not you—" Gus calls. "I think that's the takeaway here for you."

I flip him off. He mirrors me and I skulk away.

I spend the rest of the day in the sun with Hen, he's pretty shitty at me, but it is what it is.

We haven't really talked about last night. He hates it, doesn't know what to do. He was so angry when he first found out about it all, that night at Box—we'd been lying to him too. I don't really lie to Hen, not much, but Parks never lies to him—just with that we felt like we had to. And he was so fucking pissed off, half for his brother, but I reckon mostly for him. We're all too close. We don't lie to each other and then we started lying.

198

First he was angrier at her, which I get. They're something else—siblings in their own right. Magnolia said that night he yelled at her the whole drive home, the only time in her life he's ever yelled at her—that he couldn't believe her, how could she do that to BJ, and no, he didn't care that they'd broken up, that it was bullshit and it didn't matter, was she trying to kill him, what was she thinking—and she said nothing 'til they got to her house. Pulled up out front and she turned to him.

"He slept with someone else, Henry," she said. "That's why we broke up."

And then she got out of the car and ran inside.

He pivoted after that.

He was so angry at Beej that he started helping us sneak around.

I reckon that's why it's hard for him now because we drew lines back then that I don't think he's comfortable living in anymore.

"Oi." He glances over at me, takes a long drink of his sangria. "Are you mentally prepared for them basically being back together after today?"

"Yep," I say without looking over.

They've gone on a date—Beej and Parks. They're not calling it a date, but we all know it's a date. Even Tom must know it's a date, and I don't know what the fuck he's playing at, but I guess Magnolia has a nose for finding men who'll do anything for her, and letting her be whatever she wants to be with BJ is her number one dating criteria.

"I reckon they're back on from now," Henry tells me, watching me close for a response.

I nod. "Same."

"And you're good?"

I nod.

I am, for some reason. It feels like a bit of a relief. Like if they're back together, the chapter closes or something, but as long as they're not, as long as there's an open end to them, there's an open end to her and me.

So I'm ready. I'm geared up and waiting for her to sear our love story shut with the burning prong of commitment to another man.

It doesn't go to plan, though.

Their date goes to shit.

She asked him whom he cheated on her with for the thousandth time, and for the thousandth time he wouldn't tell her. He swears it wasn't Taura, so my guess is it's this girl from school, Alexis. She was always thirsty for him, never even pretended she wasn't, even when him and Parks were together. They nearly broke up over it once in school, a rumour about Beej and Alexis one night nearly burned the whole thing to the ground, but they figured it out in the end.

Anyway, he won't tell Parks—the fucking idiot—and it devolved pretty quickly.

They're fighting outside the hotel restaurant, and these two can have a screaming match for the ages. You think I'm bad with her? These two are weapons designed to end each other.

It's hard to watch, actually, when they go like this. You'd think it'd give me a thrill of hope, but not when they go this far—she's shoving him and he's letting her and he's getting in her face and fucking roaring at her and she's screaming back so much that she doesn't even realise she's crying and you've got to realise, I promise this is true, even though I'm in love with her, I love them both.

This is them at their most toxic selves. If Jo were here, he'd make BJ stop it because the way they're going they're going to pull us all apart at the seams—there wont be a Box Set by morning—but I don't feel like I can interject without Beej thinking I'm inserting myself for her, so I wait for Henry's lead, who eventually heaves him away and I give fucking England a shove to push him back in his place, but he's more solid that I'd have thought and the push doesn't go that far. Doesn't look scared of me either, the prick.

He hooks his arm around Magnolia's neck and pulls her away and I stare after her, thinking about how Daisy told me to get out the other day when I made her sad and there was no one there to pull her away from me. I wonder if she's okay.

Beej isn't okay, though. Pisses off to his room for a minute and then comes back to the hotel bar, and I can see it on him as soon as he sits down.

I stare over at him, trying to place it. "What's up with you?"

He gives me a dismissive look. "Nothing."

I watch him a few seconds longer, wonder if it's possible. Would he actually? I don't think he would, but then—I can see it on him. I lean in, grab his chin with my hand, angling him up towards the light—he smacks me off but I ignore him, hold him tighter until I see what I'm looking for. And then I see it. I breathe out, annoyed as I shove his face away. He's got to be fucking joking.

"Oi, fuck it—" I shake my head. "I'm out, boys."

"What?" Henry frowns. "Why?"

I point over at his brother. "He's on some shit."

Henry huffs a laugh like it's crazy. Like he'd never. "No, he's not—" He looks over at Beej quickly. He needs it not to be true. "Are you?" Blinks again. "Are you?"

Beej makes this dumb grunt that makes him sound guilty and apathetic all at once.

I push back from the table, raising my hands like I'm done with it, and I am. Done with this part of it all. I hate it when Beej is on drugs. It's too stressful, he can't handle himself and he becomes such a prick.

"Are we just going to pretend that you walking away has fuck all with Magnolia?" he calls after me.

I don't turn back, but flip him off as I keep walking.

He's not wrong, though. And it is about her a bit, but not for the reasons you think. It's the same reason I know Henry's up about and leaves him too, because we were there. We watched it happen, we've seen how it goes when he's like this… watched him nearly die once in Amsterdam and then again in that hotel room with that girl from our school who wasn't Parks. Parks was there fucking watching his body starting to shut down while he was in bed with someone else, and she was a wreck and he was crying and yelling, and me and Jo dragged him to the shower, and Magnolia was crying in Henry's arms, and you could see it on her face, that she thought that was it, he was going to die. The way her eyes were—forget that I loved her, forget that she's something more to me than she should be—I could have seen a stranger look the way she did in that moment and be changed forever, but seeing her like that—that scared, that pale, white as a ghost—that BJ would start using again after he promised her he wouldn't.

He's a fucking idiot.

# 35

# Julian

Weird vibe between Dais and Rome as we wrap up in Paris—which was a worthwhile trip, by the way.

Tiller's presence confirmed for me what I had suspected. That the NCA is watching and I'm going to have to plan two jobs in order to pull one of them off.

Had a good time with Soleil, always a good time with her, though.

She's a good girl. Mostly. Her taste in men wouldn't be her mother's favourite thing—from French nobility, bored of the money and the rules.

I think she knew when I called her it had to do with a job, but she didn't seem to care.

She was a nice touch to the trip. Both personally and professionally.

I imagine it'll be a bit of a headache for her, being seen with me, but she's a big girl, she'll be okay.

When I walk onto my plane to fly home it's an odd sight.

Daisy right at the very back corner, nose in a book; Rome at the opposite end of the plane, headphones in, on his phone.

I frown as I glance between them. Couple of days ago he couldn't keep his fucking hands off her and now this?

I walk over to Dais, kick her ankle so she looks up at me. "This seat taken?" She shakes her head.

I sit down. "What's happened?"

"Nothing." She looks out the window.

"Oi—" I elbow her. "None of that. Tell me what happened."

She's frowning a lot and she shrugs. "I don't know."

I sigh, rub my hand absentmindedly over my mouth.

"Face, I've been doing some thinking…" She glances over at me, waiting. "If you want to be with Rome, you can."

"What?" She blinks, sitting back a little, like she doesn't know how to process the information. "Why are you saying this?"

I sigh.

It was a mess and it was probably a bad call—they were so in love—but people tried to kill them when they were together three different times. They were practically a magnet for it. And then this one night, they were at a hotel—I fucking hate hotels and I hate talking about this night, makes me feel sick, she nearly died—so that's all I'll say. At the time it felt safest to just nip it in the bud, make them be over, send him away. Santi sent Romeo off to New York, had him finish his last few months at school over there. Daisy was ruined. Totally beside herself. Angry at me, angry at him—betrayed by us both. Found out not too long ago he asked her to run away with her and she said no. Because of me. She didn't want to run away and leave me, and I don't know if I'm sad or grateful for that.

I know me and her have a weird relationship, somewhere between my sister, my kid, and my best friend. She might be all of the above, but of all the things she is to me she is absolutely and irrevocably my way home. The way I can tell right from wrong, good from bad—if Daisy likes someone, they're worth your time; if she doesn't, they can take a fucking hike. Her instincts are insane, and I want to say it's innate but it might be learned and then sharpened from all the times people tried to kill her or kidnap her.

So she didn't run away with him, stayed home with me instead.

Didn't talk to me for about a month, though, made me pay for it big time the way teenage girls do. Started fucking about with Theseus Onasis for a little bit 'til I snuffed that one out too. Didn't like it—she was sixteen, he was nineteen. Wasn't a fan.

So then she went and slept with Declan. That's how we found him. She lied, told him she was twenty-one. He was twenty-four. I nearly killed him on the spot. He had no idea. Ended up working for me instead.

I think I've made a mess of it all for her, and I reckon if I'd let them be, she probably would have been happier and I hate that.

I nudge her. "Because." I shrug. "I'm okay with it now."

She frowns. "Why now?"

"I don't know." I roll my eyes. Fuck, girls are annoying. "Because some time's passed. I don't think anyone's trying to off you at present—"

She gives me a look.

"I want you to be happy, Dais."

She sighs, scratches her head. "Thanks," she says, but it sounds far away.

"Oi." I glance over at her, a bit annoyed she's not more enamored by my gesture. "You've wanted to be with him since you ended four years ago, and I'm sitting here now telling you you can and you're blank—" I watch my sister, waiting for a clue. "What's going on?"

She crosses her arms over her chest, huffing a bit. Shifts her body so she's facing me and I don't know—there's something weird about her face. She's scared?

"I think I'm in love with Christian," she whispers to me.

I lean back, surprised. "What?"

She says nothing.

"Fuck." I breathe out. "Fuck. How long for?"

She swallows as she shrugging like it's hopeless. "Couple of months,"

"A couple of months?" I repeat, eyes wide. I can't believe I missed it—I should have seen it. I knew she liked him more than she said, but love? Falling in love is like cancer to people like us. Gives you a weakness the whole world can see… Gives the whole fucking world something to use against you.

"Does he know?" I ask her.

"No." She shakes her head.

I nod my head towards Rome. "Does he know?"

She gives me a sorry look.

"What'd he say?"

She sniffs a sad laugh. "That it's a phase."

"Is it a phase?" I ask, watching her close for an answer. She mightn't even know herself, but I'll know. Can read her like a book.

"Um." She mashes my lips together. "I've never loved anyone besides Rome before, so maybe—" She shrugs.

I nod. "Maybe."

"Do you think he's a phase?" She tilts her head. She looks sad.

"Could be." I shrug as I toss my arm around her. "Or he could be the love of your life."

She looks back out the window.

I nod my chin towards Romeo. "Best put a pin in shagging Rome for a bit, I reckon."

She gives me a look. "You don't say."

204

# 36

# Christian

Breakfast with the boys. First one since Greece, and Beej and I haven't really talked.

We're kind of good at this, though—not paying any attention to the blaring siren in the corner of our friendship group. We've been ignoring alarms for years and today's no different as Beej reaches across the table and we do the same handshake we've done since we were kids. We act like nothing went down a week ago.

"Alright, boys." Jo drums his hands on the table. "Catch me up. I know Greece didn't go to plan for Ross and Rachel," he nods his head towards Beej, who rolls his eyes.

"BJ's using again," Henry announces, glaring over at his brother.

BJ tosses his brother an unappreciative look.

"Yeah?" Jo gives Beej a cautious look. "We'll talk about that…" Then he glances at me. "And you, man? What's the go with you and Baby Haites?"

"Nothing," I scowl.

"Christian's into Daisy," Henry announces once again.

I give him a look and roll my eyes.

"Are you?" Beej looks over at me.

I shrug dismissively. I don't know why.

"Doesn't matter, though," Jo declares. "He left it too late."

I frown over at him. "What are you talking about?"

He shrugs. "Spoke to Jules a couple of days ago—they're in Paris."

"Who?" I take a gulp of my Sazerac. "Daisy and Julian?"

Jonah nods and gives me a look. "And Romeo."

My face falters a bit, so I shrug to cover it up.

"Bambrilla?" BJ sits back in his chair interested, smiling. "Fuck, he's such a sick guy—" And then I toss him a dark look and he shakes his head. "I mean—" Clears his throat. "Sick in the head, such a prick."

Beej tosses Jo an uncomfortable face. He's watching me close—Jo's a pain when it comes to shit like this, he can read me too easy.

"I think they're together," he tells me carefully.

I shake my head. No way. "They're not."

"How would you know?" Henry rolls his eyes. "You haven't talked to her in a week."

I give my best friend a despondent look because he's a fucking pain in the arse. "What'd Jules say?"

"I don't know." Jonah shrugs. "It was right when they got there. He said something about Romeo always touching her—"

My stomach flip-flops. Fuck. Seriously?

Press my hand into my mouth without thinking and give myself away.

"Oi." Beej shakes his head at me. "He doesn't have shit on you."

I blow some air out of my mouth and throw back the rest of my drink.

This is the worst feeling. The worst fucking feeling—liking her, I don't want to like her. Liking girls never works, they always fuck it up. Or I do? I don't know which, but one of us is fucking shit up. But I hate the feeling, hate the feeling that I've lost her before I even had her. I didn't know 'til about two weeks ago that I even wanted her, snuck up on me. I'm starting to wonder if maybe I'm not the most self-aware man on the planet.

"Should I fight him?" I ask Jonah, and him and Henry both crack up laughing.

"Yeah," Henry snorts. "Why don't you joust him for her hand?"

Jonah keeps laughing like I'm an idiot and it annoys me.

"Don't listen to them, they're going to die alone." BJ shakes his head, technically the only one here qualified to give any advice because he's the only one who's been in a committed relationship for more than five minutes. And even then, his qualifications are shitty at best. "Just tell her, man."

# 37

# Daisy

Jack and I head out to one of Jonah's clubs a few days later.

Eleventh Hour. It's fairly exclusive. Mostly a place for Jonah's friends and the rich and famous.

We almost don't go there because I don't want to see Christian, but we do go because I actually do want to see him.[194]

It's been more than a week since we last spoke and well over a month since we did anything[195] and I feel weird because we're not friends, really — so I don't have a reason to call him other than for what we used to do[196].

I come to his brother's club dressed to the fucking nines. The white chain-link strap crepe mini dress from David Koma with the Bottega Veneta Lido Intrecciato-debossed white leather mules.

"As I live and breathe!" Henry Ballentine cheers as I walk over.

Christian looks up from the other side of the club — he's at a table by himself with, like, a billion girls, and my heart sinks but my face doesn't show it.[197]

I don't catch his eye and give his best friend an extra tight hug just to spite him.

Henry reaches past me and shakes Jack's hand, then he sits down, chuckling to himself.

"You're not pulling any punches in that dress, are you?" He eyes me playfully.

Jack rolls his eyes. "God, before she actually tried leaving in neglige—"

---

[194] I'm fun and straight-forward like that.

[195] "Anything"

[196] And maybe still do? I don't know.

[197] I hope.

I smack him to shut up. His mouth snaps closed and he gives me an apologetic smile.

Henry gestures to the girl next to him. "Do you know Tausie?"

She gives me a warm smile and leans over to shake my hand.

I do know Taura. I know she's slept with Christian and my brother. Gross. She's got sort of blonde hair, kind of Southeast-Asian looking[198], perfect freckles, olive skin, light eyes that are almond in shape and colour. She's very pretty. Annoying, really.

My eyes pinch at her and I leave it a few seconds too long so Jack makes an annoyed noise and he reaches past me.

"She has trust issues and we're working on them," he tells her.

"We've actually met before," Taura Sax nods, gesturing to me.

My eyes flicker from her to the boys, unimpressed. "She's kicked about with Jules."

"Well." She shrugs. "Who hasn't?"[199][200]

Jack snorts a laugh and I stare over at her, surprised. I let out one dry laugh.

Henry and Jack head to the bar to get us some drinks and Taura scooches over towards me. I watch her moving closer how you might an insect.

She sees my face and laughs. "The boys warned me you weren't the warmest, but this is another level!" She shakes her head at me as though she's mystified. "What's your deal?"

I blink at her. "Sorry?"

"What?" She shrugs. "Was your mum mean or something?"

I stare at her for a few seconds and feel this rushy-dizziness of being understood that's sort of exciting and sort of scary. Mostly it feels like some sort of trick[201]. "Yes." I peer over, suspicious. "Very."

"You're not mean," she tells me after a few seconds of aggressively close watching.

"I'm very mean," I tell her resolutely.

She shakes her head. "You're not, you're just insecure." She says that like it's a fact and I don't think she's trying to be a bitch.

---

[198] I think her mum is from Singapore.

[199] The gall.

[200] Also, LOL.

[201] Also filed under: Does Not Trust Other Women.

I watch her, a bit fascinated, but she's not even looking at me, she's staring across the club at Henry.

I frown as I watch her. "I thought you were sleeping with Jonah?"

"I was." She purses her mouth. "Am. Kind of. I've slept with all of them except for Henry—"

"Why?" I scowl at her, defensively. "Henry's perfect."

"Yeah," She gives me a small smile. "I know."

I sit up a little straight, suddenly rather interested. "Do you like him?"

"Yeah." She bites down on her bottom lip. "I'm obsessed with him, I think he's... every constellation in the sky."[202]

"Then why haven't you—"

"—Because," she interrupts me even though she isn't watching me, she's still just watching Henry. "I can't tell whether I'm infatuated with him because I haven't had sex with him so he seems extra fascinating, or whether it's because I'm just properly in love with him."

"Oh." I blink, unsure of how to proceed or help.

She looks over at me and sniffs a laugh. "That last part's a secret. Don't tell anyone."

"Why would you tell me a secret?" I frown at her because she's maybe a bit insane. "You don't know me at all."

She shrugs, unbothered. "A girl like you would have to be pretty good at secrets."

"Yeah, but I don't have to keep yours," I tell her, crossing my arms over my chest.

She shrugs, standing up. "Yeah, but you're not as mean as you think you are, so you will."

And then she walks away.[203]

I stare after her, a bit confused and then BJ Ballentine pokes his head into my peripheral vision and grins at me.[204]

"She's weird, ey?" He moves in next to me.

I nod solemnly. "Very."

"What brings you out tonight, Baby Haites?" He gives me that famous smile of his and I feel my legs go to jelly, but that's not my

---

[202] !!!! Adorable.

[203] Did I just make a friend?

[204] God, he's handsome.

fault, it's just the physiological reaction to BJ Ballentine grinning at you. [205]

"Heard you were going to be here." I give him a playful shrug.

"Oi—" He whacks me with the back of his hand. "Don't you flirt with me, Baby Haites. We don't need another log on the fire."

I laugh and he nods in Christian's direction. "How's it going with you two?"

"We are… just friends." I give him a tight lipped smile and a shrug. "If that."

"Bullshit," he snorts and he's definitely high. Pupils are massive, completely blown. [206]

"We are!" I say defensively while desperately hoping he knows something I don't.

"I've had a lot of 'just friends' in my time, Baby — and you are not his friend."

I shake my head at him. "He doesn't see me like that."

"What?" BJ frowns. "Romantically?" I nod. "He's sleeping with you, isn't he?" [207]

I scoff. "I feel as though you of all people should know that when it comes to boys like you and him that actually means fuck all."

"Oh." He sniffs a sad laugh. "Right. Want to know a secret?" I nod. "I've spent the last three years sleeping with girls who aren't Magnolia Parks because I'm in love with Magnolia Parks."

My heart breaks a little because I think, probably, it's the same for Christian.

"It's not just about the sex." Ballentine elbows me gently. "You mean more to him than that."

"How do you know?" I blink, my eyes too wide and hopeful. [208]

He shrugs, leaning back into the chair behind us. "He's never once told us what it's like with you."

"Sex, you mean?" I stare, a bit horrified. That can't be a positive.

BJ pushes his hands through his hair and shrugs. "The boys and I,

---

[205] The medical term for this is: he turns women into putty.

[206] I don't like drugs. Julian does them sometimes.

[207] 'Not as much as he used to' is one point I don't say out loud because it feels embarrassing.

[208] And I know he can see it on me.

we swap war stories. Locker room shit, you know? The only person I never tell them details about is Parks."

"Why?" I frown.

"Because she's mine."[209] He gives me a small smile that, even though it's not about me or for me, my heart thumps like a maniac anyway because I'm a sucker for romance and I love love and Magnolia Parks is a fucking idiot if she doesn't pick BJ Ballentine. But if she doesn't, then great, maybe I'll have a crack because that smile is perfect.

I stare over at Christian, who's actually watching us, frowning — all these girls fawning over him, touching him, pulling his shirt for his attention. Vanna Ripley's the worst of them all[210] with her hand on his knee like it's a permanent fixture. Then she reaches over and picks a piece of lint off of his shirt — and she does it like it's nothing — like she's comfortable there, like she's always picking things off of his body, and I'm just dying. I think I'm dying. My chest feels tight. I want to cry. I hate watching her touch him.

"He has a lot of 'just friends,'" I say out loud accidentally.

BJ follows my gaze. "Yeah, he does." He gives me a look. "But you're not one of them."

I take a big breath and tear my eyes away from Christian right as Vanna leans in to kiss him.

"So—" I stare up at BJ, trying not to look rattled[211]. I breathe in and out quickly a few times to compose myself and he gives me a smile that makes me think he knows and he's sad for me, and I fucking hate that. "How's that girlfriend of yours?"

He gives me a look. "Don't have a girlfriend."

I ignore him. "How's that girlfriend of yours feel about you getting high at clubs without her?"

He gives me a tight smile as his eyes pinch. "Not that good."

"Does she know?" I ask, eyebrows up.

He shakes his head. I poke him in the arm.

"You're an idiot." I tell him and then I hear a tiny bit of a scuffle behind me and someone says, "Oi, watch it, f—" And then he calls

---

[209] I die.

[210] And she bloody would be. The Nickelodeon Nymphomaniac, that's what the papers call her sometimes.

[211] And I look rattled, I know I do.

211

someone a word that I won't say because it's revolting, but it rhymes with maggot.

I turn, and it's Jack that these guys are speaking to.

"Oi—" BJ jumps up at the same time as I do.

They're only a couple feet from us, these big, buffoon, sexually repressed meatheads who think that talking about "pussy" will drown out their desire to buy Men's Health for the pictures.

"What the fuck did you call him?" BJ asks, stepping forward.

The lad looks over at BJ, sizing him up. I've never seen BJ in action, but I've heard about it.

"I called him a—'" Meathead calls my best friend the word again.

I pull Jack in next to me.

"I'd like you to take it back and say sorry," I tell Meathead.

He sniffs a laugh, looking me up and down. "Do you want to know what I'd like?"

BJ takes a step forward to fight him, and I hold my hand up to stop him.

"I've got this," I tell him without looking at him. I don't take my eyes off Meathead, staring him down. "I'd like you to say sorry to my best friend because you called him a bad word."

"Dais—" Jack shakes his head. "I'm fine, it doesn't matter—"

"—Yes, it does." I give Jack a solemn look. I look back at Meathead. "Tell him you're sorry."

He sniffs a laugh, and he glances at his friend. "She's kind of cute."

The friend nods. "I'd take her home."

I give him a look. "I don't think she'd let you,"

"You'd rather go home with this queer?" Meathead nods towards Jack, and BJ — that sweetheart — he's at the ready. Fists clenched, jaw tight.

"Every day of the week—" I nod once. "Now, this is your last chance…"

Meathead and Friend exchange amused looks and I sigh, shaking my head, muttering under my breath how I hadn't really wanted to fight a bigot today, but here we are. Meathead's face falters as he stares at me, painfully confused, and then I do it all quite quickly — I thrust the heel of my hand up his nose, breaking it instantly. Then grab his shoulders, pulling him down towards me as I knee him in the groin. All of it is over and he's on the floor before the room can even ripple out as much as a gasp. Meathead falls down with a thud, and the friend stares down at me, sort of stunned, and then he lunges towards me — I'm not sure why. Reflex maybe? And I'm about to swing and hit him and so is BJ and then someone grabs my wrist, so BJ gets his punch in and I don't[212]— and then Christian's pulling me behind him and shoving the Friend.

"You never touch her," he yells in his face, holding him by the collar of his shirt. "Never. Try it again, and I'll kill you myself."

Miguel's at my side now, gun out, aimed at the Meathead.

"Say the word," Miguel gives me a look, but Christian shakes his head at him.

"I don't work for you." Miguel gives him a look.

"It's fine, Miguel." I push his gun away. "I'm f—"

"What the fuck was that?" Christian demands right in my face now and he grabs my wrist, pulling me out of the club and down on to the street where he practically tosses me.

"Easy on—" Miguel calls after him[213], like Christian would ever actually hurt me — at least not in ways people can see with their eyes.

Christian shoots him a look.

"Daisy, what the fuck was that?" Christian yells again.

"Nothing." I scowl at him, not meeting his eyes.

"You picked a fight with a man for nothing?" Him, angry.

"He called Jack a—" I mouth it. "Twice!"

"Okay—" Christian shrugs his shoulders. "So come get me and I'll fight him!"

"I don't need you to fight for me!" I spit. "I can fight for myself."

"But for what?" Christian asks loudly.

"Because he called my best friend a bad word!" I yell[214].

"And that's disgusting, I agree! It's entirely not okay—"

"—Exactly!" I jump in but he ignores me and carries on.

"—And I hate that that happened to Jack — but BJ was there. So you let him fight for you or you fucking come and get me."

"Oh okay, right—" I nod wildly. "So where were you?"

"What?" He pulls back.

"Where. Were. You? Where were you, Christian?" I ask louder.

---

[212] Which isn't fair, really.

[213] And most certainly deducting points for such behaviours on the invisible tally Miguel keeps in his mind for Christian.

[214] And stomp my foot.

"When I was with BJ and that man called my best friend a bad word — where were you? What were you doing?"

"I—" He chokes on his words. I know what he was doing. I could I see it out of the corner of my eye.

I shake my head at him. "Why the fuck would I ever come and get you?" I snap.

He looks a little taken aback, blinking all sad and caught.

And then, right on cue, Vanna Ripley walks out of the club and onto the street, her head snapping around, scanning for us. Her eyes land on Christian and she crosses her arms over her chest, waiting by the door a little uncomfortably.

I wave my arm one in her direction. "She's waiting for you," I tell him, my eyebrows standing up as tall as they can, hopefully making me look tougher than I feel.

Christian looks over at her, then back at me, and something dances across his face and it seems like it could be regret — but why would it be?

"Dais, we—"

"—I know what you and I are," I interrupt him. "It's why I'd never 'come and get you.'"

He blinks, bewildered with an edge of hurt. "What the fuck is the matter with you?"

"Daisy!" Jack appears at my side. "There you are, I lost y—" He senses the tension and stops mid-sentence, glancing nervously between Christian and I. I link my arm with Jack's and pull him towards the car. Miguel's waiting with the door open.

I peer over at Vanna then back at him. "Have fun tonight."

Christian stares after me, shaking his head. He flips me off.

"Good girl," Miguel nods from the front seat.

# 58

# Christian

I didn't tell her, not when I saw her walk into Jo's club. I wanted to, but by then she'd already seen me at that table of girls, already looked hurt, and busied herself quickly with talking to Taura. I wanted to tell her, thought about it, maybe I was even about to—and then she started talking to Beej and I got angry. Felt hot in my chest and under my skin. Of everyone to talk to? BJ? Are you fucking kidding me?

Not that she knows, but—

Anyway, then I lost my focus.

Vanna kissed me.

I let her.

I shouldn't have let her. I wanted to make Daisy jealous, remind her that she likes me more than she likes Rome, but I don't even know if that's true and it didn't work anyway, because now all I have is a clingy, slutty, ex-Nickelodean star thinking we have a thing when we don't, and I've pissed off the girl I like.

The girl I like who's a fucking idiot. Fighting a fucking giant by herself? And I'm furious, because what if something happened? She's a fucking idiot.

That's what I think as I drive Vanna Ripley back to my apartment. Her hand's on my leg and she's rubbing it—her hand getting higher and higher and then I put my hand on hers without even thinking.

I frown over at her. "Where do you live?"

She sniffs an amused laugh. "New York?"

"Where are you staying then?"

She looks past me to my apartment behind me, lifts her eyebrows.

I shake my head. "Not tonight."

She snatches her hand back. "Excuse me?"

"I'll drop you to your hotel—where are you staying?"

"Are you joking?" She blinks.

I stare at her, this insanely hot, sort of famous girl in front of me. Any guy would be so stoked to go home with her and I've her got her, she's home with me, we're like fifteen steps away from what I'm pretty sure would be a spectacularly hot night, and I'm out. I don't want it—don't want her.

I want those dumb big brown eyes glaring up at me, frowning because I've made her angry because I'm a prick but she likes me anyway. I want my hand caught in her hair because there's too much of it and I wear a ring that gets stuck, and I've thought before that probably I should take it off so it doesn't happen, but the way she says my name every time it happens—it's this laugh-growl—makes me not want to stop. That probably should have been the sign… That I like literally being stuck to her, that says something—I'm just an idiot and a slow learner.

So I drop off Vanna—who is not pleased with the night's developments, that's for sure, but I don't care—and then I drive straight to Daisy's. Honestly, I'm a bit scared about what I'll be walking into—a few hours have passed since the club, plenty of time to call an Italian guy over to your house to hook up with if that's what you're into.

Julian opens the door and he looks down at me, a bit surprised. "Was wondering when you'd show up."

"She here?" I walk inside.

"Mmhm." He nods up towards the stairs. "Did she really try to fight a body builder at the club tonight?"

I flick him a look. "Yep."

He shakes his head, annoyed. "Pain in the arse."

"Yep." I nod and I don't waste my time chatting, I just jog up the stairs to her room.

Stand outside the door for a second, steel myself for whatever I might see—I'd hope if she was here with Romeo that Julian might have given me a heads up, but he can be a dickhead, so who knows.

I knock once and then open it, not waiting for an answer.

She's lying in her bed and props herself up as I walk in. There's a frown as soon as she sees it's me.

Looks self-conscious, actually.

Glances down at herself—old black Harley Davidson T-shirt—I think it's mine actually? And she springs out of bed. No pants on.

I stare down at her bare legs, smile a little.

"Oi." I nod my chin over at her.

Close the door behind me.

Her eyes pinch and she looks angry straight away. "Finished already?"

I grit my teeth. "Shut the fuck up."

"Excuse me?" She blinks, head pulled back, and I walk over to her quickly and stand toe to toe with those brown eyes I can't get out of my head.

"I said shut the fuck up, Daisy—" It doesn't go down any better the second time, so I shake my head. "I didn't go home with her."

Her face falters.

"Well," I reconsider. "I took her home. I didn't sleep with her."

"Why?" She asks cautiously.

"Because I'm not sleeping with her!" I give her a look.

She blinks a few times. "Why?"

"Because I'm not sleeping with anyone!" I yell loudly and she just stares at me.

I breathe out loudly, shove my hands through my hair, take a few steps away from her. "You went to Paris?"

She stands still, crossing her arms over her chest. "Yes."

"With Romeo?" I eye her.

Her mouth pulls. "Kind of."

I give her a look. "Kind of?"

She sighs, pressing her hands into her eyes. "It's complicated."

"Uncomplicate it for me then." I fold my arms over my chest, waiting, and she just stares over at me, eyes wide with this sort of confused-looking nervousness.

"Are you sleeping with him?" I ask.

She breathes out of her nose, licks her bottom lip, shakes her head. "That's also complicated."

"Bullshit it is—" I scoff. "It's a yes or no question."

"No, it's not—" She shakes her head, taking a step towards me.

I rub my face, already feeling tired of talking about things out loud. It doesn't feel good. Feels like shit.

"Did you sleep with him while you were in Paris?" And she says nothing, but her mouth twitches in this way that looks sad, like she feels guilty, and I make a sound in the back of my throat, press the heel of my hands into my temples. "Fuck!"

Daisy stares over at me defensively. "What's it got to do with you, anyway?"

"How's that now?" I blink a few times and take a few steps towards her. "What does you sleeping with someone else have to do with me?"

"Yeah." She shrugs. "Because we're not together—"

"Well, we fucking are now, yeah?" I yell loudly and her head pulls back a little. "So you stop fucking about with him—"

"What?" She blinks, but her cheeks are pink.

"I'm done—" I give her a look. "I'm done with other girls, okay? I just want to be with you—"

She blinks. Four. I count each time. Calling her eyes brown is underselling them. Like the inside of a Galaxy bar. The caramel one.

"Are you being for real?" she asks, voice quieter now.

"Yes."

"Really?" She sounds actually confused and I feel like shit.

"Yeah." I shrug. "What? You don't want to do this?"

She gives me a cautious look and swallows. "What is… this?"

"I don't know?" I shrug, my cheeks going pink and I don't want her to see it. "We're just… you know—whatever."

Her face falters again. "Whatever?"

"Together." I shrug like it's no big deal even though it is a pretty big fucking deal.

"Together?" She repeats, smiling a tiny bit, and I bite one back, shaking my head at her instead.

"You're just fishing now," I say and she laughs as I grab her by the waist, pulling her towards me.

"Maybe I am." She stares up at me defiantly but still slips her arms around my waist anyway.

I look over her face and shake my head at her. "You don't have to play games with me, Dais—" Shrug a tiny bit. "I'm in."

She presses herself up against me. She's on tiptoe and can barely reach my mouth, but kisses me quickly and I shift my hands so one's at her waist and one's in her hair. I move her backwards towards the bed, when she pulls back, looking up at me curiously.

"Were you jealous?"

"Of you?" I blink. "Sleeping with him?" I nod once. "Yeah."

She smirks a little. "We don't do jealous…"

I give her a half smile. "We do now."

What happened? Tell me everything.

He came over and kissed me and said he's not going to sleep with anyone else anymore and he doesn't want me to either and I think we're together....

oh holy day.

praise him

an end to the madness!!!!!!!

And all thanks to someone calling you a bad word.

Are you okay?

Fine, babe.

Thrilled now, actually.

You definitely broke that man's nose.

Good.

Thank you.

Anytime xx

# 39

# Julian

Me, Declan and the Old Boys are in Oberndorf, Germany because it's the best place in Europe for weapons, I don't care what you say.

The Russian shit is fine, the Italian and the Austrian manufacturers do okay too, but I can't go past the lads in Oberndorf.

Been dealing with them since I took over and it's always been smooth.

Always obliged me with being the first one they show new devices to, the first one they'll sell things to, private showings, etc.

Flew in this afternoon.

Declan looks over at me as he picks up a new rifle, flipping it over in his hands, trying it out for size.

"Who were you with this morning?" he asks without looking over at me.

"Quinn Miller," I say as I pick up a different gun. Open the barrel, peer around.

Declan looks over. "Who?"

"The hot waitress from Greenhouse."

Decks shakes his head a bit amused. "Fuck, you're good with names…"

"Yeah, I'm a real prince for remember the names of the people I have sex with."

I am good with names, though, always have been. Intentionally. People respond well to that sort of shit. Makes them feel seen, makes them feel validated. They do more for you that way.

"You stayed there?" He looks over, frowning.

"Hotel," I tell a different gun.

He puts his gun down, looking confused. "Why?"

"Because—" I pick it back up. "Daisy and Christian are full steam ahead and there's only so much sex my little quasi-paternal heart can handle." He doesn't laugh at that, gives me a weak smile at best, so I guess his thing for Dais is still in full swing.

"That going good then?" he asks, not looking me in the eye.

"Yeah." I shrug. "She seems pretty happy."

He nods. "Right, so anyway—" Clears his throat. "What do we need for this job?"

I scratch my chin. The truth is, I don't completely know. It's not falling together how I want it to—Scotland Yard has been keeping too close an eye on me for us to just pull a robbery. I think I have a plan, but it's a lot of wheels in motion.

"I think we're going to do a misdirect—" I squint over at him. "I can't figure out how to get them off my arse otherwise."

"Scotland Yard?"

"And Interpol." I give him a look.

"That Tiller's a fucking pain in the arse."

I nod. "He's switched on."

Declan gives me an unimpressed look. "He's switched on your sister—" A bit rich coming from him, I know, but he's not wrong.

"Huh—" I squint over at Declan, thinking.

"What?" He frowns.

I shake my head. "You just gave me an idea."

# 40

# Daisy

He's been talking about it all week, this date—this proper date we're going to go on—and even though we've been whatever we are[215] now for well over a week and we've barely parted ways besides me going to university, this date has been a thing he's talked about non-stop.

He didn't stay over last night—hated that—he left after dinner and said it'd be more fun for the date if he wasn't there when it started. When I asked what time, he said all day.

"I'll see you at 9 am," he said, kissing me[216] on my doorstep before he left.

I wake up extra early the next day, like it's Christmas and I'm five.

I spend hours getting ready, which I never do. I do a face mask, I do my hair, I wear more make-up than my usual mascara and that Gucci lipstick[217] I use on my mouth, cheeks and eyes—and it's all absurd if you think about it, because he's already seen me naked 900[218] times. He knows what I look like undone, he has undone me many, many times—but nevertheless, it's 8:45 and I'm in Brandon Maxwell's black one-shouldered cutout, ribbed jersey gown. The usage of the word "gown" is perhaps misleading, I'm not dressed as though I'm going to a gala, but maybe like I'm about to go on a super yacht for the most important date of my life—because who knows, maybe I am?

---

[215] "Together." It's now my favourite term in the universe while also being one of the broadest.

[216] A lot.

[217] Rouge à Lèvres Voile Sheer Lipstick in 518 Amy Blush.

[218] Jury's out on the official count, but I suspect it's actually closer to the lower hundreds. I'll have the Silicon Baddies run the numbers.

A yacht?[219] A plane to somewhere?[220] A private dinner in the Eiffel Tower?[221] I don't know what we're doing, and I don't really care either, with him is the part of it I like best.

My bedroom door knocks a few minutes later. "Come in," I say to my reflection as I put in the Mini Daisy stud earrings from Jennifer Meyers.

"Woah," Christian says from behind me.

I turn around to face him, but when I do, though, he doesn't look how I thought he would.

He's in the black Chitch Boneyard jeans from Ksubi, a grey tee from Balenciaga and—as per usual, black Converse and that necklace.

"Oh," I accidentally say with a frown. His face twitches, amused.

I get this stressed-out pang of sadness that he's putting in this little effort—he just looks how he always does?—and a lot of me is self-conscious of what I'm wearing. I put in effort—which seems to be a metaphor of us… that I'm nothing worth putting in effort for, that he'll not try for me at all and I'll die trying for him.

I glance up at Christian, clear my throat, trying to sound casual. "We're in quite different clothes."

"Yeah." He nods and gives me an awkward grin. "You need to get changed, you're way over-dressed."

"Oh." My cheeks have burst into flames. "Okay. What are we doing?"

He rubs the back of his neck. "Nothing special."

I frown over at him and a smile cracks over him.

"Just normal shit." He shrugs.

My mouth falls open as I try to process what's happening and wonder whether I'm a bit of joke to him. Then he takes a step towards me, takes my hand in his and knots our fingers together.[222]

"That's the dream, right?" He tilts his head, looking for my eyes. I look up at him. "Normal life, normal people, the mediocrity of it all—to not be what we are?"[223]

My eyes go round.

---

[219] Don't worry, my expectations are tempered.

[220] No, really. They are.

[221] Alright, they're not really that tempered.

[222] Pushes the hair that isn't on my face behind my ear anyway.

[223] Oh my gosh.

"A whole, normal day." He grins over at me proudly. "I'm thinking a supermarket, a petrol station... Ikea, maybe?"

"I've never been there!" I marvel over at him and he starts laughing, his eyes flickering down at me, smiling a bit.

"I like this." He tugs on my dress before he tugs it off my body.

It pools at my ankles and then he holds my face in his hands, kisses me differently than he usually does—no wandering hands, just holding me against him, his mouth hovering over mine—and then he pulls away.

"Come on." He nods his head towards my closet. "Get normal."

He sits on my bed and watches me change and it's a funny sort of thrilling, him looking at me like the mundane thing I'm doing is this complicated task, swallowing heavy as his eyes drop down my body as I pull on the light blue boyfriend jeans from Saint Laurent.

Plain white T-shirt. Normal. The black Gucci crystal-embellished leather Chelsea boots. Normal.[224]

"Let's go." He nods his head towards the door and offers me his hand and a smile and I ignore the part where it feels like a promise without words.

We drive straight to the petrol station and he has one hand on the wheel and the other on my knee—my heart, really—and he doesn't say that much but he keeps looking over at me and smiling in this way[225] that keeps making both of us nearly laugh, and I think it's so strange to be human, don't you? How my mouth has dragged over every part of Christian Hemmes's body, he has seen me completely bare, he's seen me furious, we've yelled at each other, I've never cried in front of him because I don't do that with anyone but my brother[226] but he's seen me and he knows me, I think. Properly. Knows me how you want someone to know you and he still likes me anyway. He's over there in the driver's seat, squashing away a smile, licking that bottom lip of his, not saying a fucking word, and I'm all shy? I'm never shy. I don't mind it, though. Sitting next to him saying nothing feels like taking off a corset. A great undoing, if you will, and he will. In every way.

---

[224] ...ish.

[225] Mostly with the corner of his mouth and a tiny bit of tongue pressed against his top lip.

[226] And Romeo, but let's not pull at that thread right now.

"Right—" He pulls into a BP and drives up to a pump, ignition off. He looks over at me. "All you, Baby." He flicks his eyebrows playfully as he unclips my seat belt. "Do you know how to open the tank? "

"Of course I know how to open the tank, I'm a fucking doctor," I growl at him, even though I definitely don't. I look around for the button, running my hands over the dashboard, peering around. I don't have a lot of experiences in cars, see? And each one is different, I'm learning.

Christian's mouth twitches, amused as he watches me. Sits back in his chair a little, folding his arms over his chest, eyes up.

"Okay, Doctor—" He clears his throat. "There is no button on a G Wagon. You just press the fuel door."[227]

He gives me a curt smile and I glare over at him—he starts laughing as I climb out of the car, following me out.

He leans up against the car, coolly watching me.

"I don't need any help." I give him a tall look.

"No, I know." He shrugs but I can tell he thinks it's funny. "You've got this." I stare at the fuel choice. Lots of options for a newcomer, actually. Diesel. Gas. Unleaded. E10. Premium Unleaded.

I purse my lips as I stare at them all, certainly not asking for help because I'm a fucking doctor.[228]

He lets out a little laugh and comes up behind me, slips one arm around my waist, and then puts the other on top of my hand and guides it towards Premium.

He moves with me, holding my hand as I hold the petrol nozzle, as he holds me against him.

Kisses the back of my head and I lean back into him. It's all spectacularly unremarkable and I let myself drift off into a daydream where, for a second, I'm not who I am and he's not who he is. There are no bodyguards, no dead parents, no dead sisters. I don't know Krav Maga and I'm not practically an expert at knife-throwing. I'm just a regular twenty-year-old who still goes home to do her laundry.

Next on the list: Ikea.[229]

Have you been? It's actually kind of horrible. It's too big, feels like a maze.

---

[227] Stupid design, really…

[228] Sort of.

[229] Don't get too excited, because I was and I was wrong to be.

There are lots of rooms to make out in, though, I'll give it that.

"And then you build them yourself?" I stare over at Christian, a bit horrified at his explanation of what this place is.

He nods, smirking.

"Why?"

"Because they come disassembled in a flat pack."

"But why?"

He shrugs. "I don't know, to keep the cost down?"

"But time is money?"[230] I tell him and he starts laughing, pushing me backwards and up against the wall of a fake kitchen, hand on my cheek, his thumb brushes over my mouth and then he kisses me while smiling then pulls back.

"Alright." He nods his head at the kitchen bar behind us. "How do we feel about this?"

"For what?" I frown a little.

His face flickers a bit of a frown. "Our dream kitchen…"

And even though I know it's a game, the assumption that somewhere, sometime, in some dreamland, Christian Hemmes and I have a kitchen together steals my breath for a second.

I swallow, hoping my eyes aren't as big as they feel. I breathe out my nose to steady myself.

"Nothing comes from a flat pack in our dream kitchen." I give him a look that he matches.

"Baby,[231] we're normal now." He takes my hand and pulls me into another kitchen, kisses my cheek. "Where do we live? Paddington? Fitzrovia?"

I shake my head, feeling shy again. "We're not in London."

He blinks, surprised. "Woah."

I give him a small smile and he nods once before then pointing to a pine-y rattan dining set. "Is this our vibe?"

I give him a sharp look. "It most certainly is not."

He gives me a look, gesturing to the tables around us. "Go on then."

"It's a colonial-style home," I tell him.

He nods once. "I like those…"

"Yeah?" I grin up at him.

---

[230] That's what Julian always says. And Benjamin Franklin, I suppose.

[231] He gives me a look.

226

He pushes some hair behind my ear, smiles down at me. "Yeah."

This is how the whole day feels. Completely, perfectly benign. We take a slow walk around Kensington Gardens, he feels me up under Queen Anne's Alcove, we feed the ducks, we go on some swings, we go to a supermarket, go to Nero's[232] and when the sun's finally starting to go down, we get a fish-and-chips and he pulls up on Chepstowe Place and sits there for a second before peering over at me, looking a bit proud of himself.

"The finale of your normal day..."

I give him a confused look and he points out the window.

Sparkle Laundrette and Drycleaners.

My mouth falls open a bit and he smiles more. He jumps out of his car and lugs a giant bag of laundry from his trunk, standing in front of the shop, waiting for me.

I walk over to him slowly and he offers me his hand, pulling me inside.

"Where is everyone?" I peer around the empty store. Silver washers line both white-tiled walls, gold clothing bags running over them. There are scattered white baskets on the floor, and it smells like linens and dryer sheets[233] and the quiet music playing sounds like what Christian listens to. Quiet, folky, calmer than the things you'd think he'd listen to.

"Oh." He gives me a look and lowers his voice. "I hired it so we could have it to ourselves." I pull a face and he waves his hand, dismissively. "Very normal."

I sniff a laugh as I start sorting his laundry.

"You don't actually have to do that," he tells me, looking a bit self-conscious.

I frown at him a bit and keep sorting, looking around at all the washing machines fondly. "How did you know about me and laundry?"

He licks his bottom lip. "Your brother likes me more than you think he does."

"Julian told you?" I blink, surprised.

"He said it was your favourite room in the house and I thought he

---

[232] Not the best coffee, if I'm honest... Why are there so many?
[233] Heaven for me.

was being an arsehole and kind of sexist, but then he said the thing about the coins when you were little, and I realised—"

I purse my lips to keep myself from smiling as much as I want to and push past him as he puts all his whites in one machine and then Edith Whisker's version of "Home" starts playing[234] and Christian walks up behind me and slips his arms around my waist.

"There is a fatal flaw to your normal plan, you know," he tells me.

I turn to face him, lift my brows but make sure he doesn't let me go. "And what's that?"

He locks the door behind me. "You have that face and that brain and you'll never be normal—" Shakes his head. "Couldn't be if you tried."

I swallow nervously and so does he.

Takes my hand in his and puts the other on my waist, pulls me into him, kisses my forehead and I don't know what good fortune my fates found to weave into my life right now, but I find myself slow-dancing with Christian Hemmes in a laundromat and there's nothing normal about it—

The universe, actually, is ablaze. The planets lose track of their orbits, the birds are poets now and all the songs written before this and all the ones that'll come after this are about this moment; about how when we're standing my ear rests right where his heart is, how one hand of his swallows a whole half of my waist. The beautiful nothingness of this, the most intimate moment of my life to date, a life that, actually, has been dotted with much intimacy and I think nothing will ever beat him resting his chin on top of my head.

I pull back a tiny bit and glance up at him.

"You've got something on your shirt." I point at the nothing on him.

He glances down, eyes flicker back up to me, smiling amused. "Do I?"

I nod once. "Yes."

He swallows once. "Are you going to do something about it?"

I reach for the buttons of his shirt, undo each one slowly. His eyes don't move from mine, watching me, waiting for me—and his gaze is so much, it's so weighted and heavy with a new sort of want that I can't even look at him because I'm a flower and he's the whole entire sun and he'll wilt me away, I know he will—so I focus on the buttons,

---

[234] Listen, immediately.

undo them with the precision I do with practice cadavers, and when the shirt falls open I trace down his chest for a second before he lifts my chin up with his finger and his thumb, eyes flicking down at my T-shirt and then back up to my face.

I lift my arms in the air, waiting.

He sniffs a laugh. Swallows. Lifts it up off me slowly, running his hands up me as he does. He tosses my T-shirt to the side and before I even know what's happening, he hooks an arm around my waist and his mouth is on mine and I'm off the ground, moving backwards and up and on to a machine behind us.

His hands are on my face, then in my hair and he's leaning over me, and he's kissing me in this way that feels like a ship breaking through fog, it's fresh water, clear skies, smooth sailing, birds chirping... the planets of us aligning out there like our bodies are in here, and I undo the top button of his jeans and he smiles against my mouth. I bite down on his bottom lip because when I do I know he'll smile more. He pulls me forward so I'm against his waist, tugs my jeans down and off my legs, and then stares down at me for a couple of seconds. I think I understand for a fleeting moment why everything that's bad and painful and sad is worth it if you love someone, because I'll remember how he's looking at me now forever. His eyes flickers over me face like leaves on a breezy day. He presses his tongue into his top lip, swallows heavy. Holds my face with one hand and kisses me gentler than you'd think he could down my neck and he leans me back against the machine, kissing me all over and down me—taking his time and I love my skin around him. I'm never aware of my skin at any other time of the day, the only time I think of it is when it prickles all electric because Christian Hemmes is touching me or he's about to—and when he does, his lips on mine, it feels like on my tiredest day I'm falling face first into a pillow-top mattress. Like rain hitting water and you can't see where one starts and the other ends, that's what our mouths are like. He pulls me back up so we're level, pushes his hand through my hair, then he presses himself into me.

The feel of him is my favourite feeling in the world, for all of history and all of time, write it down, ring the town bell and tell the scribes—I'll wear it on my heart's sleeve forever that I love him. I can feel myself drifting further and further from a safe harbour, though, and I should have tethered myself to something, but I didn't. I can feel it now. Me tethered to him.

He grips my waist, his mouth doesn't move from mine and my breath is caught in my chest, and when we're finished, and he shifts his head a little and our eyes catch and he's staring at me like he's hearing "Don't Think Twice" for the first time—kind of terrified, kind of awed and I wonder if maybe he's tethered to me too.

He gives me a half smile and pushes some hair behind my ear.

"Now," he says, breathless, looking down at me as he wipes his forehead gruffly. "I know you're new to laundromats, but this is generally not what they're used for."

# 41

# Christian

So, look. Since our date the other night—which went spectacularly well, by the way—Daisy and me, we've sort of just been in each other's pockets.

I haven't gone home much, just to grab some shit here and there. Can't stay too long at home anyway without Henry rolling out a fucking parade for himself to celebrate his rightness. He was right, though. Don't tell him.

That aside, it's easier to kick about at hers.

Miguel isn't hovering when she's at the Compound, Julian isn't texting her every couple of hours to check in, she has her kitchen and her laundry, which are things she cares about, I've learnt.

Doesn't like my kitchen—learnt that too.

Four burners isn't enough, my food processor is a "fucking joke" and "Where's your vegetable-spiralizer? What do you mean you don't have one, are you an idiot?" And when she asked me what shape do I like my carrots cut in, and I said, "Carrot-shaped?", the look she fucking gave me…

Batonnet, it turns out. That's my favourite carrot shape to eat. I didn't know that a week ago, but I do now.

We're in her bed and we're four seasons into *The Great British Bake Off*, and I wish I hated it but Noel Fielding really gets me.

"Holy shit—" I yell.

"What?" She comes running out of the bathroom with a face cloth. "What's wrong?"

"Paul just called that girls cake faultless! Paul, that grumpy bastard—"

She frowns at the TV. "And was it?"

I shrug. "Design could have been better, in my opinion."

"Have you ever killed anyone?" she asks sort of out of the blue, leaning back against my chest. She doesn't look up when she asks, doesn't take her eyes off the TV.

I press my lips together. "Yep." Swallow. "You?"

She nods. "Yeah. "

"How many?"

She purses her lips. "Just the guys that were trying to kill me."

I tighten my arms around her, shift her a little so I can hold her more, blow out the air of how much I hate that someone tried to lay a finger on her.

"I got into a fight," I tell her even though she didn't ask. "Stupid. It was stupid—"

She turns back to look at me. "And he died?"

"Yeah."

"Did you shoot him?"

I shake my head. Beat him, I don't tell her but she knows anyway, I can tell. She turns back to the TV, breathes out her nose, says nothing. And I wonder if that's too fucked up to have told her, like maybe she'll be weird with me now? Feel different about me? Because I feel different about me—

She picks up my hand and kisses the back of it before she hugs it to her chest, and I kiss the back of her head, and I'm not saying we're in a relationship, because I don't know what we're in, but I get why people are so about them now, they're nice—and she's so easy to be with. I'm happy when I'm with her, it's not convoluted, it's—

"DAISY!" Declan's voice bellows out of nowhere.

Daisy sighs, annoyed.

"DAISY!" he yells again.

"I'm busy!" she yells back, not moving.

"DAIS—" Declan growls and something about how it sounds makes her sit up straighter. "NOW."

She makes a sound in the back of her throat and rolls out of her bed, grabbing a T-shirt of mine on the floor and pulling it on over her head. Something about watching her do it makes me feel happy. I follow after her, pulling on the black Escobar sweatpants from John Elliot, and jog after her.

"What?" she calls out halfway down the hallway. She peers down into the foyer and freezes. "Shit." She whispers under her breath and sighs.

It's Julian. Slumped on Declan's shoulder, being held up by him and Kekoa.

232

Blood everywhere, face beaten.

"What the fuck happened?" I run down the stairs towards her brother, but she just trots down them, shaking her head.

"By all means, Dais—" Declan calls to her. "Take your fucking time."

She ignores him, grabs the crown of her brother's hung head and pulls it backwards by the hair so she can see his face.

"'Ello!" He grins, bleary-eyed and bloody-faced.

She glares over at him, grabs his chin with her hand, and manoeuvres his face around to check him out and I have no idea what the fuck is going on.

I'm just standing there, watching them.

She's not worried, she's angry.

She gets on tiptoe, wipes some blood from his cheek with her hands, and squints into a big gash.

"Love you," Julian slurs all drunk and sincere.

"Shut up." She scowls at him because she flicks her eyes over at Declan. "Take him to the dining room and get the kit."

She looks upset when she turns around to face me.

I shake my head at her. "What the fuck is going on?"

She swallows and shakes her head. "Fight night."

Julian's lying on the dining room table, sprawled out, laughing, drunk as fuck.

"Take your shirt off," Daisy tells him and he does.

My hands are pressed into my mouth, eyebrows low—still don't really understand.

"Cage fighting," she tells me as Kekoa hands her her suture kit.

I hover behind her, sort of working out how I feel about it all, and I feel a few things… It's weird. I'm super into how level-headed she is, it's pretty hot watching her be a doctor and shit, in the way where it's just sexy when people are good at what they do. She gets this look on her face when she's gone full-doctor. Brows low, nose a bit pinched— she's feeling down her brother's ribs.

"Broken," she says as she feels down his right side. "Broken…" She shakes her head a bit. "That one—" She points to it. "Could have pierced a lung."

"Didn't, though," Julian tells her.

She gives him a look. "You're a mess," she tells him.

He shrugs. "It's not so bad."

"Butterfly stitch." She points to a cut on the bridge of his nose. "Butterfly stitch." She points to one of the ones on his cheeks, then looks closer at the other one, her face pulling. "This one probably needs a couple of stitches."

She keeps looking over him, sighing as she does—and I've worked out how I feel about it now: I feel sad. I'm sad because I can see it now, she's sad.

She stares for a long moment at a pretty jagged cut on his arm and breathes out loudly through her nose.

Grabs some gauze, dabs away the blood.

"Julian," she says, staring into the cut.

"Mm?"

"Why is there glass in this cut of yours?"

No one says anything.

She glances up expectantly, looks around, waiting for someone to say something but they all say nothing.

"This wasn't from a cage fight," she tells no one in particular.

She grabs her tweezers and starts digging through the wound, fishing out glass—Julian's there, both laughing and crying at the pain.

"I won," he grunts at her, like maybe she'll be proud of him.

She flicks her eyes over at her brother.

"No shit," she says, and I have this weird feeling that I just want to put my arm around her, take her back upstairs, not let anyone talk to her for the night. Her eyes look weighed down or something. Embarrassed, maybe? I can't place it, but either way I hate it.

"He came and bottled me after," Julian tells her even though she didn't ask.

She sighs and then glances between her brother and his best friend. "And where is he now?"

Julian swipes his hand across his face gruffly. "Gone."

She shakes her head again, letting out a little puff of air, then grabs her needle and suture thread and starts stitching him up without warning.

"Ow!" Julian growls through gritted teeth, glaring up at her. And it's that moment that I work out that I don't like it when people glare at her.

"Get me a fucking local!" he tells her.

"No." She gives him a pointed look., and I wonder if it looks like she's about to cry. I haven't seen her cry before, I don't know how to

234

spot it. "You want to fight like a man, you can get your sutures like a man."

He blows air out through his mouth and looks away.

She finishes stitching him up and bends down, inspecting her work. Then—if you can believe this—Declan fucking Ellis tilts his head to the side and stares at Daisy's arse.

She's in fucking nothing, tiny knickers that aren't for his eyes and my T-shirt, and before I even really know what I'm doing, I give him a little shove.

"You right there?" I scoff, indignant.

"Oh, fuck off," Declan snorts.

Dais turns around, frowning. "What's going on?"

I grab her arm, pulling her behind me. Declan shoves me. "Don't fucking grab her like that—"

"What happened?" Daisy looks confused.

"Don't touch me, bro—" I shove him back.

"What happened?" Daisy asks, louder this time. She's looking between us but Ellis ignores her.

"Are you going to stop me then, bruv?" He rolls his shoulders back and I start to square up and then Daisy shoves me away.

"Stop it." She shoves me again. "Christian, stop—" Grabs my face so I have to look at her and I drag my eyes away from my brand-new nemesis and down to the girl I guess I'm fully into now. "What happened?"

I shake my head a little, press my tongue into my top lip.

"He was… staring at you—" I do my best not to sound like the territorial, jealous prick I think I am with her now.

She looks down at herself, like she's forgotten she's in a T-shirt and knickers, like she's forgotten she's the hottest girl on the planet. Looks embarrassed about it too—she tugs the shirt down, all self-conscious, shifts herself behind me a little and I grow four feet.

I point at Declan. "If you ever look at her like that again, I'll fucking kill you on the spot."

Then I take her hand and lead her back up the stairs.

"Christian—" Julian calls after me.

I look back at him.

And all he does is give me this smile. This dumb, drunk, bleary-eyed smile.

I pull her into her bedroom, shut the door behind her, and look down at her, head tilted. I'm trying to get a feel for her, get a read on her face—which isn't that hard to do, actually—because it's all over her. She's gutted.

"Happen a lot?"

She glances away. Swallows. "Which part?"

I give her an exasperated look. "Fuck, Dais—pick one."

She lets out a staggered breath I don't think she means to. "Jules fights when he feels out of control."

I nod once. "Drunk?"

She shrugs, looking away.

"And Declan?"

She pauses. "What about him?"

"Is he like that with you a lot?"

"I mean…" She scratches her neck. "There's a quiet assumption among the boys that he's a tiny bit in love with me."

"Oh—" I give her a wide look. "Great." She rolls her eyes and I clear my throat. "Oi, just so I know what I'm up against—how many of these boys have you slept with?"

She lifts her eyebrows, surprised.

"We do jealous now, remember?" I remind her.

She scoffs, shakes her head a tiny bit, crosses her arms, sighs. "Declan and I slept together a long time ago—right after Romeo and I broke up and I was so angry at Julian. I was seventeen, he was twenty-four—" My head pulls back, surprised. "I lied—" She interjects. "I told him I was twenty-one. He believed me because—" She gestures to her chest, and I lick my bottom lip, waiting for her to keep going.

"That's how he started working for my brother." She shrugs. "And then TK."

I nod.

"And sort of Booker."

"Sort of?" I repeat, frowning.

"Do you want me to draw you a diagram?"

I give her an unimpressed look.

She squares her shoulders, looks defensive. "Is there a problem?"

Sort of, but I don't understand it.

This weird, tight feeling is suddenly in my chest, thinking about those fuckwits seeing her how I see her. Makes me feel off-kilter.

I slip my arms around her waist and pull her into me.

"No." I nudge her face up so she's looking at me, stare at her for a few seconds—hope she can see it in my eyes that I don't give a shit about it even though I do, but not in that way. In the way where I'm jealous and I don't fully understand what's happening in my head anymore, so I kiss her in a way that makes me feel like she's mine, just.

She slips her arms around my neck and her hand snags on that heart-tag necklace I never take off.

"You wear this every day." She lifts it up.

I nod.

"Where's it from?" She flips it over in her hand, staring at it. "Hemmes" engraved on it. "Tiffany's?" I shrug.

She nods once and her brows shifts a tiny bit and I guess I must know her pretty well these days because that one nod she does, it's all weighed down in jealousy and a question she's chewing on.

"Did Magnolia give it to you?" she asks after a quiet few seconds, and I wonder if she knows. About me and my dirty, fucked up secret?

But how would she? It's probably just because who the fuck else would give me a heart necklace from Tiffany's?

I nod, flash her a quick smile. "Yeah. She gave them to all of us." I look for her eyes because they aren't meeting mine anymore. "Do you like it?"

She still doesn't look up at me, but nods.

And I don't really think about what I do next, it sort of just happens. I take off my necklace, slip it over her head and onto her.

She stares up at me, blinking. "What are you doing?"

I shrug. "Yours now."

# 42

# Julian

"Come on—" I give my best friend a look. "It'll be fun."

"I don't know." Carmello scrunches his face up at me. Folds his arms over his chest, leans back into the chair opposite my desk. "What's in it for us?"

I blow some air out of my mouth.

"What?" I give him a look. "My friendship won't cut it?"

Romeo—lying down on that chaise his brother was bleeding all over a while ago, flicking through a *GQ*—looks up and over at me. "Yeah, right."

"What?" I frown.

"You're stealing two Klimts? What's that worth?" Carm asks.

"Street value, it's—" I start before getting cut off again.

"Nope." Rome shakes his head. "*Value* value."

I roll my eyes, that little shit. "About £70 m."

Carms scoffs.

"I'll give you £2 m," I say.

"A piece," Carmello tells me.

I roll my eyes but it's fair. Nod. Shake on it.

"Why do you need us anyway?" Carms asks. "Are you short on men?"

"Kind of—" I shrug. "I'm sending the cavalry to Paris."

"What for?" Rome frowns, and I give him a little look.

"TBC, man," I tell him and then I hear the door open, my sister chattering away. "Oi," I call to her.

She moseys on in, Christian behind her.

Romeo props himself up on his elbows, staring over at them— brows low.

"Hey, Rome," she says, looks a tiny bit nervous.

He nods his chin at her coolly.

"Where've you two been, then?" I ask, keen to keep it moving. I can feel the tension and I don't love it.

"Picked her up from school," Hemmes says before tossing an unimpressed look towards Rome.

"How was it?" I nod at her.

"Fine." She shrugs and steps further into the room. I can tell because I know my sister that she's hovering because of Romeo. Doesn't know how to function without his approval. Needs it, even if it's about her being with another guy. "What are you lot doing?" she asks, peering between us.

"Business." That's all I offer her. Rather keep her out of it.

"Right." She nods and Rome stares over at her, unflinching.

Daisy crosses her arms and Christian comes up behind her, slips his arms around my sister, chin on her head, knife in Rome's heart, and clocks me.

"How are the ribs?"

"A bit sore." I shrug. "My doctor's withholding my pain medicine."

My sister gives me a look. "Your doctor thinks you should learn your lesson and not cage-fight."

I give her a tight smile. "My doctor should mind her own business."

That's not how you get the drugs," Carmello whispers to me.

"This a thing, then?" Rome sits up, swings his legs around, and rises. His eyes flicker from my sister to Christian. "Officially?"

Carmelo and I trade looks, watch on a bit closely.

Daisy opens her mouth to speak but Christian cuts her off.

"Yep." He gives Rome a tight smile and tightens his grip on Daisy.

"Officially?" I blink over at them a bit amused—Daisy looks back at Christian.

"We've actually not had that conversation—" She looks at him, unsure.

And then there's this shit moment—Christian looks embarrassed, Daisy looks caught off guard, and Romeo and Carmelo are sniggering away. Me? I'm just enjoying the show, waiting for my sister to pop off how I know she's about to.

"What are you laughing at? Shut up," she snaps at the two brothers before she turns back to Christian, who has been frowning at her this whole time while he watched. "Are we official?"

He lets out a shallow laugh, his mouth pulls. "I mean, I'm not giving you a ring—"

"I don't want a ring." She shakes her head.

"Then yeah—" Christian shrugs, pushes some hair behind her ear. "We're official." He says "official" like it's a dumb word but I can see he's actually pretty stoked on all of this.

She stares at him a few seconds, all wide-eyed and shit, then she gives him the smallest smile, and I don't know how—maybe it's because I've known him all his life, but I can feel the crushing of Romeo next to me in real time. It's fucking bleak, and I know how he goes—I remember what he was like when Daisy wouldn't run away. He fucked his way through half the prep schools in Manhattan—his mother was livid. Delina begged me to fly out there, scare her boy straight—it didn't work. He didn't give a shit. For one, he blamed me for my part in it all—fair enough, as I was a massive instigator in the demise of their relationship. But if someone kept trying to kill your sister when she was out with her boyfriend, what would you do? How many attempted murders is too many? I'd say one, but three and you're having a fucking laugh, mate—my hands were tied.

Rome looks over at them, gives my sister a look I hate but I'll let slide considering the circumstances and that she just carved up his heart like a motherfucking pumpkin.

"I give you a month," he tells them.

"Oi," I grunt, a bit annoyed now. Daisy stares over at him, wounded.

"How about I give you a month to fuck off?" Christian stares over at him, moving Daisy behind him and I know what that means.

"Come on, then—" Romeo takes a step towards him.

"No." I point a finger threateningly at him and Daisy's yanking Christian's arm towards the door.

"Don't, just leave it," she tells him, flicking her eyes over at me, looking anxious.

Try not to look annoyed at her, try not to think about the implications of what it would look like if things really went south. It wouldn't just be my two best friends in a shit position if Romeo kept on with my sister, but their families. It would be trouble if they were at odds.

I flap my hand, telling Daisy to leave and Carmelo gives his little brother a shove. Utters under his breath, "*Sei un cretino*," then shakes his head. "You gonna start a fucking war because you're jealous?"

Romeo gives him an impetuous look. "Maybe."

Carms shakes his head. "Not on my watch."

# 43

# Christian

Full Box Set dinner but it's a weird vibe because Parks is with Tom in that weird way that they're together. Course she also nearly fucked BJ in a Gucci change room, that's what Jo said, anyway.

And here they're at dinner, properly like a couple, her and Beej holding hands and shit—maybe one level down from how they used to be, and I'm fucking pissed off about it. I don't know why—the whole thing makes me angry, mostly because I sort of think she's shit.

Doesn't bat an eyelid at me the whole dinner—and I don't need her to. Fuck, I don't even think I want her to anymore. It's kind of embarrassing that I love her, but I still do. That pulls a fucking number on me too, actually. I love Parks, I have for too long now—don't really like her anymore, though. And Daisy is all I think about. She's the one who I want to touch and spend all my time with. I like her, I like who she is—but I know I'm not in love with her because I'm been in love with Magnolia for years and it doesn't feel the same to me.

When BJ goes to settle the bill, it's the first look-in I get with her the whole fucking evening.

"Like that sweater—" She pokes me. "Virgin wool colour-block logo detail jumper. Off-white," she tells me, even though I didn't ask.

I give her an unimpressed flick of my eyebrows and I see it on her face, this rolling confusion about my indifference towards her and it gives me a little kick.

Parks gets on tiptoe and peers down the neck of my sweater. A frown appears like a fog over her. "Where's your necklace?"

Henry pulls a face, makes an awkward noise.

I shrug like I don't give a shit. "I gave it away—" And to be honest, I haven't thought about it since I did—except when I see Daisy wearing it and I think about how it's my name she's wearing.

"Sorry—what?" Magnolia blinks a few times. "You gave it away?"

I breathe out my nose, nodding.

She blinks twice. "To whom, might I ask?"

I run my tongue over my teeth. "Daisy."

And then her face falters like she can't compute it. "But... I gave it to you?"

I give her a tight smile. "And now I've given it to Daisy." Tack on a little shrug at the end there.

She huffs out her nose. "Why?"

I pull a face. "Because she liked it—"

"So you just gave it to her?"

"Yep."

"Have you no sentimentality?" She stomps her little foot.

Shrug with my mouth mostly. "Not with you."

Her head pulls back and she takes a little staggered breath, all wounded and shit. Stares over at me with this confused frown like I've just smacked her or something and then BJ walks up behind her.

"Hey." Beej looks for her eyes and she interlocks her hands with his, puts her arm around her like the shield he'll always be to her. "What's going on?"

She shakes her head. "Nothing."

BJ frowns looking from her over to me, back to her. "You look upset."

He eyes me down. Parks shakes her head.

"Christian's just in a pricky mood."

Beej gives me a dark look. "Why—what'd he do?"

She crosses her arms over her chest, gives me a look. "He gave the necklace I gave you all away." She pouts and I roll my eyes because it's not fair. She doesn't play fair. He'll always take her side, he can't not. She could have said, 'He won't give me his right lung' and BJ would still think I'm a prick.

"The heart one?" he asks her, then looks over at me. "With your name on it?"

She nods, eyes big as a puppy, and BJ gives me a scowl. "Why?"

I nod my chin at Magnolia. "Ey, where's Tom tonight, Parks?"

"What was that—?" BJ points a finger in my face and I shake my head at him.

"You're a fucking idiot, Beej."

"Swing that one by me again, big man—" He eyes me down and I give him a look then sigh at them both. Walk the fuck out. I can't be bothered.

Henry jogs after me, grabs my arm, pulls me to a stop then gives me a look.

"Bro, what the fuck are you doing?"

I scoff. "Shouldn't you be asking your little best friend that?"

"No," he tells me, jaw set. "I know what she's doing. She's flailing—" He points back in the direction of her. "She's doing what she always does when she feels unstable in a relationship with someone she loves, and she's pandering for your attention and you're fucking eating it up—"

I give him a look. "Am not."

"Bullshit." He shakes his head at me.

"I'm not!" I insist, but maybe I am a bit.

Henry gives me this look. "Just stop, Chris."

"Stop what?" I ask, eyebrows up but I think I know.

Henry gives me this long look that makes me feel like an arsehole because Henry gives good long looks.

"You're happy that she's sad," he tells me.

"No, I'm not." I scowl at him. "I don't give a shit."

"Yeah, you do." He grabs my shoulders and stares at me. "I can see it and it's fucked up, Christian. And it doesn't mean what you think it means."

I jut my jaw. "And what do I think it means, then?"

Henry licks his bottom lip, like he's sad for me or something. "That she still wants you—" I scoff again but he ignores me. "And she doesn't, man. She's only ever wanted him."

"Fuck you." I give him a little shove. "I don't want her to want me." And I reckon that much is probably almost true. I don't want her to want me how I did before—I don't daydream about her like I did before—but there is something validating about her pandering for my attention and I fucking hate that he sees through my shit. Because it's shit, I know it is. I'm shit.

"Good." Henry shrugs a bit haphazardly. "I hope to God that's true because Daisy is shitballs out of your league—"

I glance over at him.

He gives me a look. "And you better not fuck it up."

# 44

# Julian

I've tried it a bunch of different ways at this point, I really have. Turned this plan inside out and upside down—I'm spending millions to get this fucking job over the line—and I hate to say it, but I need her.

"Daisy," I call for her.

Nothing.

No answer.

The Lost Boys all shift in the place, a bit amused at the indifference my sister shows towards me.

"Daisy!" I yell louder.

Carmelo and Rome exchange looks.

About thirty seconds later, she appears in the doorway wearing a big, black hoodie that isn't hers and it isn't mine—pants may or may not be accounted for—and about five seconds later, Christian appears behind her.

Romeo makes an audible noise of displeasure and Daisy flicks her eyes over to him, but I ignore it.

"What?" She folds her arms over her chest.

I sigh and then squint up at her.

"I need you to come on a job," I tell her and I know what comes next: her face lights the fuck up.

"Really?" She beams.

I roll my eyes. "Really."

She claps excitedly, but Christian's frowning away behind her. Dais lets out an excited little squeal and scurries over to the dining room table to get a look at the plans.

"You barely ever let me come on jobs despite the fact that everyone knows I'm the most skilled member of your team," she announces to a chorus of: "Oy!", "Ay—", "Woah, hey—" and "Easy on." I give her a look.

"You're not on my team." I cross my arms as I stand up.

"Well—" My sister gives me a pointed look. "Firstly, that's no way to boost morale, Julian—and honestly you're smart to be bringing me on now when you are because knowing you, you'll ju—"

"Wait." Christian interrupts, shaking his head staring over at me. "Tell me you're joking."

I lift an eyebrow. "You talking to me?"

"Yep." He nods once, unflinching. "You're going to let her go on one of your jobs? You?"

He nods his chin at me. "You, who won't let her walk around the corner to grab a fucking litre of milk without a bodyguard?"

I scoff, amused. "You think I'd do anything to put her in danger?"

"Well, I didn't." He shrugs. "But clearly I was wrong—"

Declan stands. "You better watch that tone, man."

Christian tosses him a look. "Do you think?" He looks back at me. "I think it's fitting…" And I can tell my boys all think I'm about to rip him limb from limb, but I'm not because I like him. Anyone who likes my sister enough to be this riled up about her safety is pretty good in my books.

"Alright." I shrug. "You come too then."

Christian points at himself. "Me?"

"No," Declan groans.

I give him a sharp look. "What was that, Decks?" He pipes down and I look over at Christian. "I'll give you £2M for it."

He shakes his head and Daisy frowns over at him.

"I don't need your money," he says as he pulls Dais back into himself, wraps his arms around her. Both Romeo and Declan shift their gaze from her and I reckon I can smell trouble on the horizon, but I don't have time to deal with it right now.

"But yeah." He kisses the back of her head. "I'm in."

I shrug. "That's good enough for me."

# 45

# Daisy

It's an in-and-out job, Vienna, but it's a large-scale plan.

We've sent our men, all of them, them to Paris.

Interpol have had ears to the ground too much lately, they're too tuned in for my brother's liking, so he went big.

Anonymously funded a charity gala for the children's department of Hôpital Necker, which is being held at the Louvre, thanks to the help of Soleil. Interpol thinks we're going to rob the place. To make it look like we are—we're sending in all the boys. The Old Boys, the Silicon Baddies and all the underlings and the footmen. Little do Interpol know that the sizeable donation for the children is a red herring.

The Belvedere Museum also has a gala, which I'm attending with Christian, to purchase a painting for my brother's upcoming thirtieth birthday.[235] This is the only part of the plan you need to know right now—and we're already off to a rollicking start.

The tensions are high. Rome is annoyed that Christian's coming and Christian's annoyed that Romeo's coming, and my brother doesn't give a shit about any of it, that much is made apparent, when he flings Romeo a Kevlar corset that's made custom for me.

"Fit her," he tells him.

Romeo nods and I stand, slipping out of my trackpants only for a few seconds before Christian's up on his feet, horrified and standing in front of me, snatching the corset from Rome.

"I'll fucking do it—"

Rome snatches it back. "I'm good, mate."

I roll my eyes.

Christian grabs it back. "I'm sure you are, bro—I'm still gonna do it."

---

[235] October 30th.

246

"What if you fit it wrong and she dies?" Miguel interjects, a bit bored from the other side of the room. Our eyes catch and I roll mine, because he's just being a pain.

"Pretty shit way to break up..." Carmelo interjects.

"Why am I getting shot at?" I frown.

"I don't know, pain in the arse." My brother shrugs. "Maybe because you're in a chaotic love triangle with two baby gang lords?"[236]

"Why'd you put 'baby' in front of that, then, ey?" Romeo mutters at the same time Christian's shaking his head. "Felt disrespectful—bit unnecessary—"

I roll my eyes and speak over them. "There's no love triangle."

"No," Miguel pipes up again. "Probably more of a love square once you factor in that police officer."[237,238]

Rome snatches the corset back from Christian. "Let's not factor him in—" He shakes his head as he holds it up for me to slip into.

Christian shakes his head, and he's genuinely upset, I can tell—Rome touching me, watching Christian as he does it—not saying a word, antagonising him all the same.

I give Christian a look. "There's no triangle."

Romeo's eyes weigh heavy on me[239] and I ignore them all the more as he puts one hand on my back and with the other tightens the laces.

"Snug as a bug," he gives me a little smile that makes me feel a little sad.

Christian grabs my hand and pulls me over towards him, putting his arms around me, staring over at my ex-boyfriend.

Julian glances between them. "You know, next time you could just like take a piss on her. That'd be quicker than this shit."

"I'm not really into that." I shake my head as I pull up my skirt.[240]

Christian stares at me for a few seconds, pushes some hair behind my ears, and I feel self-conscious that Romeo and Julian are seeing him watch me like that, because how he's watching me makes me

---

[236] Mean.

[237] "Maybe even a love pentagon if you count for Decks." Carmelo scratches his chin.

[238] We shan't.

[239] Because maybe there is a triangle, and maybe the corner of it is stabbing him.

[240] I had our seamstress alter the embroidered fishnet hi-low gown from Marchesa into a big, beautiful skirt that matches with the corset flawlessly.

wonder if maybe he loves me back and them seeing it makes it feel like it's somehow probably less true.

"Alright, love birds." My brother gives me a look then nods his head at the door. "You two have a plane to catch."

Vienna is just a two-hour flight from London, and as per the plan, Christian and I take the Hemmes's jet. Rest assured, Christian and I make use of the alone time in the ways that we always have,[241] but now it feels different and I can't tell whether it's in my head or it just really is different now. Like he holds me different, lingers longer.

"What?" I frown, cheeks a bit flushed from what we were just doing. He shifts himself so he's on top of me, props himself up on his elbow, covers his own eyes and reaches out to touch my face. The corner of my top-right lip, to be precise. Then he moves up a little, taps about halfway between my eye and my mouth. Then down to my chin, the centre. Then over to my other cheek, just above my mouth.

I blink a few times as he uncovers his eyes.

"I know your freckles too," he tells me.


The Belvedere[242] is one of my favourite museums on the world because it's just so beautiful itself. The collection aside, it's a marvel, and the collection shouldn't be aside because it's spectacular too.

But the palace was built as the summer residence for Prince Eugene of Savoy in the early 18th century.[243]

I've never been to a museum with Christian before but I love the feeling of it, walking in there with him—two things I love under one roof.

He's in a black wool tuxedo from Tom Ford, white collared shirt, no bow or tie, buttons a bit less done up than you'd think they should be, rosary beads underneath. He looks the sort of handsome where every girl in the place is staring at him, and I feel a bit bubbly that it's my hand he's holding.

"The Evil Mothers," Christian says, staring at the piece by Giovanni Segantini.[244] "This one's kind of fucked up."

---

[241] Albeit some access was restricted on account of the aforementioned corset.

[242] Technically, Österreichische Galerie Belvedere.

[243] By Baroque architect Johann Lucas von Hildebrandt.

[244] Also known as "*Le lussuriose ; L'infanticide*". 1894. 120cm x 225 cm, oil on canvas.

"Yes." I nod. "Evil mothers often are."

Christian gives me a look then kisses my cheek, pulling me through to the next room. That's where I spot him from across the way and our eyes catch. I turn my head, tap the almost invisible comm in my ear, and whisper without moving my mouth.

"Plan C is a go."

"Oh, fuck." Christian rolls his eyes as Tiller approaches us with a stiff smile.[245]

"Dais." He nods his head at me then tosses a look to Christian. "Hemmes."

"Fancy seeing you here, mate—" Christian eyes him. "Didn't real-ise you were taking your stalking of my girlfriend international?"

Tiller gives me a tall look. "Girlfriend?"[246]

I tilt my head, not taking the bait. "What are you doing here, Tils?"

And then he shakes his head. "That's not the question, Dais."

"Oh, yeah?" I blink. "What is then?"

"What are you and your internationally known art thief of a brother doing here?"

"What are you talking about?" I frown at him. "Julian's not here—"

Tiller rolls his eyes. "Yes, he is."

"No, he's not." Christian shakes his head with a frown. "We came by ourselves."

Tiller frowns a bit.

"It's his thirtieth soon." I eye Tiller. "I was going to try to convince them to let me buy *The Cook*."[247]

He looks confused and I give him an unimpressed look.

"Le Père Paul?" Still nothing. "Monet?"

Tiller shakes his head.

"Don't you work for the SOECC?" Christian frowns at him.

"Yes." I nod. "In the Art and Antiques Unit, no less." I glare over at Tiller. "How embarrassing."

"Your brother is here," Tiller says, ignoring us. "Just saw him."

---

[245] And yes, he does look very handsome in that navy suit.

[246] And I think I see a whisper of jealousy.

[247] Also known as *Portrait of Père Paul* by Claude Monet. 64.5 cm x 52.1 cm. Oil on canvas.

"Here?" I blink, pretending to be confused.[248]

Tiller nods right as my brother rounds the corner.

"What the fuck?" Julian says on cue. "What the fuck are you two doing here?"

"What the fuck are you doing here?" I ask, putting my hands on my hips.

"I'm just having a gander." My brother frowns then looks around. "Where's Miguel?"[249]

I point off to him in the corner. Julian gives him a little wave, before he nods his chin at me. "What's your story?"

"I'm not telling you what I'm here for," I tell my brother proudly.

"Oh." He nods. "So you're here for my birthday."

I frown, then look past him, give Carmelo a smile. Ignore his brother.

"Face—" Rome eyes me up and down with a smirk that immediately irks Christian and Tiller both.[250]

Christian lets out a little groan and pulls me back into him. "What the fuck are you doing here?"

Romeo gives him a look. "I could ask you the same question—"

"Where are the boys?" I look around.

Julian squints a little playfully. "Paris."

"But you're not in Paris." Tiller watches him closely.

"I don't need to be." My brother smiles smugly.

"This is nice." Rome nods over at me, gesturing to my corset, sort of grazing his hands on me as he does. Christian smacks him away, instantly fuming.

"Fuck off—"

Rome pulls back, smiling in a bad way. "Touch me again—"

And Christian, he's so measured normally, stoic and calm and all of that instantly goes out the window as he shoves Rome backwards. Hard.

Romeo chuckles and pushes him back.

Christian throws the first punch, Rome gets one in after—Julian rolls his eyes. I run towards them, grabbing Christian's arm, pulling

---

[248] I'm good at pretending.

[249] Who, by the way, did not enjoy the flight over as much as I did. Haha. And also sorry, Miguel.

[250] And I pray to God neither of them notice.

him away. It all happens so quickly, but he elbows me out of the way—right in the face, splits my lip open—

And there's this strange sort of echo gasp from everyone watching us. Christian turns around—he looks devastated more than anything—and reaches for me at the same time Romeo does and I smack Christian's hands away. I don't meet his eyes but shake my head at them both as I back away to have a minute. Tiller jogs over, head tilted, staring at my mouth.

"Are you okay?" He offers me a handkerchief.

I glare up at him. "It was an accident."

"I know." He nods then shrugs. "It's what happens when you date children."

"He's twenty-three." I give Tiller a look and he rolls his eyes.

"Is he allowed to stay out past ten?"

I give him another look and he steps towards me, tilts my chin up with his hand so he can see me more in the light. Takes the handkerchief back, dabs it on my mouth himself.[251] He's closer than he needs to be. We've never been this close before. I like how he smells.

He smells good. And I mean that like "good" the noun. Clean, like water. Fresh and light.

"What are you wearing?" I ask without thinking.

He dabs my mouth again. "What do you mean?"

"What do you smell like?"

He glances up at me, clearly pleased with the question. He swallows, looks back at my mouth, and licks his bottom lip.

"You're okay," he tells me. "You don't need a stitch."

"Thank you." I roll my eyes. "I am a med student."

He stares at me a beat longer than he should—especially with my brother, my boyfriend and my ex-boyfriend all watching on.

"You have a good mouth," he tells me like he shouldn't, holding my eyes for too long too. And that's when it happens.

Rapid-fire gunshots.

Screaming ensues from everyone around us and about ten masked men round the corner.

All in black, head to toe. Balaclavas.

"Alright," says an Irish accent. "This, ladies and gentleman, is a hold-up."

---

[251] He's being quite gentlemanly, actually.

He aims his semi-automatic[252] at one of the guards and then shoots him dead on the spot.

Then he swings around, finds another guard whose arms are already in the air, and shoots him dead too.

More screaming.

I freeze. Stare over at my brother, who does nothing but stare back.

Tiller's hand moves slowly towards his gun.[253]

"No," I tell him, shaking my head.

He eyes me, instantly suspicious, and I feel his judgement on me and I hate it. "Do you know who they are?" he whispers.

"No," I whisper back, glaring. And it's true.

"Now, if you don't mind—we'll have you all up against the walls—" They start aiming their guns at the people. "Come on, everyone up against the walls, that's it—face in. Just, like that—good—"

Christian's staring over at me from the other side of the wall, his chest is heaving, eyes heavy—and then he darts over towards me—one of the balaclava men swings around, gun on Christian.[254]

"Where the fuck do you think you're going?"

Christian raises his arms, but keeps on moving towards me. "Just over here to my girlfriend…"

"Aw." Another chimes in, a gun on each of us now. "How sweet. Isn't she pretty?" Christian glares at him. "You feel like dying for a pretty thing today?"

"Any day." Christian blinks, unphased, but I stare over at my brother, wide-eyed and panicked. Julian just barely shakes his head.

"That could be arranged." The man points the gun at Christian's head.

"Do you know who I am?" Christian asks calmly.

The gunman shrugs. "Don't care."[255]

"You might care about who I am, though." I step in front of Christian.[256]

The man glances over at me, annoyed. I don't like his eyes. All I

---

[252] Heckler & Koch SL8. .223 Remington caliber. 10 mag. capacity.

[253] Obviously a Glock 19 because what else would he use? 9 x 19 mm caliber. 17 mag. capacity.

[254] And my heart flies to my throat.

[255] So he does.

[256] Who tries to pull me back behind him but I shake him off.

can see of him, really, is those eyes of his. They're too blue, light blue, and his pupils are too small. It's a tacit threat on my behalf because anyone who's anyone knows that the only person in England who's more dangerous than Julian is me on a bad day. I have the weight and backing of my brother's entire empire fully behind me and about half of his restraint.

In the background, the other men are tearing pieces off the wall. First the Judith and the Holofernes, and then *Adam and Eve.* They take a Waldmüller,[257] and the way they're handling them—God, I could throw up. They're so rough. So indelicate with these pieces of history painted and frozen and invaluable in a way where people who don't get art won't get it, but I do, and my brother does, and it feels a bit like torture. Everything is so loud and so chaotic, and half the men are shoving the people up against the wall, dragging their guns over the back of their heads, and the others are going for a fourth painting—but there's one straggler who hones in on Tiller, pointing at him.

"You're a cop." He eyes Tiller and I get a sick feeling in my stomach. "Aren't you?"

Tiller doesn't say anything.

"A detective," the man thinks to himself, which must mean they run in our circles. Tiller stiffens up a little and his breathing shifts. It's getting faster. I'm feeling nauseous and my brother's brows are low—none of this was part of the plan.[258]

"Actually—" The man cocks the trigger. "You're a dead man."

And then what happens next—it's not even really conscious, it sort of just happens—I smack the man's arm away and he misfires, hitting the wall behind him, and I'm fast, I'm trained now to be fast, so before Tiller or the gunman realise it, I've reached behind Tiller, grabbed his Glock and shot the man trying to shoot him.

He falls down dead.[259]

There's this awful silence for a second where Tiller's staring at me in disbelief and I'm staring at the guy I killed—the way he's fallen, his

---

[257] Early spring in the Vienna Woods (or Violet pickers in the Vienna Woods) by Ferdinand Georg Waldmüller. 1861. 52 x 66 cm. Oil on wood.

[258] I can tell that much from Julian's face.

[259] So if we're keeping track, that's three people I've killed now. And we probably should be keeping track of things like that.

wrist exposed now when it wasn't before. A tattoo.[260] And I recognise it immediately and I know instantly what's happened here. I glare over at my brother who's staring over at me, eyes wide and caught.

The balaclava man who appears to be in charge swings around, completely furious, and points his gun at me. A chain reaction follows.

Julian pulls out his guns,[261] double-fisting now, then Romeo after him[262]—eyes wild, because he's hardwired to protect me. Miguel has a gun[263] and a knife,[264] Carmelo's next,[265] and then beside me, Christian me pulls out two[266]—and suddenly, this seemingly ragtag group of disorganised art thieves are staring down the barrel of a gang war.

I shift my gun,[267] pointing it at the man who's pointing his at me, terribly unafraid because I know he's got no moves.

He's staring at me, his eyes are slits, and he's furious. Men like him don't like having their power taken away from them in general, let alone by someone I think they'd themselves deem as a little girl. And while I might be little and I am a girl, he knows as well as I do that I am, to him, entirely untouchable, even though it appears[268] I've just shot his brother. I feel bad for a moment, I don't like killing people, it's why I became a doctor, but I didn't even think of it, I just did it. It didn't seem fair, killing Tiller like that for nothing. That's not what they're here for. No one was supposed to die.[269]

"I think you've got what you came for," I tell him, cocking the gun again.

He stares at me. "This isn't over."

---

[260] The Celtic snake.

[261] Heckler & Kosh. VP9L OR. 9 x 19 mm calibre. 20 mag. capacity.

[262] Left hand: Beretta Px4 Storm Carry. 9 x 19 mm calibre. 17 mag. capacity.
Right hand: Beretta 92X Performance. 9 mm calibre. 15 mag. capacity.

[263] Heckler & Kosh. HK45 Compact Tactical. .45 ACP calibre. 10 mag. capacity.

[264] Cold Steel Recon 1 Spear point knife. 5.5-inch blade.

[265] Beretta Manurhin MR73 Sport. .38SPL/.357MAG calibre. 6 mag. capacity.

[266] 2 x Sig Sauer P229 Legion Compact Pistols. 9 mm Luger. 10 mag. capacity.

[267] Which is technically Tiller's gun, and I really hate Glocks. You know me, I'd much prefer something lighter and more well balanced in the hand, like the Springfield Armory EMP4 pistol (9 mm).

[268] Judging from their shared strangely light blue eyes…

[269] And if they were, Julian's about to cop an earful.

I blink at him a few times, indifferent. "If you say so." I give him a careless shrug.

He whistles and all the balaclava men begin to retreat—paintings in hand, guns still on us as they back out the doors they came through.

Tiller's staring over at me, and I can't look at him because it feels dangerous to do it, so I just stare at my brother—jaw tight, shaking his head—and he won't look at me, which is a bad sign. He looks over at Christian, nodding his head towards me.

Christian grabs me and pulls me towards the fire escape, and I catch Tiller's eyes as he does, and he's frowning, watching after me and I say nothing and he says nothing but his eyes say thank you.

# 46

# Julian

A fucking clusterfuck, that's what that was.

I hate having my sister on jobs because she's too fucking emotional and it instantly makes everything more substantially dangerous. The only reason she was there at all was because I had a feeling Tiller would be and he has such a fucking hard-on for her that I knew she'd distract him if he showed.

We get into the car that's waiting for us by the fire escape. I practically toss Daisy into it because I'm so angry at her. Christian gives me a shove, that ballsy little fuck, as he moves past me, pulling her onto his lap.

He runs his thumb over her lip where he elbowed her—part of the plan too—the run-in, the fight—all of it was a part of it.

"You okay?" He frowns.

She nods, touching his face quickly before she stares over at me. "What the fuck—"

I stare over at her wildly. "Was about to say the same thing to you—"

She glares over at me, looking angrier by the second. "You hired Roisin MacMathan's men?"

Shit. Didn't know she knew about that. The MacMathans are on Daisy's no-fly zone list.

I roll my eyes and give her a tiny shrug. "It was a last-minute plan—"

"We don't work with them!" she yells at me. "Julian—she's a trafficker!"

"I know." I shake my head. I know she's not going to drop it, I can see it when my sister goes like this, like a dog with a bone. I've broken her rules and now she's pissed. "I just needed someone convincing to pull it off—someone they wouldn't trace back to me."

She's shaking her head, mumbling under her breath. "I can't believe you—"

I stare over at her, annoyed. "How'd you even know?"

"He had the Celtic snake on his wrist." She sighs, looking out the window.

The MacMathan family symbol.

"And you killed him, Daisy—fuck." I shake my head at her. "It's going to be such a fucking headache."

"He was going to kill Tiller!" she tells me, eyes wide and horrified. It's in that moment that I work out that Tiller isn't necessarily the only one here with a crush. Fuck me sideways, girls are headaches, aren't they? How many lads does she need up her sleeve?

"So what?" Rome shrugs, looking over at Daisy. "He's a fucking cop—"

She stares over at Rome, eyes all wide. "So he should die?"

"Yes," Rome says, jaw tight, mostly just to piss her off because I reckon he knows what I know too.

My sister shifts on Christian's lap, him putting his arms around her, using them a bit unconsciously as shields.

He kisses the back of her head mindlessly and it's all a fucking mess—I can see it unravelling now. Rome still loves her, Christian's falling in love with her, and don't even get me fucking started on Tiller—

Girls, you want to make sure someone falls for you hard and fast? Pull out a Gen4 G19 and save his fucking life, you'll never be rid of him.

I rub my temples, blow air out of my mouth.

Christian catches my eye, looking stressed. "Is she in trouble?"

I push my hands through my hair, shaking my head.

Maybe? That's the real answer. The MacMathans are as reactive as Daisy. Roisin gives her boys a long leash, and I can't say for certain, but I reckon that the one Daisy shot dead was Cian Gilpatrick's brother Darragh. For context, that would be like someone shooting Declan's brother.

"Nah—" I shake my head, and Miguel catches my eye. He knows.

"Bullshit she's not," Romeo says, shaking his head. He glares over at her then switches his focus to me. "Why the fuck did you bring her? She's a fucking liability, she's too emotional—"

Daisy looks both hurt and confused. Hurt, I reckon, because he's being callous about her in front of her and she wears his opinion of her like a hat on her head whether she wants to or not, and then confused because she cannot, for the life of her, comprehend how people can ever be capricious about life. "They were going to kill him for no reason!"

"Who gives a shit?" Rome shakes his head at her.

"Me!" She shrugs in a hopeless kind of way. "We are not like that, that's not what we do—we don't just let people die for no reason. That's disgusting—"

Rome gives her a look. "You're such a fucking idiot—"

"You might want to watch that tone, man." Christian eyes him.

Romeo gives him a measured look. "Nah, I think it's fitting."

Daisy shifts again, leaning more into Christian, who adjusts his arms around her.

"You did the right thing," he tells her quietly. "If you didn't do it, I would have."

And I kind of get it, in this new light, why she's so mad on him. They're kind of the same. She's worse, but neither of them want to be here, neither of them like what our families are—but you adapt, that's human instinct. It's what we do to survive—so they adapted, made what we all are work for them. But deep down they quietly resent it still all the same. And then it occurs to me that they might be a more dangerous combination than her and Rome. Romeo loves what we are and what we do, he's proud of it, who would die for honour and loyalty any day of the week; the idea of him and Daisy always made me uneasy. Because Face, who, for all intents and purposes, she's my kid, I raised Daisy, she's like me. Impulsive and all instinct, but unlike me, she's completely emotionally driven. I'm innately reactive, but I've learnt control—I've had to.

She's never had to. She lives in the padded castle I built for her, this cushy void, no consequence or reaction for any decision she's ever made because I shoulder it all, and I'll shoulder this one too.

Press my hand into my mouth, pull out my phone, text Kekoa.

> Daisy shot a MacMathan

> Tell me you're joking.

> I think we're in some hot water

No shit

heading back now.

Daisy looks over at me, and she looks a bit nervous—hate it when she looks nervous, can't not see her as that eight-year-old on the beach watching her parents die.

"It's fine, Dais." I give her a smile. "I'll sort it."

# 47

# Daisy

About a week passes and I'm sort of just holed up at home for all of it. Julian's more worried about what I did than he's saying, I can tell.

Would I have done it if I had known the man I was shooting was a MacMathan? I want to say no, but honestly, I didn't even think about it—I just shot him. I don't know what Tiller is to me,[270] but maybe now that I am, I guess he is something… I don't think he's my friend, I don't think we're allowed to be friends, but then I don't know what else I'd call him. Whatever he is, I didn't want him dead.

Christian's a bit on edge too, the corners of his smile seem laced with a concern for me that once upon a time I thought was in my head, just something I hoped was there but wasn't really, and now I'm waking up face to face with him every day and slowly wrapping my head around the idea that he actually seems to want me back.[271]

Wanting me back comes at a cost for him, though, because I'm under unofficial house arrest. No one's said I can't go anywhere, but no one's really letting me go anyway. Just university, and even then I've got Miguel and Happy and sometimes Kekoa too.[272] Christian walks me to class. I think he's trying to make it less weird, but it is weird, because he's there once class is done too, and I'd say I don't know what they think is going to happen, but I suspect that we all know exactly what they think is going to happen.

People in our world are big on retribution. They think the MacMathans are going to come for me with a vengeance.

Personally, I think they're overreacting because it's not like I killed Roisin herself, I didn't even kill her brother. I killed maybe her 3IC's

---

[270] I guess I've never really thought about it before in a coherent, conscious way.

[271] Eee!

[272] Three! Three of them! Who do they think I am, Obama?

260

brother, and in my defence, he went very off-script from the job he was hired for.

Also, I would be remiss not to mention that killing me would create absolute bedlam. The entire underworld would fall into pandemonium and my brother would never stop[273] if something happened to me. It'd be pure carnage.

So I don't think I'm a dead man walking, I doubt that anyone thinks that 3IC random's brother is worth all the crime families of the EU descending into utter chaos.

Anyway, it's a big night at one of Christian's venues, and no one tells me not to go, but he sort of shrugs it off. There's a bit of a like "I don't even want to be there, I'll nip in for a minute, be in and out, I'll come straight back, honestly not even worth you getting dressed for" kind of feeling about it. There was once a time where him saying that would have spiralled me into a state where I'd be deeply convinced that he was just trying to hook up with other girls, and now I think it's because he's worried about me and having him worry about me is[274] one of my favourite feelings. It's indicative of how he cares about me, and that's still not not novel yet.

He's not gone for too long before the doorbell rings.

I don't answer it because I don't want Kekoa having a nervous breakdown, so I just ignore it and keep playing Tomb Raider on my brother's Xbox in one of the downstairs living rooms. Someone clears their throat by the door and I look back.

Killian Tiller in the flesh, in the doorframe.

I stare over at him, baffled. "You're inside my house."

I sit up straighter.

He tilts his head.[275] "You didn't come to the door."

I roll my eyes, tossing the controller down and walking over to him. "Yes, well apparently the MacMathan clan are trying to kill me now, so—" I give him a suspicious look. "Who let you in?"

"Your friend that follows you everywhere—" He cocks his head back towards Miguel, who's definitely just outside the door.

"It's very ballsy of you coming in here." I give him a look.

---

[273] I think sometimes that I am his tether to not go too far.

[274] Sorry, Christian.

[275] He looks sort of shy.

261

He sighs, frowning as he crosses his arms over his chest. "You saved me."

"I guess." I roll my eyes dismissively. "A bit."

He licks his lips. "Why?"

I scoff and roll my eyes. "What do you mean why?" I shake my head at him, feelings a bit hurt. "Do you think I'd let you die?"

He scratches the back of his neck, shrugging. "Maybe."

I cross my arms over my chest, feeling cross and huffy. "Well, then you don't really know me at all."

His face softens a little. "Less than I thought I did, I guess." I glare across at him and he tilts his head, swallows. "Sorry—" He lifts his brows and gives me a quarter of a smile. "And thank you."

# 48

# Daisy

"Change of plans," Christian tells me as soon as I get in his car.

I frown, pressing the necklace he gave me into myself. I'll probably never take it off.

"We're meeting my mum[276] and brother at the Berkeley." He gives me a big, apologetic grin.

"What?" I blink. "No—"

He reaches across me and clips my seatbelt. "Yep."

"No, I'm not dressed for that."[277]

He glances at me as he pulls out of the Compound. "You look good."

"I'm in a denim dress[278] and rubber boots!"[279]

"Yeah—cute as a fucking button, Baby." He gives me a big smile, trying to win me over.

I give him a look. "Not for the Berkeley."

He shrugs. "We're just going to the beach huts. You're fine."

"This isn't mother-meeting attire…" I glance down at myself, my cheeks on fire. "Turn around."

"Nope—" He shakes his head. "Can't be late. Besides, I'm in jeans."[280]

---

[276] Oh, God.

[277] I'm not fishing either, I'm really not. I'd probably have spent a week trying to work out the perfect outfit to wear to meet his mother. If I were desperate enough I might have even contacted Magnolia ruddy Parks for a word of advice…

[278] Sur sweetheart-neck denim mini dress by Staud.

[279] Betty logo-embossed rubber boots by Chloé. Black.

[280] Which is true, he is. But hardly the same thing because Christian Hemmes could wear a garbage bag for a shirt and he'd still look like a motherfucking angel.

I breathe out my nose, glance over at him, annoyed. "What happened to our lunch at Annabel's?"

"Hijacked."

"I can see that," I say, my chin in my hand, staring out the window.

"My mum wants to meet you." He shrugs.

"Why?"[281]

"Because I never come home anymore, apparently—" He gives me an amused look. "I don't know why that's suddenly an issue. Haven't lived at home in about six years."

"Anyway, I've met her." I cross my arms over my chest.[282]

"Yeah, well—" He shrugs. "That was different."[283]

"How?" I ask. I'm petulant now because mothers make me this way.

He gives me a look because I know how, and it makes me feel happy that he answers that with a look because answering with a look, that's the sort of thing couples do...

Mothers make me nervous. Not just his, all but Delina, not just "even my own", but especially my own. I think it was her utter indifference for me. I could get past her obsession with my brother pretty easily, because I get it—Julian is a force to be reckoned with and there's something about him, even when he was a kid, where you just wanted his approval.[284] My mum, I don't know, it's hard to land in a completely coherent way because all the ways that I knew her, I knew her through the lens of a child. She died on that beach before I got to have a look at her with adult eyes, but were I a betting woman—if I knew her at all the way you're supposed to a mother—I think I'd find that her mother was probably mean to her too.[285]

Mum never had friends around, I don't remember any women around me growing up. That might be a bit because crime

---

[281] I'm terrified.

[282] I'm nervous sweating already.

[283] In about a million ways. For one, I was a child.

[284] Everyone does, it's why he is who he is and why we are who we are. My dad was good at what he did, but Julian is better without even trying to be better. There's a natural lean in with him that you see only every now and then, like a once-in-a-lifetime sort of leader. He'd probably win if he ran for PM, actually.

[285] But then, I've never met my maternal grandmother. I don't know anything about my mother's side of the family.

organisations are largely run by men, but she didn't seem to have girlfriends, and I didn't know that was weird until I met Jack's Aunty Eileen and she was so, so funny and so zany, and when we left her Boxing Day party I said something to Jack about how she didn't really look like his mum, and he said, "Oh, we're not actually related, she's just one of those people I grew up around. Like an aunty, you know?"

But I didn't know.

Santino would come to my soccer games with my dad. Happy and Smokeshow would come to my dance recitals. Koa would come to my parent–teacher interviews when my brother couldn't. I was raised by a village, but the village was made of men.[286]

I breathe out my nose and look out my window.

Christian reaches over and squeezes my knee. "You look nervous."

I purse my lips. "Historically I don't fare too well with mothers…"

He glances at me while keeping an eye on the road. "I thought Delina loved you?"

"She does." I sigh. "I meant mine."

"Oh. Hah." He sniffs, amused. "Well, that's just one mother…"

I give him a look. "Arguably the most important one, no?"[287]

I push my hand through my hair, look back out the window, chin in hand.

"So, what was she like, then?" He asks as he slips his hand into mine. "I know I would have met her, I just can't remember her."

I pick at my finger. "Um. Selfish… Self-involved… Vapid, cold—" I flash him a smile. "Not overly fond of me, as it would turn out."

Christian shakes his head as he frowns. "That's in your head, Dais."

I give him a tiny smile. "It's not."

He licks his bottom lip and I can tell he doesn't get it the way where people who have parents who want them just can't possibly fathom a world where a parent could ever harbour a spectacular apathy towards their own offspring.

"It's not possible to not be fond of you," he tells me as he pulls over to the side of the road.

I glance around—we're not at the Berkeley yet. He's taken the back way. We're near Cadogan Place Park.[288]

---

[286] Except for Delina Bambrilla, my bright and shining female-star.

[287] Yes.

[288] A long-cut if I've ever seen one.

265

"What are you doing?" I frown.

"Talking to you—" He faces me, crossing his arms over his chest. "Talk."

"You're not going to get it—" I give him an apologetic smile. "It doesn't matter—"

"I won't get it?" He blinks.

"Your parents like you," I tell him and he blinks at me a few times.

"After my sister died, my dad left."

That's not right. I frown. "What?"

"He's technically there—" His head rolls. "They're still technically together, my parents—he's checked out, though. When Rem died, he died. He lost her, and then he gave up on us—" Christian shrugs, but his eyes look heavy. "So, go on, tell me what I won't understand..."

I flash him an apologetic smile, wonder how it is that the more you know about a person the more you can love them.

"It was my dad—" I purse my lips. "He wanted another kid. She didn't. He pushed for it—but what was she going to do? If she refused him, he'd have found another way to make it happen anyway, you know? You didn't say no to my dad—"[289]

Christian nods.

"So she got pregnant." I shrug. "Prayed for a boy—"

"How do you know that?" he cuts in, brows low.

I give him a tight smile and I swallow. "Because she told me."

"Fuck." He breathes out as he reaches over, hair behind my ear. "That's why you're close to Delina?"

I nod. "That's why."[290]

"And your dad?" he asks, peeling out, driving again.

"He was good, I think. Weird, probably—" I shrug. "Tried to keep what he did away from me, but you know how it seeps in?" He nods. "Into who he was in... a fundamental way?"[291]

---

[289] No one ever said no to Hadrian Haites.

[290] Also, it was with her youngest son that I navigated every sort of terrain life could throw at me, but that's neither here nor there.

[291] Fundamentally, my father was born a very good, very loyal, kind man. But did he die that way? I honestly don't remember anymore. I can't tell. He lives on a pedestal in Julian's mind but that begins to crack in my mind if I let myself hear through the coins in the washing machine.

"Yeah." His eyes are heavy with the weight of all the shit we've done because we were born into the families we were born into.

"I do know that he loved me... and he fought to have me... tried to protect me from the weird shit I'd have otherwise seen."

"Yeah?" Christian smiles, tilts his head a bit. "Like what?"

I swallow. "Like people dying in his office."

His mouth pulls. "Did you see it anyway?"

I nod.[292]

His eyes drop from mine, and I think he's thinking about what to say.[293] This life of ours, it's so unspeakably shitty so much of the time, so horrifically abnormal that there's nothing he can say.

"Right." He peeks over at me as we pull into the valet of the hotel. Christian takes a breath and looks at me out of the corner of his eyes. "So a few things you need to know about my mum..."

I look over at him nervously. "Okay..."

He lists them off his fingers. "She's really bad with boundaries."

"Okay."

Next finger. "She's invasive."

"Great."

Next finger. "Doesn't miss a fucking trick."

"Perfect."

Next finger. "Doesn't have a good filter on her."

"Right." I nod. "You think she's not going to like me..."

And then Christian glances over, chuckling all amused. "No—I think she's going to eat you up." He gives me a look. "And you're not going to know what to do with it because you're weird with other females and don't trust women because of your mum, but oi—listen to me, right—" He pokes me in the ribs. "You can trust her."

He hands the valet his keys, shakes his hand and slips him £20, then opens my door. "And if you don't trust her, she'll force her way in anyway, so you might as well." He pulls me from the car.

She stands up as we walk to the table, eyes all lit up in a way that feels like in a movie when a mother sees her son.

She's completely gorgeous, Christian's mum. Of course she is with sons like hers. Olive skin, brown hair, hazel eyes, top-heavy red lips.

---

[292] Don't play hide-and-seek in the closets of a gang lord. Especially not before garbage day.

[293] But what can you say?

Her face is warm, which is strange because Rebecca Barnes[294] is arguably the most formidable person in the country after my brother.

"Darling." She opens her arms to Christian. Kisses both his cheeks.

"Barnesy." He gives his mum a squeeze and she pulls back, holding his face in her hands.

"So handsome in that colour, don't you think, Jo?" She looks past Christian to me. "And you, my darling—" She reaches for my hand and her eyes flicker from Christian's to mine to Christian's and they're excited and big and I feel like the best way I could describe her is like a hummingbird. Buzzy and precious, fast movements, enchanting to be around. She pulls me in towards her, but I suspect Rebecca Barnes might pull most people into her gravity with very little effort. I don't not hug back, but I probably don't hug her back with the enthusiasm someone in my position should. She might be the second female on the planet I've ever hugged.

"Jonah, say hello—don't be so rude, darling."

"Hello, Daisy." Jonah rolls his eyes.

"And you, my darling girl—" She looks me up and down.[295] "You mightn't remember me, it's been some time—"

I nod quickly. "I remember you."

"You were quite small. Running around with the little Bambrilla boy."

Jonah makes an uncomfortable sound and Christian balls up a napkin, tossing it at him.

Rebecca looks between them, eyebrow up. "What?"

"That's her ex-boyfriend." Jo nods his head towards me.

"Oh, dear." She pulls a face. "A recent ex?"[296]

"Mum—" Christian groans.

"Very recent."[297] Jonah grins, because he's the human version of Loki.

"Jo—" Christian groans.

---

[294] Barnes, not Hemmes. The boys have their dad's surname, I know that much. And Rebecca's family are the ones with the crime legacy.

[295] Probably because I'm not dressed appropriately to meet a mother.

[296] Shit.

[297] Shit x 2.

"Oh." Rebecca sits back in her chair, looking from Christian and I curiously. "How recent?"[298]

And Christian tenses up a bit—it's a new thing he does with me now that we do jealous. Not jealousy this time around, but jealousy's older brother protective. He licks his bottom lip and stares over at Jonah, annoyed. I know you'd think I'd be sweating bullets but I'm not. I'm built for this shit.

I give her a quick smile. "Romeo and I broke up when I was sixteen. And we nearly got back together a few months ago but he slept with Tavie Jukes—"

Rebecca gasps dramatically. "No—!"[299]

"Yes." I nod once, happy she accepted my paraphrased dating history. "Hey, Jo, how's it going with you and Taura?" I give him a curt smile. "I know it must be getting really difficult for you with how both you and Henry are in love with her—" I give him a shit-eating grin and his eyes go to slits as his mother turns to him dramatically.

"Fuck you," he mouths at me over his mum's head and I flip him off, Christian smirking next to me.

"Is this true, Jonah Isaiah?"

"Cute." I grin over at him.

"Thank you." She nods, receiving the compliment.

"No, Mum—she's trying to—she's just—but it's—" He groans. "We're here for them—"

He points his hand towards us. "Grill them."

Rebecca turns, looking back at Christian and I after shooting a withering glance back at her eldest. "We will talk about this, though—Henry, your oldest friend."[300]

"BJ's my oldest friend," Jonah corrects her and she smacks him in the arm.

"Am I not your oldest friend?" Christian asks.

Jonah rolls his eyes.

"Wouldn't my brother technically be your oldest friend?" I pipe up and Jo points over at me, with a (mostly) playful glare.

"That's enough out of you, shit-stirrer."

I flash him a smile.

---

[298] Help!

[299] I like her more by the second for that reaction.

[300] Shakes her head, disappointed in him.

"Well, Jonah," his mother gives him a measured look, "it takes one to know one." She gives me an amused look and pours me some wine. "So, you two." She eyes Christian. "How long have you two been together?"

"Yeah, Christian," Jonah chimes in. "How long have you been together?" he says and he says it in a way where it becomes apparent that he knows nothing about us being actually together and for a second I feel stupid and my eyes drop a bit and—

Christian clears his throat. "Well, Mum, we've been sleeping together a few months—"

"Lovely," she says dryly.

"But," he continues, "we've been official for... what?" He scratches his neck, gives me a shrug to confirm. "A week or something?"

I nod. "Two."

"Seriously?" Jonah sits back in his chair.

Christian nods. "Seriously."

His brother folds his arms over his chest. "You two've been going out two weeks and you didn't tell me?"

"Yeah, well..." Christian throws back some wine. "You're a bit of a prick, man, so—"

"Yeah, but—I didn't realise that being a prick meant you wouldn't tell me shit." He grins over at us, nodding. He picks up his wine glass and clinks it with his brother's. "Good for you man, not fucking it up—"

"Anyway, Daisy." Rebecca says loudly, harnessing the direction of the conversation. "What do you do?"

I fold my hands in front of me, trying to seem put-together. "I study medicine."

"No!" She claps her hands together. "You're quite clever then?"

"She's clever," Christian tells her proudly[301] as he tosses his arm around me.

"How old are you?" she asks.

"Twenty."

"And you're in your...?"

"Second year." I nod.

"Very clever." She sits back, impressed. "You finished secondary school early then?"

---

301 !!!!!

270

I let out a small laugh. "After our parents died, Julian began to run a rather tight ship—" I give her an apologetic smile. "I didn't have much of a social life."

"So you studied?" She smiles, amused.

"Mmhm." I nod and Christian kisses the side of my head.

She stares over at us for a few seconds, then smiles. "Very good."

# 49

# Christian

Daisy and me, we've had pretty different life experiences. Similar in some ways. In the bullet points, pretty similar, I guess. Family business, the wealth and the power, some losses between us; but we're kind of only similar in the headlines. Someone like Henry, right? His life—completely normal, yeah? Mum and dad, a brother, a bunch of sisters, went to school, nothing tragic, nothing traumatic, hard-working, good at most things, just a normal life. Then you look at Daisy and it's the other end of the spectrum; riddled with tragedy, constant trauma, no parents, kind of isolated, raised by her brother. I thought I got it, kind of thought that's why we've been hanging out so much, because we're just cut from the same cloth and we just get the weird shit that happens around us. But the more I'm with her, the more I see that I'm neither. I'm in the middle.

My parents, they're together still. Technically, at least. That's the sad part about it all, I guess.

They used to be in love. Never a marriage of convenience, not even close. I remember when we were kids, they'd talk about the inconvenience of loving each other and it's taken me my whole lifetime trying to piece it together—Mum doesn't say shit about it, Dad doesn't talk to anyone.

My uncle—the good one, not Callum—the one I like, Harvey—lives over in Australia with his two girls. He didn't want anything to do with this life—it shouldn't have been his anyway. The oldest of them all, Beau, was shot at a Liverpool game when he was too young to die, and so it went to Harv. All this should have been his, the Barnes Empire, but he didn't want it. He went over to Australia to play AFL instead and he just never really came back.

The crown fell to Mum (much to Callum's horror).

We visit them a bunch, Harv and the girls. The girls are a similar age to me and Jo. Their mum died.

Anyway, Harv's filled in a lot of the blanks for me and here's what I do know:

My parents met at a Manchester United game when Mum was seventeen. She was going to be a teacher at the time. They fell in love quick, my parents. My dad, Jud Hemmes, he comes from a pretty standard background. Small-town boy, grew up in Little Cawthorpe up near Louth. His dad was a farmer. I think that's all he ever wanted to do himself 'til he met Mum and then that went out the window.

Mum is... the sun. Everyone loves her, she walks into the room and it gets brighter. Instant buy-in for whatever she said and whatever she wanted, and when he met her at that Man U match, it was game over for him. At the time it was a perfect fit, a teacher and a small-town farmer.

Dad was already in love with Mum when Harvey left England to play football over in Australia and by then it was too late. It didn't matter to my dad anymore that mum was now the head of a crime syndicate, it was my mum and he loved her because you can't not once you know her.

It did cause some friction, though.

Dad's family, they cut them off. Small-town Irish. Grandad wanted nothing to do with them, thought it was disgusting, despicable, beneath him, beneath his son. Dad thought it was worth it to keep my mum.

Me and Jo, we're pretty close with Grandad anyway. He lives in England now. All that shit aside, when we came along, Grandad was too decent a man to not know his grandchildren. I think he took it upon himself to try to instill some sense of moral rightness in us—real salt-of-the-earth guy. Even now when I go to visit him, he takes my phone off me. Locks it in a drawer for the weekend. We go fishing, do puzzles by the fire, sheer the sheep—that kind of shit. I love those weekends with him.

Anyway, Mum and Dad were golden, gross in love, embarrassingly in love, until Rem died. I was ten when it happened.

Jo and Beej found her drowned in the pool. She had been upstairs playing all morning with Mum and Dad, left her in her room to make us all some lunch and it seemed to happen in about fifteen minutes.

There's a lot about it we don't understand. It was an indoor pool, because this is London and who the fuck is swimming outside? There are two doors into the pool, both are bolt-locked with a keypad. Rem didn't know the code and she wasn't tall enough to reach it.

But accidents happen, I guess?

Anyway, Jo and Beej went to go for a swim, found her floating face down.

BJ dove it, fished her out—Jo started screaming for help. I ran in, wish I didn't. She was blue, worse than that, though, was how limp she was—so painfully, obviously dead. I hadn't seen a dead body back then. I didn't want my baby sister to be the first one, but anyway—there you have it.

It went to shit after that. Dad blamed Mum, Mum blamed Dad, very quickly it became apparent that he didn't want to be involved in the family business anymore, but what part of his old life did he have left?

Mum's kind of religious. She wouldn't divorce him. Dad became entirely apathetic, lives in his office at the other end of the house from Mum.

I see them together on Christmas, sometimes he'll come out for our birthday dinners, maybe Easter? That's about it.

Anyway, we're out at No Tales, a club over in Fulham. It's one of the few cool venues about that isn't mine or my brother's, but we're all there anyway, the entire Haites cavalry, Bambrillas included—everyone's still on pretty high alert from the other week.

Haven't really gotten past that stunt Rome pulled then either, feeling her up in front of me with the corset. Still get angry every time I think about it, but I guess the part where Daisy's in my bed and not his softens the blow a skosh.

Spend the first bit of the night just hanging around Daisy, finding myself wondering when it'll get old. If it even will—everything she says is the funniest, cleverest thing, and I think about kissing her all the time, think about doing other stuff with her all the time too. I hate it when she goes to school. I'm bored as soon as she leaves—and I know I've become this disgusting sap of a man whom I'd hate and mock if I met, but I just like her, I guess.

I see an old boy from Varley on the other side of the room—catch eyes with him. Haven't seen Thatcher Hendry in a few months. Good bloke. Plays for the Lions now. Won't come over here, though, and for good reason, I'm sitting among Britain's most notorious men—so

I give her a kiss on the cheek, tell her I'll be right back and make my way over to him.

"Hemmes, my man!" He hugs me. "It's been a minute, how are you?"

"Good, bro." I nod. "How's the team looking this year?"

He shrugs. "New coach, always a bit of a scramble." He nods his head over at Daisy. "Is that your girl?"

I glance back at her, get a smile on my face like a fucking idiot, and cover it up before I look back at him. "Yeah."

"Been together long?"

I wobble my head about as I try to work out how to answer. "In some capacity or another...?"

He chuckles, smacks my arm. "Say no more."

"Are you seeing anyone?"

"Yeah, actually. I just started seeing V—"

And then there's this loud sound and even though I've heard it before, I don't immediately register what it is until it happens again and people start screaming—and then it all slips into slow motion.

People start scrambling—some people just dive onto the ground—I stare across the room at Daisy and she stares back at me, eyes wide and frozen, and I make myself a promise that I won't leave her alone again if I can get to her.

There's another shot and people are scrambling to get to the exit. Yelling. The lights go up. It's strange how disgusting a club looks with the lights on, don't you think? I push my way through the crowd to get to her, but she's disappeared now in a pile of the Lost Boys. I've heard about this—about Julian's protocol—how if something happens, if something ever goes down, it's Daisy or bust. Daisy at all costs. Protect her or die trying, she's what matters. I used to think it was a bit much, that he was a fucking psycho of a brother, but here I am now trying my hardest to get to her as fast as I can, wishing I was the one shielding her body with mine—

I get closer and there's still a river of people running between us but I can see her now, she's on the floor. There's blood—I'm gonna be sick.

"Daisy!" I call out but she can't hear me.

She's crying. I've never seen her cry before.

"Daisy!" I call again. She's looking around frantically and urgently, yelling—I can't hear what, though. Waving her hands in the air. She's covered in blood. Mostly on her hands. I can see her screaming at

Declan, he's shaking his head at her and she keeps yelling at him. Then he takes his shirt off and tosses it to her and I realise there's a girl on the floor—the one who was sitting next to her a minute ago—and she's bleeding out everywhere. It's everywhere. And then Julian picks Daisy up off the floor and she's fighting him, bucking in his arms, clawing at him, trying to get back to the dying girl and he shakes her in a way that makes me want to kill him on the spot and I'm about to right when Romeo shoves Jules, snatches Daisy from her brother, grabs her chin with his hand and makes her focus on him.

It jolts me for a second, watching him touch her with a familiar authority, a bit like he has a right to be there. More than I do, even. I push my way through towards them in time for me to hear Romeo say to her, "…was for you, Daisy. Those bullets were aiming for you."

Kekoa does a hand signal in the air that everyone but me seems to know and they all start moving except Daisy.

Her face looks how I've never seen it. Eyes wide and unfocused, watching nothing. Frozen still but sort of trembling.

My eyes go blurry.

"We have to go now." Julian pushes her against the current of people towards a back exit that no one really knows about. Romeo takes her hand, pulling her with him and that gets her moving. And I sort of stand there, stupid, like an idiot until Declan shoves me and I'm walking down the stairs and out the door and then I'm on the street. Everything feels like a skipping CD and I want to try to get to Daisy but she's not even looking for me anymore.

Her hand's in Romeo's, and even though his eyes are darting around, scanning for danger, on high alert—her eyes are on him. Big, round, horrible and sort of in awe.

"Come on. We gotta go—" Miguel shoves me towards the car behind theirs but I just stand still on the street, watching as Romeo throws open the door to one of the Haites's bulletproof cars.

"Christian," Miguel says again.

"I'm—" I stare over at them, my mouth's gone dry. I shake my head a bit. "I'm just—" I swallow. "I'm gonna go."

Miguel looks over his shoulder at Daisy in time for him to see what I see.

Romeo's hand on her face, holding it like he's sorry and sad, and I feel like it's important to say that Daisy's not looking for me at all as Julian shoves her into the car, closing the door behind them.

Miguel looks back at me, grimacing a little. Shakes his head, looking sorry for me.

"It's a reflex," he tells me.

I press my tongue into my top lip and nod slowly.

"Right." I nod. "A reflex."

Still turn and walk away, though.

+44 7724 771 959
2:13 AM

hey

are you out tonight?

nope... Just at home—

how come?

ok good

what??

nothing

this is a weirder text message than usual...

hah.

are you ok?

yep

Really?

Yep x

xx

# 50

# Daisy

It happened so quickly. I'm not like this… There have been other times when something like this has happened, but I've never once shut down. Maybe with my parents I did?[302] But then tonight I froze. Not at first, not when I hadn't realised it was for me, but it's always for me, and I'll never know why.

I hate this life. It's all I've ever known and I hate it. There are perks and pluses, and there are moments of tenderness, but being loved by my brother, merely existing in his orbit[303] has been a death sentence.

Tonight—I don't remember what happened, if I'm honest. There were the gunshots and there was the girl next to me. There was no helping her actually, even though I tried.

Shot twice, one almost square between her right deltoid and the infraspinatus and once through the neck. They were aiming for the carotid, no doubt. She was bleeding everywhere and even on an operating table, if I'd had one, I couldn't have saved her. After that, it all went a bit blurry. The stairs, Romeo pulling me down them, him keeping me safe how he always does.[304] My brother behind me and shoving me into the car. I sat in the middle, they took the windows.[305] The middle is safer. And now I'm here in the foyer of the Compound and all the Lost Boys pour in through the doors and I realise I haven't seen Christian since… I'm not sure. When the shot first fired, maybe? We must have gotten separated at the club.

I peer around the boys.

"Where's Christian?" I ask no one in particular.

---

[302] I did, thinking back to it, but I was eight, so…

[303] Every day but especially since the day our parents were the acquired targets.

[304] Always has.

[305] I love a window seat. I'm never allowed in them.

Declan glances over at me. Says nothing.

Miguel swallows, a weird look rolls over his face. "He left."

"He left?" I repeat loudly.

"What?" Julian steps forward, frowning.[306] "What do you mean? Why?"

Miguel looks past my brother to me and he gives me a little flick of his eyebrows and it is then and only then that I realise that Romeo has both of his arms slung around me, holding me back against him. How long have we been like this? I have no idea. I look down at his arms and back at Rome, and he blinks before he comes into the moment too, waking up to the weirdness of us.[307] I step out of his embrace awkwardly and he lets me—all the boys watching this strange thing between us unravel how it always does and it always will and everyone knows why and no one says a fucking thing.

"He just left?" I blink at Miguel. I feel a bit faint, actually.

Miguel tilts his head, breathes out, shrugs a bit helplessly—the rest of the boys start clearing the room. Not Julian, not Romeo.

"What would you have him do?" Miguel asks with a frown, gesturing towards me and Rome.[308]

"What about not leave?" Rome offers and Miguel shoots him an unimpressed look.

"I have to talk to him." I shake my head, walking towards the door. "He doesn't get it—it looked bad, but it's—"

"Nope." My brother grabs my wrist.

I jerk away from him. "I need to see him—"

"Are you crazy?" My brother blinks. I try to push past to the door but Julian picks me up and carries me backwards a few feet with a fury in his eyes. After tossing me onto the ground, he gets right in my face. "Someone tried to kill you tonight—"

"You don't know that." I shake my head.[309]

"Yes, we do." My brother nods.

"Don't be a fucking idiot, Dais," Rome butts in. "If they weren't trying to kill you, they were in the least trying to send you a message."

I roll my eyes. "And what message might that be?"

---

[306] Instantly fuming.
[307] And how mindless we must be around each other to not even notice.
[308] He doesn't like Rome much either.
[309] Though I suspect he's right.

My brother gives me a long look.[310] "That they can get to you."

That makes me feel sort of nauseous. Or maybe I feel like that because Christian just left?[311]

"I don't care." I shake my head.

"I can see that, Dais." Jules nods. "Fifteen people willing to lay their lives down for you tonight, an unwitting girl dead already, and you're ready to throw in the towel so you can talk to your fucking boyfriend."

"Get out of my way—" I growl and shove my brother, which does nothing at all. Julian stares me down with a set jaw.

I shove him again and again and again[312] and how much my brother doesn't move makes me start to cry and makes me feel frightened that this is what it'll always be—me losing the people I love so I can stay alive a little bit longer.

But "alive" is all relative, isn't it?

The door knocks and all three boys, Julian, Rome and Miguel, pull out guns and point them towards it.

My brother pulls me behind him and I peek out behind him nervously.

The door cracks open.

Julian cocks the trigger.

"Woah." Christian blinks a few times, frozen in his place. "Not my warmest reception."

Julian makes a noise in the back of his throat and rolls his eyes. His gun is tucked away now. "Not massive fans of deserters around here."

"Shut up," I growl at Julian as I push past him.

Romeo sighs, shoves his hands through his hair. After a single shake of his head, he leaves the room.[313]

"Can we talk?" Christian asks, pushing some hair from my face.

I nod.

"Where can we go?" he asks my brother.

Julian nods towards his office and Christian takes my hand, pulling

---

[310] He looks worried. Sad. I hate it.

[311] I can't believe he just left. Romeo would never just leave… But then, maybe that's the root of all the problems.

[312] And he looks sad and worried and sorry and it's always been like this, him trying his best to keep me alive and I'm not meaning to be ungrateful, I swear, but somehow it all feels unfair. I know other people have paid prices, but my whole life has been a paid price.

[313] Avoids my eyes.

me there. Closes the door behind us and I rush him, throw my arms around his neck, kiss him so hard he falls backwards into the door.

He holds my face in his hands, kisses me with that sad urgency that happens between people when you feel like you're losing them.

He pulls back a little. "Are you fucking around with me?"

"No—" I frown.

"Biding your time till you and Rome work your shit out?"

"What?" I blink. "No! I—"

He shakes his head at me. "I'm not doing that dance again, Dais. If you want me, you want me."

I nod, bottom lip wobbling a bit. "I want you."

He shakes his head at me and gestures back toward the door. "Then what the fuck was that?"

I press my hands into my eyes, shake my head, and walk over to my brother's desk, perch on it.

I stare over at Christian, who's glaring at me a little, like I've hurt him and I guess I have. I try to imagine how I'd feel if I watched him holding Magnolia's hand, pulling her out the door, leaving me alone in a high-stakes situation. I sigh. Leave my face in my hands.

I never talk about what happened.

Julian put me in therapy for a whole year afterwards, but it didn't really work.

He tried to get me to talk to him about it, I wouldn't.

It's too much to say out loud and I don't want to tell him because it is the out-loud confession of what I inwardly know already but I've never wanted Christian to hear it: loving me only leads to bad things.

Christian walks over to me, pulls my hands from my face, and lifts my chin up. Brows low, so serious and so handsome, it hurts me square in the chest.

He waits.

"When I was just seventeen, Romeo and I were at a hotel in Marylebone. We'd just—" I give him a look. "You know."

He nods.

"He left for a couple of minutes, went to go get a bucket of ice for some champagne or something and I ran a bath—it was a big bath." I take a shallow breath and he waits. "You know, one of those ones with the claws? Deep."[314]

---

[314] Deep. That part is important.

His frown deepens but he nods.

I wipe my eye. "I got in the bath… There was music playing. The lights were off, there was just a candle lit, I think."

"Okay…" He nods, crossing his arms over his chest.

"My eyes were closed, so I didn't hear him come in—and um—" I take a big breath as though I'm scared I won't be able to breathe again.[315] "Then this man—I don't know how he got in, I should have heard him—" I flash him a quick smile. "Well, he started choking me."

Christian's face goes still.

"Pushed me under. Drowned me for a bit. I tried to fight but it wasn't much use." I shrug. "He was so much bigger than me, and I was naked and slippery—" I give him a weak smile. "Bit of an uphill battle."

The man was giant—at least that's how he felt. A puggish face, thick neck. A necklace that wasn't meant to be a choker was a choker around it.

"Crushed my larynx in the end, actually."[316] I nod, touching my neck absentmindedly.

I can see Christian's breathing change, the pace picking up.

"And I was dying, I knew I was. All I can really remember thinking is 'I hope he kills me before Romeo gets back' because by that time we'd figured it out. Really, for the most part, it was about me, not Rome. About getting a message to my brother—and I thought that maybe if I died before Romeo was back that they'd leave him alone, and then the choking stopped and I don't know, I think Rome cracked a mirror over his head, dazed the guy for a few seconds—"

Romeo pulled me out of the bathroom and was headed back into our room to get a gun, but he was stopped before he could get clear of the door. I watched him slowly back into the room with his arms raised.

A different man was there with a gun pointed at Rome. Orange-ish hair, thick beard that was well kept. Dark eyes.

Thick Neck staggered up from the floor and grabbed me, pulling me back into him, a gun now to my head too. I didn't have clothes on.

"Don't move," Dark Eyes said as he cocked the trigger at Romeo.

---

[315] PTSD does that to you.

[316] I couldn't speak for a couple of weeks.

His eyes flicked over to his partner and then he nodded his chin at me. "Not a part of the plan, but when opportunity knocks…"

Thick Neck ran his hands up my body and Romeo lunged towards me. Dark Eyes turned his gun to me.[317]

Just his bottom lip trembled, but the rest of Rome froze.[318]

"It's okay." I mouthed over to him wordlessly. "I love you."

"I'm so sorry—" Romeo mouthed back as Dark Eyes sat down on the edge of the bath, gun casually pointed back at my boyfriend who was watching on as his friend groped me. Rome was crying—he was maybe just nineteen at the time. Eighteen? Nineteen at the very oldest. And he was so sad, so wrecked watching this person trying to do this terrible thing to me, but I knew he wouldn't risk doing anything that might get him shot. Not because he wouldn't die for me, he would in a second, but he was doing everything in his power not to die in front of me too.[319]

And then I sort of thought—fuck it, I'm dying anyway, I might as well go out swinging. So I switched tactics and instead of fighting him off, I fell limp in Thick Neck's arms and miraculously it worked how I thought it might—his hand holding the gun to my head slipped and I grabbed it and fired it at his friend on the edge of the bath.

It didn't mortally wound Dark Eyes—it was just lodged in his arm but it was enough of a stir for Romeo to charge him. He knocked him into the bath, began wrestling the gun from him—he was always a good fighter, my Rome.[320] You kind of have to be in this life, but he especially had to be because that was the third time someone had tried to kill me when we were alone together.

Romeo was fighting Dark Eyes and I tried to leverage my weight to destabilise Thick Neck, but it was hard because he was so much bigger than me. Instead of bringing him down, I turned his arm around and over in a way and hung my weight off of it—snapping bones. He cried out in pain and swung his good arm at me, got me once, but then I went low. Glass everywhere. Huge shards.

You think quick when people are trying to kill you. Our survival

---

[317] And this is why Julian won't love a girl.

[318] The most afraid I've ever seen him, and we were once in a restaurant shooting on a Good Friday one year where twenty-three people died around us.

[319] He wouldn't do that to me.

[320] I probably shouldn't still call him that, but then maybe he always will be.

instincts really are incredible. I grabbed one of the shards and drove it into his calf. Distracted and crying out in pain, I grabbed another and drove it into his stomach, slicing through his skin in a way that made me feel funny. It's hard to articulate, but it almost felt like I was pushing a knife through wet sand with how deep it went. He was doubled over, so I stood quickly and took the biggest shard I could find and shoved it up through his digastric muscle.[321] His eyes went wide and this panicked look came across his face. I know the look. I've sported it several times myself. This man had seen it in my eyes just a few minutes before. It's the one you get right before you die.

Thick Neck moved backwards and away from me, a weird, terrible gurgling was spilling from him, and then there was a loud crash as he fell. I watched him for a few seconds—my chest heaving like I had just finished sprinting—to make sure he's really dead. Then I grabbed his gun and swung it around to Dark Eyes and Rome, who were still fighting in the bath. The sound was terrible. The gasping for air—the yelling—both of them fighting for their lives.

Rome was under the water with Dark Eyes pressing his entire bodyweight down on my boyfriend's throat. Then I put the gun against the back of his head.

"When opportunity knocks," I whispered to him,[322] and then I pulled the trigger and everything changed forever.

Have you ever seen a head all shot open?

That's not why the world changed.

"Something bad happens, and we just…" I shrug, looking up at Christian. "We just… gravitate. I don't think we were born that way, just rewired."

"Fuck." Christian whispers, eyes round. Glassy, actually.

I flash him a quick smile that is my best defence for not crying.

"Dais—" He shakes his head. "I'm so sorry that happened to you."

I give him a little shrug. What else can I do? "It's okay."

"It's not."

"I'm sorry for tonight—it wasn't on purpose, we're just—"

"You don't need to explain." His mouth pulls as he shakes his head more. Christian sighs, pushes some hair from my face, leans in, and

---

[321] The soft spot on the bottom of your jaw, just under the chin.

[322] But barely, because larynx. I do hope he heard me, though, because that was a nice full-circle moment for me.

brushes his lips over mine. He breathes in and out. Swallows. "I'm sorry I left."

"No I—" I shake my head. "I know it's a lot."

"Yeah." He nods, not letting me go. "But it's not too much, though."

# 51

# Christian

All that shit with Daisy, everything she told me, it's been on a loop in my head. I feel sick about it every time I think of it—every time I see a bath—my throat goes tight. She says I keep hovering around her now. I can't tell if she's happy about it or not. She's had a lifetime of people hovering around her and I used to think it was stupid and kind of weird, but I get it now. Now that I know her how I know her—and you know, there's that whole feminine trope of a girl who needs to be saved, doe eyes fluttering, damsel in distress, all innocent and virtuous and that's not what it is. She's not like that, she doesn't need my help, she doesn't need me to save her—but I'm going to try anyway. Now that I know what I know, now that I've seen how she still thinks about a stranger choking her for no real reason other than she was born into the wrong family...

"Oi." BJ whacks me in the arm. "Where's your head at, man? You're completely out of it."

"Sorry." I blink. We're on our way down in Newquay for a bit of a surf. Big swell coming in off the Celtic Sea after a storm. We only ever come down here for the big ones, the ones that make the drive worth it. It's just the boys. Better that way. Wouldn't want to see Parks right now anyway. She's pissing me off. I was already pretty off her after the necklace thing, but we're sitting here and Beej is telling us all about how she's kind of just dating them both—him and Tom.

Queen of having her cake and not just fucking eating it, but, like, ploughing it too.

"It's kind of rough, man," Jo tells him and Henry's quiet because he feels caught, like he knows it's fucked up but she's brainwashed him too, so he can't say a bad thing about her.

BJ shrugs. "I fucked up. She doesn't trust me now."

And I don't personally think that's much of an excuse for her, so I don't say shit. There's nothing I can say that won't land me in hot water. If I take his side, I've got to talk shit on her and he doesn't want people to talk shit about her, he just wants people he can talk shit about her to. If I don't take his side, then I'm on her side, and I'm only on her side because of what happened and then I'm shit too. There's no winning. But there never is with them.

And actually, the more I think about it, the more I think about Magnolia these days—and in a lot of ways, I actually think about her a lot less—I think that maybe she's just trash.

I don't know how I can love her how I have for so long, I don't understand how she was all I thought about, everywhere I looked, she was everything to me for such a long time and now she's just... not. She's sharing the space with someone else—someone better, someone I like and I want to be with, who I am with. And it doesn't seem to matter how much I like Daisy, how light she makes my head, how done up I feel in myself when she's asleep next to me in her bed—because I just hear Magnolia's name and it fucking weighs me down all over again. She's like a bear trap my leg's caught in. And I could try to pry it open, but there's too much blood and it hurts too much. I don't know. I think it's been too long. It's gone septic. Loving Parks, for me—it's infected now.

She dating them both? Fuck her. Honestly.

Beej is rolling with the punches here on the outside, but I know him—she's everything to him. And yeah, he's a fuck-up. And yeah, he fucked up first, but she's worse. I'm sure of it.

"Anyway—" Beej tosses his drink back. "How's it going with you and Baby?"

"Yeah, good." I nod.

"He's never home anymore," Henry tells them and I roll my eyes.

"It's just easier being at her house with all the—you know—" I trail off, not really feeling bothered to explain it.

Jonah squints over at me. "You hate not sleeping in your bed."

That's true actually. Suddenly seems a bit worth it these days, though.

I shrug. "Her bed's pretty good."

My brother makes a loud crowing noise from the driver's seat and I ignore him.

"Look at you, bro." BJ chuckles as he turns around. "In a relationship and shit."

I sniff a laugh, scratch the back of my neck. "Yeah, I guess."

He nods once, gives me a quarter of a smile. "Suits you."

# 52

# Julian

At the speakeasy with the boys, and we're all having a good laugh at how Carmelo accidentally spent £45,000 last week on clothes he hates because he was trying to sleep with the shop girl but in the end she was gay. Brilliant shit like that happens to him all the time because he's got those Italian eyes that see the entire world as a romantic prospect and every pretty girl he passes might be the one. I swear to God, the number of "the ones" I've met of his is in the vicinity of Elizabeth fucking Taylor.

First time I've been out of the house in a few days. Just waiting for all the drama to die down—Kekoa's on high alert after the shooting. No real lead yet, though there's an obvious lead. We can't directly tie it to any of their people—that has him worried. Koa likes a trace, likes to know our enemies. We have a lot of them and all of them know that my sister is the chink in my armour.

We think that the shooting wasn't a near miss for Daisy as much as it was a message to me that if they wanted to get to me, they could.

Dais seems to be doing okay, Christian is practically her shadow these days anyway, but that feels well timed. I never noticed before, I didn't think he used to carry one, but now he's always got a Nighthawk VIP on him, which is a nice little piece, actually.

Him following my sister around seems to be softening the blow, but probably only in a superficial way. Band-Aid over a bullet wound sort of thing, because if history has taught us anything, it's that her being in a relationship doesn't preclude her from danger. It invites it.

Jonah leans back, wipes his eyes from laughing so hard at Carmelo's story and gives him a look. "Oi, how's Rome doing?"

Not good, I can tell you that much myself. He's fucking about again with Tavie Jukes, a couple of Instagram girls, posting the shit out of it all. He goes like this when he's cut up about Daisy and it always serves me as a healthy reminder that girls are more trouble then they're worth.

Carms sniffs and tosses Jonah a look. "Yeah, look—he's taking it pretty hard." I cross my arms over my chest, pretend like I don't already know. I'm good at reading people, but people don't often like being read. "Yeah?"

Carmelo shrugs, looks sad for him. They're close, and not just in the way brothers are, but in the extra way you have to be when you do what we do.

"I think he always thought they'd work it out in the end."

"Might do," Jonah shrugs. "Wouldn't put it past Christian to fuck it up."

I peer over at him "He'd better not."

Jo shrugs helplessly as Declan appears behind him with a frown.

Nod my chin at him. "What's up?"

He scratches his neck, thinking. "He hasn't made the payment."

"What?" I yawn, stretching my arms over my head. "Who?"

Declan gives me a look. "Brown."

I sit up straighter. "What?"

He shrugs. "Paid the deposit—nothing else."

"You're shitting me."

He shakes his head and I let out a hollow laugh.

"Fuck—" I laugh. "And he already has the painting?"

He nods. "Handed it over the day after we got back. He said the money was in escrow—"

"And we didn't check?"

He shrugs again and I'm getting angry now. "You didn't check?" I point at him.

"Not really my job." Declan gives me a look and I stand up, get in his face.

"You work for me. Your job is whatever the fuck I say it is." I point to the door. "Go get my fucking money."

# 55

# Daisy

There's a lot to be said about my brother and a lot is said about him. Yes, he has a reputation.[323] Yes, he can be dangerous.[324] Yes, he has hurt people,[325] but also he's saved them. He saved me. Literally and metaphorically. He was all of eighteen years old when he accidentally become a sort of father to a sister who was already up to her eyeballs in issues and complexities from a mother who didn't want her, and he's navigated it all in a way that's never made me feel like I was an inconvenience or a burden, even though I know—beyond know—that I was and I continue to be both of those things for him.[326]

So, say what you will about him. Focus on the bad things he's done—on the bad things he will continue to do—but he's not like everyone else, and he doesn't abide by everyone else's rules. Me? I will sit happily and proudly in his corner every day of my life, apologising for his abruptness, making excuses for his misgivings, laughing at the things I shouldn't, but mostly just being grateful for him.

When I creep into his room this morning, I'm happy to find no random girl asleep in his bed,[327] just him. Thirty today, must be all that personal growth.

Julian's horrible to buy presents for. Do you think there's anything on this planet that if my brother wanted he wouldn't just take for himself? He's impossible. He has it all. Art, sometimes. Feels indulgent at the second, what with the Holofernes hanging in his bedroom over there like his very own Lady of the Lake. For his twenty-fifth

---

[323] No, it's not all bad.

[324] But so can a lion and an orca and a tiger; no one says that they're innately bad.

[325] This one is harder to defend.

[326] I know this because I'm astute, not because he'd tell me.

[327] Praise be.

birthday, Koa and I arranged to acquire the Wallace Hartley violin that he played the night the Titanic sunk—he liked that one. Last year I got him a Seymchan Meteorite slab for Christmas. Anyway, all we really do for his birthday is just spend the day together. Watch an entire movie franchise in one sitting, eat our body weight in Galaxy Minstrels.

Tradition also dictates that I make him breakfast in bed.

Same thing every year since I was ten and that's because when I was ten it was the only breakfast that I knew how to make.

Corned beef hash. It's better now than it was then.

I used to boil the potatoes, fry them afterwards but that was wrong—they have to be tiny and they have to be roasted. It's the only way to do it.

Brown and purple onion, sautéed first with garlic and in beef broth. Shredded beef, not diced, fried up until the edges crisp. A bit of grated Swiss cheese. Eggs poached just below 63°C, just how they should be.[328]

I sit on the edge of his bed, wait for him to wake up, which happens with a big yawn.

"Happy birthday." I smile.

He sits up, blinking wide, gives me a tired smile.

He clocks Christian at his door, nods his chin at him.[329]

"Happy birthday, man," Christian says from the doorframe.

I hand Jules his breakfast tray with a proud smile.

"She's been up since 5 am roasting those potatoes," Christian tells him and Julian looks over at me, eyebrows up.

"Yeah?"

I nod, nose in the air. "Probably my best yet."

He shovels some into his mouth. "Agreed." He claps his hands. "What's the plan today?"

"Well." I stand up. "We're going to go to lunch with the boys. Declan said you might like to go car shopping this morning? In the afternoon I was thinking we might be able to squish in a couple of Batmans? Skip *Batman Begins*—"[330]

---

[328] And I won't hear another bloody thing about it!

[329] I'm not sure that the reminder we're sleeping together is the best awakening for his thirtieth.

[330] Awful.

"Naturally," my brother interjects.

"Then tonight we have a dinner with the Bambrillas." I flash Christian an apologetic glance, but not too apologetic because we're together now, so he has to come.

"Best behaviour—" Julian points at him.

Christian shakes his head. "Oi, I don't tend to be the problem." He shrugs.

"And then tomorrow night's your party at Jonah's." I nod. "It was going to be big. Now it's just about 200 people."

"Just a small gathering, then—" Christian smirks.

"Ko's gone apeshit on the security—ID, physical invite matching the ID, one way in, one way out—bag searches, body searches, metal detectors…"

"Geez." Julian blinks wide but shakes his head. He stares over at me and something sad breezes over his face. "No, it's good—that's good. Alright." He shovels some food into his mouth. "Go get dressed—I've got my eye on a little 1965 Aston Martin DB5."

## 54

# Christian

I don't know whose idea of a joke it was to sit Daisy between me and Romeo last night at Julian's dinner, but it wasn't particularly funny, even though Jonah thought it was.

It was a shit vibe, though. Romeo Bambrilla gets prickier and prickier by the fucking second and we're getting closer to coming to blows, which is stressing Daisy out, I can tell. He talked about all this shit they used to do when they were kids, holidays they went on, a summer they spent treasure-hunting in Punta del Hidalgo. And he's chatting away to her about it and I'm watching these things, these memories make her happy, and my reasons for feeling like shit are two-fold. One is that she was happy like this with someone else before me (we do jealous) and the other is that I feel like shit that her being happy with someone else makes me feel like shit. I know that makes me a small person, and maybe that's just what I am. I knew he was doing it all to shit me, because he was only speaking to her half the time, and the other half he'd be saying things like, "Remember when we snuck into that museum after hours and that nun caught us when we were—" and then Daisy would elbow him and he'd start laughing. Then she'd give me an apologetic look, but he wasn't saying it to her, he was saying it to me. To compound how fucked up it all was, he bought Tavie Jukes with him to the dinner. Don't know why. It was at his parents' house, so maybe that's why. Danny Jukes was there too, who's a good time but I've never been a fan of him. Thinks he's a bigger man than he is. Who gives a fuck about what's happening in Birmingham? It's Birmingham.

The whole thing shitted me. Daisy cooked this dinner for her brother for days and then she sat through it being tense the whole time, trying to placate Rome, trying to include me, trying to ignore Tavie. She divided her attention equally between me and Rome, but I'm not sure why because I'm her boyfriend, not him.

Anyway. Julian's party tonight. I arrive with Daisy, feel pretty tall about it, actually. She's in this tiny white dress, long sleeved but real short. Legs are out and up to her elbows, and we're holding hands as we walk in—some cameras flash and I pull her inside, kiss her in the stairwell on our way up.

Jack's there with a boy he's been interested in for a while that Daisy's losing her shit over. Hot Dom is what she keeps referring to him as. Try to tell her to stop because it's a bit of a giveaway with how Jack feels about him, but she assures me that everyone thinks he's hot so it's not very revealing at all.

I don't get it personally. Brown eyes, brown hair. Good cheekbones, I guess. Jack's better looking, though. And as I watch Daisy and him interact with Hot Dom, I get the underlying feeling that he's somehow flipped the tables, made Jack think that he's lucky to be spending time with him, but he's not. Jack's better.

"I don't like him," I whisper to her when they're not paying attention to us.

"Dom?" she asks, eyebrows up. I nod. "Why?"

I shrug. "He's making Jack jump through hoops. It's bullshit."

"Well." Daisy sighs with a little shrug. "Jack's had a crush on him for a very long time."

I shrug back. "He should have had a crush on Jack for a long time."

She gives me a pleased smile and kisses me. I kiss her back longer than I need to—I try to remember if I have a key to my brother's office upstairs here, but I don't.

Jo arrives after a while with Henry, Taura, BJ and—wait for it—Magnolia. I didn't think she'd be there. Haven't thought much about her lately at all because whenever I do I'm just instantly angry. I don't know what to do about it. It feels like a foreign object that I'm holding onto these days, loving her. Like an old antique—it's all ugly and outdated, dusty. I don't know what to do with it. Mostly it just lives on a shelf in a dark corner now, but it's been around so long that I can't just throw it away.

Part of me wonders if I feel Daisy stiffen up as I spot Parks, and I wonder what she knows. How would she know, though? I'm not obvious about it. No one knows we had a thing and there's no paper trail that gives me away.

I kiss Daisy's cheek anyway. Try to show her and Magnolia both that I don't see anyone but her, and that's when Julian struts over.

"Ballentine," he jeers, a drink in each hand. He's pretty buzzed already but he downs one drink and then passes the other one off to Magnolia with a wink. He grabs BJ up off the floor, jostling him around affectionately.

"Happy birthday," Jo says and grabs him by the shoulders. Jules claps his face, grins, and then something weird happens.

Julian's eyes catch Magnolia's and he smirks down at her in a way that throws me.

"Magnolia." He nods at her.

She squashes a smile away. "Jules."

I'm watching Jo and he has no idea what the fuck is going on either, so I know it's not just me. Whatever's playing out in front of us is news to everyone.

"What the fuck?" Daisy whispers with a frown.

My face sort of scrunches as I watch Magnolia, wonder what's happened that we've all missed.

Beej sniffs this shallow laugh and his face pulls. "Didn't realise you two knew each other." He looks between Magnolia and Julian.

Jules lets out this this cocky "hah" and sort of shrugs it off. He gestures towards Magnolia. "Everyone knows this one."

"Right—" BJ's stares over at Parks, his mind moving as fast as mine I reckon, trying to piece it together. "How's that now?"

Jules tosses Parks this look, too casual and playful to ease anyone's concerns, lifts his eyebrows, and waits for Magnolia to answer the question for him.

Am I staring? I guess I am but I can't look away. She's a car crash. I'm horrified—Magnolia licks her lips, and gives Beej a broad smile. "Would you believe me if I said we're in a book club together?"

He shakes his head, unimpressed.

She purses her lips and slips her hand into BJ's back pocket and I roll my eyes, breathe out my nose. So fucking over her shit.

"Julian loves… historical women's fiction and is also quite partial to a biography."

Jules starts laughing, but Beej isn't and I just feel sad for my friend.

"I offered to help her out with something." Julian catches Parks's eye. "She never took me up on the offer, mind you—" He elbows BJ playfully. "She's still slumming it."

Magnolia tilts her head at him with a stern look. "Behave," she tells him, but Julian grins back.

296

"But for real, Parks, if you're ever looking for a good time, with an actual bad boy—not one of these silly *Vogue* bad boys—you call me, yeah."

And fuck her—because I can see it on her that she is stoked. She's not just bathing in the attention, she's fucking swanning around and doing the backstroke in it. She tempers how pleased she is and gives him a curt little smile. "Perhaps let's just get me through this present love triangle I'm in? And once I sort that out, you'll be next in line."

I scoff, shake my head a bit. I honestly cannot fucking believe her.

Julian nods. "Yep, fair—" He gives Beej a smack in the arm and walks away.

I stare over at them, and I don't know what I am. Shattered a bit, but I don't think for me? I think it's for my best friend. Who's standing there learning that the girl he's spent his whole life loving is, I don't know, a man-eating train wreck?

I take a big breath and steady myself for how much shittier this night will be now that it's started to turn.

I can't believe her.

Julian's next in line? Like, fuck her. I don't want to be next in line, by the way, but she's an arsehole. It's not really my problem anymore. I don't want it to be at least, even if it still is a tiny bit.

I blow some air out of my mouth, look away from all the bullshit, then Daisy stands up and walks over to the bar without saying anything. Seems a bit weird and I wonder if I should go after her, but I'm pretty quickly distracted when I catch a look at BJ and I can see his brain's ticking into overdrive and we all know how he goes when he's like this. I look over at Jo, wonder if he's thinking the same thing. I discreetly tap my eye and my nose. My brother nods once.

I wait 'til Parks flits off to Jonah and Carmelo, and then I walk over to Beej, trying not to grimace too much as I do.

"You okay?"

"Yeah." He frowns, shakes his head a bit.

"It was a while back, yeah?"

"Yeah, I guess—" He nods, distracted. Pushes his hands through his hair, glancing over at Parks nattering away to Carms. "Right after we broke up."

"Right." I nod once. Before me then. Stings a bit.

What the fuck is the matter with her?

"Did they—"

"No." He gives me a sharp look and I nod once, but then he looks past me, frowning. Points his chin behind me. "What's going on there?"

I follow his eyes and then my stomach falls down a trap door.

Daisy toe to toe with Romeo Bambrilla. His hand around her fucking waist.

I push past BJ, cross the room in three steps. I can feel a storm building up in me. I grab his hands off her and step between them, staring down at her.

"What the fuck are you doing?" My chest feels tight.

She just stares up at me, blink a few times.

She gives me a weird smile, makes me feel all off balance. "You and me? We're done."

I scoff. "Oh, are we? Since when?"

"Now," she says without flinching.

I nod, frowning at her. "You mind telling me why?"

"Of course." She gives me a calm smile. "I know what I am to you, Christian."

"And what's that?" I ask, jaw tight.

And then she says with perfect, straight-faced delivery, "I'm the girl you're fucking while you're thinking of your best friend's girlfriend."

I stare over at her, mouth fallen open.

I breathe out. Feel like she just punched me in the stomach.

"Daisy, I—" I stutter.

"Oh—" She shakes her head lightly like she's not just pulling my whole world apart. "Did you think I didn't know?" She does this laugh that catches in her throat, kind of sounds like a cry and I'm sick about it. This one single tear slips from her eye and she smacks it away. She shakes her head at herself, swallows, then looks up at me with eyes that make me feel a bit afraid. She clears her throat.

"See, you're confusing me for someone who has a tiny bit of self-respect, because I've known the whole time what I am to you—and me and Rome—" She gestures between herself and him, grazing her hand on his shirt. I stare at it. My breathing's gone shallow and my eyes are wide and round. I can't get a handle on all the thoughts I've got.

"I don't know whether we're friends, I don't know what me and Rome are, but one thing I know for certain is that when I take him home tonight, he sure as fuck won't be thinking about Magnolia God damn Parks."

I stare over at her, open-mouthed. My eyes are bleary and the rest of me is completely frozen.

Holy shit.

She turns to Romeo. "Take me home?"

"Always." He nods once, slipping his hand into hers, and I should kill him. Make a point out of him that no one touches her now but me, but I can't kill him, I can't even fucking move. I can't see straight but I can see enough to watch Romeo fucking Bambrilla pull Daisy out of the club and away from me.

I stare at the spot on the ground she just walked from. I don't look up, don't look left or right. I can feel my brother's eyes on me, I can feel BJ staring at me and Parks, well, she might actually look a tiny bit afraid.

I stare after Daisy, watch her walking out to go home with someone that isn't me, and I feel like I'm about to cry on the spot. I don't cry. I'm not a crier. Magnolia's never made me cry in all the years I've loved her, in all that time and on all those night's I've watched her go home with BJ, with Tom, with whichever fucking flavour of the month she was using as her own personal flack-jacket. I've never felt like this and it's now, right now, this exact second that I realise I am in love with Daisy Haites. And then it is immediately after, in that exact second, that I realise I've lost her.

I push my hands through my hair, shake head, try to steady my breathing for a second, then I push past the boys to get to the emergency exit.

Jonah's charging after me because he's irrational about BJ, like he owes him shit because he was the one who dredged Rem out of the pool. I can't be bothered with fighting with him but I know it's coming anyway.

Punch a wall a couple of times and I don't need that doctor I love here to tell me I've broken a knuckle.

"Fuck!" I scream and I punch it again anyway.

"What the fuck?" Jonah spits at me and I spin around to face him. Honestly, I'm ready to hit him.

My brother's shaking his head at me, a finger on my chest that's meant to threaten me but it doesn't because I could beat him if I wanted to.

Jonah thinks he's tough shit because he's the first in line once Mum's done, but he can't fight like me. He forgets that because I never think it's worth it to fight him back, but it might be tonight. No matter how I slice it in my mind, fighting my brother and his best friend feels like a good way to distract myself from the fact that Daisy's in the back of a car being felt up by Romeo Bambrilla.

"What the fuck is she talking about?" BJ asks me. His eyes look ragged.

I glance over at Parks just for a second before BJ ducks his head, looking for my eyes. "Don't look at Parks—look at me."

Jo gives me a shove and then I shove him back, hard.

"Don't fuck with me tonight." I give him a look.

"Boys—" Henry jogs over, stands beside me. He pushes his sleeves up. I reckon that shits Jo more for some reason, because he grabs me by the neck of my shirt and slams me against the wall.

"Jonah!" Parks yanks his arm. "Let go of him—what are you doing?"

And my brother turns to her, glaring down.

"What the fuck are you doing, Magnolia?" Jonah barks back.

And Beej—he stares at me and Parks and lets out this sound, almost like a wolf's howl in the night.

"Are you fucking kidding, Parks?" He stares at her with wild eyes. "Is two of us not enough?"

"Beej—" She reaches for him, her eyes are all teary. Hate it when she cries, makes my heart feel twisted in my chest, so I look away because what else can I do?

"Did you know?" BJ barks down at her and I swear to God, for a second her face falters. And then she shakes her head. "Of course I didn't know!"

I bang my head backwards against the wall then shove my brother off of me.

Beej shakes his head and I don't think he believes her, but it's her, so he hooks his arm around her neck anyway. Kisses her cheek in this sad, pathetic way. Pulls her away from me. "Come on." He nods his head towards Main Street. "I'll take you home."

She nods obediently before she looks back at my brother. "Jonah— don't hurt him, okay?"

Jo just grunts at her and she looks over at me. Our eyes lock and I get this weird surge of adrenaline that's wrapped around everything I feel about her these days—good, bad, exciting, ugly, complicated, shameful, embarrassing, stupid, pointless—this is what loving her felt like. Our eyes hold and then, for probably the first time ever, I'm the first to look away.

"What's the matter with you?" Jonah asks, shaking his head at me.

Henry steps forward, shakes his head. "Not tonight, Jo."

"It's tonight if I say it's tonight," my brother tells him, stepping forward a bit and I know this is less about me as much as it's about them and Taura.

But Henry's stoic and gives my brother an unimpressed look. "Not tonight."

Hen gives me a little shove towards Main Street. "Let's go."

We sit in silence on the way home for the first few minutes, then Hen glances over, grimacing a bit.

"You okay?"

I rub my face, breathing heavy. "I'm in love with her, man—"

Henry gives me this look. "I know, bro, and I'm sorry, but it's not gonna happen. It's never gonna be you. She's always going to pick Beej—"

"No—fuck." I shake my head staring over at him. "Not Magnolia, no. I love—" I shake my head. I've never said it out loud before. "I'm in love with Daisy."

"Oh." He blinks. "Shit."

"Yeah."

"But she thinks you're in love with Magnolia."

"Yes." I nod once.

"Fuck." He gives me a steep look. "Are you?"

"I—yes." I shake my head. "Maybe? I was."

"And now?"

"I don't know—" I shake my head. I shove my hands through my hair. "I don't—" I sigh, because I don't know how I feel about Magnolia anymore. I take a couple of big breaths, poring over the night in my head, a lot of things I don't get.

"Daisy knew. How the fuck did she know?"

"Anyone's guess." He shrugs, confused. "Are you going to go speak to her?"

I give him a look. "No—" Shake my head. "She left with Rome—"

"So?" He frowns.

"So?" I stare over at him. "So, how could she do that to me?" I say, but I feel stupid even saying it out loud so I try to shrug it off. I feel like a fucking paper bag, empty and crumpled. Is this how I made her feel? I feel like she's stuck a fucking vacuum over my mouth and turned it on. Romeo? Of everyone, why Romeo?

The one fucking guy in her life I can't compete with. The boy she grew up with, the one who saved her life, the one whom she instinctively turns to when she's in danger. Maybe she thought she was in danger.

Maybe she was.

"Christian—" Henry gives me a look. "Bro, you have spent your whole relationship in love with someone else."

It's kind of true, kind of isn't. It's not like I picked it, not like I willed it to happen—I'm just kind of stuck there, that's all. So I just shake my head at him.

"What are you going to do about Beej?"

"I don't know, Hen." I look out the window, tired. And actually, I don't give a shit. I'm done giving a shit. Because I've done this fucking dancing before, and I don't know how I'm back here—how for the second time in my life, I've fallen in love with a girl too late for my own good, and she's off fucking someone else because of it.

# 55

# Daisy

Christian went weird the second she walked in—the very second.

And here I thought for a minute that maybe he was past all his shit with her—maybe now I was what he saw—but it wasn't true. Because when Magnolia made a dumb joke about her and my brother[331] being next in line or something mind-numbingly benign… And forget how his face went when he saw her, forget that he was staring over as the whole bloody mess unfolded like a fucking moron—it was this scoff that Christian let out, the one that no one but me heard—that's what pushed me over the edge.

I don't know why exactly it crushed me like it did. This little puff of air that blew the house of cards I was trying[332] to build with him down.

I wasn't overreacting—I know his breathing, I've learnt over the last few months, meditated on it while he's slept. I practically have a doctorate in it. I know what it meant when he did that, and it means I am exactly what I always worried I was to him.

I thought I might have been more. I'm not.

So he scoffs and me? I didn't react. I went still. I don't think he knew that I'd heard him, but I did, and my heart burst into flames instantly, and not in the good way, in the vampire-in-the-sun way.[333]

So I stood up and cut my losses, of which there are many. Think fast, I told myself. Make a plan, don't look back. Shift your attention to surviving and saving face.

I've had people come for my head all my life, but I've never really

---

[331] Which—by the way—what the fuck?

[332] Always trying.

[333] And not *Twilight* vampires in the sun, proper ones. Burnt to a crisp, blowing away in the wind.

had someone come for my heart before,[334] but here we are. Much of a muchness when it comes to surviving, if I'm being honest. Did you know our brains haven't yet adapted to being able to tell the difference between emotional pain and physical? Our secondary somatosensory cortex and our dorsal posterior insula both flare up the same way regardless if you're in physical pain or emotional pain. Our brains can't tell the difference. It just knows something's hurting us. For all my brain knows, I've just been stabbed through the heart. Christian wants to hurt me? Well, fuck him. I'll hurt him more and all roads lead to Rome.

I walked across the bar, locking eyes with the pair that had been on me all night, even when they shouldn't have. I have a new wave of gratefulness for them and their inappropriateness.

"Where's Tavie?" I asked Romeo as I saddled up beside him.

He glanced down at me, lifting his eyebrow. "She wasn't made to feel exactly welcome last night."[335]

I gave him a look. "I wonder why."

He flicked me a quarter smile.

"Are you two back on then?" I glanced up at him.

He shrugged. The shrug was to bait me.[336] "Maybe."

I took a step closer towards him. "Maybe not?"

His eyes flickered over my face and his brows dropped low. "What are you doing?"

"You were right." I flashed him a tight smile.[337]

He frowned a little. "About what?"

"We lasted less than a month."

Romeo's face faltered. "What are you talking about? I just saw you kissing him twenty minutes ago."

I shook my head, breathed out my mouth long and low, like in yoga. Kept myself level, kept myself contained. "And now we're done."

My voice didn't tremble as I said it.

He touched my arm. "What happened?"

---

[334] Tavie, maybe.

[335] As a side bar, the fucking gall on that girl, showing up to my brother's thirtieth with Romeo? Class act.

[336] He doesn't know that he doesn't need to. I'm all in already.

[337] Pray to God he doesn't see the hurt prickling through, and if he does that his infernal drive to save me kicks in and he'll kiss me anyway.

I shook my head again and gave him a tiny shrug. "I made a mistake, that's all."

"Yeah?" His brow furrowed a tiny bit. "And what was that?"

I stared at his mouth, flicked my eyes up to his eyes, back to his mouth.

He bit down on his bottom lip, looked at me suspiciously but still slipped his hand around my waist because he can't help it and I know that. "What's going on, Dais?"

And then you know what happened next.

Christian saw.

He probably got embarrassed to be losing face in front of Magnolia or some shit like that. Then I tell his secret to the world, which I almost feel bad about because—I guess I started to think he wanted... not her.[338] I didn't ask to be with him. He made me stop seeing Romeo and it was him who came to me that night.

At the bar with Romeo, I feel stupid and hot in my hands. My throat feels tight and I hate him for making me feel like this, so I look up at Romeo with eyes I know he'll never say no to. "Take me home?"

He nods once. "Always." Then he slips his hand into mine and pulls me out the door.

"Are you okay?" Rome asks me once we are in the car.

"Fine," I tell the window, still holding his hand.

I won't be letting it go anytime soon.

"I'm sorry, Dais," he tells me and I know he means it because we're programmed this way—to hurt when the other is hurting.

He starts looking for my eyes to try to make me feel less like I'm drowning, but he can't find them. Instead, he stares straight ahead and I count the street lamps to my door.

Romeo's brows are low when we get home. He's wearing the look men get on their faces when they're around a fragile woman—like they're navigating what they should do, how to proceed with caution. Like they're afraid to take advantage of you. But what if I want to be taken advantage of? What if I want caution thrown to the wind?

I've never had sex with one person while I'm in love with someone else.

---

[338] Also known as me.

305

Not consciously, anyway.[339] Once I knew I loved Christian, I stopped it with Rome. Tonight I'll just plough through.[340]

It's strange, actually. Surreal. Almost a bit of an out-of-body experience. I feel like I'm detached and watching down on myself in mystified horror.

Once we are back in my room, I know that if I don't just get it over with I'd find a reason not to.

My bedroom is full of reasons not to. Completely, hideously ripe with them.

Christian's T-shirt thrown over my pillow for one.[341]

His glass of water on his side table.

A pair of his shoes in the corner.

A packet of his condoms in my drawer, which I'll use with Rome just to spite him.

When we left my room a few hours ago, there was no part of me that didn't think Christian and I would be coming back here together later, so the room is literally full of reasons that this is wrong,[342] but my room is also full of reasons that prove to me that I've always been wrong.

I should have never fallen in love with him.[343]

All the reasons I shouldn't sleep with Rome immediately to me become reasons that I now must and, on the spot, I try my best to switch my mindset about sex from being an application of love to a waterboarding of self-correction.

This doesn't make it less weird, in case you were wondering.

As I move towards Rome, sliding my hands up and under his shirt, he grabs my wrists and gives me a wary smile. "Dais, don't you think we—"

"Rome," I interrupt. "I don't want to think."

"You just broke up with him. I just think we should give it a fucking minute—"

"I don't want to give it a fucking minute," I say, the words sharper

---

[339] I definitely have, in retrospect, but not on purpose. 'Til now.

[340] Pun semi-intended.

[341] I smack that away and kick it under my bed as quick as I can.

[342] Nay, deeply fucked.

[343] Me and in love… it doesn't work.

than I mean to. "I want you to stop thinking, stop talking, and just take off your God damn clothes."

"But you're sad." He frowns and something about his face looks like it did when we were in school[344] and my chest starts hurting in a different way. Multi-level hurting.[345] I'm a combine harvester ploughing through a bed of roses.

I swallow. Refocus myself on the endgame. The endgame here is survival.[346]

"Then make me feel better, Rome," I tell him, unflinchingly.

And then a look flickers over his face. His eyes trail down my face to my mouth and then he just grabs my face with both of his hands and moves me back towards the bed.

I trip, he catches me, and he throws me backwards and I'm relieved.

Relieved he's not pussyfooting around. Relieved for the distraction. Relieved to have his hands on me because it's like my body has a thousand lacerations all over where my blood is pouring out from and his wandering hands are what's stopping me from bleeding out.

I undress quickly, and I'm grateful that Romeo is[347] such an extraordinary kisser. But from this point forward, I don't open my eyes once until it's over.

And he's good. Good at what we're doing, I mean. He always has been, especially with me, because he just knows me, knows how to get me, where to touch me, where to kiss me, how to hold me to yield the best results for everyone involved.

Also, you know how you can sort of tell with boys when they're good it means they're sort of slutty, or in the very least, experienced.

I slept with a virgin[348] once after Rome and I first broke up and it was really bad. Apparently after I broke up with him he went on such a sex-bender that he's a real pro now, so you're welcome, world.[349] Romeo was never like that, though. He's one of the boys who was a good kisser, even back then. The kind of boy who knows their way around the bedroom because they've been in a lot of bedrooms.

---

[344] So painfully and unimaginably beautiful.

[345] Hurting Christian, hurting him, hurting me.

[346] As it's always been for me

[347] And always has been…

[348] Angus Breckinridge

[349] And sorry, Angus.

Christian knew his way around a bedroom. How much I love him grips my heart's ankle like a monster hiding under a bridge, but I kick him off.

It's not over quickly. Romeo's got stamina. He hits all the right places because he knows them by heart, and if my heart wasn't smushed under a pair of Magnolia Park's Aquazzuras maybe I could have enjoyed it, but I can't. I squeeze my eyes closed and I think Rome thinks they're closed because I'm enjoying it and maybe I'm all lost to the moment, but they're closed because if I open them and I see Romeo Bambrilla and not Christian Hemmes I swear to God I'll break in two.[350]

My mind is gunning my heart down with a million thoughts a minute.

Is Christian okay? Did they hurt him?[351] Is he with Magnolia? Did my brother hurt him? Did Christian ever actually like me at all or was it always only about the sex? Why did he make such a spectacle about us being together then? Romeo is so good at this. Is this fucked up?[352] Am I doing the wrong thing right now?[353,354] Wrong to who?[355] Wrong to me, yes, definitely. Wrong to Romeo? I don't know. He was with Tavie last night—which he only ever does to hurt me—so maybe it is fucked up but maybe that's okay because maybe Romeo and I are just like that. Maybe me and all men are like that. Not having a father can do that to you, you know? It's called emotional transference. I was raised by a slutty teenaged gang lord. Casual sex is his bread and butter, he doesn't do relationships.[356] Christian didn't either when I met him. Is that what I was to him? Bread and butter? Why did he come to my house and tell me we were together? Why did he start doing jealous? Was it all a lie? Is he completely full of shit?

My head stays here the whole time.

I don't want to do it a second time, but as soon as Rome pulls out

---

[350] I am in two.

[351] Did he fight back?

[352] Yes.

[353] No.

[354] Maybe.

[355] Everyone.

[356] And he didn't have time when he was raising me anyway.

I am engulfed with a searing pain. Visceral pain. I feel it everywhere. All over me, every single inch.

You know how after you burn your hand and you run it under the cold water, there's two seconds of it being okay after you've taken it out and then the burning comes roaring back? How it's like someone turns up the volume of your pain? Pain in stereo.

That's how my body feels.

The absence of Christian is all over me, and I realise that it hurts less when Rome touches me, so I need him to touch me more. I need Romeo to never stop touching me. I'm afraid for him to stop because I can't feel how I feel when he stops because I am unbearably in love with Christian Hemmes in a way I didn't even know until now that we're done—and you best fucking believe that we are done. I will never forgive him, never come back. I'll never look at him, speak to him again. He will be nothing to me even though he's everything. I will make him pay for the rest of his life for tricking me into loving him unrequitedly.

Round three, I force myself to keep my eyes open.

I make myself stare Rome right in the eyes. He likes that, and that makes me feel shitty. He brushes the hair from my face and looks at me like he loves me[357] and I mirror his face[358] because I don't care, fuck it, I'll burn this place to the ground if it means I can walk out of here alive.

I stare Rome right back in the eye, touch his cheek. He kisses the palm of my hand, and you don't need to tell me—I'm a fucking monster.

Let's call it electroshock for the heart.

Let's call it immersion therapy.

Let's call it the most difficult thing I've ever done.

But I wouldn't let myself close them.

And it was good. Amazing even? I came twice. I thought of Christian the whole time, wondered how far he'd gone with Magnolia. Had they slept together? What was he like when he touched her? Did his hands linger on her how they do on me? Did he touch me how he'd touched her? Where did his mouth go? Where would it stay? Does he like those places on my body because they're mine or because they're

---

[357] He does.

[358] Even though I don't.

309

the same parts she has but he can't touch them anymore?[359] Did he close his eyes when he was with me so he could see her? I never really noticed.[360] I think he used to, at the start, I think his eyes used to be closed a lot, but they felt like they were on me towards the end.

Maybe I was immersion therapy for him.

Do you know much about supernovas?[361]

There are two types. Type one is when the star accumulates matter from a neighbouring star until it ignites a nuclear reaction. Type two is when the star runs out of nuclear fuel and collapses under its own gravity.

My heart is a type two supernova.

I loved him so much, so quickly, too soon, and now it's done and I'm collapsing under the weight of it all. I'm imploding.

I'm thinking about my imploding heart and how empty I feel while Rome is still inside of me, and that fucks with my brain more than I can tell you.

Books and movies and TV shows portray having sex with one person when you're in love with another as something with a lot of angst and guilt and a sublime lack of enjoyment because the person doing it, ultimately, they're so in touch with their feelings and they're just a God damn fuck-up who's so incredibly human that they stop midway through and they're redeemed by this moment of clarity where they realise that the sex is not what they want because they're not having it with who they actually want to be with. But I knew going into this that Romeo Bambrilla is not the man I that am in love with. Instead, I will hold his body against mine as tight as I can, like a human shield. And you know what, I know that it won't work, but fuck it, at least I'm trying.

I don't know what this says about me as a person at this point, but I enjoy the coming. In some ways maybe even more than when I'm having sex with Christian.

With Christian, coming is a sign of the end. It's the final act of the only sort of intimacy I'll ever have with him[362] and then the intimacy

---

[359] That is a revolting thought. But maybe he is a revolting man. I hope he is. That might make this easier.

[360] I wish I had noticed.

[361] No? Just me then?

[362] And never have again.

will be pulled off, wrapped inside a tissue and thrown away. But here with Rome, coming is sixty seconds of rushing pain that feels mostly like pleasure and is my heart breaking or is it on fire? Definitely on fire, but is it the good kind or the bad kind? I can't tell. It just needs to be put out and I can't think of anything else for that whole minute, that whole perfect minute where the world rushes and shakes and I don't think about how I'm fucked up crazy in love with a man who doesn't give a shit about me.

# 56

# Julian

I don't completely understand what happened on my birthday.

The boys did a good job from keeping it from me—sort of appreciate the effort, sort of don't. She's my responsibility is all. And whatever happened, it's fucked up and it's fucked her up, she's gutted about it, but she's also not speaking to me about it either.

I didn't even know 'til the next morning that anything had gone down. That made me feel like shit. It was Romeo, shirtless in my kitchen, drinking milk from the carton.

"What the fuck are you doing here?" I frowned at him.

He gave me a cocky half smile. "You and Dais have some catching up to do—" Smacked me on the back. "Happy birthday, bruv."

Me and the boys are on the way to a little intervention with Ezra Brown.

It's been about a month since the job and he's only paid half. I'm a forgiving man—I'm not that forgiving, though, and I'm done with his bullshit.

I'm sitting in the armoured Defender with Miguel and I look over at him.

"Oi, level with me—" I nod my chin at him. "How bad is this with Face?"

He presses his lips together, thinking. "Yeah, pretty bad."

"Worse than when her and Rome broke up?"

He thinks for a second, nods once. "Probably."

I shake my head at him. "I haven't seen her skulking about."

"That's because they haven't left the bedroom." He gives me an unimpressed look. I pull a face. Disgusting. Like I want to know that.

I lean back in my chair and sigh. "What happened?"

Miguel clicks his tongue a couple of times, trying to work out what to say, what not to say—he's more loyal to my sister than to me.

A bit annoying. Can't really fault him on it, though, pretty stand-up quality in a man.

"She figured that Hemmes's in love with Magnolia Parks."

"Fuck." I blink, surprised. I didn't know.

Miguel shakes his head. "She's not taking it well."

We pull up to Ezra Brown's house in two cars. Kekoa, Miguel, and myself in the Defender. Happy and Smokes in the Escalade.

Climb out and over the front door of his Cobham estate.

Smart man. A place with the family down here, and apartment with Lyra up in Westbourne Green.

I knock twice.

Wait.

The door swings open and it's a girl. She's like—I don't know—eight? Nine? Fucking hate it when people have kids. It's too humanising.

I also don't like it when people let their children answer the door. It's fucking 2021. Pull it together, Brown. You owe £75 m to a gang lord, answer your own fucking door, you pussy.

The girl's eyes go a bit nervous when she sees me and I don't like it—I'd never hurt a kid.

"Is your dad here?" I ask her.

She just swallows and then a woman appears behind her. "Can I help you?"

"I'm looking for Ezra Brown," I tell her and her eyes dance from me to the boys. She bends down and tells the kid to go upstairs.

"What's this about?" she asks, frowning. Looks genuinely confused. She doesn't know that her husband got into bed with a very dangerous crowd.

"Is he here or isn't he?" Happy asks, grumpy. Not a tonne of patience up his sleeve on the best of days, let alone a day where I've interrupted his daytime soaps to come and threaten a man's life.

"Who is it, sweetheart?" Brown asks rounding the corner. He freezes when he sees us.

I raise my hand, give him a merry wave.

His brow furrows. "Darling, can you go get my lunch ready, please?"

She nods, leaves.

I check my watch. Santos de Cartier. A gift from the Hemmeses for my thirtieth. Very nice.

"Bit early for lunch, no?" I give him a look.

He clears his throat and steps out front with us. Closes the door behind him.

"Does your wife not know you owe me £75 million quid?"

He swallows.

"She not know about your little girlfriend either?"

He stands up a little straighter, tries to man up. "It's come to my attention that while you were in Vienna you acquired a secondary piece of art."

Smokes scoffs and I lift and eyebrow. "Has it?"

He nods once. "Valued at approximately £70 million."

"Now, how's that any of your business?" I ask, folding my arms over my chest.

He gives me a long look. "I think that about makes us even."

Koa starts laughing as Happy flashes Brown a gun concealed under his waistcoat.

I smile a little, shake my head—honestly, I'm pretty impressed with the balls on this guy.

I squint over at him, purse my lips. "It's a nice family you've got here—"

"That wife of yours," Smokes interjects. "She's pretty."

I'm good with reading people. Always have been, kind of have to be in this job and also when you're raising your kid sister.

Good at facial cues, body language and shit.

Fear is universal. Everyone looks scared the same way—and this fucking joker here now, when his wife is threatened, doesn't even bat an eyelid.

Some men, they'll move heaven and earth for their wives. Throw everything they have at you to keep their woman safe, but not this guy.

He doesn't give a shit about her, which usually means he's out of love but there's a prenup.

I'll be looking into that.

I give him a little smile. "If your kid wasn't home right now, I'd kill you right here on this doorstep."

He swallows again.

I walk towards my car, call back at him without a glance. "You'll be seeing me."

# 57

# Christian

I went to Grandad's after the party and spent the week up in Little Cawthorpe. He didn't really ask why I was there, he just knew that there was a why. Either way, he's not really the sort of man who pushes, at least not at first.

We went fishing in Saltfleetby, down in the Theddlethorpe Dunes. He was pretty quiet for the first hour. Works for me. I'm not a talker either, really. Happy to be in silence, most of the time. People say I get it from my dad, but I don't know my dad for shit. I say I get it from Grandad.

"So." He casts another line. "What sort of trouble are you in?"

I glance over at him and he doesn't look back, just keeps watching out over the water. "What makes you think I'm in trouble?"

He glances over again and sniffs a laugh. "Because y'are."

I sniff.

"It's your face—" Gestures between his eyebrows. "They're too low. Too much on your mind."

I nod once and think about side-stepping the conversation, but what do I have to lose, anyway?

"Do you remember BJ? Ballentine?"

He nods.

"His girlfriend?"

"The pretty one?"

I nod, scratch the back of my neck. "I've been in love with her for a really long time."

He nods slowly.

"Maybe I still am—" I shake my head. "But I fell in love with someone else too. I didn't mean to, it just happened. And she loved me back, the other girl, I think—and then she found out about Magnolia and, I don't know… It all went to shit. She hates me—" I shake my head. "Everyone's angry at me."

315

He stares over the ocean, nods a few more times.

"The girl you love now—where's she?"

I press my lips together. I shrug.

"Called her?"

I blow some air out of my mouth and stare up at the sky. "She left that night with her ex-boyfriend. She hasn't spoken to me since."

"Ay, but I asked if you've called her."

"No—" I frown over at him proudly. "Did you not hear what I said?"

"I did." He nods, squints at the sea, then goes quiet again. "This has been yer problem since you were a boy."

"What?" I frown over at him.

"You're proud," he tells me, his old eyebrows up. "It's not good fer ya."

"I'm not proud." I frown, annoyed.

"Aye." He nods. "Y'are. And yer clearly blind too if you don't know that about yerself."

I reel in my line, cast it back out again. Don't say a word because I don't know what to say.

"Talk to your friend," he tells me. "You've known him twenty years."

I shake my head. "I don't think he wants to see me."

"Maybe not, but after twenty years, it's a lot to lose."

A few days later, I drive back to London, not really sure of what more I could do other than speak at least to Beej, and probably Parks too.

I know I should talk to Daisy—she's the only person I want to talk to, actually—but fuck her because the night I realised I loved her was the night she went home with Romeo Bambrilla.

I knock on their door at Park Lane and my brother opens it.

"Oi." He nods his chin at me and steps aside to let me in. "Mum said you were in Louth?"

"I was." I nod.

"How's Grandad?"

I shrug. "He's got a new pig he's very proud of."

My brother chuckles then gives me a steep look. "He talk some sense into you?"

I give him a look but I don't really know what it's saying, because I don't need sense, I need three wishes.

316

"Is he here?" I look around.

"Downstairs." He pats me on the back.

I stand outside his closed door for a second, trying to work out what I'm going to say and how to start.

It's a hard thing about relationships, isn't it? Doesn't matter what type it is, if it's worth keeping, sometimes you have to say shit you don't want to, pry it out of your own mouth and toss it over a fence your mate's building now because that's what people do when you hurt them—build fences, raise walls, dig ditches, pitfalls, etc. If you're the one making the first move towards reconciliation, you sort of have to just stand there and see if their head pops up over the other side of the fence, see if they'll toss the ball back.

I knock once and don't wait for him to answer before I open it. Beej stares over at me and I lean against the doorframe. He looks back at the TV.

"Where'd you fuck off to then?" he asks the Man U rerun.

I shove my hands into my pockets, walk in a little more. "Just needed a minute."

He says nothing, just stares over at me and I shake my head. It's been years of this shit.

"I'm in love with her, Beej—"

His jaw goes tight, then he sniffs this little laugh, shakes his head. He looks angry but not necessarily at me.

"What?" I frown.

He presses his lips together. "You're just not the first person to tell me that lately."

I shake my head as I walk over to him. "That's fucked up, Beej." He kind of nods, distracted. "She's fucked in the head—" I tell him, but it's a mistake because he growls instantly and I sigh, annoyed that she can fuck us all around and no one can say shit about it.

"She is, man," I tell him. "She needs everyone to love her. You, me, Tom, Jules—it's fucking shit. And she—"

"Stop." He shakes his head. "What are you doing, Christian? This isn't about her."

I think that's mostly untrue. For him, it's always about her. Always has been, probably always will be.

"It's about you being my best friend and being in love with her," he says.

"I didn't mean to." I give him a look but he scoffs.

"You fucking dated her. Behind my back."

"Beej—" I bang my head against the wall behind me absentmind-edly. "It was an accident. We were hanging out—we've been friends forever—longer than you." He didn't like that—tosses me a warning with his eyes, so I give him a shrug. "I was just hanging out with her, the same way I'd hung out with her a billion times before that day, all our lives. And then one day we just kissed."

"Oh." He gives me an exaggerated look. "One day you just kissed!"

"It was rainy, in a phone box…"

"Fuck, Christian—" He starts shaking his head like crazy. "I'm not asking for a fucking play by play."

"Then what are you asking?" I yell a bit.

"Why her?" he yells back.

"Because she's Magnolia fucking Parks."

Which is the answer. It's the only answer he'll get and the only answer he needs, really—because I know he gets it. She's just one of those girls, you know? The kind that you'd do anything for, be anyone for, ruin your life for, throw away all your friends and scruples for forty seconds alone with her in a foggy phone booth because it was raining and she smelt like she did the summer you first lost her. Mag-nolia Parks is a million different things. A bitch, a pain in the arse, an enigma, a fucking super-blood moon—people do insane things to get a vantage point of those eclipses. I did an insane thing. Paid the price ever since.

BJ glares over at me and I shrug, as helpless to all of this now as I was then.

"She was sad and I wanted to make it better." I give him a look. "But she was sad because of you, Beej. Because for her, it's always you—"

He gives me a look that's weighed down. "That's not true anymore."

"Yes it fucking is, man." I roll my eyes. "How can't you see that? Everything she does is because of you, or about you, or trying to fuck you up because you fucked her up first."

He lays down on his bed and stares up at his ceiling. He blows air out of his mouth and peers over at me. "Why didn't you tell me?"

I sit down next to him. Sigh. "Because she's yours. And even when she isn't yours, she still is."

BJ looks back up to the ceiling and I stare at my hands.

"And I don't want her, Beej. I just—" I trail and sigh. "I don't know how to get past her."

He breathes loudly out of his nose.

"Yeah—I know the feeling."

I watch him carefully for a second. "Beej, I've gotta talk to her."

He grinds his jaw absentmindedly. "What are you going to say?"

Fucked if I know, that's my answer. Haven't got a fucking clue.

"I don't know." I lift my shoulders. "But I have to."

He frowns, nodding once. "I trust you."

# 58

# Daisy

Me and Romeo, we're complicated—obviously. What we're doing at the minute is not complicated, it's actually very transparent.

But what he is to me, which once upon a time was innocent and bushy-tailed, has now become convoluted and confusing.

It has been ever since that night with the bath and those men who tried to kill me. They couldn't do it—they just killed us. What we were before then, they changed it. They changed everything.

My boyfriend scrambled out from under the dead man on top of him and pulled me out of the bathroom, putting both guns in his pants.

I was shivering so much—less from the cold, more from the shock—so he put a robe around me. Didn't let me go.

Our brothers and his parents came for us soon after. They tried to take Romeo home but he wouldn't go, wouldn't let go, he wouldn't leave me.

They gave us a day.

When we woke up sometime in the late afternoon the next day after a night of barely sleeping—my throat was bruised and purple, I woke up swinging every half an hour, still fighting the men off in the sleep I don't think I was getting—our families, they sat us down and told us we had to break up. They said that these things kept happening when we're together, so we couldn't be together anymore. They said that Romeo was going to go to school in New York to finish out his final year. I couldn't say anything, I couldn't speak—I cried this weird, stunted cry that didn't even sound like myself and I felt like I was letting Romeo down even though I wouldn't let go of his hand. And he said no, put up a fight, hit my brother. Jules let him. Carmelo dragged him away.

They physically pulled us apart. Julian has a scar on his face from where I clawed him trying to get back to Romeo.

That night at about two in the morning, Romeo snuck into my room. I think Kekoa helped him in because he'd never have gotten in by himself. He pulled me out of bed, kissed me like crazy.

"Run away with me," he told me. Leave everything behind, our life, our families, Julian.

I couldn't talk. I shook my head.

"We don't need anyone else," he told me, holding my wrists. "New Zealand or Bali or somewhere far away where they can't get us."

I shook my head.

"Anywhere you want then—" He shrugged. "I don't care—"

"I can't leave London," I barely said. It hurt me so much to say it, it was such a spectacular strain that it made me feel nauseous afterwards.

But I knew he knew it wasn't about London. It was Julian.

"You can," he told me, giving me a look. "I'll take care of you—"

I shook my head.

"Dais, if we don't run they're flying me out tomorrow—we'll be apart for months."

I covered my face, started crying the foreign cry—he pulled my hands away, held them. "Come with me. You don't need him."

And I wish that was true, because if it was I would have gone with him, wherever he wanted, in the dead of night. I would have slipped away and left it all behind, because that really is the dream—but it's not true. I do need Julian. He's not just my brother, he's not just my best friend, he's my father and my protector and my family and my home—and Romeo meant the world to me, but my brother meant the universe.

I shook my head a tiny bit and Rome took a step back from me and a staggered breath.

"No?"

"I'm sorry—" I didn't really say out loud.[363]

Romeo let out a sad, dry laugh.

I reached for him.

He smacked my hand away.[364] And then he left. Flew to New York the next day.

That weekend he was plastered all over every magazine in England

---

[363] Though I did try.

[364] That hurt me as much as anything from the night before.

and America for hooking up with two girls from the same terrible reality TV show. Fucked his way through New York City, broke my heart wide open when he came home that Christmas and I didn't speak to him at all, even when our families spent the day together. New Year's Eve we both got drunk and slept together and so it began, the fucked-up version of our togetherness was born and lives on still. I can't tell where loving Romeo ends and being traumatised with Romeo beings. It's all muddled.

Muddled here no less as he falls down on my naked body, panting. He pushes his hand through my hair with a tenderness in his eyes I'm quite sure will make our precarious situation all the more dicey in due time.

We've been doing this for days. Non-stop. We only really stop to eat and sometimes shower.

It is a complete and total disaster, I know that. I am a walking train wreck. I loved Christian so much more than I knew I did—and I knew I did—but now here I am, in the wake of his absence, just a shell of a person who is ready to be filled by any means necessary.

Romeo is the means, and believe me when I say that he is necessary.

He's the hand punching through the ice I fell through.

He's the shot of anti-venom after a snake bite.

He's the climbing axe I'm clinging to on the side of the cliff I've just fallen off.

Romeo rolls in towards me, brushes his mouth over mine.

"Just gotta call Mum." Gives me a small smile. "Hasn't seen me in days. She's starting to worry."

I nod and look away, wondering how long it will take because when my mind is left to its own devices there's only one place it goes and it's a place I've forbidden now.

The door bell rings.

I sigh, annoyed I have to leave my room but quietly pleased to have the distraction of it all the same.

I wander downstairs in one of Romeo's T-shirts and lacy knickers, swing the front door open.

Tiller pulls back. "Woah."[365]

Rude. I pull a face.

---

[365] And I suspect—by the look of him—he doesn't mean that nicely.

He opens his mouth to say something but he pauses and looks at me properly.

"Are you okay?"

I take a shallow breath. All my breaths are shallow now. "What do you want, Tiller?"

"Is it true?" he asks.

I cross my arms over my chest. "Is what?"

"You and Hemmes are over?"

Searing pain. Straight face. "Yes."

He looks a bit sad for me, actually. Breathes out, shakes his head. "Look—Daisy, if you ever want to talk or, you know—like—"

"She doesn't," Rome says from behind me, slips his arms around my waist, and pulls me backwards into him all shirtless and obviously fresh from a shag.

Tiller holds my eyes—looks sadder still—then he glances past me to Rome. "Wasn't talking to you."

Romeo steps forward, pulling me behind him. "Should have let them shoot you—"

I yank Rome backwards. "Well, that wasn't your choice, Romeo." I glare up at him. "Go wait upstairs."

He glares over at Tiller for a few seconds and then kisses me in a way that makes me feel like I'm trash because it's a showy display and a point he's trying to prove, but I don't know what he's displaying and I don't know what his point is.

Tiller watches him walk away then looks down at me, eyebrow cocked.

"Geez." He scoffs. "You got past Christian qui—"

"Don't say his name," I say quickly. Low, back of the throat.

Tiller blinks, surprised.

"Or not," he says quietly, backing down the stairs. "I meant what I said. You want to talk—"

I nod once but I don't smile. I don't really know how anymore.

# 59

# Christian

I'm on my way to Holland Park and I'm sick to my fucking stomach.

This is worse than talking to Beej. At worst, Beej could just punch me. But Parks—I don't even—fuck, she could rip my soul right out. Has, in fact, several times. It's why I'm driving to her now, I guess. Ask her to give those pieces of myself back.

Marsaili lets me in, eyes all pinched and suspicious. She didn't like it when me and Parks were together, but I guess that just makes her a responsible parent or whatever she is. Who in their right mind would choose for their daughter to be with someone like me? Just an idiot, really, so I can't hold it against her.

I jog up the stairs, push open her door because it's not clicked shut. She's just sitting on her bed. Head down, nose in a magazine, so beautiful it's fucking disgusting and I immediately remember why I'm in this mess in the first place.

She feels eyes on her, looks up—glances around and over.

Magnolia's eyes go wide as she rushes over to me, pulling me into her room, yanking the hood of my sweater off my head.

"Did they hurt you?" she asks in a small voice. I shake my head and she sighs, relieved. "You did, but…" I tell her.

"What?" She blinks a lot.

"Honestly, Parks, fuck you." My tone comes out more aggressive than I mean it to, but I guess I'm pretty angry so I just roll with it anyway. "Like, really, fuck you. I mean it."

"Christian—"

"You're a bitch, Parks."

That one hits her like a slap. Hates that word, always has. She looks over at me with those fucking Bambi eyes, all big and wounded.

"I'm in love with you," I tell her, shaking my head. Kind of just spilt out—no permission, no forethought—like it saw it's chance for the first time in three years and made a break for it. I figure I'll just roll with the punches now because what do I have left to lose? I slip my hand around her waist.

"What?" She blinks, panicked. Then I kiss her.

And it's a strange kiss. Good, important—could be the most important kiss of my life actually, because it's very clarifying.

I've thought about kissing her for years since the last time we did it, made kissing her again my Everest, and here I am, in her bedroom in the middle of Holland Park with my hand on her waist, kissing her how I've wanted to for so long and it's not what I want and I know why.

"And actually—" I glare over at her. "I hate you."

She looks a bit shattered at that. "Why?"

"Because you let me be," I yell, exhausted. "There's a reason you turn to me over the other boys—"

She shakes her head quickly. "Yeah, because we—"

"Don't." I eye her. "You know why."

Then her fucking bottom lip starts shaking. Doesn't like it when anyone in the world is offside with her, really—but one of us? Me? She can't handle the rejection.

She gives me a weak shrug. "The other two, they're loyal to Beej. They'll lie to me for him. And I know you'd—"

"Do anything for you." I nod. "Yeah, I would. But fuck you for letting me. What's the matter with you? Do you need the whole fucking world to love you?"

"Christian," she says and her eyes go teary and then I just can't help it. I'm rushing towards her, got her wrists in my hand and I push some hair from her face.

I stare at her for a few seconds, run through my brain what I'm thinking, make sure I mean entirely what I'm about to say to her next. No takebacks—this is irrevocable kind of shit.

"I'm done with this now, yeah?"

"Christian." She sighs.

"And I need you to let me be, Parks." I give her a look. "Let me be over you."

She nods, looks a little bit like she did in school and she'd been scolded by Ms Bain. She also looks a little bit scared. "Are you not going to be my friend anymore?"

"I'll always be your friend, Parks, but I haven't been your friend for a really long time."

Her eyes drop from mine, embarrassed.

"From now on," I look for her eyes, "if you wouldn't ask Jonah to do it, don't ask me."

She shakes her head, I think at herself. "I'm so sorry—I don't know what's wrong with me, I—"

I press my tongue into my top lip.

"I let you." I shrug weakly. "We could have had this conversation three years ago but we didn't because I didn't want to." I flash her a half smile. "Loving you was a good reason not to love anyone else."

She blinks a few times and her eyes look brighter. "Do you love her, then?"

I nod, sitting down on her bed. "Yep."

She sits down next to me. "Lucky girl."

"Oi." I point at her, squashing down a smile, "None of that shit, Parks. We're strictly business now, you and me."

"Is she okay?" she asks.

I press my lips together, shake my head. "I don't know—we're not speaking."

Her face falls a bit and I wonder if I see a bit of guilt there. "I love you, Christian. You know that, right?"

"I know." I nod. "Not how I've loved you, unfortunately."

She purses her mouth. "I did once."

"Never how you love him, though." Give her a look, squeeze her knee playfully.

It feels like the end. After so long, so many years of bottled-up, tortured shit feelings, it feels like I'm watching the bonfire of how I love her go up in flames and I'm actually less sad about it than I thought I'd be. Mostly I'm just relieved.

I kiss her cheek, stand up, and walk over to the door. "Don't fuck it up with him, Parks—" I shake my head at her. "I'll be so fucking pissed if you do."

# 60

# Daisy

There's never been a time in my life that I can remember where Romeo and I have had sex and we didn't finish at the same time.[366] And I'd love to say I have anything to do with that, but I don't, it's him. Rome knows me, he always has. And he'd watch me and wait for me, and even now he does that, here in my bed, there in my shower, downstairs in the theatre room, on my kitchen bench, anywhere, everywhere, all the time. It's constant and we don't stop because I can't. If I do, I'll feel it all, it will rush back to me and I don't want to feel it anymore. I can't. I won't let myself. So he holds me against him again for the third time today, our bodies tense and rigid until the moment rolls through us and passes. And just like every time before this one, Romeo's head flops back and he smiles with his eyes closed, sniffing a laugh, and I, without conscious thought, bury my face in his neck and kiss it. Just once. Like I always have. Tastes salty, like it always has.

And, like always, that's the signal fire for round four.[367]

It's been about a fortnight since my brother's birthday happened, and we haven't really stopped. I haven't been answering my phone, I haven't even looked at it, even though I probably should. What happens next probably could have been avoided if I'd just looked at my bloody phone, but instead Rome's on top and I'm staring at him[368] when my bedroom door flings open.

Romeo looks back over his shoulder, glaring and ready to fight, but his demeanour changes completely the second he realises it's Jack.

"Well, well." He leans against the doorframe.

"Jack!" I growl "Get the fuck out."

---

[366] Is that too much information? Sorry.

[367] Don't be judgemental.

[368] Because it's the only way I don't see Christian.

"No," he says pointedly as he walks over to my windows, thrusting open the curtains.[369] "Do you even know what day it is, Dais?"

"The day we stopped being friends?" I say hotly as I yank a sheet over myself to cover up.

Jack makes a 'hah' sound, throwing me a fake smile.

He sits on the bed and Rome sits up, grinning over at him.

"Jacky—" They do the same handshake they've done since the night I introduced them and they got drunk and made it up approximately seven years ago.

Jack waves his hand between us. "So you two—this is happening?"[370]

Rome juts his chin in Jack's direction. "What do you think, Giles?"

"Me?" Jack gestures to himself. "I mean, personally, I think you're a Trojan packet away from an intervention—"

Rome starts laughing and I roll my eyes again.

"Jack—" I give him a look. "We're kind of in the middle of something…"

"Yes." He tilts his head. "Missionary! Riveting stuff, you two."

Romeo laughs more as he shoves his hand through his hair. "I mean, we put on a hell of a show this morning, man. You should have seen it, it was acrobatic."

"I don't doubt it—" Jack gives Romeo a tall look. "Look at that back, Rome—what are we benching these days?"

Romeo smirks, glancing over at me. "I don't know, what do you weigh?"[371]

"And, I mean, Daisy—" Jack gives me a look. "Mazel tov."

"Giles." I give him a warning look.

"What?" He frowns and gives a little shrug. "Rude not to acknowledge the elephant in the room."

"Jack!" I squawk.

He starts laughing at his own joke.

"I've got to say, though," Jack glances between us, "you two being back together is a lot to handle for the rest of us."

I roll my eyes. I can't be bothered to tell him we're not really together, we're just doing this.[372]

---

[369] Romeo and I both blink violently as though we've forgotten what direct sunlight feels like.

[370] He doesn't sound totally pleased.

[371] About 8.3 stone, thank you very much.

[372] I also don't know what Rome knows.

Rome leans back against the head of my bed, knees up, and cocks an eyebrow at our old friend. "How's that now?"

"Well, the two of you, you're very temperamental. On and off, up and down. Murder..." He eyeballs us.

Romeo pulls a face. "Attempted murder."

Jack smiles tightly and nods. "Much better."

Romeo laughs and leans over, kissing my cheek. "I'm gonna grab a shower." He grabs a pillow to cover himself as he rolls out of my bed.

Jack smacks his arse as he walks past and Romeo shakes his head, laughing at his old friend.

The whole thing makes me feel fifteen again, when these two were my only friends in the world and all I really had was them. It's still kind of true now, I guess. And for a brief moment the nostalgia of it all overtakes all the burning hurt I'm trying to smother out with Rome's body—it subsides and just for a second I'm afforded some cool relief. Then he shuts the bathroom door and the sound snaps the cord I've tethered from me to Romeo. That line between the two of us which, for all intents and purposes, is an IV drip for me because when you have an orgasm, something wonderful happens: dopamine and serotonin[373] are released into your system, which is basically morphine for a heart like mine.[374]

So me and Rome, we're having a lot of sex. Obviously.

I'm my own pain management specialist and Romeo Bambrilla is the drug dispensary. Thankfully, he runs a very loose outfit. Quality product and so much bang for my buck.[375]

It is a complicated fix, though, because at this point, where we've done it more times than I care to count,[376] it still hasn't erased Christian. Every time we have sex, my brain notes all the things Rome does different from him.

Rome prefers to be on top, Christian prefers me on top. Preferred.[377]

---

[373] (Also, I feel obligated as a med student to tell you something called oxycontin is also released but I don't want to think about that because I'm pretty sure that was the neuro-hormone that got me into this mess in the first place).

[374] Broken, to clarify.

[375] Pun absolutely intended.

[376] Than I could count, even if I tried.

[377] I'll say it again so I remember: preferred.

Romeo always seems to have his hands on my arse, Christian would have one around my waist, and the other around my neck.

Rome starts from the top and works his way down, Christian was a grazer.

And I don't want to think of him—but I can only ever think of him.

Jack gives me a long look, crossing his arms over his chest, looking both hurt and serious. "Where the fuck have you been?"[378]

"I—"

"I called you, texted a hundred times in the last week. Where have you been?"

"Nowhere!" I shrug, a bit helpless. "Just… here."

He points at my bed. "You've been here for a week?"

"Two, actually." I tell him, nose in the air.

He blinks a lot then shakes his head. "And Christian? Where's he?"

I shrug, my eyes instantly filling with tears at the mention of his name. I blink them away, shake my head at my stupid self, and Jack's face softens.

He sits down on the bed and wriggles in closer towards me. "What happened?"

"He's still in love with her."[379]

His face falters a little. "How do you know?"

"I know." I tell him solemnly.

He presses his lips together then nods his head towards the bathroom door. "So what is this, then?"

"It is—" I pause. I think I know what it is, but it's too ugly and cruel for me to acknowledge what I think I'm doing with the body of my best and oldest friends, but I'm dying here, and he always saves me when I'm dying. This is just in a different way. "I don't know. We're figuring it out."

Jack nods a little at me but he's frowning. "Don't forget what you are to him, Dais."[380]

"What am I to him?" I ask defiantly.

He gives me a look. "Everything."

---

[378] I hate it when Jack is disappointed in me.

[379] I manage to say this without dry-heaving.

[380] And whatever it is, I know I don't like the insinuation.

# 61

# Julian

"Right, boys." I sit back in my chair, look at all my men assembled at our dining room table. "We've gotta have a chat."

I sigh, look over the dinner my sister's made us. Ten-hour slow-cooked lamb ragu. Had to wait for her to clear out for this chat.

Kekoa stands, folds his arms over his chest. "Brown won't pay up."

Smokeshow scoffs, Happy shakes his head.

"Now, these two—" I nod towards the Silicon Baddies. "They can just drain his account. Pull from him everything he owes us, but—" I shake my head, Miguel mirrors me.

"It's bad for business," Declan says and gives the rest of the boys a look. "People can't think you can do this shit with us."

Kekoa nods.

"Right." I clap my hands together. "So we're getting even."

A murmur among the lads, agreement for the most part. Not necessarily from Miguel, but he wouldn't be on board for whatever stunt we're going to try here. Pretty Catholic. And you know what, I like God as much as the next guy, but sometimes you've just gotta do what you've gotta do.

"What about that wife of his?" Happy asks.

"We looked into it." Koa shakes his head. "We'd be doing the prick a favour."

I scratch my neck, thinking.

"He got a girlfriend?" Smokes asks.

"Yeah." Declan nods and gives him a look. "Lyra Iordanou."

"Oh, fuck—" Smokes sniffs laugh. "So that's a no-fly zone." Touching her would piss off too many people.

"Kids?" Happy throws out there and I give him a look.

"We don't fuck with kids." I shake my head.

Decks gives me a long look like he's thinking about it. "I don't know, Jules. It could be the right foot forward."

I shake my head again. "We don't fuck with kids, boys," I say loudly, mostly in case Dais is listening in. I can't be bothered with the crucifixion.

"We don't have to kill them—" TK shrugs. "Just take 'em for a minute. Squeeze some more money out of him."

Declan nods. "Teach him a lesson."

I look between them both. "You want me to kidnap an eight-year-old and a five-year-old?"

Declan gives me an irreverent shrug whose sole purpose is to get under my skin. "I just don't want anyone thinking you're a joke, bro."

I run my tongue over my teeth, shake my head a bit because I know that was to bait me and it worked.

The truth is I didn't love the feeling of this fucking nobody defying me. No one defies me. No one dares not pay me what they owe and this brand-new money fucking gee shows up out of the blue, asks me to steal him a motherfucking Klimt, and then has the fucking balls to only pay me half?

I'd kill him without question, but I'd rather teach him a lesson, let the fear he'll live with every day for the rest of his life serve as a living, breathing billboard that nobody fucks me over and gets away with it.

I give the lads a steep look. "No one hurts them, yeah?"

Kekoa nods. "Never."

"Okay." I jut my chin out, nod my head. "Let's do this."

# 62

# Christian

Me and the boys jiff off to the Netherlands. Don't remember whose idea it was, me or BJ's. Probably a bad one, if I'm honest. Beej and Parks had this wild fight. Worst one I've ever seen with them—tearing each other to pieces out there on Harrington Street for the whole world to see. We're all usually pretty conscious of keeping this shit in the family, inside where no one but us can see it, but that one snowballed too quickly, and he went too far, and he got too high. When she worked it out she was as devastated as you'd imagine. More, probably.

Amsterdam felt inviting for that reason, I reckon. Absolute escapism—which, honestly, none of us thought through properly before we got there. For BJ, escapism is all drugs and sex, and we've been down this road before.

There's no "say when" with him. He doesn't know how to say when.

It's as bad as you think it'd be, and he's more of a mess than any of us would ever let Parks know. Even me, a few months ago when I probably would have tried to let it slip to her how shit he's been, I'd probably have covered his tracks a bit here because the truth is too much.

We all take turns babysitting him and he's too fucked up to notice.

It's Henry's turn, so Jo and I go grab a bite.

Jo dusts off his hands, leans back in his chair at Renzo's Delicatessan, and looks over at me.

"Oi, so how are you doing with all the Daisy shit?"

"What are you talking about?" I frown.

He frowns a little. "Like, her and Rome—"

I blink a few times. "What about them?"

Jo crosses his arms over his chest and frowns, and then I get a shit feeling. Just like a low-lying nervousness that starts swirling in my stomach.

My brother scratches the back of his neck. "Bro, they are, like, fully back on."

I stare over at him. Shake my head. "No, they're not."

Can't be. That night, it would have just been a one-time thing.

He frowns, nodding. "They are."

"People talk so much shit, Jo. That's not true."

My brother looks at me a bit confused. "Christian, I saw them."

"Saw them doing what?" I shrug.

"Knitting." He gives me a look. "They're together, bro. Julian said they're never apart and that he…"

He keeps talking but I'm not listening. I sort of feel dizzy. Nauseous and dizzy. I don't know what I thought she was doing all this time—just missing me, I guess. I'm a fucking idiot, of course she'd go back to Romeo. I don't know why I didn't think she would. Maybe I thought he wouldn't take her back after me, but why wouldn't he? Who wouldn't?

"Are you okay?" My brother tilts his head. "You look weird."

"Do you think they're having sex?" I ask him.

He gives me a weird look. Nods once.

"A lot?"

He presses his tongue into his bottom lip, frowns, nods once. "I'm pretty sure it's all they're doing—"

And it's like an avalanche in my brain, all the things I've done with Daisy, all these things I actually never put a stop to in my mind. It wasn't conscious, it's not like I was there all pathetic and shit thinking we'd be together forever, but I just never really thought about it stopping—us stopping. And we've stopped, I know, these last few weeks, but I thought we'd stopped because she did the wrong thing by me, fucking him that night, and in a couple of weeks when I'd cooled down and she'd realised that she really fucked up and overreacted and that she loves me back, that we'd start up again and we'd keep starting back up forever, I guess.

But she's there in her room with him? Now? Her room where I left my favourite trackpants from Bassike? Where half my underwear is? Where my phone charger's still plugged into her wall? I swear to God if that fucking prick is using my phone charger—

My socks are there. What if he's wearing my socks?

I bought condoms, left them in the drawer on my side of her bed. What if he uses them to fuck her?

I make a weird sound, press my hand into my mouth. "I think I'm gonna be sick."

He scowls over at me. "What the fuck is the matter with you?"

Does he touch her like I touch her? I love her waist, love how I can hold it in one hand. The freckle under her eye that always seems like a call to arms to kiss her, the corner of her jaw that I trace over every time we have sex. Is he doing that? Of course he is, the shape of her face fucking demands it.

I look up at my brother. I think I've gone pale.

He shakes his head. "What's wrong? Do you... do you love her?" He chuckles.

I just stare over him, my breathing's gone fast.

Her breathing goes fast when she's getting close to finishing, these quick, breathy pants that are so sexy and I don't know, every time she did them I felt so fucking proud of myself. I wore making her breathless like a badge of honor, but then, I wonder, is she breathing like that for him?

I throw back the rest of my Greyhound. One gulp. Eye Jo's glass of whiskey. Grab it. One gulp.

Jo stares at me, looking at me a bit foreign. Jonah doesn't love people. Or when he does, he does it very reluctantly.

"Are you being for real right now?" He blinks. "Are you a crazy person in love with her?"

"I—I—" I shake my head. "I don't know what that means, Jonah."

"This." He gestures towards me. "You're fucking twigging out, man."

I push the tips of my fingers into my closed eyes, shake my head. "I'm properly in love with her, Jo."

"Then what the fuck are you doing in Amsterdam?" He shakes his head.

"You just told me she has a fucking boyfriend!"

"Well, she does, I think—" He shrugs.

I shake my head at him. Pinch between my eyes. I hate girls. They're fucking monsters, all of them.

I honestly thought she loved me too.

But here we are. So fuck her.

I look over at my brother. "Where are the boys?"

Fuck it. I'm going Full Beej.

# 63

# Daisy

Romeo and I decide to go to Annabel's for dinner and Julian tags
along. It makes me feel like I'm fifteen again being out with the two
of them,[381] but I'm not who I was when I was then. Back then, somehow,[382] I was quite hopeful. I believed in love, I thought Rome and
I would be in it forever, thought forever was a destination, not just a
thing we say to make ourselves feel better. I remember being fifteen
and feeling like I'd never love anything as much as I loved Rome.
Then came Christian, who jumped the fence, gunned down my hes-
itations and inhibitions, and blew a hole right through the centre of
me. I loved him in a way I didn't know I knew how to love someone.
Loving him has made me sure I'll never love anyone that same way
again, because that hole he left reminded me of a case study I saw in
a medical journal that documented injuries from the American Civil
War.[383] There was this solider for the 149th Pennsylvanian Infan-
try who was wounded by a massive shell fragment and it blew right
through him—tore away the dorsal integuments and horrendously
lacerated the subjacent muscles—but there was no injury to his spine,
not even his ribs. He was, for all intents and purposes, fine. I think
after six months they actually sent him back out into the war. A hole
right through him and everything. The illustration in that book—it's
me. I am the fine man with the gaping hole through the middle of
him.

Christian is the artillery shell that tore my life to pieces just because
I loved him how I did and so now I think I hate him for it. I feel the
absence of him in my life the way you can feel the sun slip behind a

---

[381] Which I suppose has a sort of nice nostalgia to it…

[382] I don't know how.

[383] Just for fun. Some light reading, you know how it goes.

cloud and wish you were fifteen again, full of stupid hope and unbroken and able to love properly, but here we are. Immeasurably fucked up, fucking my oldest friend in the world and fucking him over all at once. I won't stop, though. I don't think I could even if I wanted to.

Rome tosses an arm around me while he and my brother talk about the Liverpool / Man U game on the weekend. I'm making a Pinterest board of things I want to cook for Christmas when I feel eyes on me. I glance up. Look around.[384]

It only takes a second to find them and I look away as soon as I do.

Christian Hemmes has no right whatsoever to be looking over at me like I've skinned his fucking dog by being here with my brother and my childhood sweetheart. None. Zero rights.

I stare intensely down at my half-eaten plate of the Mussels Marinière. Not because it isn't delicious, but because I also got the Lobster a L'Américaine.

"You good?" My brother nods his chin at me.[385]

I barely glance up, nod back.

Rome looks over at me with a frown at the very same second Christian just waltzes up to our table, I can tell it's him without looking up. New shoes. Black J.M. Weston Nubuck Sneakers. Old black jeans of his that are all torn up and showing a knee I love. I stare down for a few seconds as I try not to let the weight of how much I love him flatten me dead.

I look up. "What do you want?"

He looks a bit sad that that's what I opened with, I think, and it gives me a thrill. I wish it didn't, I wish I wasn't like this, that we weren't like this, that I wasn't used to having to forage through his actions and the way he blinks to find a shred of evidence that he, at least in some way, liked me how I loved him.

But I am like this, and I don't know how else to tell that anything between us was real besides taking the knife he put in my back and prodding him with it.

Christian nods his head away from the table. "Can we talk?"

Romeo leans back in his chair, looks up at Christian incredulously as he folds his arms over his chest.

---

[384] You get a Spidey-sense for these things after an attempted murder or two...

[385] Try to remind myself that it's technically nice, not annoying, that Julian's as observant as he is.

"No." I shake my head, not holding his eyes.

Christian sighs. "Dais, come on—"

Romeo stands. "She said no."

Christian looks down at him, annoyed. "What the fuck are you standing for? Sit down, no one's talking to you."

Rome's head pulls back in surprise.

I stand up between them, shaking my head at Christian. "Just go—"

"Daisy." He gives me this look, sort of desperate, kind of tired. "Please, I just want to talk—"

But Rome steps around me and shoves Christian away. "She told you to leave."

Christian sniffs this sort of hollow laugh that makes me feel nervous because I know Rome thinks he's a better fighter than Christian because he's never really fought him. He's only seen him in that constructed one at the museum in Vienna, but I know how Christian fights. I know why he doesn't usually do it.

Christian catches himself and shoves Rome back, quickly following it up with a crazy punch square in the jaw.

Rome wasn't expecting it, but it only takes him a second to recover lunge at Christian, knocking him backwards into the table behind him. Food, plates, glassware smash everywhere as Christian wrestles Rome and starts punching the shit out of him. Rome gets the occasional punch in, but not really, and everyone is staring—everyone.

I look over wildly at my brother—who actually, if I'm honest, looks a little bored.[386] I know my eyes are wide with embarrassment. "Would you fucking do something, Julian?" I yell.

He grunts and pushes back from the table, walks over, and pulls Christian to his feet—hurling him away from Rome and pointing a threatening finger at him.

"She told you to go, man. So you better fucking go."

Christian gives me a long look, his chest heaving—fists bloody, so is his nose—he stares at me like I've wronged him, like it was me who tricked him into loving me, like it was me who threw his heart under a bus, but we both know the truth.

He presses his tongue into his bottom lip, wipes the blood away

---

[386] Like the two loves of my life fighting here in this restaurant is just a dime a fucking dozen.

338

and I stare at him a second longer than I really should before over to Rome, checking over his face. He pushes my fussing hands away when I get there, embarrassed and angry. I grab his face so he has to look at me, so I can hurt Christian one more time by making him watch me touch Rome like this. I don't even know if it will hurt him, but I'm willing to take the chance for a moment's reprieve, trade my hurting for his, even if it's just for a second.

# 64

# Julian

I had another fight last night.

Didn't end that well—not for the guy in the cage, anyway.

Felt a bit bad, but it's the risk of an underground fight, isn't it?

Could have killed me as easily as I killed him. I guess that's maybe not altogether true either.

I wear a long sleeve shirt so Daisy can't spot the bruises—if she does, she'll know and she'll be angry.

"Oi." I walk into the kitchen, sit down at the counter.

"Hi." My sister looks up, flour smeared across her face.

"Baking?"

"No, just having one of those renowned flour facials..." She gives me a look, that little shit.

The kitchen's a disaster. Like she's cooking eight things at once. She hasn't cooked in weeks, not since she and Hemmes called it—weird for her, she never doesn't cook. Even when she was a kid. Actually, even when our parents died, she cooked. Didn't talk, but she'd cook.

It's the following a recipe for her. Measuring, pouring, creating a plan and it working because cooking is just physics. It's quantifiable reactions, that's what she told me when she was twelve. The results don't vary if you follow the recipe.

I've never seen her cook more than one thing at a time, it'd feel counter-intuitive for her because she does it for the method, and here she's darting from countertop to countertop, bowl to bowl, spoons everywhere, burners left on, oven door cracked open—she'd never do that if she was fine, but I guess that's the point.

She's not.

"What's this?" I dip my finger in the bowl she's stirring.

She smacks my hand away. "Blueberry filling for a pie I'm making."

I look past her to the oven. "Are you making eclairs?"

340

"And millefeuilles," she says without looking up. "Pass me the butter."

I do, then I lean back against the counter, watch the sister that I raised—try to read the room even though she doesn't want me to, that's why she's moving around it so fast, like a hummingbird that won't land.

"I'm worried about you, Dais."

She scratches her nose with her forearm, somehow emerges more floury. "Well, don't be." She flashes me a look that tells me everything I need to know. "I'm fine."

"You and Rome trying to break some sort of record?"

She glares over at me. "You're one to talk—you have a different girl in your bed every night."

"Always have, though." I shrug, point over at her. "But you? This isn't like you."

She ignores me.

"Miguel said you've been skipping class—the laundry's backed up for yards—"

"Do it yourself." She tells the bowl she's mixing.

I shake my head. "It's not about the laundry, Dais, I'll send it out. But you love laundry and you love cooking and you love class and you love boxing and you love reading and you're doing none of it anymore—"

She looks away for a few seconds then turns back, a little defiant look across her face. "Well, maybe I don't really want to feel like me anymore."

I stare over at her and shake my head, feeling a tiny bit afraid. "What the fuck did he do to you?"

She shrugs, staring unfocused at the pile of dishes in the sink.

I tilt my head, looking for her eye.

"Want me to kill him?" I ask, just looking for a laugh.

She looks over at me, says nothing. Blinks a few times. "I'm going to make a Huntsman Pie," she eventually says, nodding to herself.

"What about the desserts?" I ask, eyeing the blueberry filling.

She picks up the bowl and dumps it in the sink.

"I'm out of slab bacon," she tells me. "Will you run out and get me some?"

# 65

# Daisy

I step out of the shower and Rome passes me a towel. He's got one eye closed and he's smiling at me how I wish he wouldn't.[387] He brushes his mouth over mine how he shouldn't, but I kiss him back because this is what I'm like now.

I move past him and look at myself in the mirror, marvel at how I can look the same on the outside and feel like a shitty, terrible shell of myself on the inside. Façades are impressive like that.

I pick up my toothbrush, toothpaste on. Marvis Jasmin Mint. Stare at myself, trying to look for a familiar thing, but there's nothing familiar in me left, just Rome. I'm grateful he's here even though I feel terrible he's here. I can tell that all the things I'm lying to myself about aren't true.

He loves me.

I love someone else.

Who loves someone else.

It's all very... Greek. And you know how those stories end—someone dies. There's always tragedy. I'm the death. I'll be the tragedy.

Rome comes up behind me, slips his arms around my towel-clad body, buries his mouth in my neck.

"Oi, so, Mum wanted you to come for dinner tonight—"

"Oh," I say. I open my mouth to say more but nothing really comes. I can't go to family dinner with Romeo for about a million reasons—one of them being I can't let Delina see me like this. If she does, she'll know. Am I healthy? No. Am I functional? Barely. Am I using her son? Completely.

"Um—" I turn and give him a tight smile, shake my head dismissively. "I don't know, I don't really feel like it."

---

[387] It reminds me how shit I am being.

"Like dinner?" He blinks.[388]

"Yeah." I shrug. "You just go now and then come back later and we'll like—whatever—"

He blinks a few times then swallows once. "We'll whatever?" he repeats, brows lowering.

"You know what I mean—" I shrug, trying to move past whatever's happening as quick as I can.

He shakes his head. "I don't actually, Dais."

"It's not a big deal." I lift one shoulder up and down. "Just you go, give them my love, and then come back after and we'll pick up where we left off." I lean in to kiss him and he pulls back, and how he stares at me makes me feel frightened. He's never really looked at me like that before. Like I'm a stranger, like he's lost sight of something he recognised too.[389]

"What are you doing?" He frowns.

I press my lips together. "Nothing—"

"Bullshit." He scowls and steps away from me. Back turned from me, he pushes his hands through his hair. He shakes his head and then he whips around, presses his hand into his mouth and glares over at me.

"Daisy, I love you," he tells me, unflinching. Shit.[390] "I'm in love with you."

And here is what I say, "Rome, don't do this—"

He scoffs. "Do what?"

"This!" I wave my hand at him vaguely. "What are you doing this for—"

"What?" he interrupts.[391] "Me telling you I love you?"

"Yes!" I huff.

His mouth moves but sound doesn't come out. He stares over at me, painfully confused. "What the fuck are you talking about?" He shakes his head and then looks at me a bit like I'm a stranger. "What are we doing?" He stares at me, and his eyes look blurry.

I say nothing, because what the fuck can I say?

---

[388] Not understanding.

[389] I guess he has.

[390] Shit. Shit. Shit.

[391] And I wonder if he might be about to cry? His eyes look like it.

He looks nervous as he asks louder, "What are you doing with me, Dais?"

"I don't know." I shrug hopelessly, press my hands into my eye sockets. "I—I—I'm—treading water—"[392]

Which is true, but I don't mean to say it out loud[393] and but when I do it's done. Hits him like a bullet, dead centre. A kill shot.[394]

His face falls, the breath leaves his body and I've crumpled him up for a second, this boy I've loved for as long as I can remember but I'm not in love with anymore, who's fought for me and protected me, who's killed for me, who I have killed for. I'd kill someone for less than all the ways I'm hurting him right now, but none of that matters now because I needed him to survive.[395] I was sinking, couldn't keep my head above the water, and then I saw him across the bar and now here I am, killing him differently than the ways they've tried to kill us before, but dying is dying, I guess, and I can see him die a little as I say that with him I'm just treading water.

"Drown then," he tells me.[396] "I don't give a shit."

He stares over at me, eyes dark, jaw tight, nostrils flared—and all of those things are true, but the truest part of his face is the part where it's broken.

He pushes past me, slams the bathroom door. A few seconds later my bedroom door slams too.

And then my breathing goes to shit because the dull ache I've been smothering with Romeo's body cranks right back up in his absence.

Instant, searing pain.

I make this sound that sounds like the cry of a stranger as I sweep varying items off my bathroom vanity and on to the floor.

Glass breaks all over the floor and I stare at the shards and pieces for a few seconds[397] before I get the vacuum to clean it up. If Romeo was still here, he'd say that was the most aggressively me thing he's ever seen, breaking something and then cleaning it up immediately.

---

[392] Oh my God.

[393] Oh my God.

[394] What have I done?

[395] Need, maybe?

[396] His entire face shifting to stone.

[397] See myself in them more than I do a mirror.

Pain is a good distraction from pain, I think to myself as I sit on the bathroom floor and pick out glass from the soles of my feet.

I do it slowly, try to make it last, let myself be as distracted as long as I possibly can from the feeling I have, but I can't, because that fire in me that we all have—that Christian left for dead—that Rome was stoking 'til just now—it's down to its last embers.

I need to do something.

I wander downstairs and into the kitchen. It's a bit later now, around 8 pm.

Declan's in there, just him.

And that's okay, it's fine—preferable, even.

He looks up at me, nods his chin at my feet with the bandages on the soles of it. "What happened?"

I shrug dismissively. "Stepped in some glass."

He stands up and walks over to me, frowning—grabs one of my feet and looks up at me a bit incredulous. "How much fucking glass, Dais?"[398]

I ignore him.

He boosts me by my waist onto the kitchen bench behind me, picks my foot up again, and pulls back one of the bandages. It hurts a lot but I don't even wince.

He frowns up at me. "Did you give yourself stitches?"

I nod once.

"What the fuck happened?"

"I just dropped some glass upstairs and then I stepped in it."

"By accident?" he says[399] to me as he searches my face.

I say nothing, reach past him to the half-drunk bottle of vodka, and pour some into a dirty glass by the sink. Toss it back.

Declan watches me, frowning. Blows some air out of his mouth, moves back to the table he was sitting at.

"Where's Julian?" I ask, pouring myself some more.

He leans forward on the table and gives me a long look. He knows I know where he is. Josette Balaska is in town. A repeat offender of his. They're at a hotel. "The Rosewood," Declan tells me anyway.

---

[398] He's worried. They're all worried, though.

[399] (He hopes.)

"Is he heading home soon?" I ask casually. I know the answer to that too.[400]

He looks at me out of the corner of his eyes. "Home for breakfast, he said."

"Oh." I nod once, my eyes floating around the kitchen. "Where's everyone else?"

Another long look. "Miguel's in his room. Smokes and Happy—I don't know. The Baddies are on the town."

"Right." I purse my lips. "So, what are you doing, then?"

"Now?"

"Yeah." I shrug.

He gives me a weird look. "Nothing."

I nod once and he huffs a laugh, bites his bottom lip and picks up the newspaper.

I frown and feel huffy on my insides. I don't like Declan ignoring me, so I perch myself up on the kitchen counter directly opposite him and just watch, waiting for him to look up.

He doesn't for a long time. At least a minute or so at first.

A full minute of ignoring me. That doesn't sound like a long time, but it is when you remember that Declan Ellis has spent the last four years entirely un-ignoring me.

But he reads the newspaper intently, even making facial expressions as he does, sniffing laughs here and there.

This makes me want him more than I did when I initially thought of this idea.

It's an impure want—I'll give you that. Polluted by a burning desire to not feel like my heart is about to blow out, a little bit of pride, and a lot of lust—but I want him on my body. Now.

So I sit there, waiting, kicking my legs, picking at my nails, drinking shot after shot—at room temperature, mind you![401]—waiting for Declan to look up, which he does—finally!—before he quickly looks back down.

This happens a few times.

"What are you doing?" he eventually asks the *Daily Telegraph*.

"Me?" I fake-clarify. "Nothing." Pause. "Is there something I should be doing?" I ask lightly.

---

[400] It's no.

[401] Gross.

He presses his tongue down on his lips, squinting at the paper. "Daisy—"

"Declan." I mimic his tone.

He glances up at me and our eyes hold.

He wants me too. Not that I thought there was much of a question about that but, to be clear, when he looks at me, even from a few meters away, I know he wants me.

I can feel it in the room and, also, I can read it on his body. His pupils are dilated, he's pressing into the marble with his hands so hard they're white, he's trying to steady his breathing.

I shift my weight around a little, not dropping his eyes.

He stands up and walks over to me, tilting so our eyes meet. "Stop."

"Stop what?" I blink innocently. I know he doesn't want me to stop. He's come and stood in front of me, between my legs, nothing but a few inches between us.

"This."

"What?" I bat my eyes at him.

"This," he says clearer.

"Why?"

He barely shakes his head. "What's going on?"

"Nothing." I shrug airily. "I'm fine—"

Delcan's eyes flicker over my face. "Where's Rome?"

I breathe out a controlled breath. "I believe that we currently aren't on speaking terms."[402]

My presses his lips together. Nods once. "Hence the vodka."

I shrug. "Sure, if you say so."

I take another shot.

Declan takes a conscious step away from me, pushes his hands through his hair. "Goodnight then—"

"Where are you going?" I pout.

He gives me a look. "To bed."

I swallow. "Here or your place?"

He crosses his arms over his chest, trying to look unimpressed. "Here."

I bite down on my bottom lip and peer over at him. "Would you like some company?"

He gives me a look. "Daisy—"

---

[402] To put it mildly.

"What?" I ask brightly.

He shakes his head. "You seem drunk."

"I am drunk." I nod.

He sniffs, shakes his head, and backs away a little more.

I feel a panic ripple through me as he does, like it's slipping through my fingers—my night's chance at not feeling as though my insides are up in flames, so I decide to go in a different direction.

"Are you scared of my brother?" I ask him antagonistically.

Declan scoffs. "No, I'm not scared of your brother."

"Then why?" I ask and he says nothing. "Nothing we haven't done before," I tell him and I know I sound desperate. I am desperate. It's ugly. I should be embarrassed. But I'm not and I don't care. Call me a slag or a slut or tart or whatever the fuck you want, I'll be them all, I don't care as long as I don't have to think of Christian.

Decks gives me a look. "I know."

I go for the second antagonistic swing. "Have you forgotten how?"

"Well, I know you haven't," he says too quickly,[403] like he's angry at me.

"Wow—" I let out a dry laugh,[404] nodding. "Fuck you then."

I jump off the bench and push past him. He grabs my wrist, turns me around, and now that I'm standing up, I realise I'm the sort of drunk where my hands and feet feel warm and tingly.

Declan's eyes wander over my face and he pushes some hair behind my ears.

"How drunk are you?"

I blink a few times. "Very drunk," I nod. "But very willing—"

He turns his head away from me then peers back, brows furrowed. And then it just hangs there. Both of us looking at each other like kids at a school dance too scared of one another to make the first move.

I walk over towards the cellar. "Do you want some wine?"

"You don't need it." He gives his head a little shake as he follows me down the cellar stairs anyway. "Neither do I," he tells me solemnly.

I swallow a little, nervous but the good kind—the kind of nervous a drug addict feels when their skin is burning, desperate for a hit and they know it's coming. In a minute I'll stop feeling so awful.

---

[403] He's been saving that one up for a while, I can tell…

[404] Stung a bit, I guess. I'll take all the stings I can.

I stand there, waiting for him to make a move, but he doesn't. He cocks an eyebrow. "If you think I'm starting this, you're out of your fucking mind."

And then all I do is raise my arms in the air. As soon as I do, Decks rushes me, pulls my shirt off, picks me up off the step and slams me into the wall behind us. It's sandstone and grazes my bare shoulder. It hurts, but what doesn't these days?

We tear each other's clothes off in record time, both of us too scared that if we pause for even a second the moment will break and we'll have to stop. I don't want to stop. I want him on me and in me, and I love skin on skin. I love him on me—or anyone on me, I think, because it stops it.

The dull ache fades to nothing.

I feel like I can breathe again.

He pulls me against him, breathing heavily in my ear—he's wanted this for so long. I'm wrapped up in four years of want and it comes hurtling back to me, all the reasons Declan was so good at this. He always been good to me... kind to me. Selfless when it came to me, and here I am, selfish and thoughtless and using him and I curse Christian's name under my breath for making me this pitiful, hateful version of myself.

Sleeping with Declan is harder than I wanted it to be, though, because as soon as I'm doing it, I can feel it, feel me, ripping holes in the fabric of our friendship. Every time he pulls back just to look at me, I feel a stitch pop and I wonder if someone were to rate how cruel I'm being right now, 1–10, would I be an 11?[405]

Afterwards, my breath keeps catching in my chest as I lie on our cellar floor, looking over at this person I know has feelings for me that I don't feel back,[406] and he's watching me.

His eyes are funny and I can't read them.

I thought maybe I could? Like after we had sex I'd be able to read him how I used to.

Sex is funny like that. Instant intimacy but only for a second.

There's sixty seconds of pure, unadulterated intimacy and you feel like you could never be closer to a person than now, not even if you tried, but it's a trick.

---

[405] Yes.

[406] A trend, I guess.

349

It's momentary closeness.

It passes.

Declan grabs his shirt, pulling it over his body, even though I'm not sure I'm ready to be done yet.

He pulls on his jeans and looks at me, shaking his head. "Julian can never know."

# 66

# Christian

Henry walks into my room and falls face-down on my bed. He lets out a tired groan. It's been a big few days.

I look over at him from my desk. "Spoken to her?"

He peers up, nodding.

"Where is she?" I stand, folding my arms over my chest.

Everything's gone to shit. Parks and BJ got back together, and it was actually good, they were actually happy—she was so happy. They brought us to the Rosebery to tell us all and when Parks got there—I don't know how—but somehow Magnolia clicked that the person who BJ cheated on her with was Paili fucking Blythe.

I didn't know and Henry didn't know. Turns out that we three—Magnolia, Hen and myself—were the only ones of the group who didn't know.

And Magnolia, fuck. She probably honestly would have legitimately preferred it if you'd shot her dead.

It was fucked up. How sad she was made me feel sick. And Beej—holy shit. Crying on the front steps of the Mandarin in my brother's arms—it was a fucking disaster.

Henry sits up, sighing. "She's in New York."

"With Tom?" I ask.

"I think he's there now. Bridge flew there first." Henry scratches his neck, looks over at me. "She says she's not coming back."

I roll my eyes. "Bullshit. It's nearly Christmas."

"No." Henry shakes his head. "The whole family's flying in for Christmas."

"Her family knows?"

Henry gives me a look. "Everyone knows, bro. It's everywhere. Every paper, every tabloid, every website—someone got it on video and it's gone viral." Henry shakes his head again. "She's not going to come back. What the fuck is she coming back to?"

I blink a few times, trying to imagine what it'd even look like. London without Magnolia? Besides him betraying her, the embarrassment of it would be too much for her. She'd be so ashamed that he cheated on her in general—I know that was always a hurdle for her, that he did that—but that he did it with her best friend? And now strangers know? Fuck.

I nod my chin at his brother. "How's Beej doing?"

"I don't know." Henry shrugs, gruffly.

"You haven't spoken?"

"No." Henry scowls. "Fuck him, he's a fucking idiot."

"Where's Pails?" I lean back against my desk.

Henry tosses me another look. "I don't give a shit, the tart."

"Hen." I roll my eyes. "She's been our friend since we were seven."

"Right." Henry nods. "So who does that to someone they've been friends with for sixteen years? Dead to me." He's resolute on that, loyal as a fucking Labrador, he is. He shakes his head. "Happy if I never see her again."

Funny how tides turn. Henry probably would have decked someone in the face if they'd called Paili a tart a week ago and now—

"I'm going to fly to New York this weekend, see how she is," he tells me.

I nod and he looks over at me, thinking.

"Are we stupid?" Henry shakes his head. "For not seeing it?"

"Maybe." I shrug. "I feel like the signs were there, now that we know, you know?"

"Like what?"

"I don't know, like—remember when we were in school and Jo and BJ threw a party at our house but we all ended up upstairs in my room playing spin the bottle—?"

Henry shakes his head.

"Magnolia spun and got Jo? Before they were together. And then BJ was so shitty at him about it that Jo rigged a seven-minutes-in heaven game the next week to make up for it?"

"Oh yeah." Henry nods, vaguely.

"Paili spun Beej—remember she wouldn't shut up about it? And then she got me for seven minutes and she spent the whole time in the wardrobe complaining about why BJ took ten minutes in the wardrobe with Magnolia because that's not how the game works—"

"Yeah." Henry nods, pursing his mouth. "She always stares at him, I guess."

I shrug a bit. "Most girls."

Henry shakes his head. "I can't believe Jo knew."

"I can." I shrug again. "Those two keep all their shit close to their chest."

"And Perry?"

"Yeah, well." I lift my eyebrows. "That makes it a bit more miraculous that they all kept a lid on it." I look down at my hands, feel a bit shit as I look back up at Henry. "I always kind of thought it was Taura and Beej was just lying."

"Yeah," Hen nods. "I used to till…"

He doesn't finish the sentence but the end of it is: till he started liking her.

"She must be feeling vindicated."

Henry shakes his head. "She's not really like that." Pushes his hands through his hair. "She said she worked out about a year ago it was Paili. Decided it was better for Parks to think it was her still because she thought it was too sad for her to lose her boyfriend and her best friend at once."

I stare over at him and then rub my tired eyes. "Oh, fuck."

"What?" He frowns and I pinch my nose.

"You like her." I blow air out my mouth. "A lot."

"Calm down." He scowls. "A regular amount."

I shake my head at him. "There's no such thing."

"Anyway." Henry yawns, walking over to the door. "How's your girl?"

"I don't have a girl." I give him a tight smile. "She's made that very clear."

Henry gives me a look. "Has she?"

# 67

# Julian

Pretty spectacular night with Josette. We've been hooking up for a while. Whenever she blows into town. Her mum's an American, dad's from here. Bi-coastal. The kind of girl I'd maybe date if I dated, but I don't.

She's always fun, though.

I get home in the morning and Daisy's nowhere in sight, no surprises there, though.

I miss the stupidly big breakfasts she'd put on for us. She's a better cook than half of the big chefs in the city.

I walk into the kitchen and pour myself a coffee, ruffle Declan's hair as I pass by him, and he gives me a quick smile.

"How was last night?" he asks.

I laugh, shaking my head. "She's fucking hot."

"Balaska?" Kekoa asks.

I nod and he gives me an A-OK symbol.

Decks yawns and I nod my chin at his arm all grazed. "What happened?"

He glances down at himself, frowning. "Scraped it in the cellar."

I nod. "What'd you drink?"

"Oh, uh—" He blinks, shakes his head. "Nothing in the end."

I nod, a little confused but don't care enough to ask about it.

"Where's Dais?" I look around.

Koa shoots me a glance. "With Romeo, no doubt—"

Declan pulls a face and shakes his head. "Nah, I don't think so." I look over at him, waiting for more. Declan rubs his nose. "I think they called it last night."

"What?" I frown.

"Yeah, I don't know." He shrugs. "She said they're not talking."

I trade looks with Ko and he pushes back from the table. "I'll go check on her."

I shake my head and toss him a wink. "I got this one."

I knock on her door. She doesn't answer. Open it anyway—peek my head in.

"Oi," I call. "You decent?"

She doesn't answer and I spot her sleeping away in her bed. I walk further in and as soon as I do, I can smell it, that stale alcohol stench of someone who has been binge drinking.

I stare down at my sister, confused—crack open a window, pick up the glass of water by her bed, sniff it. Straight vodka.

I sit down on her bed. Shove her.

"Oi—"

She blinks awake, looks over at me for a few seconds, then sits bolt upright. Looks around quickly.

"You're good, Face—" I touch her arm. She startles easy when you wake her up. She leans back against her bed head, glancing around her room, and I frown at her a little less sure. "Are you good?"

"Yep."

"Something happen with Rome?"

Her bottom lip pouts. "Nope."

So yep.

Won't push it, though, because it gets you nowhere with her.

She presses the heel of her hand into her forehead.

"How much did you drink last night?"

She rubs her eyes and blinks, giving me a shrug. "I don't know. A bit."

I jut my jaw, nod a little. "You finish that bottle of vodka downstairs by yourself?"

She scowls at me. "So what if I did?"

Fuck me—this is worse than having a teenager.

"Nothing." I force a smile. "Just making sure you're okay."

"I'm fine," she tells me, shifting so she's hugging her knees.

I nod and lean forward to check, but as I do, I catch sight of her shoulder all grazed.

I grab her and move it so I can look closer. "What happened?"

"Nothing—" She covers it with her hand.

"No—" I shake my head. "What happened?"

"I just—it's nothing. I was in the cellar. Scraped my shoulder."

I squint at her. "How?"

She shrugs.

I sit back, starting to cotton on. "What'd you drink?"

"What?" she asks, blinking.

"From the cellar?" I ask, standing up and folding my arms over my chest.

"Oh, uh—" She clears her throat. "Nothing, actually, stuck with the vodka. Didn't want to mix." She flashes me her lying smile.

I nod slowly, backing out of the room. She must see it on my face because she springs out of bed.

"Julian—" She reaches for me but she's too hung over and stumbles a bit. I catch her and give her a steep look. So angry that I could be confused with calm, but I'm not calm.

My second-in-charge is getting my baby sister drunk and fucking her?

I stare over at her, her eyes getting wider and rounder with panic.

"Declan!" I roar as loud as I ever have and then I barrel out of her room.

"Julian—" she calls, running after me, chasing me down the stairs.

Decks is standing in the foyer, face still. I know he knows I know—I stare over at him.

"Did you fuck my drunk baby sister?" I ask him and Koa runs out. He looks over at Declan, frowning.

"Yes." Declan nods once and Daisy freezes.

"While she was shit-faced?" I ask, getting up close to his face.

"Julian—" Dais grabs my arm and I jerk it out of her grasp, point it in the face of the man she fucked last night.

"Yes or no?" I ask him.

Declan blinks a few times. "Yes."

I look over at Daisy and it's worse than I thought—she's too sad, too undone by it, so unlike herself. She's not like this, she doesn't do this, she doesn't drink too much, she doesn't fuck random guys to feel better, doesn't feel embarrassed. I watch her as she's staring at this one marble tile and there are tears on the tips of her eyelashes. Because we're too connected, because I know her better than I know anyone, I can feel it on her that she feels like shit. And he helped her feel like that, so before I even think about what I'm doing, I grab him by the neck of his shirt and toss him across the room.

And then I don't really know what happens. I think I put him through a table, throw him into a grandfather clock—Daisy's screaming, crying, and my fists are flying at this old friend of mine and he's not even trying to fight back. First he tried to get away, but then he sort of just stopped, which made me angrier because I know that means he knew it was wrong. Daisy keeps crying and jumping on me, yelling my name, begging me to stop, trying to yank me off of him but she can't.

Kekoa and Miguel both try to pull me off him, but they can't either, and Declan's body stops flinching when I hit it and his face stops looking like a face. I keep hitting him until I realise I've broken my own pinky finger on his face and then I throw his fucked up, bloody body down onto the floor. Spit on him once and turn to face my sister.

She's scared.

Makes me feel like shit instantly, I have instant regret and I reach for her and she flinches away instinctively. Makes me want to die.

I swallow heavy. Daisy pushes past me.

"He needs to go to a hospital," Daisy says, reaching for my friend, who's still not moving.

"No shit." Kekoa scoffs, glaring up at me.

"Don't touch me—" Declan growls at her in this mangled voice and I know I've fucked up. I've gone too far.

But she was drunk and she's my sister.

"I can help you—" Daisy tries to shift some hair from Declan's face.

"No!" Declan slurs, trying to move away from her but he can't move and so she perseveres, running her hands over his body, trying to count the injuries I've caused him in her name. Daisy nods once and looks up at Kekoa, pressing a shaking hand into her mouth.

"Kekoa, are you listening?" she asks, and he nods—but she's not looking at him, she's just staring at Declan, whole body shaking. "Tell Merrick he has a broken nose, a suspected orbital fracture, s-several broken ribs—" She lifts his T-shirt and exposes a gash in his stomach where a massive shard of glass from the table is still wedged in him and I swallow heavy.

Fuck.

Daisy looks up at me, eyes all teary.

"An approximate 8 cm lac-laceration—" She's stuttering because she's shaking so much. "Placement could be piercing a k-kidney."

Kekoa nods.

Miguel holds her arm. "He's going to be okay," he tells her, just her, not me. They're all angry at me.

Daisy barely nods.

Miguel catches her eye. "Are you going to be okay if I go to the hospital?" He glances from her to me—asking her without asking her if she's okay to be left alone with me.

I could vomit.

She nods, mouth wobbling as she tries her best to keep it together.

"Let's go—" Kekoa nods towards the door, scooping Declan up and carrying him out to the car.

I watch them lay my friend down all bloody in the back of my Escalade. When I turn back around, my sister's disappeared.

# 68

# Julian

It doesn't take a genius to work out I went too far. I know I did, felt it as I was doing it—didn't know how to stop, though, because it shouldn't have happened. I could tell by the state of her the morning after that whatever happened the night before happened completely bereft of her sobriety, and, honestly, I wouldn't have cared for this much if she was fully sober. But drunk? No fucking way.

It's not what we're about.

And he wasn't drunk, I know that much because his eye wasn't doing the thing it does when he's hungover. So I know she was shit-faced and he wasn't, and I'd be fucking mad if he slept with anyone who wasn't as sober as he was, but my sister?

Nope.

But he's in the hospital, pretty roughed up. Everything Daisy said about him, bar the punctured kidney, plus a dislocated jaw and too many stitches to count—it was bad.

Declan's at a private hospital in Ordnance Hill that isn't actually a hospital for people like us, but it is. The boys bypassed Merrick, took him straight there.

It's been two days and he's still in.

It's been two days and I haven't said sorry.

A bit because I fucking hate saying sorry, a bit because I'm not completely sorry. And a bit because I don't like admitting I lost control, and I'll have to.

I never say sorry, actually. Not really. Not to anyone but Daisy, but she won't even speak to me until I apologise to Declan. Tried a bunch of times, she just walks out of the room.

The hospital's a good one, the best that illegitimate money can get you and it can get you a lot. The best doctors (who are willing to turn a blind eye to gunshot wounds and you being covered in someone else's blood) that you can buy. State-of-the-art equipment and progressive procedures, rooms like hotel rooms—and I'm footing the bill, but between us I probably should be because I put him there.

"Oi." I nod over at him, standing in the doorframe. Lock eyes with Smokes, tell him to leave the room without telling him to leave the room. "Give us a minute?"

Smokes nods and Declan looks away, stares out the window.

I walk over. Sit in the chair by his bed.

"I fucked up." He looks at me. "But so did you—" I give him a look. He looks away again. "She's my fucking sister and she's a fucking mess, everyone knows she's a mess right now—you've said it to me yourself—"

He's back to looking out the window.

"You're supposed to protect her—and you fucked her while she was drunk?" I stare over at him, incredulous. Have the urge to put a pillow over his face. Fight it. "You and me, we've literally killed people for less."

"Jules, she came on to me," he tells me and I give him a look.

"Yeah, I don't give a fuck, man—would she have done it if she was sober?"

"These days?" He pulls a face I don't like, shrugs a bit gruff. "Yeah, probably."

I pull my head back. "Fucking say that again—I dare you."

His eyes drop from mine.

"I went too far," I tell him. "But so did you."

And then I walk out.

# 69

# Daisy

It's been a lonely few days.

I haven't spoken to Julian since, a bit to punish him, a bit because it made me afraid. He was so angry, so unreasonably angry, it made me wonder if this is what he's like when I can't see him. Was that a glimpse behind the curtain?

Is that who he's become?

Someone who's lost control of himself beyond belief? Because what I saw wasn't a man in control—it was someone afraid he was losing it. Actually, it was someone who's lost it.

Everyone else isn't really speaking to me either. The Baddies are scared of me[407] and behaving like if I look at them sideways my brother's going to beat the living shit out of them too. Kekoa is disappointed in me,[408] I can tell, even though he's saying nothing. So is Miguel.

Romeo's still not talking to me.

Julian said we're not going to go to the Bambrillas this year for Christmas, which means it'll be the first year other than the year where we broke up when I was thirteen that we haven't gone to his parents' house for Christmas. I can't even imagine how cross that means Rome is.

That's scary.

But nothing more scary than the fact that my loneliness is under a magnifying glass now that I'm not numbing how much I miss Christian down with anything. I'm just feeling it all. And it is constant.

Constant. Keep you in bed, don't shower, forget to eat, half a glass of water that you don't touch for a whole day, sit in the dark, no music,

---

[407] Or of my vagina?
[408] The worst.

no TV, no books, just the overbearing hum of missing him 24/7 in my ears, constant.

Julian apologises to me eventually, though that seems like a misplaced apology—he said he'd already spoken to Declan, and that, yes, he went too far, but so did Declan. Julian said he'd do it again in a heartbeat without thinking even once.

"I'd like to go see him," I told my brother.

He gave me a despondent look. "Yeah, okay—just keep your clothes on this time."[409]

Miguel drives me there. It's so quiet on the way over. I've never really felt judged by him before, but I guess I do now.

"You're angry at me," I say eventually, staring over at him.

He looks straight ahead for a couple of seconds, then looks over at me. "I just don't really get you these days…"

I sigh.

"Why'd you do it?" He frowns.

"I don't know—" I look back out the window. "Christian—he was never it, I know that. He didn't want me back, so I know he wasn't it. But I guess I thought he was. It felt like he was. And I didn't know, not really, not properly, 'til we were done, that I loved him how I loved him. I mean—" I shake my head. "I knew I loved him but—um—" I shake my head again. "I didn't know I loved him in the sort of way where when you lose them you lose you too."

"Oh." Miguel nods once.

"I've never loved anyone like that before." I purse my lips. "Nor shall I again." I breathe out my nose.

"Daisy—" Miguel gives me a look.

"Nor shall I again," I tell him louder.

He sighs and keeps driving.

There's this horrible moment when I hover in the doorway of Declan's hospital room and he stares over at me in a way that's both blank and vacant. I wonder whether he's about to send me away when he lifts his eyebrows up and pulls a bit of a grimace.

"I think your brother knows."

I press my lips together, trying not to smile because it seems inappropriate considering.

"Are you okay?"

---

[409] The prick.

362

He gives me a steep look. "I've been better…"

I walk over to him and take his hand. "I'm so sorry."

He moves his hand away from me carefully. "None of that anymore, probably—"

I sigh. "I feel terrible."

"Don't—" He shakes his head. "It's only maybe 20 percent your fault."

"Decks." I frown a little. "I know I came on to you—"

"Yeah and I knew you were drunk." He shrugs. "I knew I was taking advantage of you."

"It was mutually advantageous." My eyes fall from his and I swallow. "Perhaps less so for you now—" I pull a face.

He smiles over at me through a black eye. "I don't know what you're talking about, I feel great."

"Shall I stay a while?" I perch on his bed, not necessarily upset at the idea of some company.[410]

"Nah." Declan shakes his head. "Best be on your way. I can only see out of one eye at the minute, I'd never see you coming if you tried to make a move."

I sniff a laugh, hope it sounds more amused than sad, but I suspect it doesn't. I squeeze his hand one more time and head back down to the lobby where Miguel's waiting for me.

I stand at the elevator door, waiting, and when it dings open I see that there's a body in there. Baggy jeans, black and white converse, grey T-shirt, hands on the rail as he leans against the back door.

"Tiller." I give him a curious look as I step inside.

The doors close. He glances over at me. "Why's your brother's 2IC in the hospital?"

I click my tongue twice, trying to work out whether I should tell the truth.

"Because he had sex with me."[411,412]

Tiller licks his top lip and nods once.

"Did you come all the way down here just to ask me that?" I ask him, eyebrows up.

---

[410] Or a distraction.

[411] I watch closely for his reaction.

[412] I don't know why.

"No—" He shakes his head. "I came here to say I think you're brother's maybe starting to fly off the handle."

I'm beginning to worry about the same thing, actually, but I hardly want Tiller to know it, so I fold my arms over my chest and give him a defiant glare. "How's that now?"

"I know he hired Roisin's men—" Tiller shakes his head. "I just can't prove it."

"He didn't," I lie and Tiller knows it, rolls his eyes.

"You have those rules, don't you—you and Julian?"

"How do you know about them?"

Tiller shoves his hands in his pockets. "He told me."

"My brother told you?" I ask, incredulous. Tiller takes a step towards me.

"Tell me then, what's your brother meeting up with Matta Tosell[413] for?"

I freeze. Shake my head. "He's not."

"He is." He nods.

I grind my jaw and squint at him. "You're lying."

The elevator dings open and Miguel is standing there, waiting. His head pulls back, surprised to see Tiller. He steps into the elevator and pulls me away from him. "You okay?"

"I'm fine." I shake my head.

"Yeah, she's fine," Tiller tells Miguel with a bit of an eye roll. "I'm actually going to give Daisy a ride home."

I look up at Tiller, eyes wide.

"Are you just?" I say at the same time Miguel scoffs, "Yeah, right."

"Yeah—" Tiller nods. "Right. You can follow us," he says to Miguel.

"Why?" I frown.

"We have some things we need to discuss," he tells Miguel and not me, but Miguel just shakes his head. Tiller rolls his eyes, and reaches into his pockets, hands him his phone, his wallet and unholsters his weapon and hands everything over to Miguel, who stares at it all in his hands, confused.

"Do you really think I'm going to hurt her?"

Miguel's face looks conflicted and he looks over at me. "Do you want to go with him?"

---

[413] The trafficker, remember.

Yes.[414] Can't say that, though, so I just shrug. "It's like a fif-teen-minute drive."

He nods slowly and then eyes Tiller. "Acacia to Finchley, then onto Wellington Road. Left at the A5205 roundabout, then turn onto Park Road. Take the A41 to a right on Gloucester Place and right on to Bryanston Street—"

Tiller's nodding. "I have been to the Compound before." He gives Miguel a look, who ignores him and keeps going.

"Right onto Bryanston Street, left at the Marble Arch. Follow the A4202 around the park, turn off and follow Duke of Wellington Place the whole way around—"

"Is this the most you've ever spoken in your life?" Tiller interrupts again and I stifle a laugh. Miguel is not amused.

"Left at Grosvenor Place," he continues. "Left on to Brampton Road then left on Hans—"

Tiller frowns. "Why not Brampton the whole way round?"

"Do you want to drive her home or not?" Miguel asks, eyebrows up.

Tiller rolls his eyes. "Left on Hans—"

"Walton Place on Walton Street, right into Yeoman's Row. Left onto Egerton Gardens Mews and then left onto the terrace. Do you understand?"

Tiller nods.

"You pull any shit, take any deviation from the instructions I just gave you, I shoot you on sight."

Tiller gives me an exasperated look.[415]

"It's the Walkabout Route, Dais." Miguel gives me a look and I have a surge of affection for him because he takes my safety so seri-ously. "Do you remember it?"

"Yes." I nod and Miguel hands me Tiller's gun.

"Shoot him if he takes a wrong turn."

Tiller blows some air out of his mouth and leads me to the car.

He opens the door for me, closes it behind me and then gets in. "I hope you know the way because I only remember about half of those instructions."

I sniff a laugh.

---

[414] Yes!!

[415] It makes me feel like I have a friend for the first time in a week.

"What was all that about?"

"Oh—" I shake my head dismissively. "We take different routes on different days so it's harder for someone to kill me."

Tiller stares over at me, frowning the way people who don't have people trying to kill them do.

"What did you want to talk about?" I frown back.

"Are you okay?" he asks and I stare over at him, surprised.

"Is that really what you wanted to ask me?"

He shrugs, looks embarrassed almost. "Kind of."

"Were you lying before?" I ask. "About my brother and Matta—"

He shakes his head and stares at the road in front of him.

"Whatever you think my brother did, it wasn't him."

Tiller gives me a dubious look, but I shake my head. It can't be. He wouldn't.

"We've just completed Day 7 of the Classic Christmas Movie Countdown—" This is true. It's definitely been our worst Christmas movie marathon to date because I've been pretty stroppy with him about Declan and he's felt like shit about it, but tradition is tradition.

"Okay." He nods slowly. "What are the top ten, then?"

"In ascending or descending order?"

"Descending." He frowns like I'm an idiot.[416]

I roll my eyes, like he should know. "Ten, *Die Hard*—" He tilts his head, considering. "Nine, *The Grinch*."

"Okay." He turns right on to Bryanston.

"Eight, *Nightmare Before Christmas*."

"Decent placement." He nods.

"Seven, *It's a Wonderful Life*."

"Don't like it—next."

"Six, *Elf*."

He nods.

"Five, *Home Alone*."

"One or two?"

"One."

He nods. "Interesting."

"Four, *Miracle on 34th Street*. Three, *The Santa Clause*—which we just watched."

"Yeah, that's pretty classic," he concedes. "What are your top two?"

---

[416] And he feels like my friend again.

"Coming in second is *Home Alone 2*."

"You think two is better than one?"

I nod emphatically. "And I'll fight anyone who says otherwise."

He gives me a look as he turns into Yeoman's Row. "I say otherwise."

"Give me a time and a place." I play-glare at him.

"How's Friday at eight?"

My eyes go wide. "Was that a date joke?"

"It was." He grins, proud as he turns into our cul-de-sac.

The guards at the gate nearly have their eyes fall out of their heads when they see me in Tiller's car.

I give them a merry wave.

Tiller pulls in and looks over at me. He presses his tongue into his top lip, puts his chin to his chest and looks down for a couple of seconds.

He's quite strong. I hadn't paid attention to that before, but looking at him now without the distraction of his eyes, he's broader and taller than I'd realised.

"Mostly, I just wanted to drive you home," he says, glancing back up at me and I wonder if I can see a hint of pink on his cheeks.

I look at him skeptically as I sniff a laugh. "Why?"

"I don't know." He shrugs. "So I could see if you were actually okay?"

I lift my eyebrows, a bit amused. "And am I?"

He breathes out a frown. "I don't know."

Honestly, me either.

"Why, though?" I shake my head, a bit confused. "Why do you care?"

"Because I'm being nice!"

"Why?" I blink, baffled.

"Because I'm being a gentleman!"

I shake my head, amused. "But you're a police officer!"

"Can't I be both?" he asks with a confused laugh.

I glance over, shaking my head. "Not to me."

He licks his bottom lip and cocks a smile. "Watch me."

And then he laughs and I can't tell if what just happened was serious or all a joke. He shakes his head a little.

"What?" I pout.

And he sniffs a laugh. "Just trying to work out how I went so wrong here that I've ended up alone in a car with the sister of the gang lord I'm investigating."

"You went out of your way to bring her here."

"I know." He gives me a look.[417] "That's the problem."

"What is?" I cross my hands over my chest.

"I'm meant to be pulling information out of you and all I'm doing is trying to work out how to kiss you." I pull back, blinking, and he laughs at my face. "That surprises you?"

"Kind of."

"We flirt all the time."

"Yeah, but—"

"Doesn't mean anything." And then Tiller nods, eyes down. "Got it."

I tilt my head, looking for his eyes. "Well, it can't mean anything because you're—you know…"

"Right." He nods once. "And you're…"

"Yeah." I nod, frowning.

"Besides, the last person I hooked up with my brother beat within an inch of his life."

"Ah." He flicks me a playful look. "It could be worth it."

I shake my head, laughing. "It's not."

He gives me a tiny smile. "You might be."

And I'm not, I know I'm not—I'm the worst version of myself I've ever been. I promised myself after what happened with Declan that I'd stop, I wouldn't sleep with people to avoid the giant Christian-shaped hole in the centre of my life, but here I'm presented with another option in front of me, another chance for that searing pain to stop. It's hard to say no to.

Especially hard to say no to someone like Tiller, who I have—in one way or another—day-dreamed about being with since I was sixteen. "With" could be taken to mean any manner of ways—the biblical with, romantically with, with on a date in a normal place, in a normal town, just with. But in all the ways I'd imagined Tiller and I, I never thought it would be because I'd love another man so much that in the mirage of what I thought we were I'd lose myself so much that I'd go looking for me in every other man around me instead.

I did it with my oldest friend in the world, though, so why not the

---

[417] He looks burdened.

sexy policeman? I consider as I stare over at him, trying to work out if I should lean in so he'll kiss me and I'll feel better for a second—

There's a tap on the window behind my head. I turn and Miguel's there, eyebrows up,

I look back at Tiller, pressing my lips together. He fights off a smile.

"And I reckon that it's about time," Miguel says, eyeing me, mostly.

Tiller gives Miguel a little nod, then looks at me.

"What's number one?"

I give him a tiny smile. "*Love Actually.*"

He nods a couple of times. "You Brits and that movie."

"It's the best one!"

"Merry Christmas, Dais." He flicks me the face you give someone you were maybe going to kiss but you didn't but you wish you did.

I climb out of his car and duck my head down to see him again.

"Merry Christmas."

He pulls out of our giant driveway and I spin around to face Miguel with his judgy look and folded arms.

"You need to tighten the fuck up, kid."

70

# Christian

I don't know—this is embarrassing but there's something about Christmas that gets me. It's my mum's fault. She'd make us watch those completely shitty American rom-com Christmas movies by the dozen every year. They've had a bit of a resurgence lately on Netflix, though, ey? That one with the chick from *Sex and the City* and Rob Lowe in Africa? That was pretty good. Anyway, those movies have made me an idiot and I feel like everything's going to be fine at Christmas time. Like, half of me fully expects Magnolia and BJ to be completely fine—but they're not going to be.

We G-ed him up, convinced him to fly in to New York Christmas Eve, try to win her back. She wouldn't even see him. Him and Harley had a bit of a dust up. He's on his way back now.

But me and Dais—part of me wakes up with this feeling that it could happen. It could. We all go to the same church on Christmas morning. St Agnes of Perpetual Hope. I know that's true because we have all our lives, for one, and because Father Harry Devlin is the brother of James Devlin, head of the Belfast outfit that lives under Julian's thumb. Father Harry turns a blind eye to all of our sins.

The other reason I know is because last Christmas was probably the first time I saw her as, like, a fully fledged hot adult. Sitting in the pew with her brother, surrounded by the lads, she was in this red dress that I couldn't even really see properly but it was red, and I was staring over at her, kind of rattled about how hot I thought she was because it felt like a crime. She was Julian's kid sister for so long, and it's not like I'm fifty years older than her. She was maybe nineteen at the time, I was twenty-two. But a hard and fast rule to live by in London is not to fuck around with Daisy Haites, so it never crossed my mind until I saw her that Christmas and I realised she wasn't a kid anymore, she was trouble.

She caught me staring at her from across the aisle and she stared

370

back for a few seconds before poking her tongue out at me. I would literally give you my fucking kidney if she'd look across the aisle at me today and poke out her tongue.

I do love St Agnes—it's like a little version of the London Oratory. My brother slides into the pew first, then my mum, then my dad, who—if you can believe it—left the house today. I'm about to sit down next to him when something catches my eye. A flash of red slipping into the pew a few rows down and I'm a fucking moth to a flame—I don't even think about it, I just push in front of whoever's about to sit next to her and sit down wordlessly next to her.

She stiffens up straight away.

"Hi," I whisper as close to her as possible.

"Hi," she says quickly back, staring straight ahead.

"Merry Christmas," I whisper again, looking for her eyes.

She angles her face but doesn't look at me. "Merry Christmas."

The service starts. We all stand up and I steel myself as her perfume hits my nose. I breathe out—steady myself again—sing the Christmas hymns—"Come Thou Fount of Every Blessing", "Hark the Herald Angels Sing", "Adeste Fideles"—all the good ones, and I'm not messing around. Every chance I get to edge myself closer to her, I'm taking them. By the last chorus of "Adeste Fideles" we're arm to arm and my heart is pounding just touching her again, even if it's in this dumb fucking way—an arm graze? Who gives a fuck about an arm graze? Me, apparently, because I reckon I could die happy now that I'm touching her again. This is all I want. To be near her and around her, my arm up against her, all of me up against her, and I'm starting to feel that Christmas magic because she doesn't move her arm away—she's just staring straight ahead.

And then the song ends. She shuffles away from me a bit.

Bit of a blow as she leans forwards, holding on to the pew in front of her. She takes a deep breath. So I do it too.

She leans forward, hands gripping the pew in front of her how I used to grip her. She stares up at the ceiling so she doesn't have to look at me and how controlled she's being makes me feel hopeful too, so I move my hands, brush my fingers up against hers and again—she goes still—I keep them there. So does she. I take her not moving as a tacit invite and I place my hand on top of hers, and I fucking can't believe it—it's a Christmas miracle. The prayers have been answered, Agnes was right to be hopeful—and then Daisy pulls her hand away.

"Stop," she whispers savagely.

"Daisy—" I start, trying to not let her hear in my voice that my heart's shattering into a thousand fucking pieces.

She pushes past her brother, past Miguel, out into the aisle and she speed-walks out of the church.

I'm after her a second later—we're causing a scene—or I am, I guess. And I don't give a shit. Maybe this is the magic of Christmas? Maybe this is the part in the movie where everyone's swearing under their breath but then it's okay, they fix it and they're together. She's running down the steps of the church and I'm jogging after her as fast as I can—she's pretty fast, though. I catch up eventually, grab her wrist and spin her around to face me.

"Daisy, wait!"

"What do you want?" she yells as Declan, Miguel, Kekoa and the rest of the Lost Boys sort of assemble behind me, watching on.

I shake my head, feeling flustered. I just want everyone to fuck off and give me a minute with her.

"I just need to talk to you, Daisy. Please." I try to hold her hand but she shoves me off, taking a step back towards her brother's boys.

I'm staring at the girl I love with a formation of London's Most Dangerous men behind her.

"Touch me again," she dares me and actually it frightens me a bit because there's no emotion in her face.

"Daisy—" I shake my head, taking a step towards her and then my eyes catch Declan's behind her. He's fucked up. I mean, he genuinely looks like shit, like he's been through a garbage disposal. He looks bad enough that in the middle of what I'd been assuming was going to be my Christmas miracle, I stop and stare at him. "What the fuck happened to you?"

Then something weird happens. Daisy's face shifts a little, she looks sad when she glances over at Declan, who keeps his eyes low and doesn't flinch, doesn't move, doesn't say a fucking word. Then Daisy swallows heavy and it kind of feels like I'm hit by a wave—you know when you're not paying attention and it's a big swell and you get hit by a wave that's so big that it knocks you under and the undertow is so strong, it yanks and jerks you around, pounding you against the sand, dragging you over it—that's how it feels when I realise she's slept with him.

I take a step closer towards her, and I don't mean to sound how I sound when I say it—like that's fucked me up, which it has, like that's ruined Christmas for me, which it will, like the thought of her body being touched by anyone but me, but especially him, makes me want to put my fucking hand through a wall—but my voice does sound like a combination of the above. "What are you doing?"

And the fucking worst thing happens. Her perfect mouth starts to shake and she yells. It's this weird, panicked squeal, like a dam burst in her or something. "Getting over you!" she sort of screams and presses a tear into her face.

I lower my voice, wanting this conversation to belong to just us and not the entire nosy congregation of St Agnes. "Dais, can we just talk?"

"No!" She shoves me away. It's a big shove. It's a fighting shove, actually, like she's actually trying to start something with me on the front steps of a church on Christmas morning.

And then Julian steps forward, standing behind his sister. His face, I can't fully read it, but I think he's sad for me. For us, maybe. But there is no us, she's making crazy-sure of that.

Jo jogs out of the church and down the stairs towards me, puts a hand on my chest and says quietly and calmly, "Christian, get in the car."

But my eyes don't break away from Daisy's. "Please, Dais—"

"Get in the fucking car, Christian," Jonah tells me more sternly. I'm shaking my head as I stare over at her, feeling sick that I love her how I love her and that I've hurt her how I've hurt her, and that the total sum of the above is that she's too fucked up from it all to even give me twenty seconds to tell her I was wrong and I'm in love with her, which I was and I am.

I mash my lips together, take a staggered breath, hang my head and leave.

# 71

# Daisy

I burn it into my medial temporal lobe, the feeling of Christian's hand on mine in church. I spent the rest of Christmas Day and the few days following 'til now drinking.

Not sloppy-drunk drinking, just a nice, steady-flow kind of drinking. Always-in-a-good-mood drinking.

Julian's New Year's Eve party appears annually in *Harper's Bazaar's* list of best parties.

The guest list is tight, hand-curated by my brother.

There's never a theme. There's never a dress code. There's never a plus one. You're either invited or you're not.[418]

Everyone submits their phone to security at the door, if you're caught with a camera inside, you'll get thrown out.

Lots of celebrities show, but only the cool ones because the pussy ones are scared of my brother.

Last year Chance the Rapper DJed the party.

This year I think Kygo is. I might have a crack at him for my midnight kiss because that's a pretty good way to bring in the new year.[419]

I wander downstairs from by bedroom at about 9:30, pleased to make a late entrance and also because Jack and I got into a mini fight about what to do in the hypothetical instance that Antoni Porowski were to show up tonight,[420] who'd get to go home with him. As per usual, Jack said him because they're both gay, which is fair enough, I suppose, but I couldn't with "Yes, but Antoni hasn't met me yet—"

Jack rolled his eyes and got stroppy and then I had to trade him my first-dib rights to *Pearl Harbor* Ben Affleck for him to stop freezing

---

[418] But everyone who's anyone is.

[419] And he's hot AF.

[420] He won't, I've thrice-checked the guest list.

me out. Joke's on him, though, because in the trade-off I got 1997 David Duchovny, whom I've wanted all along.

Anyway, we wander downstairs and it takes me all of a minute and a half to spot Christian Hemmes perched on our couch. I don't know why he's here. I can't believe he's here, actually.

He's holding a beer loosely in his hand, laughing. Henry, Jonah, BJ and Taura are there too. BJ looks drunk in a way that makes me feel nervous. He's talking to a model who has a bad reputation, and I don't really know what happened with him and Magnolia, but I heard that he cheated on her with her best friend. He looks so fucked that I feel sad for him—sad for Magnolia, if I'm being honest.[421] He has this look about him like he's already lost her, so fuck it—he'll lose the fuck out of her.

Christian spots me—I know he does, because his eyes light up—but I drop his eyes before they really have a chance to catch. I only have so much willpower.

I feel myself go pale in the face and simultaneously see red.

I spot my brother on the other side of the room and gallop down the stairs.

"What! The! Fuck!" I push the girl he's talking to out of my way.

Julian gives me a despondent look before he chuckles and looks at the girl I shoved. "Sorry—" He shakes his head. "My sister's got no manners. I raised her,"[422] he tells her. It's one of his tricks he pulls out to bed women. Doesn't need the tricks. He still uses it anyway. "By myself[423]—" He keeps going. "I was a kid, practically. It was really hard."[424]

"Julian!" I stomp my foot. "What the fuck is Christian doing here?"

He tilts his head considering the question. "Felt like it was time."

I stare over at him, confused. "Time for what?"

"For you two to have a chat—"

I roll my eyes at him. "That's not really your choice, is it?" He shrugs and I shake my head at him. "You're such a fucking areshole."

"Maybe," he concedes. "But you're chicken shit." He gives me a small smile.

---

[421] So just imagine how truly fucked he must really look.

[422] Oh, here we go…

[423] He's incorrigible.

[424] Hhhhhhhh.

I frown instantly. "Fuck you! I am not!"

"Go on and talk to him then."

"No!"

Julian gives me a triumphant look. "Why?"

"Because I just don't want to."

"Chicken shit." He smiles.

I look at my brother very seriously. "Not wanting to do something that's going to hurt me doesn't make me chicken shit."

"You are my sister—" He gives me a look. "You don't shy away from hard things, you're not scared of things that hurt you—you look them in the eye and stare them down until they're on their knees and doing exactly what you want them to do."

I'm not in the mood for one of his Napoleon speeches so I just sigh and his face softens.

"Dais, do you really think that I'd tell you to do something if I thought that there was even a chance of it hurting you?" He shakes his head and then walks away.

I storm into the kitchen in search of Cristal. I pop it but can't find a glass.

Romeo walks in and I freeze. We haven't spoken since.

He stares at me for a minute, something breezes over his face. "You okay?"

"What the fuck is Julian's problem?" I growl.

He rolls his eyes. "Everything Jules does is what he thinks is best for you." I give him a skeptical look, and he shrugs. "It's a flawed outworking, I'll give you that."

"So you're talking to me again?"

He throws me a look. "For now."

"Is that because you want to kiss me at midnight?" I ask, a bit hopeful.

He laughs throatily, pointing a finger. "Fuck off."

"I was joking!" I shrug innocently and he gives me a look.

"You're not—" Romeo shakes his head. "That's the problem." He takes the champagne off of me and takes a big swig. "You use sex to feel in control."[425]

"No, I don't!"[426] I frown, defensive. "Fuck you!"

---

[425] Woah.

[426] I do.

"You already have, Dais." Smarmy look. "And yes, you do." He nods super casually. "You haven't always—it's a fun, new development." I frown as he shrugs. "Post-Christian. You didn't before, but now you do."

"I do not."

"It's a control thing. I think it probably makes you feel like you've got a handle on everything—and maybe you do for a minute—but it's not controlling what you want it to control."

I hate this conversation. So much. I stare over at Rome defiantly. "And what do I want to control then?"

He gives me a look. "You fell in love, Dais. And he broke your heart. You've got no closure." He waves his hand, despondent. "I mean, truly imagine how much this must fucking pain me to say, but you've gotta to talk to him, Dais." He shakes his head. "Only way around this shit is through."

I look up at him with big, scared eyes.

He kisses my forehead. "You're going to be fine, Face."

I walk back into the party. Christian spots Romeo and I leaving the kitchen together and he frowns, but I ignore it and walk straight over to him.

"Baby Haites!" Jonah says,[427] leaning in to give me a kiss but I swat him away.

"Not now," I mumble.

Henry snorts a laugh.[428]

"You want to talk to me?" I stare pointedly over at Christian.

He nods quickly and stands.

"Good luck." Jonah grimaces.

I lead Christian Hemmes upstairs wordlessly.

How many times have I lead him wordlessly up these stairs?

Rushy hands and our breath all mixed, not able to climb them quick enough, tripping up them as we go, him pressing me into the bannister so hard it hurt. But now we walk in silence.

We get to my bedroom and I sit on my bed.

He shuts the door behind us.[429]

---

[427] I miss him.

[428] I miss him too.

[429] Easy, girl.

I fold my ankles, lay my hands in my lap. "You keep trying to talk to me," I tell him in the least emotional voice possible. "Why?"

He lets out a single laugh as he intentionally donks his head on one of the posts of my bed. He peeks over at me. "How are you?"

I frown at him, confused. "That's why you keep trying to talk to me? To ask me how I am?"

He shakes his head. "No, I—"

"I'm fine!" I tell him loudly.

"Really?" he asks, quietly.

"No!" I yell, exasperated. "What do you want?"

He kneels in front of me. "We have so much to talk about..."

I shake my head. "No!" I push past him, standing up and away. "I have nothing to say to you!"

"But I have things to say to you."

"I don't want to hear them!"

"I would never hurt you—"

"Yes, you would!" I yell, a bit manic, tears filling my eyes. "You have already! You do."

"Not on purpose," he tells me sadly. He shakes his head, looking confused. "What did I do, Dais? I don't know what I did. I know I was I still caught up in all that shit with Parks when we started, but what did I do that made you hate me so much?"

I wipe my eyes that are giving me away. "You made me fall in love without you."

Christian looks taken aback, shakes his head a little. "Is that what you think?" He pauses, looking as baffled as he is sad. "Daisy, you're my best friend."

"Yeah, same!" I shake my head incredulously. "And you still let me love you by myself."

"Dais—I lo—"

"No!" I shriek,[430] and it's sounds external of my own body. I don't recognise it. "Don't. Please don't."

And the strangest thing is, Christian doesn't look alarmed by the sound. In fact, his face softens all over, his eyes go wide, his mouth falls open.

"Baby—" He shakes his head.

"Don't call me that."

---

[430] I think I even cover my ears.

378

"I need to explain to you—"

"Please stop," I sniff.

He ignores me. "The only time I've ever been in love with anyone was with Magnolia, and everything I felt, everything that I then associated with being in love was, like, guilt and regret. And I was embarrassed and felt like shit all the time. I was so fucking angry that I loved her, and so when I met you and everything felt good, I didn't know that I was falling in love with you."

I press my fingers into my eye sockets, hoping that'll stop me from crying. "I want you to stop talking."

"Why?" He takes a step closer to me, hand on my waist.

"Because it's all fucked up now."[431] I push him away from me. "I've slept with Rome, I've slept with Declan—"

"I don't care." He shakes his head as he steps towards me again.

"I care!" I wipe my face. "I don't like how—" my chest is heaving as I cry how I told myself I wouldn't, "loving you made me feel."

He touches my face. "I don't think loving me was the problem." He shakes his head. "I'm pretty sure you thinking that I didn't love you back was."

"Would you stop saying that!" I yell.

"Why?" he asks quietly.

I cry. "Because I don't believe you."

"I love you," he tells me, eyes unwavering. Maybe he is telling the truth?

I take a staggered breath.

"Miguel!" I scream. I sound frightened and he comes barrelling in to the room, gun out, eyes wild, ready for danger. He stops short in front of Christian and I, looking confused.

"Miguel, I need you to escort Christian from the Compound."

"What?" Christian's face falls. "No! Dais—"

"He's hurting me," I tell Miguel, wiping my face madly, trying not to look like I'm crying even though I still actively am.

"Miguel—" Christian starts and Miguel looks at him with wide, heavy eyes.

"Now, Miguel." I glare at Miguel.

"Daisy," Miguel says gently.

---

[431] I believe that to the core of me.

I shake my head. "Miguel, your job is to protect me. I'm telling you, he's hurting me—" I wipe my eyes. "I need you to make him go."

Miguel gives me a long look a bit like how you might look at someone you know is too drunk to drive but insists that you give them their keys.[432] And then he nods his head at Christian. "Sorry, mate."

"Miguel—" Christian starts. "You know I'd never—"

"Come on." Miguel grabs his arm and drags him towards the door.

Christian looks back at me like I've just smashed him to pieces, and maybe I have, but... same.

Christian drops his eyes from mine, then walks away.

And I collapse on my bedroom floor and cry into the new year.

---

[432] So somewhere between me being like scum and him thinking I'm an idiot?

# 72

# Daisy

I thought maybe he'd call.

I don't know why I thought that, but I did.

Hoped is the right word, really.

Wrong of me—I shouldn't have hoped that. I know that's not how it works. If you keep pushing someone away, eventually they'll stay there.

Part of me is glad he didn't call, because men who respect themselves enough to not be treated like shit—which is how I treated him—are stupid hot. But a more emotional, less rational part of my brain hoped he'd fight my pride to its death to get to my heart.

He won't, though.[433]

I saw it on his face when Miguel dragged him away.

That was the last nail in the coffin.

Christian and I have had a lot of nails in our coffin, but that was the one that sealed it shut, I think.

Just how ragged were his eyes? I hate it when his eyes are ragged. Because Christian's eyes in general look a little bit ragged, like he's seen too much. It always looks a little like something is hurting him. It's not brooding. He's not a broody guy. He's just got a lot of humanity behind his eyes and I mean that in the way where being human is a lifetime of disappointments and heartbreaks and losses and griefs and mistakes and regrets and the weight of those things, you can see them behind his eyes. Like he's almost always thinking about how the world works and whether it's ending and how he fits into it all.

It's why I love his eyes.

It's why I love him.

---

[433] Nor should he.

He said he loves me.[434]

He loves me.

And do you know what? I actually do believe him.[435] I think he does love me.

Which I think makes everything so much worse—

I feel like my heart's been through the garbage disposal while still attached to my body, and I'm looking down at this mangled thing that's barely beating where the love of my life used to live, and all I can think about is calling him because he loves me but I can't call him because everything is so fucked up. I am fucked up. I love him in a way that's unravelled me, it's undone me at the seams of myself, and everything that's pouring out of me is ugly and awful, maybe because I let out all my good for him?

Something about Christian loving me makes me sick to my stomach that I slept with Romeo and Declan, somehow it makes it so much worse.

It's like how it's sad if you're driving and you hit a stray cat. No matter what, that's sad. But if you're driving and you hit a cat with a collar, and you know it belongs to someone, and then you back over it twice for good measure, I feel like I did the heart version of that to myself.[436,437]

I spend New Year's Day crying in my brother's bed.

Declan makes a joke about how he's pretty sure this isn't the sort of crying in bed Julian had imagined he'd ring in the new year with, which was sort of funny but mostly gross, but I was crying too much to respond. Julian threw a pillow at him and told him to get out.

Julian's got a black eye and a busted lip. I don't know when he had time to get into a fight, but his knuckles are raw and that's not from Declan, so I know he's been fighting again, which means he's stressed.

He doesn't say much—he wouldn't know what to say anyway, he's never been in love before. He just sits. Keeps clicking "Yes, I'm still here" on the remote whenever Netflix asks, so there's *Friends* playing in a loop in the background. He leaves bowls of M&Ms on his bedside table like I'm a weird, stray cat.

---

[434] Holy fucking shit.

[435] I think I could see it in him.

[436] I don't know whether I'm the driver or the cat in this metaphor.

[437] Both, maybe.

Mostly he just lays next to me on his phone but occasionally he'll glance over, give me a sad smile and kiss me on the forehead.

And it's doesn't sound like much, I know, but if my heartbreak was a fever, my brother is the cool cloth they'd lay on my forehead.

# 73

# Julian

Probably shouldn't admit this, but I felt sick the whole morning. I know it's necessary, I know Ezra Brown is an absolute fuckwit and we've gotta do what we've gotta do, but taking his kids—I mean, fuck.

If Daisy ever found out, I'd be in the absolute dog house.

Thought about just getting the boys to do it so I could stay out of it, but that goes against my ethos. I don't get other people to do my dirty work, even my dirtiest work—I'd be a pussy and a shit leader if I did. Took a valium, though, numbed myself from the whole fucking thing.

We nabbed them at school—ballsy, I know—but we wanted to be. Wanted to make a point to Brown. He can't fuck with us—with me— without suffering very real ramifications. A threat within a threat.

An unmarked white van with Kekoa at the wheel, Happy and Smokes on sniper duty, and me and Declan to do the grabbing.

Once we spotted them, it was pretty quick—we just jumped out, balaclavas on, both had a gun each that we pointed at the kids to make them comply, a pillowcase over both their heads—their nanny had a bit more fight to her than we were anticipating. Happy shot her. I don't know whether she died or not—probably did, though. Happy doesn't really shoot to miss.

I grabbed the girl, Declan grabbed the boy—she bucked in my arms—hated the feeling. She didn't not remind me of my sister— hated that too.

Hauled them into the van and sped off.

Didn't have a massive headstart, only about a minute before the feds were on us—but we had TK on the radar, watching and reading the streets.

We took a turn down a street with an underpass and waiting for us there was a different white van driven by one of the footmen, as well as a black Escalade—we had a twenty-five-second window to

384

get the kids from the van into the Escalade without anyone seeing. Our van pulled up right next to the Escalade, not even inches apart, passed the kids through a window and climbed in after them. Kekoa jumped into the driver's seat, from which a footman jumped in to the van and peeled it out of there, leading the police astray. We drove on away with the kids, watching as the police cars screamed by us, sirens and all.

We took them to an empty bungalow the Bambrillas own up in Clayhall. Drive in the garage—important for getting the kids inside without anyone seeing.

The boy cried the whole way there. The girl was stoic, she felt for his hand, found it, held it, told him she'd keep him safe—

Felt like shit again for the millionth time in the last hour.

"What do you like to eat, then?" I ask them once we've shifted inside. The house is empty. A shitty mattress in the corner for them to sleep on and a TV with DVDs so they don't complain.

It looks pretty shit but Koa keeps saying that we're not meant to be putting them up in the Shangri La, so it's okay.

"We like to eat meals from our home that our parents cook," the girl says and it makes me laugh.

I take off my balaclava. "Your dad doesn't strike me as much of a cook."

The girl's eyes pinch.

"Tell me your names," I tell her, even though I know them already.

"Edie." She glares. "And this is Philip." She frowns. "Why have you taken us?"

"I'm Julian." I tell them and Declan gives a look like "what the fuck?" I shrug because I've never done this before—I don't kidnap kids.

"Why have you taken us?" she demands again.

I sigh because when I look at this little girl all I see is my sister the day our parents died and I hate myself, but I can't back out now. Her dad can't do what he's done and think it'll fly. It can't fly. The entire model I run is predicated on shit like this not flying.

I scratch the back of my neck. "Your dad took something from me—he won't give it back. I'm incentivising him." I peer at her out of the corner of my eye. "Do you know what 'incentivising' means?"

"Yes, I'm not stupid," she tells me proudly.

"No—" I shake my head. "I don't suppose you are."

"I like McDonald's," the boy says, finding his voice.

I glance over at him, nodding. "Alright then—" I nod at Declan. "Tell him what you want and he'll go get it."

"I want to go home," Edie says and I give her a look.

"Soon. But what to eat?"

"How soon?" she presses.

"I'll have a cheeseburger with extra cheese, extra chips, a Coke—"

"You're not allowed those," Edie tells her brother and gives me a look.

I shrug. "Maybe today we let it slide?"

"And nuggets," Philip says. "And chips but more. And barbecue sauce."

I nod a few times. "And you?" I ask Edie, eyebrows up.

"Nuggets, please. With a Fanta."

After they eat their dinner, Kekoa pulls me aside with a look on his face. "Jules, you gotta go—"

"Why?" I frown.

"You're emotionally invested in the children we just kidnapped."

"Am not—" I frown. Maybe I am. He gives me a look and I roll my eyes. "She just—"

"Reminds you of Daisy, I know, but we did kidnap them, and a massive part of kidnapping kids is that they're scared, and that they think they're going to die so their parents pay the ransom, yeah?"

I roll my eyes.

"We need them scared, Jules."

And I feel like shit again, kind of regret it, kind of regret saying yes to this—but I'm here now, can't back out. I can't just let them go and let their fucking old man mosey on with my £70 mil in his pocket.

I nod once, stare at the ground, head towards the front door. Happy and Smokeshow take over. Not a lick of a calming presence between them. They look like the kind of men you move away from in the train carriage.

They walk into the kids' room and close the door behind him.

"Where's Julian?" I hear Edie say and I stop in my tracks.

Ko shoves me towards the door. Edie calls my name and this time she sounds scared but I walk out anyway.

# 74

# Daisy

It's right after uni starts up again in the new year. I'm sitting by the fire doing some work when the doorbell rings.

No one else is home. I've been fairly busy because I really let the uni ball slip lately.[438] I don't like not being the smartest,[439] so I have some work to do. The boys haven't been around much, a big job brewing I'm guessing. I don't know what. They've kept me out of this one. I can't imagine after I shot one of Roisin's guys that I'm going to get an invitation back any time soon anyway.

I wander to the front door, swing it wide open—

Bright, light blue eyes, a jawline that doesn't mess around, and very serious eyebrows. The half-cocked smile that usually accompanies them is absent, though.

"Happy new year, perv." I grin at Killian Tiller.

He gives me a barely there smile. "We need to talk."

"Okay." I shrug. "Talk."

"Alone."

I give him a look. "I am alone."

He peeks past me into the house.

"No one's home," I tell him.

"Your bodyguard?"

I give him a quizzical look. "He's in the gym downstairs,"

"Is there somewhere we can talk?" he asks, looking around.

"You want to come in?" I blink.

Tiller takes my wrist in his hands, pulling me inside the house. "I need to talk to you," he tells me, looking strangely serious.

"About what?" I blink, taking a step closer.

---

[438] What with all the drinking and sex…
[439] I still am.

He taps his ear, giving me a look, as if to say, "Who can hear us?"

I shrug. He's not off base assuming there are ears everywhere here. There are. I don't know where but it's a safe assumption.

He shifts his jacket a little and flashes me a manila folder that had been tucked away. He gives me a look that I don't like. It's weighty and implied, but I don't know why it's heavy or what it's implying.[440]

I take his hand and lead him up to my bedroom. I watch his eyes scanning my room as I pull him into the shower in the bathroom. I turn on the water and crank Spotify's Mood Booster playlist through the speakers.

"What's going on?" I ask, frowning at him.

He pulls the folder from his jacket, passes it to me. I open it, then close it again quickly. Beaten dead body. I look up at Tiller, glaring.

"Julian did it," he tells me.

"Bullshit," I spit, but I already know it's true. It'd explain his bruises. It's just the underground fights, but sometimes he doesn't know how to stop.

"There are five others."

I give Tiller a look. "What, are you saying my brother is a serial killer?"

"No, I'm saying your brother is a gang lord and people are dispensable to him."

I scoff, but that's true too.

Tiller shoves a piece of paper under my nose and I frown down at it. "What this?"

"It's proof of a wire transfer."

"Between whom?" I ask but I know the answer. I can read it.

"Mata Tosell," he says, wiping some water that's splashing onto his face. "He's on your list, right?"

I glare at him. "Yes."

"Do you know what he does?"

"Of course I do." I glare.

He does one of the never-three.

He nods once. "Your brother just wired him £3 million."

"Why?"

Tiller shrugs.

"You're lying." I shake my head but the blood is draining from my face.

---

[440] I know it can't be good.

His face softens as my world crumbles. "I'm not."

And you know what—honestly, there have been a few instances in my adult life where I've actually imagined being in a shower with Tiller. Jack has had the same daydream, we've talked about it—it can hardly be helped because the man is balls-to-the-walls hot, everything about him makes you sort of undress him with your eyes and so it's not a far leap for the imagination to picture him shirtless in my steamy shower. But never once were we clothed and never once was he shattering the universe in a way that wasn't sexual.

"What do you want?" I say, barely, looking away from him.

He's shoved a photo under my nose.

Two kids. A boy and a girl. The boy looks about six, the girl looks eight or nine.

I look up at him and shrug.

"Do you know who these kids are?"

I shake my head, but I have a nervous feeling in my stomach. I know this can't be good. Anything with kids is never good.

"Do you know who Ezra Brown is?"

And yes, I do, but it feels like a trap so I shake my head vaguely. "Rings a bell."

"We think he's the man your brother stole the Klimt for."

"You were there." I roll my eyes, covering quick. "We stole nothing, you saw us."

"Cut the bullshit, Daisy." He shakes his head. "I know. I can't prove it, but I know it—I'm not an idiot. Brown just happened to wire your brother £70M for no reason?"

I frown. £70M wasn't the settled upon price—it couldn't be, it's half its value. And that's bad.

Tiller licks his bottom lip and squints at me. The way he's looking at me, the way the air hangs between us is like the air between two boxers in the ring before one is about to deliver the knockout punch and they both know that one of them is about to go down.

"You know what he's done," Tiller tells me, and I wonder if it's so he doesn't have to say it.

"Fuck off," I growl as I shake my head, but even as I shake it, part of me knows it's true. I've felt my brother slipping for a while now. I can always tell when he's not doing so well, even without the cage fights.

"It's true." He nods.

389

"No, it's not. We don't do that." I wipe my nose. My eyes are wet.

"I know you don't," Tiller tells me.

"Yeah and neither does he!" I shake my head. "We have rules!"

He gives me a gentle smile. "I know about your rules, Dais." He locks eyes with mine. "He's breaking them."

"All of them?" I blink quickly and wonder if I'm going to faint.

Tiller's eyes look heavy for me. "From what I can tell, two of them."

I look over at him with threadbare eyes. "Are you lying?"

"No." He reaches for me but I shove him away.

"Is this what all this has been about?" I yell. "You showing up at my door for months, flirting with me, talking about kissing me in the car the other day—is all that about this… your… it's a trick."[441]

"No." He shakes his head. "Daisy, showing up at your door for months, flirting with you, trying to kiss you—" He sighs. "Are all reasons I shouldn't be doing this. I shouldn't be here. But I need your help."

"With what?"

"He's taken two kids."

I shake my head. "He wouldn't."

"Dais." He gives me a look. "He already has."

I cover my face with my hands and let out a small cry. It comes out muffled like a staggered breath, but I don't want Tiller to see me cry, it makes me feel like I'm weak and I don't want anyone to know that my brother is the glue that holds me together, because if Julian is bad then what does that make me?

This life is a landslide into muddied water.

I think Julian's been slipping for so long he's just not bothered to get up.

When you spend enough time in the muck, the filth doesn't feel that filthy anymore. I think that's what's happened because I remember when he was eighteen and he'd just taken over from Dad—he'd dropped out of school because he realised there was no point. Did Julian want to be what he is? It's hard to say. My dad never did, but I think Julian always liked the power he saw our dad wield. Julian's fallback plan was to be a professional boxer or rugby player, but he didn't need a fallback for very long.

I remember being nine, sitting on Julian's lap at the dining room table, and some of the older guys who'd worked with our dad like

---

[441] I need it to be a trick.

Kekoa and this guy, I think they used to call him Nuk,[442] and a nice man called Mayweather,[443] they were talking to him about upcoming jobs and things that were on the books. Julian told me to go upstairs because they needed to talk about grown-up stuff, but I wouldn't go because after our parents died I didn't really leave Julian's side 'til I was eleven.

He asked me again but then I started to cry, and so he shrugged and looked at Kekoa and said, "Anything we can't talk about in front of Daisy, we're not doing anymore."

Then the older I got, the more they could talk about, so the more they did.

Also, funnily enough, the more we went to church. That's when church started. That's when the praying at dinner time started.

It wasn't a thing we learnt from our parents, it was a thing Julian implemented.

I think Julian thought us going would balance us out, but all it did was fuck me up. I don't have a father, and the closest thing I have to one is my brother, who I think, from a church's standpoint, isn't necessarily a great example?

And if earthly fathers are supposed to represent the heavenly one, then He seems like a weird guy.

When I was thirteen, one of the sisters at the church gave me a slip of paper with the Ten Commandments on it. I think she knew who I was, I think most people know who I am. Julian's never tried to hide it, he's just good at covering his bad tracks and never getting caught.

Anyway, she gave me the Commandments, and I'm not sure if she gave them to me thinking it would straighten our family out. Like I'd read them and be like, "Oh shit, we aren't supposed to kill people!" But I read them. I still have them. Reading them now is worse than before because we're worse than we were then.

If we're going 1–10, assuming #1 is the most important, Jules has never failed there to the best of my knowledge. Nor have I.

I've never had another god.

I've also never made an idol. Neither has Julian. Crafting isn't our family's strong suit…

We're two in—so far, so good.

---

[442] He's dead now.

[443] Also dead.

But it's kind of downhill from here.

Have we taken the Lord's name in vain? Probably.[444]

Worked on a Sunday? Definitely.[445]

Honoured our parents? Absolutely not.[446]

Murdered? Yes.[447]

Adultery? Yes.[448]

Steal? With our eyes closed.[449]

Lied? Yes.[450]

Coveted? Wanted what isn't ours? Practically a Haites family staple.

I say we, as in the plural pronoun, because Julian's sins are mine, I think. I think the blood he spills stains our whole family. I know before I said I didn't like to think that—that whole thing about the sins of the father falling to his children, but now with some time and space and kidnappings between us, I think I need to think that that's how it works, because if his sins stain us both, then maybe I can cancel it out for us both.

And here's what worries me: those rules, they're like a basic how-to for humanity, and he is failing them. Which means I am failing him. I'm my brother's keeper, and I've lost him.

---

[444] I don't really know what this means.

[445] This one seems stupid, if I'm honest.

[446] Whoops.

[447] Both of us.

[448] Him, not me.

[449] …

[450] Spectacularly.

# 75

# Daisy

I meet Tiller at the corner of Mossop and First like he said and I slip into the passenger seat before noticing another guy in the back. Immediately I pull out my little NAA-22S[451] and point it directly at the stranger.

Brown hair styled short, impressive beard, nice eyes, tattoos up and down his arms.

"Woah, woah—" He shakes his head, looking at Tiller urgently, who I'm already glaring at. I told him not to bring anyone.

"Is this a set-up?" I ask him in a low voice. "I'll shoot him," I tell Tiller as I reach for the handle with my other hand.

"He's my partner!" Tiller says quickly.

"On the police force," the man says. "Not sexually."

I look back at him and give him a disparaging look.

"Tim Dyson." He offers his hand. I don't take it. "You can call me Dyson."

I look at Dyson then back at Tiller. "Why is he here? He shouldn't be here, you said just us—"

Tiller shakes his head. "If you think I'm going to take you into a hostage situation without backup, you're insane."

I shake my head. "You said nothing would happen to my brother."

"Nothing will." He gives me a look as he peels out on to the street.

I haven't really slept since the last time I saw Tiller, since he told me what Julian did.

He asked me to help him get the kids back and I said I would. I

---

[451] North American Arms Mini Revolver. Smallest on the market. Less than 4 x 2.5 inches. Tiny. Great for handbags and surprising police officers you don't entirely trust.

want me helping him get them back to cancel out my brother taking them in the first place, but I don't think it works like that.

None of the boys have been around much—they've been running this job. When I asked my brother about it, he said they were scouting a new "acquisition" and that he needed a lot of manpower.

None of them being around made it easier to snoop—but it's not like my brother has a file that says "WHERE I KEEP THE KIDNAPPED CHILDREN"—so yesterday I asked Kekoa to fish out my bracelet that I dropped on purpose down the sink and, while he wasn't looking, I turned on the Find My Friends feature on his phone. He's over forty, so he'll never figure out how to turn that off.

Somewhere in Clayhall. I don't know where. We don't own anything out there—not that I know of. That's the part of this that frightens me, I guess, all the things I don't know. I thought I knew it all, but I clearly don't.

I can't, anymore. I didn't even know he was on speaking terms with the MacMathans until they showed up that night in Vienna, let alone Mata Tosell. The way he beat up Declan too. What else am I missing? What else are they keeping from me because they know I won't stomach it?

How is my brother stomaching this?

He's a good man, that's what I thought.

I thought he was.

And good men can do terrible things, I know that. But it's usually by accident and just once, it's not premeditated and the behaviour doesn't repeat. I know I must sound insane, being upset that my gang lord brother isn't a good man, but I've spent my whole life trying to convince the world that he is,[452] and I don't want to be wrong. Because if I am, if he is bad and he has raised me, and he is the only family I've got, then if he's bad, I am too.

I stare straight ahead. I feel like I'm driving to my doom.

Dyson reaches forward from the back seat and puts on the radio.

"Highway to Hell" by AC/DC starts blasting.

"Our pre-game song," Dyson tells me before leaning back into his seat. I smack the music off.

"Hey—" he groans.

---

[452] He is.

394

I stare out the window. "The demise of my life as I know it doesn't need a soundtrack."

It hangs there, what this means to me. Neither of them have thought about it, I can tell that much now. To them, this is a job. Save the kids, do the right thing—to most people, doing the right thing is the goal, the right decision, the healthy decision, the decision you should make—but part of me feels that I shouldn't. I should get out, jump out at the next light and run back home, because doing the right thing for these kids, which—by the way—I know is the literal right thing to do, but it just so happens that the literal right thing to do also requires me to double-cross everyone I love in my life.

Tiller sighs, grips the wheel tighter and doesn't look over at me. "Are you okay?"

"No," I barely say, looking out the window.

The polite thing would have been for him to say "We don't have to do this", but this isn't a date and we aren't about to have sex. I'm about to betray my brother.[453]

He betrayed you first, that's what I keep telling myself. Julian's done the things he promised he wouldn't, he's working with men who traffic people, he's kidnapped kids, he's not who I thought he was and he needs to stop now because I don't know how to save him from those kinds of things. They don't have a bleach for the sorts of sins that don't leave a mark on the world like blood does, because those sorts of things leave marks on your soul. I can't clean that up.

"So, you're Daisy," Dyson says, trying to ease the tension.

I look back at him, saying nothing.

"Tills has always said you're a real chatterbox, but—"

Tiller shoots him a look.

"What?" Dyson frowns. "You have nice eyes." He peers around at me and I pull away from him, scowling.

"Tiller's single now, did you know?" Dyson says lightly.

Tiller snaps his head in Dyson's direction, glaring at him.

"I did know." I nod, coolly.

"I just thought you'd like to know," he whispers. "He's single, you're single…"

"You're dead," Tiller growls under his breath.

"Oh, Killian," he laughs airily.

---

[453] A wave of sick hits me.

I turn to him, frowning. "How did you get into the police academy?"

"Perseverance," he whispers, grinning and I stare up at Tiller.

"Does he have an off switch?" I ask Tiller.

"I wish," he says, not taking his eyes off the road.

Silence.

Dyson lets out a long whistle. "You could cut the sexual tension in here with a knife."

"I think that's just tension," I tell him, staring straight ahead.

"Nope." He shakes his head, resolute. "It's sexual."

Tiller shakes his head then sort of sniffs a reluctant laugh.

"You excited to take down the bad guys, then?" Dyson pokes me in the arm.

I don't look back at him, just bite down on my bottom lip. "I am the bad guys."

He gives me an uncomfortable look.

We pull up around the corner from the house and sit in the car for a minute.

No one says anything, so I ask the most obvious question. "Do you have any idea how many are inside?"

Tiller shakes his head. "Thermal reading suggests three adults, two children."

"Do you know who?"

He shakes his head. "Not your brother, though. We've got eyes on him at those baths he likes in the city."

"Do you promise?" I ask, feeling hopeful.

He nods and I nod back, relieved.

I look over at Dyson. "You're staying in the car."

"What?" He frowns.

"With the engine running," I tell him.

"I don't want to stay in the car." He pouts.

"And I don't want to topple my family's entire dynasty,[454] but here we are."

Tiller gives me a long look and I wonder if he looks sorry. "We do it her way," he tells Dyson as he climbs out of the car, tossing him the keys.

I walk ahead of Tiller—he's got his head down, hood up. My heart

---

[454] What am I doing?

396

is racing as we round the corner to the street and it feels like I'm rounding the corner to a new part of my life—one I've thought I've wanted for so long, but now I'm at the precipice of it, I'm not sure. Going against everyone I've known and loved because they're doing something I don't like, it seems crazy in the light of day—but it's a bad something. It's quite a bad something. I reach for the handle of the door and I hear Tiller cock his weapon.

"Do not pull that trigger unless I say so—"

He nods once.

I open the front door and a massive muscle man stands to his feet, a gun pointed to my face. Then he lowers it a fraction.

"Daisy?" I don't recognise them, but they recognise me and relax a little.

Julian's branch is so big, for all they know Tiller could work for him too.

I smile as warmly as I can muster and extend my hand—which he takes but I yank him in towards me quickly, swing my arm around his neck, and launch myself onto his back, putting him into a sleeper hold.

I lower him to the ground silently.

Tiller gives me a little look, brows raised.[455] "Did not see that coming."

I crack open the door, peek inside. The hallway's empty but I can hear the muffled sounds of a television upstairs. I pull out my brushed stainless Colt Mustang and creep up the stairs. Sitting outside a door is TK.

"Fuck," I whisper under my breath and signal Tiller to freeze. I keep walking up the stairs. Teeks looks up from his phone and reaching for his gun, but when he sees it's me he pauses.

"Dais?"

"Hey." I force a smile.

"What the fuck are you doing here?" He frowns.

"Nothing—I'm just—uh, Julian sent me here for—"

TK tilts his head, suspicious, and I keep walking towards him.

"Daisy, what are you here for?" he asks as I stand toe to toe with him, toss my arms around his neck.

"Dais—" he starts, but I brush my mouth against his as I flick off

---

[455] Impressed.

the lid to the syringe I'm holding and inject him with a non-lethal dose of propofol.

He pulls back, looking at me confused, and then he collapses.

I kneel down next to him, check his pulse and his airways before propping him up safely against the wall. I signal for Tiller to come and then I open the door.

Two kids, hands tied behind their backs, face a TV with the 90's Flintstones movie playing, and then I spot him[456]—Romeo Bambrilla in the corner[457]—legs swinging on a table, lazily turning about the gun in his hand.

He looks up at me and jumps to his feet.

"Daisy?" Rome frowns instantly. "How did you—" And then he spots Tiller. He's confused for a minute, then he lifts his gun and cocks it.

"What the fuck are you doing?" he asks me, eyes wide with betrayal.

"What the fuck are you doing?" I ask back, desperate, rushing towards him. "They're kids, Rome!"

"And he's a cop!"

"We don't do this—this isn't who we are."

The kids sort of look back and forth between us like we're a tennis match.

"This is exactly who I am, Dais—" He shakes his head at me. "But I have no idea who the fuck you are anymore."

"Not a kidnapper." I shake my head at him.

"Oh, just a traitor, then?" He nods his chin at Tiller. "I fucking knew it. You fucking him too, now?"

Tiller cocks his weapon.

"No, Romeo," I tell him, holding his eyes, trying to calm him down a bit.

"She's here because her brother kidnapped some children," Tiller interjects.

"Don't you fucking speak to me, you dog." Rome eyes him. "I can't believe you're here with him, Dais. Of everyone—him?" He shakes his head again.

"Just let them go, Rome." I sigh.

---

[456] Oh my God.

[457] My heart sinks.

"No." He shakes his head.

"What are you even here for?" I ask, a bit desperate. "You don't work for my brother—you don't have to be here—just let them go—" I move towards the children

"He asked me to be here."

"For what?" I yell wildly. "I don't understand—why would you do this?"

He gestures at me wildly. "Why would you?"

"Rome, please just let them go," I press. Romeo shakes his head again and so I turn to the kids. "Whatever happens, you go with this man." I point to Tiller. "He's a policeman, you can trust him," I tell the girl. She's bigger, she looks afraid but switched on.

I glance at Tiller. "Whatever happens," I tell him with a discreet nod.

He looks confused for a moment, but I suppose he would. We'd never spoken about the specifics of my plan. I didn't really have one until just now, that's why. I'm developing it actively, but the development was complicated dreadfully by the presence of my ex-boyfriend.

I look over at Romeo, give him a sad smile as I centre my gun on him, and cock the trigger.

Romeo presses his lips together and shakes his head. "This is what we've come to then?" he asks, a bit in disbelief. I shrug. His eyes look watery, as he points his gun past me[458] at Tiller. "You going to shoot me, Dais?" He sniffs.

"Never," I tell him earnestly and he frowns, confused, and then I turn my gun towards me, shooting myself. In the stomach was the plan, I hope I succeeded, it's hard to tell as soon as it's done. I tried to angle the trajectory of the bullet left and up, but not so up that I'd pierce a lung or hit a rib.

It's louder than I thought it'd be—the echoing bang in that big, mostly empty room, and then I collapse forward.

It's probably not as bad as I'd imagined, a gunshot. Doesn't feel that much different to how I've been feeling lately anyway—maybe just a tiny bit more literal. Worse at first, and then the adrenaline kicks in as Rome rushes forward and catches me before I hit the ground.

---

[458] Because he can't even pretend to point a gun at me.

"What the fuck have you done?" He stares down at me, blinking away tears, presses in his mouth into my forehead.

"Run!" I tell the kids, who are on their feet now, their eyes wide with terror.

Tiller's watching me all dazed and looking like he might throw up. "Daisy—"

"Now!" I try to yell, but it's too much energy to muster.

Tiller scoops up the kids and bolts and Rome doesn't give a shit, he doesn't look away from me. He's shaking his head. "What have you done? What have you done?" he whispers.

"Keep pressure on it," I tell him.

"I'm trying," he says, wiping his eyes with his hand, smearing my blood over his face.

I hear him make a call—the part where I didn't think this through is the part where we don't call ambulances. I wonder if this is how I'll die.

A self-inflicted injury with my childhood sweetheart applying pressure to the wound to stop me from bleeding out. Just like before but no longer a metaphor.

"I'm sorry," I tell him with a frown.

He shakes his head at me. "Don't be sorry, Daisy. Do you hear me? Don't—"

And then I black out.

# 76

# Julian

The first thing I felt when I got the phone call was fear. Multifaceted fear.

Something happening to Daisy has been—for at least my adult life—my primary concern. Notwithstanding the facts around her injury, it doesn't matter—she's still hurt. Daisy hurt scares me. What also scares me is that she knows. Knows what I did, knew what we'd done and was revolted enough to do something about it.

And not just something—she shot herself in the stomach to help them get away.

Rome's frantic call to me was probably the worst call of my life to date.

"She's shot!" he yelled down the phone. "She's shot and I can't stop the bleeding!"

"Who?" I asked, even though I knew. I could tell by his tone. No one else could make him sound like that.

"Daisy!" he said. I think he was crying.

I was on my feet and out the door before he even said her name.

"Where are you?" I asked.

"We're at the house—"

"What?" I stopped dead in my tracks.

"In Clayhall," he said.

"How did she—"

"I don't know," Rome said quickly. "She just turned up with the cop—"

"Fuck—" I ran to my car, all the boys running after me without a word. I turned to Kekoa. "Call TK."

Kekoa shook his head. "He's not answering—"

"Julian—" Rome said. His breathing didn't sound good. "I can't stop the bleeding."

"Pressure, Rome," I said, trying to start my car but I fumbled my keys.

A tap-tap on my window and Kekoa signalled for me to move to the passenger seat.

I slipped over without a fight and tried not to look as afraid as I felt. "What's her pulse like?"

"Faint—"

"Romeo—" Kekoa called loudly. "I have two men coming, they should be there within a few minutes, leave the kids."

"They took the kids," Rome said.

"What?"

"That copper took the kids," he told me and my jaw goes tight.

"He left Daisy there?" I could kill him.

It hung there for a second. "She told him to."

"There's a safe house across the street from the Barkingside McDonalds—they're going to take her there 'til we can get her stable," Koa told Rome.

"Okay."

"She's going to be okay," Kekoa said into his phone, looking at me as he did.

It took a minute once she was in the safe house.

She had lost a lot of blood, but Barnsey has good doctors dotted all over London, and one of them met us there. Stopped the bleeding, got Dais an okay pulse, then we moved her to Ordnance Hill as quick as we could to operate.

She pulled through. Hit her stomach. She would have done it on purpose, I know. GSWs to the stomach almost always heal surprisingly well. It took a lot out of her—it was touch and go there for a minute. Christian's tried to come visit her but the boys have kept him out—I don't know whether that's what she'd want, actually, but I have this uneasy feeling that maybe Daisy and I, for the first time in our lives, are on different pages.

I met him down in the foyer—he was crying, kind of hysterical in the way I reckon you would be if the girl you loved had been shot.

"She'd want me there," he told me, trying to push past me to get to her.

"Christian—" I took him by the shoulders. "The last time she saw you, she had you forcibly removed from our house."

"That's because she's scared of me, not because—"

"Christian." I gave him a look. "You're not getting up to see her. See her when she's out, man. When she can decide for herself."

I felt like shit, leaving him down in the foyer, doubled over, crying—but I didn't need the complications of it all. Just needed her to wake up. Next steps could come after that.

She was unconscious for a bit over two days before her eyes fluttered open.

When they do, they land on Romeo to her immediate left. Doesn't spot me straight away.

He sits up straighter, eyes wide with that sad hope they always have for each other.

He reaches for her hand.

She blinks a few times, confused as she comes to, trying to sit up quickly, looking panicked. She looks down at herself, where she was shot, looks back up at Rome, who's glaring over at her, and she frowns.

"Fuck you, Daisy." He drops her hand and stands. "We're done now," he says, walking to the door. "Don't you ever speak to me again."

Her eyes track him across the room until she spots me and freezes.

I stand up, walking over towards her, arms folded over my chest.

"What the fuck did you do?" I ask her, shaking my head.

Her eyes fill with tears instantly. "What the fuck did you do?"

This is what I was afraid of, that she's gonna make this like it was my fault—I'm already furious, already in a state of disbelief that she'd even try. She looks a bit scared. Good, though, I think to myself, I want her to be scared. She's a fucking idiot.

I press my hand into my mouth because it makes me look like I'm in control of my emotions, but I'm actually doing it because my hands are shaking. "You shot yourself in the stomach." I sound sadder than I want to. "To help some kids you don't even know!"

"They were kids!" she tries to yell.

"They were a job!" I yell louder.

Those teary eyes of hers spill over, and she looks even more afraid. My mouth twitches as I try my best not to cry.

"You promised me," she barely gets out, mouth twitching, trying not to cry. "Never kids—"

I jut my jaw out, shaking my head, lick my bottom lip, all tired and angry. "You just lost me £70 million."

"Yeah and you just lost me!" she says, voice cracking.

"Bullshit," I spit at her.

"I mean it, Julian—" She shakes her head, my little bottom lip trembling. "I'm out. I don't want anything to do with this shit." She looks at me with wild eyes. "They were kids!"

"Yeah, they were kids, Daisy—I get it! Unideal, sure, but their dad owes me £70 million which, now, thanks to you, I'll fucking never see!"

"Julian!" she cries. "Can you not hear yourself? They were children. Children! I was her age when Dad died."

I knew that part of it would stick out to her. Knew it because it stuck out to me too, but what can I do? It's done now. I've lost the money, lost the kids, reputation's probably in the hole now too, thanks to my kid sister's little fucking rebellion with the police force. I can't even begin to imagine how much shit I'll take for this. People will see this as weakness, dissension in the ranks, an opportunity to strike and take over.

"This is business, Daisy." I give her a stern look. "I run a business—"

"And I don't want anything to do with it!" she screams. "I am—I'm sick over this—"

Her voice is cracking and something about it makes my eyes go wet.

"I'm out." She shakes her head. "Don't speak to me, don't call me, don't follow me. I don't want anything to do with you."

My face pulls back a little, sort of in disbelief that she's saying this shit to me, and it ripples through me, this poison anger I get sometimes. I've never had it with her, but I can feel my pride's been hit and someone's pulling a punch that hurts. Usually I kill those people, but I can't kill her.

I give her a pointed look. "Those are some big words for a little orphan girl."

Her jaw goes tight and she bats away a tear. "I don't need you."

Her chest is heaving.

"You don't have anyone else," I remind her and I hate myself for it.

Her eyes pinch.

"I'd rather have no one than who you are now," she spits.

"Alright." I give her a careless shrug. "You got it, Dais."

She nods quickly, wipes more tears. "I can't believe you," she barely whispers.

I shrug again because I don't know what else to do. If I stop to think about what I think's happening, I'll probably start crying too.

"You're despicable," she tells me.

"And you're a traitor," I shoot back. Had that one locked and loaded because it's true. After everything I've done for her, the life I've given her, the way I've shielded her and kept her safe and loved her and—

"I'm serious, Julian—I'm done with you." She sniffs, shaking her head. "I don't want your protection, I don't want your covering or your time or your thoughts—"

"Oh—" I give her the meanest smile I've ever given her. "Don't even worry about it, Face. You won't have them." I give her a careless shrug "As far as I'm concerned, you died with them on that beach." I glare over at her. "Should have let you, you ungrateful little shit."

Hate myself for that.

"Get out," she tells me, voice shaking.

Grab my keys from the table beside me with shaking hands I hope she doesn't see. "Gladly."

I walk out, cover my face with my hands, and breathe out calm as I can. I get in the elevator, wait for the door to close. I let out one sad growl. She doesn't deserve more from me, even though she does. I punch the face in the mirror—need stitches but I won't get them, and then I walk away from the only family I have and the only person besides myself I've ever loved.

Good riddance, I tell myself as I take a deep breath. But I can't shake the feeling that I maybe just got rid of the only good I had in me.

# 77

# Christian

As soon as I heard what happened, I tried to get to her but I couldn't—it was a shit storm. I heard loosely what happened via my brother, but I didn't know much—just that she was hurt.

I went to the hospital but Julian sent me away. I nearly fought him over it but there was something wild in his eyes that made me think I shouldn't—like a dog backed into a corner, teeth bared. So I left it, because I'm shit and I'm weak and I probably should have fought him, probably should have forced my way into seeing her so she knew, but I didn't because I don't know what the fuck I am to her. I know what she is to me.

In short, everything.

In long, still everything.

I waited a week—it was a fucking long-ass week too because I couldn't speak to her. Her number wasn't going through, and when I asked Julian for her number, he didn't reply. Jo said they had a massive falling out, Daisy and him, and then all these rumours started swirling and I didn't know what I believed—she's with the cop? With Tiller? I heard she moved out of the Compound, I heard she got a place with Tiller—needed that one not to be true. I heard she got a place by herself—that one was true, I found out from Taura. Got the address from her too.

She moved into a building over on Warwick Avenue in Maida Vale.

I don't really have a plan when I show up there, I just want to see her for a second, see it with my own eyes that she's okay and I think I deserve that after all the shit we've been through—maybe tell her I love her and I won't stop and I'm sorry, who knows?

I knock on her door.

There's a long pause. I hear a sound behind the door. Another long pause.

She opens it frowning but I frown back. "What the fuck is going on?" I bark at her.

She crosses her arms over her chest, proudly. "I moved out."

I shake my head at her. "Why didn't you tell me you were moving?"

She gives me a defiant look. "We're not exactly on speaking terms..."

"Yeah, and whose fucking fault is that?" I push past her, inviting myself in.

She eyeballs me. "Yours."

"Mine?" I give her a look and look around the apartment. Kind of minimal. Lots of wood. Almost completely empty. "Baby, I would have helped you moved."

"I don't need your help," she tells me and I sigh.

I lean back against the door and stare over at her.

"What happened with your brother?"

She presses her lips together and shakes her head. "I don't want to talk about it."

"Yeah, well I do." I walk over to her and angle her chin up so she's looking at me. This startles her for some reason, but not in a way where she recoils from it. She freezes and I stare down at her. "So what the fuck happened?"

She licks her bottom lip and I'm jealous of it—she looks away.

"My rules—" She glances up at me. "Do you remember them?"

I nod. "Yeah."

She looks away. "He broke them."

Oh, shit.

Fuck.

I don't know what I was expecting—what sort of shit he'd pull to push her away this bad but those were lines I'd never thought he'd cross.

"Fuck." I blink. "Really?"

She nods.

"Which one?" I ask.

She looks over at me, brows low with a look she only gets when she's worried about her brother.

"Does it matter?"

"Dais—" I reach out for her, slip my hand around her waist without her permission but I never needed her permission before. "I'm so sorry." I push my hand through her hair and she lets me, staring up at me, eyes wide and heavy with a bunch of shit I missed but I shouldn't have.

She says nothing for a few seconds, purses her mouth, eyes all heavy.

"I love you," she tells me all solemn and shit.

I blink a few times, look down at her confused and stoked all at once. "I love you too."

She gets on tiptoe, slips her arms around my neck and pulls my mouth towards her.

I move her backwards, kissing her heavy against the wall and she lets out a muffled squeak of pain.

"Shit—" I pull a face. "Sorry! But you love me!" I grin down at her.

"Obviously," she huffs.

I give her a look. "Haven't said that to each other before—seems like a bit of a big deal—"

"It is a big deal." She nods but her face has gone sad again. She shakes her head, frowning up at me. "Christian, I'm done with this shit—"

"What shit?"

"I'm out—" she shrugs. "I don't want anything to do with that life."

I stare at her, confused and not letting go of her. "But I'm in that life."

She presses her tongue into her top lip and her breathings getting fast. "We could leave? You and me? Go be normal somewhere—"

"Dais…" I stare at her, blinking a lot. I take a breath. I don't know what to say. Never mind the part where something about what she's saying is exactly what I want—I can't? I can't. I don't have another plan, this is the plan. Me and Jo running the game together. It's the only plan we've ever had, and even that aside—Mum. I couldn't—not to her.

"Julian's out of control—" Daisy tells me, eyes teary.

I shrug helplessly, because I've heard that too. "Yeah but he'll swing back—"

"No, Christian." She shakes her head. "He won't—he can't. Not from this—not with me, anyway." I give her a doubtful look but she looks like she might cry. "I'm ashamed of him. I've never been ashamed of him—and I hate it, I feel sick thinking about what he's done and who he is when I'm not in the room with him, and I don't ever want to figure out how it feels to feel that way about you—"

I push my hand through her hair again, cradle the back of her head.

"I'm not like him—" I tell her.

Her eyes soften a bit. "Yeah, you are, it's why I like you so much."

I give her a look. "You don't believe in the Electra complex." Her words, not mine.

But she shrugs, "It's just pre-sexual programming." Because she's the smartest girl in every room. "We unconsciously develop a schema for what love is when we're small that is completely based off of the way we're treated by our primary caregivers—" She purses her lips, amused. "And then when we grow up, we're attracted to people who make us feel the same way."

I shake my head at her. "I won't break your rules, Dais..."

"That's what he said."

"But I mean it—"

She nods. "So did he."

"Come live with me, then—forget Jules. You don't have to walk away completely, you can—"

"I'm tired of people trying to kill me—"

I frown. "Do you think I'd let anything happen to you?"

And she gives me a look. "But how many times do things nearly have to happen for me to take the fucking hint that I need to get out."

I feel like I'm sinking.

"Daisy, we can figure this out—"

"I've figured it out, Christian—" she tells me, stubborn. "And I'm done."

"Baby, I can't be done. This is my whole life."

"Right. No." She nods quickly, the hope behind her eyes crushing. "It's—okay. I get it—" Her eyes drop from mine.

"What does this—" I tilt my head, looking for her eyes, trying to get my head around it. "Is this you saying we can't be together?"

"I don't know?" She looks back up at me. "I guess."

I stare at her for a few seconds. "But I'm in love with you."

"I know," she wipes her eyes. "I'm in love with you too."

"Baby, please don't do this—" I shake my head, absentmindedly rub my hand over my mouth.

She kisses me on the cheek. "When you leave, please don't come back again." She curls her finger and wipes away a tear. "I can't do this twice."

"Daisy—"

"I mean it, Christian. I just—I need to be normal now. I don't want to be jumpy when a white van drives past me. I don't want to have to take different routes home every day. I don't want a bodyguard. I want to be able to order the same things at restaurants every time I go there. I don't want to sleep with a fucking 45 under my pillow—"

"Daisy—"

"I want to be free of it, Christian, so I have to be done. Please let me be done."

I take a staggered breath, act like me understanding why she's saying what she's saying makes it hurt less but it doesn't—just push me in front of a fucking train, why don't you, but I nod a couple of times instead. Try on for size that old adage of if you love someone, let them go. Even if you've just gotten them, which I have, even if you hate how the world feels without them—which I do, I know that now. It's a hollow in me, where she used to lie on my chest at night, feel her gone like how you feel dust and dirt hit your face on a windy day. I don't want to let her go—I didn't even want to love her in the first place, but here we are and I do, and I would't take it back now. Couldn't. Even if I could, I couldn't, because I'll love her 'til I die. Whether I have her or not, whether she wants me back or not, I'm in, even if she's out.

"Okay." I nod, barely. "You can be done, Baby."

"Thank you," she whispers, chin wobbling.

I kiss the corner of her mouth, walk out her door and then we don't speak for ten months.

# New York, March

I'm staring out the window over the park, doing my best to ignore all the buildings around it.

If I squint, it could be Kensington Gardens, but it's not.

I've done my best to make my Fifth Avenue apartment feel more like home, but what can you do when home is so much more than the house you grew up in?

"Hey," he says from behind me. I look over at him standing in the doorway, drink him in.

"Hi." I give him a small smile as I walk over to him and he slips his arms around my waist.

He tilts my chin up towards him and brushes his mouth over mine.

He takes off his pilot hat and puts it on my head, tugging it over my eyes and kissing me more.

There's been lots of him kissing me more in the months since I fled London.

I flew straight here from the Rosebery—I turned up at the airport—I always keep my passport on me because we take a lot of impromptu trips. I bought a one-way, first-class ticket to JFK.

There actually wasn't a flight until the next morning by the time I arrived, it didn't matter to me, though.

I went through the gate, threw my phone away, threw up in the bathroom, bought a new phone after an hour because I was bored, bought a change of clothes, then was holed up in the lounge 'til my flight rolled round.

Normally I'd strictly use the Windsor Lounge, but obviously none of this was planned, so I just had to fall asleep in one of the little sleep pods BA has now, and it was one of those funny sleeps you have when you're grieving something—do you know the kind? A sleep that feels like quicksand, as though your brain decides "we don't want to be awake for this", and it grabs your consciousness by the ankle and drags you down into a quiet darkness.

I didn't move once, it was that heavy sort of sleep... Indentations on my face from where I lay.

It was a stewardess who woke me.

"Your flight's boarding, miss," she told me and the way her eyebrows pinched, I knew she knew who I was and I knew she'd seen the news. I didn't even know it was on the news yet, but, my God, was it on the news. There were so many camera phones out filming us as it was happening. They got the whole thing on video. Never mind that it's in the top two worst moments spanning the history of my existence, never mind that my life as I knew it was caving in on itself, never mind that I was visibly mortified and traumatised and betrayed, they ran it for weeks anyway. People gobbled it up, they lived the drama of it, and there was so much drama. People we hadn't spoken to in years from Varley popping out of the woodworks to say they knew all along, other girls saying he'd cheated on me with them too in school, at parties, in bathrooms when I was distracted. I don't know if those parts are true. I don't know if them being true would make it better or worse. And the headlines...

"Ballentine's Disgrace with Parks's BFF."

"Bad Boy Ballentine Does the Dirty with BFF."

"Magnolia Parks: Betrayed by BF & BFF."

The paparazzi followed me here for a while, maybe a month or so. It was hard. Tom made it easier.

I arrived with nothing. I went straight to Sotheby's. I told them I wanted a house or an apartment, I didn't care, just anything that looked the most like London, and then I booked myself into the Central Park Ritz Carlton 'til they found me my place here—995 Fifth Avenue, the top floor. Two stories, garden terraces on both levels that overlook the park.

London's green. I need the green.

I called Bridget as soon as I got up to my hotel room and she cried when she answered.

"Where are you?" she asked once she'd gotten a hold of herself.

"Manhattan."

"Good." She took a big breath. "Stay there."

"Is it bad?" I asked. She said nothing. "Tell Henry I'm here, would you?" I told her as I stared around my empty suite.

"Okay." She blew some air out of her mouth. "And Tom? What do I tell him?"

"Nothing." I frowned. "We broke up."

"He's called me non-stop for thirty-six hours."

"Oh. Well, I guess you can tell him I'm here then too."

Tom flew out to me the next day. I feel like it'll be a memory that hangs in my mind forever, the way Tom moved towards me from the elevator.

A carry-on and a coat draped over his arm, he dropped them both to wrap his arms around me and I buried my face in his chest. Then I cried and cried, crumpling to the floor and he crumpled with me.

I cried 'til I fell asleep again. When I woke up, he was lying next to me, just watching.

"Are you okay?" he asked.

How do you answer that? How could I answer him?

No, I'm not okay. I will never again be.

That would have at least been the truth, but instead I just nodded, and that was enough for him. Any more questions and the thread would start to pull.

A nod was concise, tacit permission to move forward how he'd rather and an unoriginal way for both of us to side-step the truth.

Then we didn't talk about it again. We just... pretended like it didn't happen. Like I hadn't dumped him for the man who cheated on me with my best friend, and we pretended like the cameras that followed me those first few weeks were following me for the old reasons they used to in London, we pretended that the reason I couldn't go back home with Tom was because I was so bogged down with work at the Condé Nast offices over here, and that all my work was pulling me to other places, and it just didn't make sense to go back to London, because what's new and leisurely about London for people from London anyway?

So no London. Never London.

We worked around it.

He split his time. Half here with me, half there. Not completely dissimilar to his life before with the flights he runs, I suppose.

I made a friend who lives in my building, technically on the other side of the top floor. A Latin-American heiress whose father owns a telecommunications company.

She ran up to me in the lobby when I was wearing the crystal-embellished parka jacket from Burberry's runway.

"Oh my God." She grabbed me and I gave her a horrified look as I pulled back.

"Please don't touch me—" I flinched. "I don't have any money."

"Your jacket—" She stared at me and I kept frowning at her.

"I love it. Can I try it on?"

I shook my head. "No."

"But it's sold out everywhere."

I nodded. "I know."

"So how'd you get it?"

I gave her a small shrug. "I know Christopher Bailey."

I hugged my mint-blue Point Crochet-Knit Clutch from Bottega Veneta to my chest and her eyes fell down me, landing on my shoes.

"Crystal Twist 105 sandals from Aquazurra," she told me and I gave her a suspicious look.

"Yes."

"An open-toe shoe in New York? My God." She gave me a look. "You must be new. I'm Lucía Nieves-Navarro."

She offered me her hand and I cautiously shook it. "Magnolia Parks."

She's studying fashion at Parson's and she's loud and enigmatic and ridiculous and beautiful—completely terrible boundaries—but when Tom isn't here and Bridget or Henry aren't visiting, it's Lu who makes me feel less alone.

"Good flight?" I ask Tom as I follow him into the bathroom.

He nods, turning around as he leans back against the vanity.

I undo the buttons of his pilot jacket and slip it off his shoulders.

"How many days do I have you for?" I ask, batting my eyes at him.

He kisses my nose. "A whole five, I'm afraid." He nods his head towards the bed. "Want to order up some wine? We'll have an early night."

A euphemism but I give him a look anyway. I give him a look. "It's mid-afternoon."

"We can have sex in the daylight, Magnolia—"

"How uncouth!" I gasp and he laughs, reaching for the remote that closes every blind in my apartment.

"How's that?" He gives me a look.

I smile up at him even though he can't see me. "Better."

After, we're lying in bed and he's flicking through the TV because he thinks I take too long to choose a show on Netflix, and it's all so mindless, because I am too these days. I have to be.

Have you ever deadened a bit of yourself to make it through? Toned down the brightness, trimmed back your edges, square peg, round hole, force it in anyway.

"Ah." He nods at the TV. "Finally a good one."

I look over at the TV and I go tense.

*Back to the Future.*

"Mmm, no," I say after about ten seconds, ultra breezily as I reach for the remote, but Tom holds it above my head.

"I love this movie—"

"No." I shake my head dismissively. "It's stupid."

He frowns a little. "It's one of my favourites."

I frown back. "Well, I hate it, so—" I gesture towards the TV. "Change it."

"What?" He keeps frowning.

"I don't want to watch this stupid movie," I tell him loudly and he pulls back from me a little, staring over.

He stares at me for seven seconds, frowning, piecing together, processing.

He blinks twice. "Is this about BJ?"

My head pulls back and my heart jumps off the balcony at the mention of his name.

"No—I—" I'm thrown. "Why would you?" I'm shaking my head.

He gives me an exasperated look. "Because everything about you is about BJ."

That scares me, what he says, because I've always worried that it's true, and if Tom's saying that to me, then probably it is.

I shake my head. "That's not true," I tell him weakly.

"Yes, it is, Magnolia, I can see it—" His head rolls back and he stares at the ceiling. "Everywhere. Every time we walk past a news stand and you turn over the *National Geographic*s to hide the covers. You haven't been in a Gucci store for months. You won't get in a bathtub—"

"I've always hated baths," I correct him but he ignores me.

He shakes his head at me. "You can't even look at a fucking negroni. If there's one on a table you turn away."

"Tom—" I reach for him but he pulls away and gets out of the bed.

"What is it about this movie?" He gestures to the TV. "Be honest."

"I just think that… it's some of Christopher Lloyd's weaker work."

Tom's eyes go sad. "And it's got nothing to do with that DeLorean tattoo BJ has on his fucking arm?"

My eyes drop from his and I press my tongue into the roof of my mouth.

"I can't do it, Parks." Tom shakes his head again and grabs a shirt, throwing it over his head. "I can't keep being in love with people who don't love me back properly."

"I do!" I jump out of bed after him.

He nods his chin at me. "Say it then."

"I love you," I tell him easily, rolls right off the tongue. It's true, I do.

He nods once, twice, mouth pursed. "Now say you don't love him."

My mouth falls open and I blink a few times, swallow, cross my arms over my chest and stare up at him, eyes all teary and defiant. Denounce him? Denounce my whole heart that lives across the Atlantic in the shape of a boy who I never want to see again even when he's all I want to see every day? How am I to do that? If you can tell me, I'll do it. If there is a way to move past loving him how I love him, I will do it—I'll do anything—and Tom rests beautifully under the umbrella of anything, but then he is so much more than that. He's everything, you might even say, and still, here he is, standing in front of me, demanding me to love him in the way he deserves, which I can't do because I'm tied to a boy and a tree in Dartmouth and I hate him so much, and I worry every day that I will never love anyone more than how much I hate him.

Tom breathes out a shallow breath and shakes his head at me, eyes like I gutted him. Maybe I did.

He shoves his hands through his hair. "I'm so in love with you, Magnolia, and you don't give a fucking shit."

"Tom, of course I do—" I reach for him again but he darts from me, grabbing his backpack and shoving things mindlessly into it.

"What are you—" I stare at him and he keeps grabbing random things and throwing them into his bag.

"I can't do it." He shakes his head.

"Tom." I wipe my face and I grab his wrist.

He swings around to face me and ducks so we're eye to eye. He licks his bottom lip, chin trembling a bit.

"Just tell me you don't love him, Magnolia," he says in a muffled whisper. "Tell me and I'll stay." He brushes his eyes with the back of his hand.

His eyes are so blue. Bluer when he's sad. They're sapphires right now.

# Thank You's

First and foremost, I will thank Ben once again. Even though I know for a fact you haven't finished reading this and I'm not entirely sure that you even finished Magnolia, but we've had a big few months and I forgive you. You are (not who BJ is based on but) my best friend, my favourite person, and because you believe in me how you believe in me, now I believe in me too.

Luke, Jay and Maddi and everyone at Avenir. I love working with you clowns so much; sorry for always wafting on in our meetings but I love you all so much even though you (@Jayboy) look annoyed whenever I ask what everyone else is eating. What a privilege it is to work with you, you creative genius and (best) friend of my youth.

Luke, you are the best brother, you have worked so hard and tirelessly for me and my books, and I love you forever.

Maddi, I know you know that I think you loving my books how you do has changed the shape of them.

Thank you all for getting it, thank you for believing in this with me, thank you for pushing boundaries and doing things with my books we've never seen before. I'm never not glad we're doing this together.

Joel, my editor. Thank you for being with me in this process even though at the time we were both saddled with complicated puppies that neither of us were entirely prepared for. Thank you for really getting these friends of mine who live in my head. I'm really grateful for how much you know them.

Euan and Kankana, for your work with me towards the end, I'm sorry for the chaos and grateful for your patience!

Amanda (or as Ben calls you, "that girl who really loves your book") thank you for really (really, really) loving my characters. You gave this book a boost of confidence when it really needed it. And to my other beta readers, sister-Hannah, Bronte, Kenzie, Shannon, Mystique, Laura, Darion, Janice and Juliette thank you for lending me your eyes and allowing me to pester you with questions. Tori, as always, for your Britishness.

Karalee, when I was very worried about this book you sent me a text message that I read every time I doubted it. I love you, you're a very good best friend. #Sassafrass2022

And Emily, because you believe in me as blindly as Ben does, if not more… Is my self-confidence overly inflated because you've compared me to incomparable authors for the last 10 years, yes. Is it helpful, is it harmful, who's to say but I'm thankful for it either way.

Camryn, for all you've done for our family. We love you. And Lindsey and Kim, for filling in the cracks of the busiest season of our lives so we didn't fall down them, we're very grateful.

Charlie Rionne, because you changed my life and I love you. Thank you for everything. Should have thanked you in the last book but I was all over the place, so thank you here for then and for now.

To the unofficial sponsors of my sanity these last few months: the Hamish & Andy pod (ahoy!), Starbucks Nitro Cold Brew, Wags & Wiggles (and the real MVP of my life, Ranaye.), the Lox Bagel from Wexler's Deli and of course, Perfect Bars. Thank you for all you've done for me. I'd also like to thank the state of California for being so opportunity-heavy (S/O X-Files), happy to be here, happy to be alive.

And lastly, to everyone who read Magnolia and loved it how you loved it, thank you. I hope you love this one just as much.

# About the Author

Australian-native Jessa Hastings lives in Southern California with her husband, two children, her cat and a Rhodesian Ridgeback puppy she semi-regrets getting. She refuses to wear long pants, but loves a sweater. Since moving to LA she has struggled with the coffee and really misses Sydney cafes and how superior their breakfasts are to everywhere else in the world. She no longer really eats breakfast, but thinks of it fondly and often. She doesn't like writing synopsises nor biographies. Writing this here has been her waking nightmare and this book is her sophomore novel.

written by
Jessa Hastings

# Magnolia Parks